Loving Elise

M.B. Smith

To my mother, who taught me to fall in love with books.
You are the reason I write.

Note to Readers

When I first wrote *Loving Elise*—during the 2020 pandemic while juggling college classes and planning my wedding—I had no idea what I was doing... and honestly, I still don't.

But I do know this: as much as I love storytelling, I love Jesus more.

Because of that, I have chosen to republish this book with some intentional changes. The storyline and emotional depth remain the same, and it's still very much a story for adult readers (18+). But in this edition, any intimate scenes fade to black, and strong language has been significantly toned down.

All future books will follow this level of modesty, while still exploring mature—and at times heavy—emotional themes.

This second edition also includes a brand new chapter from Joshua's point of view (Chapter 12), as well as a bonus chapter at the end from Ryder's perspective, offering a glimpse into his book, *Choosing Rachel*, the next installment in this series.

Thank you for your continued support and grace as I grow—both as a writer and as a woman of faith. I'm truly humbled by the love you've shown me on this journey.

TABLE OF CONTENTS

CHAPTER ONE

Elise

There's no way to tell time: seconds, minutes, hours, days—it's all a blur of drifting in and out of sleep, eating oatmeal and bread when it's brought to me, and staring at the wall.

Cuts and bruises cover my arms and legs, visible through my ripped and bloodied clothing. It's been days since I woke up in the basement, but the wounds are still sensitive and raw. My meager meals aren't enough to energize my body, and I can feel myself growing weaker. The lack of good hygiene and nutrients has minimized any healing that should've taken place by now.

I'm about to drift off to sleep when I hear the faint sound of footsteps coming down the hallway.

My eyes dart to the tray of food, steam faintly rising from the oatmeal, still warm.

If someone is coming to see me, it isn't a routine visit.

I scramble backward on instinct, getting as far away from the solid metal door as possible, but the effort is in vain.

The doorknob turns, and my visitor enters the room.

This can't be good.

Six days earlier

I wipe off the counter and listen to the pleasant chatter of customers. It's been a slow day at the bakery, but I'm not complaining. I didn't sleep well last night.

I made it three weeks without a nightmare night, but my luck ran out last night. By five, I'd given up on sleep completely, and I've been at work since seven.

It doesn't help that I can't stop worrying about this phone call with Dad tonight, but there's no avoiding it. I've pushed it off long enough, and I'm officially out of time.

I have no doubt he'll be difficult, so I replay my best arguments on a loop. One shot is all I get—once he says no, it's game over.

The sound of the door opening pulls me from my imaginary debate, and I look up to greet the newest customer. As soon as I see him, I have a difficult time remembering how to breathe, let alone speak.

The first thing I notice is how his presence seems to consume the room. There's a collective lull in conversation, and all eyes seem to follow the man sauntering toward the counter.

His hair—cut shorter on the sides than on top—is dark brown and windswept, no doubt thanks to the breezy weather. He has a closely trimmed beard that outlines a strong jawline and full lips set in a charming half-smile. His posture—which effortlessly commands the room—is confidently relaxed.

I'd expect a man like him to complete his larger-than-life look with a suit, but somehow, the dark jeans and plain gray tee fit him better.

As he approaches, customers begin looking away to return to their conversations.

If only I could do the same.

He slips one hand in his pocket, scanning the menu above my head with analytic eyes. I'm about to attempt to look away when he glances down and meets my gaze, locking me in place. Dark eyes stare into mine, and my cheeks warm at the attention.

He didn't catch me staring, right?

"Can I order here?" he asks, suppressing a smile.

He definitely caught me staring.

"Yes, of course! Welcome to Milwaukee's Finest. What can I get for you?" I have to crane my neck to meet his gaze.

"I can't decide what I want. Any suggestions?" He leans one hip against the counter, bracing his weight on one arm, flexing as he does.

"Well,"—I tuck a loose strand of hair behind my ear and avert my gaze—"I would suggest the chocolate pastry. It's made from scratch every morning. It's my favorite."

"I'll take two—bagged separately—and a large coffee."

I ring up his items and open my mouth to tell him the total, but before I get a word out, he hands me a fifty-dollar bill. "Keep the change."

I don't make a move to take the bill from him. "Sir, that's more than a thirty-dollar tip. Please, let me give you your change."

"Keep it," he commands, and his tone doesn't leave room for argument, so I take the money.

His eyes are trained on me as I prepare his order, but his body is turned outward to face the rest of the bakery. "How long have you worked here?"

"This is my third year," I tell him as I bag the pastries. "I like it a lot. Not many bakeries sell authentic, house-made pastries." I set the bags aside and grab a cup to pour his coffee. "Cream or sugar?"

"Neither."

"Here you go." I present his food with a smile.

He doesn't take it. "This isn't what I ordered."

I may be out of it right now, but I'm *positive* he asked for two chocolate pastries, bagged separately, and one black coffee.

I open my mouth to tell him just that, but he interrupts me. "I could've sworn I asked for your number, too. I'm not sure I could forgive myself if I left here without it."

I've had customers flirt with me before, but it's usually just a wink or a *have a good day, gorgeous.* I'm so caught off guard by his forwardness that I'm momentarily rendered speechless.

He digs into his pocket for his phone and places the device in the palm of my hand.

I bite down on a smile. "How can I give my number to someone I don't even know?"

"I believe it's called making friends."

"I usually know the names of my friends," I counter.

He places the pastry bags on the counter and holds out his hand. "My name is Hayden Montez. I just moved here from California. I work in real estate at an agency two blocks away, and I'm single." His smile grows. "Now you know a few things about me."

He's got a point, so I relent and shake his hand. "It's nice to meet you, Hayden. My name is Annie."

I feel a pang of guilt at the lie, but it's necessary.

I finish typing "Annie Smith" along with my number and hand his phone back to him. He messes with it for a few seconds, and as he puts his phone away, mine vibrates in my back pocket.

"I hope to hear from you soon, Annie," he says, picking up his order before leaving.

He's halfway to the door when I notice one of the pastry bags is still on the counter. I call out to him, but he doesn't turn around. He only lifts his phone before exiting.

For a moment, all I can do is stand dumbfounded and watch the exit.

After several seconds, I shake my head and pull out my phone, reading the message.

Hayden: Enjoy the pastry.

The rest of the work day passes quickly, and I'm ready to go home by the time Kaitlyn is waiting at the door.

Kaitlyn is the head of my security detail. I used to hate being trailed everywhere I go, but after six years, I barely even notice anymore. Kaitlyn is my favorite. Being the same age as me, we're more like friends.

It had taken a lot of convincing to get my dad to hire a female for my security team since there are absolutely no women in my father's line of work. He only agreed to hire Kaitlyn after months of my begging. I'd been desperate for a friend who understood the complications of my life.

"Someone had a good day," she observes.

I smile, remembering Hayden from this morning. "Were you around when that guy was flirting with me?"

Her eyes spark with interest. "No, I must have missed it. When did that happen?"

"Around noon, I think."

"I would have been running perimeter. What happened?"

We climb into the car—her in the driver's seat as usual—and I recount the events.

"I can't believe I missed all of that," she says, taking her phone from her lap. "What did you say his name was? I'll have Jace run a background check."

"No way." I shake my head at the mere suggestion. "I do *not* want my dad to find out. It's just innocent flirting. Maybe if it gets more serious, we can run an official check. Promise me that you won't do anything for now?"

Kaitlyn studies me warily before saying, "Okay, no background check yet, but be careful. Your dad would have my head if anything happened to you."

When I think back to Hayden's warm eyes, I'm confident Kaitlyn has nothing to worry about.

It's almost seven, and my hands won't stop shaking. My eyes keep flitting to my phone, and the TV does little to distract me from my nerves.

Half an hour until the call with my dad.

I'm so lost in scenarios that I jump when my phone buzzes. For a second, I wonder if it's Dad calling early, but I know better.

Dad doesn't change his plans.

I relax and reach for the phone, but my nerves spike again when I see the name on the screen.

Hayden: How was work?

Consumed by the stress of my impending call, I'd completely forgotten about my encounter with the handsome stranger.

I pour myself a glass of wine before responding, desperate for the liquid courage.

Annie: It was really nice. Thanks for the pastry. Whoever suggested that has great taste.

I press send before I can second-guess myself.

Not even two minutes have passed before it vibrates again.

Hayden: Well, she might have great taste. It depends on whether or not she'll let me take her out to dinner.

Annie: I think she'd like that.

Hayden: Then no, she doesn't have good taste.

My smile is wide as I write my reply.

Annie: On second thought...

I turn off the television, no longer needing the mindless distraction.

Hayden: Don't go breaking my heart now, gorgeous. How about tomorrow night?

My fingers fly over the screen, ready to accept his invitation, but I stop and count the days in my head.

Tomorrow is the third Sunday of the month.

The only night I'm without security. The only night my father demands I stay inside.

Disappointment settles in my stomach like a ten-pound weight, and I lean back against the couch.

This is just my luck.

Annie: Tomorrow isn't the best for me... How about later this week?

I wait for his response, and my heart drops when I read it.

Hayden: I'm going back to California on Monday to get the rest of my stuff and I won't be back for a week. I'd really like to see you before then.

The temptation to break my father's rule is strong, but I can't bring myself to do it. I've never been much of a rebel.

Annie: I'd love to see you before you go, but I can't do tomorrow night. I'm really sorry.

Closing my eyes, I picture a life without security details, background checks, or paranoid criminal boss fathers. Then I could just say yes to a date with a sweet man like Hayden.

Hayden: Don't be. You're worth waiting for. Let me know if you change your mind.

Before I can open my phone to respond, it buzzes with an incoming call from a Chicago area code, and I can't believe Hayden distracted me from the impending conversation that's been haunting me for weeks now.

Steeling my nerves, my finger slides across the screen to accept the video call.

I expect to see my father's graying hair and signature scowl, so I'm surprised when two identical grins appear on the screen. Their dark brown hair is similar to mine—that is when I don't conceal it with blonde dye—but the light green eyes are a trait they got from our father.

I'm told that my brown eyes are exactly like my mother's. Not that I'd remember.

"Elise! How are you?" Logan greets.

It's strange hearing my real name since no one but my family actually uses it. Everyone I encounter on a daily basis—including my security detail—has taken to my alias.

"I'm good. Where's Dad? I thought *he* was going to call me."

James is the one to answer. "He's with Damon right now. They're handling a time-sensitive matter."

Only Dad would send the twins to call me instead of just pushing it back an hour. If they couldn't see my face, I'd probably roll my eyes.

"Oh, when will he be able to talk? Should I call back later?" I wonder what he and my oldest brother are attending to that is so important.

Logan shakes his head. "He should be ready in a few minutes. Is everything okay?"

Being the youngest and the only girl in my family, I've always been the outcast. My four brothers act as our father's capos—captains —at our family's main Chicago base.

I, on the other hand, choose to have no affiliation with his work whatsoever.

I smile to hide the disappointment threatening to taint my evening.

"Yeah, everything is fine. I just have something I want to talk to Dad abo—" A loud crash in the background steals their attention.

Muffled grumbling follows, but it's quickly cut off when my brothers mute their microphone, and their lips move as they address the interruption.

I ignore the pang of hurt that hits my chest at being shut out.

My finger taps against the glass in my hand as I wait for my brothers to return to the call. Judging by the look of concern on Logan's face, that may take a while.

Logan hands the phone off to James, who gives me a forced smile as he unmutes himself.

"Dad will be done in just a few minutes." His eyebrows jump up when he catches sight of something beyond the camera. "Mason! Will you talk to Elise?"

I don't hear a response, but a moment later, the youngest of my brothers takes the phone.

His light brown hair is cut shorter than the last time I saw him a few weeks ago, and the look suits his sharp jaw and prominent cheekbones. His dark eyes sparkle, and the sight of his wide grin eases some of the hurt in my chest.

Mason is the only one of my brothers who also inherited Mom's brown eyes, which made us look more like twins than Logan and James in our childhood years.

"Hey, Elise. What's going on?" His deep voice continues to take me by surprise. Though he's three years my senior, I can practically still hear the voice cracks of his teenage years.

I wave my nearly empty wine glass in front of the camera. "Obviously, not very much. What about you?"

He glances in the direction the twins went. "Things are a little hectic here, but nothing out of the ordinary." When his eyes flit back to the screen, they take on a calculating edge. "What's wrong?"

"What do you mean?" I strengthen my fake smile, but there's really no point.

Mason has always been the most analytic of the Consoli family—a habit he picked up from our father. He doesn't miss anything.

One exasperated look from him, and I drop the act altogether.

"Tomorrow is the deadline to submit an application for the European Culinary Tour that my professor recommended to me. Since graduation last month, I haven't heard back from a single job I've applied for. Having this tour on my resume would make me stand out."

He gives me a sympathetic smile. "You know he's going to say no."

"Why would he? I'd still have security, and I'd maintain my fake identity. He has no reason to say no."

Mason gives me a knowing look. "And what about family dinner? You know how important it is that Dad keeps everyone informed. That's without taking into consideration the enemies we have in other countries."

The mention of family dinner reminds me why I can't go out with Hayden tomorrow night, and my face falters. Luckily for me, Mason takes it as disappointment from his words.

"I'm sorry. You deserve to do things that make you happy."

I open my mouth to respond, but a gruff voice catches my attention. "Elise! Sweetheart, how are you?"

Mason doesn't object when our father snatches the phone from his grasp. His dark hair is peppered gray and white, but that's the only sign of his age. There's not a single wrinkle on his face, which is likely due to the fact that his smile is a rare sight, though now his lip tugs upward, and his eyes soften when they meet mine.

"I'm good! I actually have something I want to talk to you about." My hand starts to shake, and I wonder if more wine would've better prepared me for this conversation.

"What's on your mind?"

His seemingly good mood has me feeling optimistic.

"Do you remember me telling you about Dr. Burns—the professor that I really liked?"

My father's poker face is excellent, but his pause gives him away.

He doesn't recall my professor at all.

I don't let it bother me. "Well, he suggested that I apply for an internship that would look really good on my resume, and I want to do it."

His eyebrows pull together, and he analyzes me the same way Mason had.

"And where exactly is this internship?"

Here goes nothing.

"Well, uh—actually—it's, well..." I take a deep breath. "It's across Europe."

"No."

"Dad, just hear me out—"

"Elise, the answer is no. I can barely manage you being an hour away. There's no way you're going an ocean away."

"But—"

"My answer is final."

I don't attempt to hide my disappointment, and my father's eyes soften ever so slightly. If I had any other dad, I might be able to persuade him with tears, but not Gabriel Consoli.

This is a man who sticks to his word.

"I'm sorry, sweetheart. You know I only want to protect you, right?"

The weight of disappointment is heavy, but I humor him. "Yeah, I know, Dad."

"Good. I'll see you in a few weeks. I already have reservations at Vincenzo Bistro to celebrate."

Buying out an entire restaurant for the night isn't exactly the same as a reservation, but I don't bother mentioning that.

"Can't wait," I tell him, but it's hardly convincing even to my ears.

I hang up the phone and stare at the blank screen, letting Mason's words come back to me.

You deserve to do things that make you happy.

Before I can stop myself, I pick up my phone and type out a message to Hayden.

Annie: Turns out tomorrow works perfectly. My place at 7?

CHAPTER TWO

Elise

Kaitlyn is at my door at noon. She looks as sharp as ever, with her blonde hair pulled up in a neat bun, black slacks, and a matching blazer. Normally, her attire is casual since she needs to blend in, but she opts for professional wear for family dinners.

"We're about to head out. Are you all good?" she asks.

I'd be lying if I said it didn't hurt being excluded from an event called *family dinner* by my own family. Though even I have to admit that it'd be stupid to risk revealing my identity when I've been allegedly dead for six years now, so I've never argued the point.

"Already? It only takes an hour to get there. Why are you leaving so early?"

She huffs, throwing an annoyed glance behind her to where the others are getting into the car. "A few of the soldiers are required for a training session, so we have to leave now to get there on time." She eyes me warily. "Is that okay?"

"Of course," I answer, a little too quickly, and add a warm smile to assure her.

I decided against telling anyone that Hayden is coming over tonight. If I did, there's no way they would let it happen, *and* they would tell my father. Technically, I'm not breaking any rules though, since I will be staying in tonight.

"I'm good. I'll see you guys tomorrow morning."

She studies me so intently that I wonder if she knows what I'm up to, but after a long moment, she nods. "Call if you need anything."

"You know I will," I tell her and wave as they drive off.

14

* * *

The hours pass in a blur of cleaning and meal-prepping for the week. I've never had a guy over before, and I'm not exactly sure what the etiquette is. My only reference is movies and the endless romance novels I've read through the years.

At quarter 'til seven, I'm done getting ready and check myself in the mirror one last time.

I'm wearing my nicest pair of skinny jeans and a loose gray blouse with a generous V-neckline. My long blonde hair is perfectly straight, and I note that my dark roots will need a touch-up soon. I've applied minimal makeup, not wanting to look like I'm trying too hard to impress him.

Even though I am.

A knock on the door pulls me away from the mirror, and my heart leaps into my throat.

I take a deep breath before approaching the door and releasing the several locks that Kaitlyn insists I have.

When I pull the door open, I'm stunned into silence.

Hayden is dressed in dark jeans and a short-sleeved, white button-up, showing off his tan arms. His broad shoulders and commanding posture give off a dangerous air, but his smile is welcoming.

"Hey, beautiful. Mind if I come in?" He lifts his arms, and I realize his hands are full—one with a take-out bag and the other with a bottle of wine.

I open the door wider and step aside for him. "Please do. How are you?"

I really have no idea what I'm doing.

"Much better now that I'm here. You have a really nice place," he says, following me into the kitchen and placing the items on the counter.

"Well, thank you. I'm glad you were able to come over."

"Me too. I haven't been able to stop thinking about you." His smile is charming but, somehow, not as warm as it was yesterday.

Unsure of how to respond, I gesture to the food. "Thanks for grabbing dinner. You can take it to the table, and I'll get us some utensils and glasses for the wine."

"Sounds good." Hayden takes the food and heads to the table.

Once we're settled in, he opens the bottle of wine and pours a glass for each of us. "So, are you originally from this area?" he asks, sipping his drink.

I didn't even consider that I'd have to feed Hayden lies about my past, but I have no other choice. As it is, I'm already pushing my luck by having him here in the first place.

I give him my well-rehearsed backstory.

"Yeah. My parents died when I was three, so I was raised here by my aunt. A few years ago, she retired and moved to Florida, but I decided to stay here. This is my home."

I've told the story enough times that it almost feels like the truth.

"I'm sorry to hear about your parents." His words are compassionate, but his expression is almost... calculating.

"Don't be. I was too young to know any different. My aunt is my family, and that's enough for me. What about you? Why did you move here from California?" I ask, using the opportunity to take a bite of food.

"Business." A cool smile graces his lips. "I decided to move here last week."

"*Last week*? You're telling me that within seven days, you decided to move your whole life across the country?"

"More or less."

"That's incredible. I wish I could just pick up and move somewhere."

"Why can't you? Doesn't sound like you have many ties."

And I've said too much.

I backtrack, waving my hand dismissively. "I mean, it sounds great in theory, but it's not for me. I'm a homebody."

He doesn't push the point. "So, tell me more about yourself."

Taking a sip of my wine, I use the pause to make a list of the true information that is safe to give him.

"Well, there isn't much to know. I graduated a few weeks ago with a major in Culinary Arts, and I'm working at the bakery until I figure out my next steps."

"And what are your ideal next steps?"

The bitterness from Dad rejecting the internship still stings, and I decide on a whim to answer his question honestly.

"In a perfect world, I'd study in Europe for a few months and find a full-time position after that. But I'll probably end up taking the first job that'll hire me and gain as much experience as possible."

"Why only a perfect world? That sounds like a reasonable plan to me."

If only my father thought so, too.

"Like I said, I'm a homebody. What about you?"

His lips pull to one side as if he doesn't know where to start, and I wait patiently for his response.

"I didn't go to college. In fact, I didn't finish high school."

"What?" I blanch. "How did you manage to get a job without any credentials?"

"It's all about who you know. Connections are worth more than any degree."

Logistical questions flood my brain, but I don't voice them. This is a first date, after all. The last thing Hayden wants is to be grilled about his educational background.

He continues, "I mostly work in management. Right now, I'm preparing to start negotiations for a property my agency is interested in."

After finishing my food, I set my elbows on the table and rest my head on my hands. "That sounds interesting. What kind of property is it?"

He mimics my dismissive wave. "I won't bore you with the details. Are you done eating?".

"Oh, uh—yeah, I am." I stand and begin to clean up.

Hayden stands from his chair, and suddenly, we're so close that I can feel the heat radiating off his body. If he weren't so tall, our noses would be touching.

I look up into his deep brown eyes and feel small, but not in an inferior way, more like I'm being protected.

Like I'm safe.

I forget that I'm holding our empty food boxes until he takes them from my hands.

"Allow me," he says, and I release them to him as if in a trance.

"You know, you're a little controlling," I tease once I'm able to form a coherent sentence.

He laughs—the sound deep and amused. "In my line of work, it's a necessary trait."

While he clears the last of the trash from the table, I take our glasses and pour refills.

"Come join me in the living room when you're finished," I tell him, and I walk out of the kitchen with a sway in my step.

My whole body relaxes as I lower to the couch. Between the small talk and the wine, I'm significantly more relaxed than when Hayden first arrived.

I lift my legs onto the couch, tucking one under my bottom and bending the other in front of me.

Hayden walks in, surveys the room, and comes to sit next to me instead of on the adjacent chair.

We lift our glasses, and I take a sip of mine while he studies me.

"What?"

"I have a hard time believing that you're single," he admits after a moment of thought.

I smile sardonically. "Does that line usually work?"

His low chuckle returns. "As a matter of fact, it does, but I suppose I'll have to ramp up the creativity to impress you."

"Please do. I'd hate for clichés to be your downfall."

"I can assure you, Annie, that I am anything but cliché."

It's only now that I realize we've both unconsciously leaned toward one another, putting our faces only inches apart.

Every feature of his face is flawless. The eyebrows are tugged together as he studies me with a gaze overflowing with interest. His full lips are lifted in a ghost of a smile that sparks heat in the pit of my stomach.

What were we talking about?

I reluctantly pull away, desperately needing to regain some clarity.

"So, what about you?" I ask breathlessly. "Why are you single?"

Hayden seems to snap out of a daze similar to mine, but his expression remains thoughtful.

"I'm married to my job. And I've never met anyone I wanted to be with."

"I find that hard to believe."

"What's your excuse?"

My shoulders lift in a shrug, and I sip my wine to cover the red that creeps into my cheeks. "I've never actually... dated anyone before."

Genuine surprise twists Hayden's features, and I hope he doesn't push the topic.

I'm not so lucky.

"What do you mean?"

His free hand rests on my leg, rubbing lazy circles on the knee. The touch is so natural that I'm not sure he even notices he's doing it.

"I was homeschooled until college, so I never really did the whole '*dating*' thing."

"But you had guys throwing themselves at you once you went to college, right?"

I shake my head, drinking the remaining wine and setting the glass down.

He lifts his hand from my knee, and his finger gently lifts my chin to meet his questioning gaze. His eyes are softer now than they have been all night; that strange edge is gone.

"Have you ever had a boyfriend?"

I shake my head.

"Have you ever been on a *date*?"

I shake my head again.

"So, this is your first date? Ever?"

"Yeah." I try to look down, but his finger holds me in place, and I lose myself in his comforting pine tree scent.

If it weren't for the fact that he's clearly put himself together for our date, I might wonder if he's been hiking today. It's nothing like the overpowering cologne of most men I pass on the street. It's subtle yet wholly overwhelming.

Without moving his finger from my chin, he sets his glass on the coffee table and leans in.

"Annie," he says, his voice low and soothing, "have you ever been kissed?"

His words aren't accusatory, but that doesn't ease my embarrassment.

I can't bring myself to speak, so I shake my head slowly.

My heart pounds faster, and all my nerves rush back when he closes the short distance between us, and our lips meet.

The kiss is slow and sweet. The hand that held my chin now cradles the side of my face, his thumb resting on my cheekbone. I place my hands on his hard chest, and I can feel that his heart is beating almost as fast as mine.

When we slowly pull away, I bite my lip to stop from saying something that could ruin the moment, and I look up at him through thick lashes. The gaze I meet is unlike anything I've seen on Hayden's face before. It's dark—overflowing with a desire that would scare me if I didn't mirror it.

That unbridled desire is my only warning.

His lips crash to mine.

This kiss—though just as sweet as the last—is rough and passionate. One of his hands still holds the side of my face, and the other takes hold of my lower back, pulling me in until we're flush against one another. I move my hands from his chest and let them run through his hair, gripping it and anchoring him to me.

I don't process my lack of experience and happily let Hayden take the lead. In one swift pull, we're lying down, and he's on top of me, dominating my mouth with his. My hands wander up his back, and with little conscious thought, I pull his shirt up.

He slows then, leaving one last kiss on my lips before pulling away and looking at me with a cold calculation—one that makes me wonder if I did something wrong.

Hayden climbs off me and stands, taking our empty glasses and giving me a tight, almost pained smile. "I'm going to get us refills."

I sit up when he leaves and bring my fingers to my lips as I try to process what just happened. I just had my first kiss, and it was *incredible.*

Until he ended it so abruptly, that is.

Hayden comes back into the room, handing me my glass and taking a seat on the couch, farther away from me than before.

Was I that bad? Maybe he just isn't that into me...

I try to control my expression, but I must not do a good job because he gives me a forced smile. "No need to rush, gorgeous. Let's just enjoy tonight."

The strange edge has returned to his expression, and I wonder if it has anything to do with our kiss. Then again, my knowledge of men is minimal, and I'm probably just reading into it.

"I'm sorry. I didn't mean to get carried away," I whisper and avert my gaze.

"You didn't. I did."

I take a sip of my drink to cover my heated cheeks and the insecure thoughts threatening my composure.

"What is it?" Hayden asks.

"It's nothing..."

His finger lifts my chin, rougher than before. "What is it?"

When I look at the demand shining in his brown eyes, a rush of something I don't recognize hits my chest and reverberates all the way down my spine. The feeling is completely foreign—a warm mix of adrenaline, boldness, and nerves.

Whatever it is, I want more.

"You didn't need to kiss me out of pity." I pull away from his gaze just long enough to down the rest of my wine.

Wow, I drank that too fast.

The world grows hazy, and I blink to clear my blurring vision.

"I didn't kiss you out of pity," he tells me, and I get lost in his eyes —in the longing I find there. "I kissed you because I couldn't stop myself, Elise."

My heart stops.

Time stops.

Everything stops.

My eyes go wide, but it's hard to focus because everything seems to be moving in slow motion.

I push away from him, and my wine glass falls to the wooden floor, shattering along with my sense of security.

"What did you just call me?"

With a slight shake of his head, Hayden's eyes narrow in an expression that sucks all warmth and safety from the room. With his lips pressed in a hard line and his jaw ticking angrily, he looks nothing like the man I let into my apartment.

I try desperately to scramble away, but he's on top of me in an instant.

"What'd you do to me?" My words are mumbled, and I shake my head to clear it, but the world is too fuzzy.

I look at the fragments of glass on the floor, tinged red with the last drops of what I now realize was drugged wine.

"Take a nap, Princess. Everything is going to be just fine."

Dark, cunning eyes are the last thing I see before I slip into oblivion.

CHAPTER THREE

Joshua

I throw my remaining wine back like a shot and gaze at the unconscious girl on the couch.

Well, that is *not* how I expected the night to go.

I replay the last ten minutes in my head, surprised by my lack of control over the situation. The plan had been simple: get in, get her, get out.

I'd only been inside the apartment for five minutes before I decided that I was not going to follow that plan.

My phone buzzes, and I glance at it to see a sixth missed text from Ryder Bates, my underboss.

Ryder: In place. Ready whenever you are.
Ryder: Waiting for your signal.
Ryder: Everything okay in there?
Ryder: Moreno.
Ryder: What the hell is going on?
Ryder: Coming in.

The last was sent less than a minute ago, and I force myself out of my trance to open the door before he knocks it down. When I swing it open, my right-hand man is stomping toward me, wearing a mix of relief and annoyance.

"What took so long?"

He follows me into the apartment, taking in the girl on the couch and the shattered glass on the floor.

"The conversation was useful, so I let it play out." I shrug like it's no big deal, but even I notice how tightly wound I am. "I'll get to work on the kitchen. You clean up the glass. I don't want anything left behind."

Ryder nods and gets to work without another word.

I wipe down dishes and anything else my fingerprints touched, then collect all garbage, but my thoughts are consumed by the girl on the couch.

Elise Consoli.

I'd known that she was attractive, but seeing her in person was nothing like I imagined. For as egotistical and malicious as her father is, I'd expected her to be the same, but that couldn't be further from the truth.

She's shy, soft-spoken, easily flustered, and innocent.

So innocent.

I wasn't lying when I told Ryder that the conversation was useful. Elise lied all through dinner, and each time was an opportunity to read her. She's a horrible liar with obvious tells—avoiding eye contact, shoulders tensing, and over-explaining.

Which is how I knew she was telling the truth about never having had a boyfriend.

What kind of twenty-three-year-old has never been kissed? Especially one that looks like her? There's no way no one has ever tried to take her out.

But damn, her inexperience makes her *that* much more enticing.

Just knowing my lips are the only ones that have touched hers is enough to make me want more—not to mention the giant middle finger it will be to her father when he has her back and finds out that I've tainted her.

"Done in here," Ryder says, interrupting my thoughts as he comes into the kitchen. "I'll get her ready while you finish this."

"You do this. I'll deal with Elise." My voice is perfectly indifferent, but Ryder still hesitates before he nods and takes the trash bag from me.

I ignore his silent question as I make my way to the living room.

And there she is.

Her tan skin is still tinted pale from when I called her by her real name. She'd been terrified, but now that her features have fallen into perfect relaxation, I let my eyes linger.

She looks different from her brothers, but there are enough similarities to assure me of their relation. Her eyes are a deep brown, unlike their green, and her face is rounder, too.

Still, the way she holds herself—with confidence her words rarely reflect—is all her father. Even her voice, though softer than the men in her family, is effortlessly compelling. I've only met Gabriel Consoli a few times, but the resemblance is uncanny.

And if my intel is correct, he'll do anything to get her back.

I pick up the bag Ryder dropped by the door when he came in and grab the rope stashed there. I keep the binds on her wrists loose enough that I don't have to worry about her circulation, and after a moment of deliberation, I decide against restraining her legs. Even if she happens to wake up, she's not going anywhere.

The possessive side of me relishes that fact.

When Ryder walks out of the kitchen carrying the trash bag, I wait for him to make a comment about the lack of effort I put into getting Elise ready to go, but he smartly keeps his mouth shut.

I pass him a pair of gloves and slip my own over my hands. "We'll leave in a few hours when her neighbors are asleep. In the meantime, let's take a look around. I don't think Consoli would've left anything here, but I want to be sure."

With a nod, he disappears down the hall.

I take my time looking through the trinkets on the shelves around the living room. Several fake potted plants line the bottom shelf, and a row of worn books rests above it. I scan the titles—mostly classics—and wonder if she enjoys reading them or if she just likes to collect antiques.

A small spinning globe and a picture of a vineyard occupy the next shelf, and I recall how her expression deflated when I asked her why she couldn't travel. Of course, I knew, but watching her answer was enough to know she isn't a fan of her confined lifestyle.

There are no family pictures in her apartment. I wasn't expecting a family gallery, but this apartment looks more like a model that would be shown to potential residents. There's nothing personal about the décor.

I'm sure this was done for a reason. After all, pictures of her family would conflict with her story about living with her aunt. Still, I wonder what this place would look like without the limits.

It almost makes me feel bad for what I'm about to do.

Almost.

The car door slams shut behind me, and I turn to glance at Elise lying peacefully in the back. We originally debated whether or not to drug her, but I'm glad we did. Since we would've taken her either way, this is easier for everyone.

Ryder wordlessly climbs into the passenger seat, and I put the car in drive, leaving a spotless apartment behind us.

After thirty minutes, we pull onto the runway, where the private plane awaits us. I park the car, but neither of us moves to get out.

I ignored his brooding and questioning glares the whole ride, but I'm not about to let it follow us onto the plane.

"What?" I snap.

He doesn't waste our time. "What happened in the apartment?"

"I already told you."

"You didn't tell me everything."

"You don't need to know everything."

"You took two hours to do a job that should've taken less than one."

"And I have more information for it."

"So, nothing happened?"

"What are you really asking?"

Ryder squares his shoulders. "Did you screw her?"

I bark a laugh. "You're kidding, right?"

His expression is unchanging. "You didn't touch her then?"

Well, that's a different question.

I try not to make a habit of lying to Ryder, but that doesn't mean he needs to know what happened in that apartment.

So, I opt to stay silent.

Contrary to the glares I've been getting all night, Ryder's chuckle fills the car. When I look to the passenger seat, I find a rare smile from my usually expressionless friend.

"What?"

"Gabriel Consoli is going to kill you."

And despite myself, my lip tugs upward. "He's sure as hell going to try."

CHAPTER FOUR

Elise

The sound of metal clinking is the first thing I process when I come to. I try to open my eyes, but it hurts, and I can't see anything clearly. My breathing is labored, and every muscle in my body is stiff. I try to move my arms, but for some reason, I can't get them to budge. I go to roll over but stumble over my own feet, which is when I realize I'm not lying down.

I pull my arms again, understanding now that they are secured above me, holding up my entire body. No wonder my shoulders are burning. I try desperately to regain my vision as another sound seeps through the fog of my brain.

Whispers.

As soon as I notice it, the whispering stops, and terror shoots through my veins as I strain to remember how I got here, but my memories are a muddied mess.

"Good morning, Princess. I hope you slept well." The voice is familiar—deep and soothing.

A shudder runs through my body, and my vision finally clears enough to reveal the speaker.

Hayden Montez.

Events from last night come rushing back—Hayden coming over, eating dinner, sitting on the couch, kissing... and then I passed out.

No, he *drugged* me.

"Welcome to the basement," he says, waving an arm around the room.

I take in the exposed brick that covers every wall of the large room.

A set of stairs that goes up in front of me and a door to my right are the only exits in sight. Chairs are scattered around the area, but only one of them is occupied.

The dark-skinned man has an even bigger build than Hayden, and judging by the way his white shirt clings to his chest, it's all muscle. He has black hair that's cropped short and a neatly trimmed beard. His fiercely handsome features are currently arranged in a glare directed at me.

Then, there's the man who stands directly in front of me.

How did I not see it? How could I have been so stupid?

In the dim light of the basement, I see him in a way I never did before. Those brown eyes that had seemed so warm are alight with malice. His broad frame no longer makes me feel protected but weak and helpless. His lips are pressed in a hard line, and it's difficult to imagine that those same lips had kissed me so gently.

I open my mouth to speak, but it's so dry that I only end up coughing. Hayden turns and walks toward a table to my left to grab something.

When my eyes drift to the table, my blood turns to ice. Fear grips me so tightly that I can't breathe. The long wooden table is crowded with devices that I can only assume bring the most violent pain—saws, knives, whips, chains, and countless other weapons that I can't even name.

I vaguely notice Hayden walking back toward me, but I can't tear my eyes off the table of tortures. My mind races, imagining all the horrible things he could do to me with the items there.

A rough hand grips my chin, forcing my head to the side as I gasp for air.

I stare into Hayden's expressionless face and work to get my breathing under control. When I finally have a steady breath, he raises his other hand, and I flinch, but he doesn't hit me. Instead, he lifts a glass of water with a straw to my mouth.

I shake my head.

He rolls his eyes, guessing my thoughts exactly. "It's not drugged. Drink."

My parched mouth begs me to accept it, but how can I? Even if it isn't drugged, I can't just do what he tells me. That would mean he wins.

Though strung up in this basement at his mercy, it seems I've already lost.

Still, my pride is all I have left.

"Either you drink, or I make you." His words are sharp, and I have no doubt the threat is real.

My mind is still hazy from whatever he put in my wine, so it takes me a moment to decide if I'm going to obey.

Unfortunately, he isn't in the mood to wait.

Releasing my chin, he reaches back and grabs hold of my hair, pulling until my head is facing straight up. I cry out, and as soon as my mouth is open, Hayden pours the water down my throat. My mouth quickly fills with the liquid, and the excess pours down my face. I choke and swallow what I can, but most of it spills out. He lets go of my hair, and I cough, dropping my head as the water drips from my face down my clothes.

When I finally lift my head, he no longer holds the cup, and his arms are crossed over his chest.

"You'll learn very quickly that when it comes to obedience, there's an easy way and a hard way. It doesn't matter to me which you choose, but what you need to understand"—he steps forward, pressing his body to mine—"is that you *will* obey me."

Fire blazes in my veins. I never thought that I could be capable of killing someone, but looking into the face of pure evil, I imagine a multitude of ways that I'd like to make this man suffer.

I swing my head as hard as I can, forehead connecting with his face. Hayden grunts, reaching up to touch the blood dripping from the cut on his lip.

I smile, but my victory is short-lived.

Before I can process his movements, his arm reaches for my side, and the most intense pain I've ever felt shoots through my whole body. Every muscle goes limp as the inflicted spot burns like a flame to my skin, and I sag into the chains, yanking on my already sore shoulders.

He pulls the taser back, and I gasp for air.

Once the worst of the pain is over, I bite my tongue, willing myself not to cry. This asshole can't see me break.

"Elise Maya Consoli, you're not at all what I expected." He's circling me now, surveying my trapped body.

"That makes two of us, *Hayden*," I spit the undoubtedly fake name.

I can feel his low chuckle against my ear as he stands directly behind me, and a shudder of something more than fear runs through my body. I wince when he, once again, pulls my hair back so I'm looking upward, only this time he's standing over me.

"I'd watch how you talk to me, Princess."

"Stop calling me that." I narrow my eyes, but with my head tilted upward, it only makes me dizzy.

"I'm not sure you're in a position to make demands."

"Who the hell do you—" My words are interrupted when the electric burn of the taser meets my side again.

I want to stay silent, but I can't help the pained yelp that escapes my lips. He releases his grip on my hair but holds the current to my body longer than he did the first time. When he finally pulls away, sweat drips down my face.

"I'll be the one asking questions, *Princess*."

I open my mouth to tell him off, but I halt my words when he raises an eyebrow, daring me to speak.

"The easy way or the hard way. You get to pick, beautiful."

I want nothing more than to spit on him, to curse him to hell and back, but when I think logically through my options, I reluctantly close my mouth.

"Good girl," he purrs.

I narrow my eyes to deadly slits, but the reaction only amuses him. Stepping close, his fingertips brush the sensitive skin on my side where the taser made contact.

More than just the discomfort, it's unnerving to have him touch me, and I feel a whole different kind of electricity. I grimace and try to pull away, but my chains keep me firmly in place. There's nothing I can do but stare daggers at him.

"I'm going to ask you some questions, and you're going to answer them. Easy enough, don't you think?" He walks toward the table of torture, and my heart leaps into my throat.

"Wait," I whisper.

He turns, raising an eyebrow at me again.

I want to beg him not to hurt me. I want to say I'll tell him whatever he wants to know, and he doesn't need to hurt me.

But I can't do that.

I drop my head, unwilling to beg this monster for anything.

"That's what I thought." He grabs something off the table and hides it behind his back as he comes closer. "When was the last time you saw your dad?"

My dad?

Of course, this is about my dad. How did I not understand that right away? That must be why he asked to hang out on Sunday. He must have known I wouldn't have security. Come to think of it, I bet he timed his visit to the bakery just right so that Kaitlyn never saw him.

The realization hits me so hard that I forget the question.

"Huh?"

That was the wrong thing to say.

I wince at the searing pain on my thigh and look down to see a bright red mark where he's slashed me with a thin switch.

"When was the last time you saw your father?"

Do I tell him the truth or not?

But isn't this the reason why I stayed out of everything? So I wouldn't have any incriminating information?

"Maybe a month ago," I tell him.

He trails the switch along my leg, and I hold my breath, knowing that, at any second, he'll strike me again. The action is so nerve-racking that I have to clench my teeth to stop them from chattering.

"You've been legally dead for six years."

"That's not a question."

I'm not surprised when the switch comes down hard on my thigh.

"Again, I'd be very careful about how you speak to me."

Staying silent seems like the safest option, so I do.

He takes leisurely steps out of my view to round me again. "Why did you go into hiding?"

The days leading up to my alleged death aren't my fondest memories, and I loathe this man for forcing me to relive them.

At seventeen, most girls are going to parties, sneaking out, or failing calculus, but not me. I was packing up everything I owned from my family home in Chicago and moving to Milwaukee to hole up in a lonely apartment while my father and brothers arranged an empty casket funeral.

Ultimately, it was my decision to leave Chicago and the Consoli criminal family behind. At the time, legally dying for my freedom had seemed like a fair price. It wasn't until years later that I realized I'd given up far more than my name for far less than freedom.

"I went into hiding to avoid psychopathic maniacs who might use me against my father. As you can see, it's not going well."

The remark is a risk I know could result in more pain, but he doesn't strike me again.

When he returns to my line of sight, he regards me with an awe that brings heat rushing to my cheeks, but I don't look away.

I won't give him the satisfaction.

Though his eyes don't leave mine, he tilts his head, shifting one shoulder back to aim his words behind him. "*Six years*, Ryder. Unbelievable."

The man—Ryder, I assume—leans forward in his chair with a solemn nod.

"Nobody questioned him when he said she died. They had a funeral and everything," he says, and his voice is eerily calming, a honey-smooth tenor that makes me want to hang on to his every word despite the shiver running down my spine.

I hate how they talk about me like I'm not right in front of them.

His hand grips my chin before I can pull away. "It's a miracle no one got to you before I did."

I match his glare in a standoff, and I know he's waiting for me to snap, to give him a reason to hurt me again, and *damn*, I want to give him an earful, but I force myself to keep quiet.

Seconds pass before he releases my chin. "How often do you talk to your father?"

"Maybe twice a week."

The switch comes down again, and I wince as my thigh throbs.

"What was that for? I answered your question!" My outburst is rewarded with two strikes to my other thigh.

There's a ghost of a smile on his face. The bastard is enjoying this.

"To remind you that I can."

"Because the restraints aren't a clear enough indication."

Though I expect the lashes, they still bite into my sensitive skin with a force that makes me grimace.

"Apparently not." He steps in close, dropping one hand to my lower back and drawing me into him in a strangely intimate gesture. "But it will be by the time I'm done with you."

He releases me. "How many days a week does your father work out of his main base in Chicago?"

"I don't know." My answer, though truthful, prompts him to brush the switch along my leg.

"I'd think harder if I were you, Princess."

"*I don't know!*" I expect my insistence to bring on more pain, but he only raises an eyebrow, and I take that as a sign to continue. "I've never been involved in any of my family's work. They don't tell me anything, and I don't *want* to know. I don't have any information that

31

would be useful to you. That was the whole point of me '*dying*' in the first place!"

His lip quirks up. "Then, it's a good thing having you is enough to get what I want."

"And what exactly is that?" I ask as if I haven't learned my lesson by now, and the switch comes down again.

I have no idea how long it goes on, but by the time Ryder releases me from my chains, I collapse onto the ground. I barely have the energy to look down and see that my skin is decorated with slim cuts and light bruises.

"Stand up," he orders, but when I try to, I crumble helplessly back to the floor.

"I'll get her," Ryder offers.

"No, you get this cleaned up. I'll handle her." As he says the words, strong arms scoop me up from the ground.

My mind urges me to resist him, but I don't have the energy, so I let him hold my aching body against his hard chest. The familiar pine scent that wafts off of him calls to me in a way that I despise because, even after everything he's done to me, it's downright intoxicating.

"Yes, Mr. Moreno," Ryder bids as I'm carried from the room.

Moreno? I rack my over-exhausted brain for any meaning to the name but find none. I truly have no idea who this man is.

I'm taken to a cold, windowless room and dropped onto a lumpy mattress. The door slams shut, but I barely hear it. Burrowing into the flat pillow and scratchy blanket, I fall into a restless sleep.

CHAPTER FIVE

Elise

There's no way to tell time: seconds, minutes, hours, days—it's all a blur of drifting in and out of sleep, eating oatmeal and bread when it's brought to me, and staring at the wall.

Cuts and bruises cover my arms and legs, visible through my ripped and bloodied clothing. It's been days since I woke up in the basement, but the wounds are still sensitive and raw. My meager meals aren't enough to energize my body, and I can feel myself growing weaker. The lack of good hygiene and nutrients has minimized any healing that should've taken place by now.

I'm about to drift off to sleep when I hear the faint sound of footsteps coming down the hallway.

My eyes dart to the tray of food, steam faintly rising from the oatmeal, still warm.

If someone is coming to see me, it isn't a routine visit.

I scramble backward on instinct, getting as far away from the solid metal door as possible, but the effort is in vain.

The doorknob turns, and my visitor enters the room.

This can't be good.

The man who was with Moreno the other day, Ryder, marches right to me. I scramble away, but before I know it, he has an iron grip on my arm.

He drags me to stand, and I yelp when he twists my arms behind my back to handcuff me. Within seconds of him entering the room, he has me restrained and is leading me out.

He guides me down a hallway of off-white stucco walls, and,

much to my disappointment, there are no windows that could indicate where I am or even what time of day it is. I try to remember the direction of the basement, but I had been so exhausted that I wasn't paying much attention.

I hope Ryder won't take me there again.

We turn down a wide hallway with doors lining either side, but it's the one at the end of the hall that draws my attention. Twin dark oak doors tower high above the rest, with intricate designs carved around the edges in no notable pattern.

Sure enough, Ryder takes me right to it and knocks.

"Come in," a familiar voice calls, and my skin crawls.

Ryder opens the door and pushes me inside so carelessly that I trip over my own feet and crash to the ground.

"Ah!" I cry out, and every inch of my body throbs from the impact.

The door shuts, and I lift my head, blinking to adjust to the bright light.

When I finally do, I observe the office—large windows dominate the far side, overlooking a wall of tall trees. Bookshelves, paintings, and statues decorate the room, but my eyes land on the mahogany desk, or rather, the man who sits behind it.

Moreno stands, making his jeans and dark T-shirt visible as he steps around the desk.

I want to move, run, or hide from him, but I don't. What's the point?

I'm not going to win.

"How are you feeling today?" His soft tone catches me off guard, but I'm not fooled by it this time.

"Go to hell," I bite.

An amused grin spreads across his face as he unceremoniously grabs me by the arm and places me on one of the seats in front of him.

I clench my teeth to conceal the amount of pain it elicits.

"I'll ask again." He leans against the desk, arms crossed over his broad chest. "How are you feeling today?"

"Like I've been kidnapped and put through hell by an asshole."

He shakes his head. "Such a dirty mouth."

"You didn't seem to think so the other night."

To my surprise, he laughs. "At least I bought you dinner first. You can't say I'm not a gentleman."

"You're a pig."

"You didn't seem to think so the other night," he says with a wink.

Against my better judgment, I stand and step toward his desk. "I can't wait until my dad kills you. He'll torture you for weeks, maybe even months, before showing you the mercy of a bullet in your head. Hell, maybe I'll get to finish you off myself, you sadistic bastard."

My chest heaves, and I'm feeling triumphant, that is, until his smile twists into a malicious sneer.

He straightens from his desk and steps slowly until he's towering over me, and my confidence vanishes.

"You have a lot more fire in you than I expected. It's cute, but it's getting annoying. I don't have time to deal with your temper tantrums, so they stop now. As far as your father goes"—he lets out a humorless chuckle and steps behind me—"I'd love to see him try."

He moves my hair to one shoulder, and I hate the shudder that travels down my spine when his warm breath tickles my neck. "Your dad can't save you from me, Elise. No one can. You'll go home if and when *I* say so."

I try to process his words, but it's difficult when he places possessive hands on my waist, inspiring conflicting emotions. Fear, of course, but it's more than that. I'm taken back to my apartment and how it had felt to have his hands on me.

There'd been no fear then.

A wave of relief washes over me when he finally steps away.

"Sit," he orders, walking back around his desk.

I glare at him but obey, prompting a smug grin from Moreno.

"Speaking of your father," he says, "it's about time we send him proof of life, don't you think?"

"You'll let me call him?"

He laughs. "I'm going to send him a video, and you're going to say exactly what I tell you to, or else we're going back to the basement, understand?"

The threat is a noose tightening around my throat. I can barely pull air into my lungs, let alone speak, so I only nod.

When Moreno raises an expectant brow, it doesn't take a genius to know what he's waiting for.

"Yes," I manage in a whisper.

As I drop my gaze, I catch sight of a small device on his desk.

A cellphone.

I don't let my eyes linger for fear of Moreno getting suspicious.

He turns to grab something on the shelf behind him, and I notice a gun strapped to his side.

A crazy plan formulates in my head, but I need to be careful. I doubt I'll get another opportunity like this.

He walks around the desk, holding a video camera and newspaper.

"Seriously?"

"Watch it, Princess. My patience only goes so far." He sets the items on his desk and moves closer to me. "Now, I'm going to take off the handcuffs. You're going to be a good girl, right?"

I grit my teeth and give him my most vicious glare.

His lip twitches upward as he crouches. I flinch away when he reaches for my face, but he ignores my recoil and gently cups my cheek with his palm.

Having felt both pain and pleasure at his touch, the conflicted feelings his touch inspires twist my stomach to the point of physically aching.

"Now, that wasn't very convincing," he chides. "You'll be good, right, Elise?"

"Get your hand off of me," I whisper, hating that his closeness is making me dizzy.

He tightens his hold.

Wincing, I look up at him through full lashes. "I won't do anything. You can take them off."

He holds my gaze for a moment longer, expression unreadable, then releases my face to remove the cuffs.

I rub my newly freed wrists, and Moreno stands before me, leaning against his desk. He tosses the newspaper onto my lap, and I instinctively catch it there, searching for a date.

It's Friday, meaning I've been here for five days—I only remember three.

"I was unconscious for *two days*?"

Crossing his arms over his chest, Moreno gives a tight nod.

How is that possible? Two days of my life just gone. What could have possibly happened during that time?

My stomach drops with the weight of dread as terrifying, perverse theories surface.

"What happened?" I whisper.

His eyes narrow, and I unconsciously shrink back.

"I mean"—I cross my arms over my chest—"no one, you know, did anything... to me, right?"

The reasoning behind the question registers, and Moreno's

expression softens the slightest bit.

He meets my gaze with perfect sincerity. "I can assure you that no one has laid a hand on you—aside from myself."

Heat creeps up my cheeks, and I drop my gaze. "And you—you didn't do anything? While I was unconscious?"

I hear a rustling, but I don't move my eyes from the floor. A second later, a gentle finger lifts my chin, and Moreno is crouched in front of me again.

For just a moment, his eyes carry the same warmth they did at the bakery.

"Elise, I have no desire to take you against your will—in that sense, anyway," he says with an unapologetic shrug. "Aside from carrying you to and from the car, you have remained untouched."

Staring into his deep, brown eyes, I see no ounce of deception. He's telling the truth.

The tension of our intimate moment breaks when Moreno pushes to stand, and any hint of the man I met at the bakery disappears.

We're back to normal—a captor and his captive.

"Ready, Princess?"

After twenty minutes, we're done with the video. It took a few tries—much to Moreno's frustration—but it's difficult to say *I am safe and unharmed* without rolling my eyes because it's not even close to the truth.

I am far from safe and unharmed.

He returns the camera to the shelf behind his desk, and I eye the cell phone and his gun once again.

If I'm going to do this, I need to do it soon.

I take a calming breath, refusing to let my nerves get the better of me.

I can do this.

"Why me?" My voice is hardly above a whisper, but I know he can hear it.

He stiffens, raising an eyebrow but not bothering to answer the question.

"Why me? And why at all? What do you even want?"

His eyes spark with dark amusement, and he steps closer.

Good.

"Elise, do you remember what happened the last time you asked me questions?" He steps closer again, then crouches to my level.

Almost there.

"What's your name?" I ask.

The question catches him off guard, and he thinks for a moment, visibly deciding whether or not to tell me.

It's just the opportunity I need.

Before he can react, I grab the gun from the holster at his waist. His head turns, but he doesn't understand what I'm doing until it's too late, and I've bashed the butt of the gun against his head. He makes a hissing sound and I hit him again.

Moreno falls to the floor, and I take the lack of groans to be a good sign. I rush to the desk, scrambling to grab the phone in my frenzied state.

Holding the gun in one hand and the phone in the other, I fumble with the keypad, and my finger accidentally hits the call button, which triggers the phone to call the most recent number. I go to hang up, but the recipient answers before I get the chance.

"You got the video done already? My dad's flipping out right now. That'll send him over the edge for sure."

I know that voice. I grew up with that voice. I love that voice.

It's my brother.

It's Mason.

CHAPTER SIX

Joshua

"What's your name?"

The question gives me pause, not because I think Elise needs this information but because of her expression when she asks it.

Thin brows furrowed, delicate lips parted, big eyes searching mine for answers. Even now, when her clothes are tattered and her hair is matted and tangled, she's beautiful.

There's a tug in my chest that makes me want to tell her the truth.

I'm about to open my mouth to do just that when a flash of movement stops me. Before I get the chance to look around, pain explodes on the left side of my forehead.

The force momentarily blinds me, and I reach for my gun, but it's gone. Just as I realize what's happened, the gun comes down in the same spot a second time. My body slumps to the floor while being cursed to hell and back by my mind, which has already put together Elise's plan.

Blood drips down my face to the carpet, and I can already feel a nasty bruise forming on my skull.

When I raise my head, I find the exact scene I expect.

Elise stumbles to my desk, the gun shaking in her timid grasp, and takes the cell phone I carelessly left sitting there.

The phone that only has one contact.

I push to my feet despite the debilitating headache she's given me, but it's too late. Her fingers clumsily hit the keypad, and the phone only rings once before he answers.

Mason's mumbled voice comes through the line, and it's as if all the air has been sucked from the room.

Elise's eyes widen in horror, all the blood draining from her face as the phone clatters to the desk, and she falls to her knees.

I take advantage of her shock and shove myself to my feet, taking the gun from her limp hand and lifting her by a tight hold on her arm.

"Ryder!" He bursts into the room at the same time that I shove Elise over the desk and pull her hands roughly behind her.

When his eyes flit between the discarded burner phone, the gash on my forehead, and the look on Elise's face, he quickly puts the pieces together.

A small whimper draws my attention to the girl in my arms and the death grip that I have on her wrists. It's not until that moment that I realize she's not resisting me. There isn't an ounce of defiance in her.

When her hands are cuffed, I notice the blank expression on her colorless face.

She has *no idea* what she's done.

Ryder wordlessly takes hold of the girl, pulling her from the room while I reach for the phone that's still on the line with Mason.

The heavy pit in my stomach turns as I bring the phone to my ear.

"Mason."

"Tell me that wasn't who I think it was." His voice is tight.

"I'll deal with it," I tell him, though I have no clue how.

"Deal with it? What the hell is there to deal with? The whole plan just went off the rails!"

"Watch it," I warn, clenching my fist to contain my frustration. "I told you I'd deal with it. The plan will go on as normal."

"How the hell did she even—"

"The plan goes on as normal. Don't check in unless you absolutely need to. I won't risk your father getting suspicious of you."

There's a pause, and despite the fact that we both know he has a lot more to say about this, there's only one acceptable response.

"Yes, sir."

Friday, April 10: six weeks earlier

I burst through the door, cutting off all conversation in the conference room. The five capos of my main base here in Los Angeles surround the table. They straighten respectfully at my entrance, but their attention is directed at the man who stands regally at my side.

Though Mason Consoli has worked with the Moreno family for

40

years, his physical attendance is a rarity that puts all my men on edge. The hesitation is understandable but unnecessary. He's followed every order to the letter, never once giving me a reason to doubt his loyalty despite his bloodline.

My capos don't bother hiding their glares, but Mason doesn't seem intimidated in the slightest. He takes his place on the left side of the conference table, but I remain standing behind the head chair.

Ryder sits to my right, face utterly expressionless as always. Donovan Riley, Alec Tonis, Tripp Singleton, and Kade Manning fill the remaining chairs and look at me expectantly.

Each of these men has worked their asses off to earn their spot at this table, which is how I know I can trust them with the details of the plan I'll be implementing in the coming weeks.

Ryder and Mason share an icy look, but I don't interfere. They've never been particularly friendly with one another, but it hasn't affected their work, which is all I care about.

"I'm making a move to claim the remaining southern territories that would give us control over the Mexican border," I state, getting right to business.

I lower the video screen and press the button that turns it on to show a map of the United States of America, colorless aside from the dots that mark various bases occupied by the five major American criminal families.

The Morenos, Consolis, Marsollos, Diazes, and Riveras.

Hundreds of mafia families reside in each of our territories, but all with the permission of their designated family.

I look over the green dots that represent my West Coast empire with pride. It's been a long journey to accomplish everything I have, and I'm far from done.

Consoli's red markings span over three regions—Midwest, Southwest, and Southeast. Though his strongest bases are Midwestern, his influence is nothing short of admirable, albeit annoying as all hell.

"Gabriel Consoli is planning to put a base in Austin to be established by his Dallas and Houston locations. We're going to beat him to it and take Houston from him while we're at it."

"Why not put all our resources into taking Austin first, then go from there?" Kade asks.

I point to the map. "Because with El Paso being our closest base to Austin, we won't be able to sufficiently protect it if Consoli attacks from his Dallas and Houston bases. By taking Houston, we weaken him and have a fully armed base to help develop and protect Austin."

Donovan straightens in his chair. "And how exactly do you plan to take Houston? As you said, we can't fight against his two bases there."

"Well, Mr. Riley." Mason stands from the table and straightens his blazer. "We won't be taking it by force."

Though no one asks, the question hangs heavy in the room.

Mason throws me a look, and I nod for him to take over.

"Elise Consoli. Recognize the name?"

Tripp rolls his eyes. "Your dead sister, we know."

He's never been one for sympathy.

Mason sharpens his glare and says, "She's alive and has spent the last six years in hiding."

My men aren't easily surprised, but I can hardly blame them for their shocked silence.

Ryder gives me a look, and though nothing in his expression changes, I read the message: *are you sure about this?* The lowering of my head is my confirmation. It's only been a few days since Ryder and I learned of this development and formulated our plan.

The news was initially infuriating.

Mason's been under my command for four years now without a single mention of his sister. It's a secret that he deliberately kept from me, and I nearly put a bullet in his head for that alone, but the value of the information saved his life.

Up until this point, Gabriel Consoli has been an impenetrable fortress, but Elise is his weakness.

"You get her, and my father will do anything to get her back, including surrendering these territories."

"Consoli's don't surrender," Alec says. "Everyone knows that."

"Which is why he staged her death after the attack on our family home six years ago. He made it look like she got caught in the crossfire, then sent her to Milwaukee, where she lives under the alias Annie Smith."

Tripp barks a humorless laugh, and we all turn to him. "Why would you keep this a secret for so long? I don't buy it."

"What are you suggesting?" Ryder asks.

Tripp leans back in his chair. "I'm not suggesting anything. I'm only pointing out that it's a big secret to keep."

Instead of giving reasons or excuses, Mason simply pulls out his phone. He puts it on speaker, and the ringing fills the room.

"Mason, what's up?" The voice is unmistakably feminine, soft, and melodic.

"Hey, Elise. Nothing really, just thought I'd call to check up," he answers, eyes never leaving Tripp's glare.

The girl groans. "You're worse than Dad. You'd think half a dozen security guards would calm you down some, but nope."

"Where are you?"

"Nowhere anyone can hear me, don't worry. I'm not new to this, you know."

"Excuse me for questioning your stealth."

She laughs, and the sound is like music. "It's like you guys forget I'm just as much a Consoli as the rest of you."

Mason raises a challenging brow to Tripp, who cuts his eyes in response.

"You're right, you're right," he says." When are you coming home next?"

"Um, next Saturday?" It's more a question than a statement.

"Why do you say it like that?"

"Because it's been on Dad's calendar for three months now, just like *every visit ever*."

Mason laughs, and though the sound is effortless, his face remains stony. "You'll have to forgive my forgetfulness. I haven't been to the base much this week."

"Good. You work yourself too hard. Take it easy, okay? I love you."

"Love you too. Bye, Elise," he says before ending the call.

There's a beat of silence as my capos come to the same conclusion I had only days ago.

Elise Consoli is a gold mine.

Mason tucks the phone back into his pocket, folding his arms over his chest. "Any more questions?"

Present day

I brace myself on the wooden rail that lines the windows of my office, gripping it so tight my knuckles turn white from the strain.

My head still throbs, but the cut is cleaned and bandaged.

There's a knock on the door, but I don't bother calling him in. Ryder opens the door a moment later, though I don't turn to face him even when the door swings shut. We're encased in a thick silence as we process the implications of our situation.

"How did it happen?"

"She's craftier than we gave her credit for," I bite, releasing the railing and stretching my aching fingers as I stride to my desk.

"What are we going to do?"

"What is there to do?" I shake my head. "There's no way we can establish these bases without Mason. I can't let her screw this up for us."

"There's no way we can *get* the bases without this deal going through. Consoli won't bend for anything aside from her. You can't just refuse to give her back. You'll start a full-on war."

I rack my brain, desperate for anything that could help me figure out what I can do about this.

"I need time," I tell him. "I'll call Consoli first thing in the morning and schedule a meeting for Monday. Maybe I can buy us a few more days with these negotiations."

Ryder nods. "I'll make arrangements for the trip."

"Have Donovan make a list of reasonable negotiations we can work with. Alec can pick the meeting point and analyze all routes and possible ambush points along the way. Kade will need to keep an eye on their digital activity to ensure they're not planning to blindside us with anything. If we're doing this last minute, we can't afford to be sloppy."

He makes the notes on his phone and leaves my office the second I finish giving orders.

My mind, which was full of strategies and ideas only a moment ago, wanders to the girl who put me in this mess. Despite the headache that her stunt has *literally* given me, anger's not the emotion that accompanies the thought of her.

Her expression when she was in here, pale and broken, tugs on something in my chest that I don't understand or like.

I tell myself she brought this upon herself, and I can't be held responsible. Giving her back for the territories was always my plan, and it's her fault that can't happen now.

If it weren't for the incessant pounding in my head, I'd allow myself to feel bad for Elise. I can't exactly blame her for trying to contact home. Who wouldn't in her position?

Unfortunately, this girl has a luck streak from hell.

It's these confusing thoughts that lead me out of my office and across my base. When I reach the door, I wave a dismissive hand to the soldier on duty there, and he leaves with a respectful nod.

As soon as my hand touches the knob, I hear scuffling on the other side of the door. I push it open and find the wide, puffy eyes and red, splotchy face of a terrified girl. Her small frame is curled into a ball with her knees pulled to her chest on the pathetic excuse for a mattress.

If the thought of her tugged on my chest, then the sight of her crushes me in a way that urges me to turn from this room and never return.

Even so, I can't bring myself to do it.

But I can't bring myself to comfort her, either.

"Daughter of the most notorious mafia boss in the country, reduced to tears. I thought you were stronger than this, Elise."

She closes her eyes, drawing a shaky breath. "You don't know anything about me."

"I usually wouldn't be inclined to agree, but you continue to surprise me."

Her eyes snap open at that. She hadn't been expecting me to agree with her, and really, I hadn't either, but it's true.

She hadn't shed a single tear during our time in the basement, a fact that nearly knocked me on my ass. Her witty retorts were ready on the tip of her tongue no matter what I made her endure.

It was a stark contrast to the timid, stuttering girl I went on a date with.

"What's that supposed to mean?"

"You're resilient," I admit, fully expecting the confusion that twists her face.

She says nothing as she studies my expression, and I walk toward her. I've made it one step before she shuffles to a standing position, hands raised protectively in front of her.

"Calm down," I say in an easy tone, but she shakes her head.

"Get away from me," she mutters hoarsely.

I don't. Step after step, each one slowly draining the color from her face until she's concerningly pale. As I get closer I see the subtle shaking from her panic.

I reach for her face, wanting the color to return to her rounded cheeks simply because I miss the shade of pink.

My fingers are outstretched, but right before I can make contact, she darts past me.

There's nowhere for her to go—the door was locked the moment I walked in—but I still catch her arm. My grip is tight, and I wait for her to resist, but she doesn't.

"Where the hell do you think you're—"

She turns just in time for me to see the green that colors her face before she leans forward and vomits all over my shoes. Eyes rolling back in her head, Elise collapses to the ground.

Damn it all.

CHAPTER SEVEN

Elise

Sunlight hits my eyes, and I roll over in bed, burying my face in the soft pillow and hoping to fall back asleep. I'm on the brink of consciousness when my thoughts catch up to me.

Sunlight? Soft pillow? I open my eyes, and a shooting pain pierces my head. I quickly shut them and take a deep breath before trying again.

Slower this time, I ease my eyes open. It hurts at first, but as I blink, the pain dulls, and I take in my surroundings.

I'm in a new room, though this layout is similar to the last. The bed is still against the right wall, the bathroom on the left, and the door that leads out of here is on the far wall that I face now. Only, in this room, the wall behind my bed isn't empty. There's a window allowing sunshine to spill into the small space.

Drywall replaces the prison-like concrete from before, all painted light gray aside from the wall that holds the window, which is a rich burgundy. A table occupies the corner between the bathroom and exit, with two chairs on either side. The dresser is also a new addition, and it looks to be made out of marble or some other heavy stone. On top of it is a stack of books—all classics—a small elephant statue and an alarm clock.

An alarm clock.

Just knowing that it's 9 a.m. makes me feel like a human again.

I climb out of bed, my bare feet hitting wooden floors instead of cement, and I rush to the window. My heart drops when I see the heavily gated courtyard before me. The lush garden is vast and absolutely beautiful, but it's still a cage.

I walk into the bathroom and gasp as I look in the mirror for the first time since my kidnapping.

I look disastrous.

My thick blonde hair is a tangled mess, and my body looks worse than I imagined. Dark bruises cover my arms and legs, though they've had days to heal. My clothes are bloodied, and the various tears make the fabric nearly see-through.

Not only is there a shower, but there's also a beautiful bathtub that looks more like a small hot tub. To my utter shock, both the shower and bath are decked out with various soaps, salts, scrubs, razors, and loofas.

I'm relieved to finally be in a room that makes me feel more like a person than a prisoner, but there's no mistaking it: no matter how beautiful the room is, it'll always be a prison.

I don't even consider trying to open the door—I know it won't budge.

I want to shower, so I check the drawers for any clothes. To my continued surprise, it's full of T-shirts, sweatpants, shorts, jeans, bras, and underwear. They're all modest and close enough to my size.

After picking out a plain black shirt and gray sweatpants, I step into the shower before the water is fully warmed up, afraid someone will walk in on me if I take too long. The hot water stings against my cut and bruised body, but the ease it brings to my tense muscles makes it worth it.

I decide on a whim to shave my legs as best I can, hoping it'll give me some comfort since I don't normally let the hair grow as long as it is. As I start to shave, I realize that, in this new room, I have access to razors, small statues, and heavy drawers.

Maybe it'll be enough to escape…

Drying my body is a painful experience. Most of my cuts re-open, and by the time I'm finished, the towel is speckled with blood. The clothes I wore here lay on the floor, looking more like dirty rags than my once-favorite outfit. I stuff them into a small trash bin under the sink.

Within thirty minutes of stepping into the shower, I'm dressed in clean clothes with damp, brushed hair. I haven't felt this much like myself in… I don't know how long it's been.

The sound of the lock clicking sends ice through my veins. I take a seat on the far end of the bed, knees to my chest, arms wrapped around them.

It's morning, so I assume it's just another goon bringing me breakfast, but when Moreno enters, my heart drops. Blood rushes to my face at the horrifying memory of puking on his shoes.

Oh, please don't let him punish me for that.

He steps into the room, holding a tray of food.

Real food.

Nothing like the bland oatmeal and bread I've been eating for a week. This tray is full of bacon, eggs, fruit, and a cup full of steaming coffee. I'm practically drooling when he places the tray on the table.

I wait for him to leave, but he sits instead, gesturing to the chair across from him. "Take a seat."

My stomach turns at the idea of being anywhere near him. There's no way I can throw up again, right? My excitement for food urges me to run over, but fear of being so close to this man begs me to stay put.

I slowly shake my head, but even that simple motion elicits pain. "I'm okay over here."

"I wasn't asking. Sit."

I do, but only because I *need* that food, not because of his order.

Being so close to him makes me nervous, but a small (and stupid) part of my brain reminds me of the last time we sat like this.

Our date.

Embarrassment brings a shameful tear to my eye. I lower my head in hopes of hiding my weakness.

"Eat." He pushes the tray closer to me.

I eye the food, but him being here makes me feel sick all over again. "I'd like to—"

"Elise, look at me when you're speaking to me." His words are unmistakably an order, though his tone is controlled.

I glare up at him, but that's when the tear escapes.

I'm sure I look as pathetic as I feel.

Moreno raises his hand toward my face, and I flinch. His hand freezes in the air, expression purely analytic. I take a deep breath, and his hand slowly continues toward me until his finger gently wipes away the single tear from my cheek.

"You were saying?"

The tender action has me at a momentary loss for words, but I finally get my thoughts in order. "I'd like to wait until I'm alone to eat."

I'm surprised by his small smile. "I have no intentions of hurting you, so you can calm down. If you eat, I'll play nice. Deal?"

I shouldn't trust a single word he says, but the food looks so delicious, and he seems genuine enough, so I nod.

He leans his head to one side like he's waiting for something.

A response, of course.

I clear my throat and reach for a piece of bacon. "Deal."

"Good girl," he says with a nod. I narrow my eyes, but that only seems to amuse him."How are you feeling?"

"Huh?"

"After your fall, how do you feel?" There's an uncharacteristic tenderness to his tone. I wonder if he's mocking me, but his expression is thoughtful.

"Not great," I answer honestly.

Moreno nods. "The doctor said a headache is normal, but he didn't seem concerned about a concussion. He said malnourishment is the only reason you lost consciousness."

He had a doctor come to check on me? Unfortunately, the gesture isn't enough to ease my bitterness.

"And whose fault is that?"

He ignores the jab, which is probably for the best.

"Now, the real reason I'm here," he starts. "You have questions, and I've decided to give you a chance to ask them. Of course, there are things I won't tell you, but I'm giving you this opportunity to ask what you want without fear of being harmed."

He leans back in his chair as if he's bestowed upon me the offer of a lifetime. I'm sure he thinks he has, but I'm not so easily won over. I refuse to be a Stockholm Syndrome victim just because of a scenery change.

Accepting the potential repercussions, I sit up straighter and cut my eyes at him. "How very *kind* of you."

"Watch it, Princess. My generosity is limited."

"Generosity?" My laugh is bitter as I push to my feet. "That's what this is? After days of captivity, starving, and beating, I'm supposed to be grateful for the chance to ask *why* the hell you're doing this to me? If you think for one second that a nicer room and real food make up for the hell you've put me through, then you're not just cruel. You're stupid."

A storm rages just behind those brown eyes, and anger mars every crease of his face.

Suddenly, I'm not feeling so brave anymore.

He stands so fast the chair flies back, tipping over and crashing to the floor.

"You know what I think?" He leans his hands on the table and lowers his head to my eye level.

My heart is racing, and I silently accept that I'm about to feel a lot of pain.

"I think the princess needs a time-out."

I don't have time to be confused by his words because before I know it, he's swept me up over his shoulder and thrown me onto the bed. I scramble as far from him as I can, but he doesn't seem to mind because he's too busy… taking off his belt.

I didn't even consider the other kinds of torture I might face here.

Fear paralyzes me. He can do whatever he wants. No one would hear me, and even if they could, they wouldn't care.

"Wait, d-don't," I stutter through trembling lips.

It's pathetic, but it's all I can do.

He ignores my plea and grabs my wrists, using his belt to secure them to the headboard. By the time he's done, I'm effectively trapped, arms raised uncomfortably above my head.

I expect him to continue to shed clothing, but he doesn't.

Instead, he picks up the tray and sets it at the base of the bed. Right where I can see and smell it, but just far enough away from my toes that it's hopelessly out of reach.

He steps back and smiles to himself. "I think this will be good for you—maybe teach you some manners." His eyes roam my body, not bothering to conceal the hunger there, and my cheeks flush bright red.

"Go to hell, you sick bastard," I bite out.

His smile widens, and he leans in until our noses are inches apart.

"You're in hell, Princess, and I'm in charge."

With his face so close, I make the reckless decision to swing my head forward, hoping to catch his nose with my forehead. He pulls away just in time to miss being hit, and my head throbs from the motion.

"You just added an hour to your time."

My eyes widen, and my voice jumps an octave. "An hour? You can't leave me here that long!"

"Watch me," he says, not bothering to look back at me as he walks out the door.

The alarm clock turns out to be more of a curse than a blessing. At least before, I didn't realize how slow time was moving. Now, all I can do is watch each grueling minute pass by.

It's been two hours and thirty-six minutes since he left me here. My shoulders stopped burning in agony forty-three minutes ago and are now numb. The food is, no doubt, cold now, but its alluring scent still mocks me with every breath I take. My stomach is aching, and my eyes droop with the exhaustion of facing nonstop pain.

I don't even react when I hear the turn of the door handle. I don't have the energy. He sets something on the table, but I don't bother looking to see what it is.

I figure now is as good a time as any to get the answers I want.

"Why did you change my room?"

I hear steps and finally look up to find him grabbing the chair he knocked over earlier. He flips it around and straddles it, hands resting on the back of the chair. "I wasn't sure how much longer you were going to survive in those conditions. Well, that and I don't want to keep buying new shoes."

I roll my eyes. I only ruined one pair.

I consider asking what he wants from my father, but it wouldn't change anything, and I doubt he would tell me anyway. "Where am I?"

"Watch the eye-rolling." He doesn't sound angry, simply informative. The ease with which he speaks to me like a child should piss me off, but I'm too tired to care.

"Okay," I whisper. "I won't do it anymore, but answer my question."

My compliance seems to catch him off guard. Opening his mouth to speak, he's interrupted by my growling stomach. It's not the first time it's happened in the past two hours and forty-three minutes, so I don't react.

Sighing, he rises from the chair and makes his way toward me. Even in my exhausted state, I process this as a danger. My heart rate kicks up again, and I'm on alert, but he simply reaches to untie my hands.

I stay quiet, reluctant to give him any reason to keep me restrained.

Once my hands are freed and he's returned to straddling the chair, I slowly lower my arms. They're sore but feel better the more I stretch them. A feeling of gratitude washes over me at being free, but I reject it.

He's the one causing my suffering. It is not kindness that he releases me from it. It's a game, and I refuse to play.

"You should eat," he suggests. "It's cold, but it's still food."

I pull the tray closer to me. The scrambled eggs and bacon are chilled, but I still scarf them down, then the fruit, and lastly, I down the mug of room-temperature coffee.

He regards me as I eat and finally answers my question. "We're at one of my bases. You don't need to know anything more than that."

I drink the last of the coffee as he stands, turns the chair to face me, and gestures to it.

"Sit. I'm going to treat some of your wounds." He crosses his arms, waiting for me to obey.

I consider my options. Logically, there's no point in opposing. Sure, there's a chance he'll hurt me, but that chance becomes a guarantee if I stay put.

I silently climb off the bed and take a seat.

He grabs the item he put down on the table when he entered—a first aid kit. Pulling out some sort of cream, he begins to apply it to my aching wrists. The cool sensation feels heavenly on my burning skin.

"Second drawer on the right has shorts in it. Go change, and I'll treat the cuts on your legs."

Grabbing a pair of shorts, I walk into the bathroom and close the door behind me, exiting within seconds wearing cotton shorts. As I return to the chair, a very silly part of me is grateful that I shaved today.

My thighs are a mess. Various shades of blue and purple create a horrific picture, though it does look better since my shower.

He grabs the supplies and sets them on the floor, tending to my legs. His fingers work gently across my skin, effectively distracting me from my pain. Everywhere he touches, my skin tingles, but I scold myself each time.

I can't let him have any more power over me than he already does.

"Why am I still here? I thought I was going home soon."

"Things have changed," he says, looking up to meet my eyes. "The plan was to exchange you for what we want from your father. Obviously, that can't happen now."

"What do you mean *'that can't happen now'*?"

He studies my expression like he's waiting for me to come to some conclusion. "You didn't think you could just go home, did you? After knowing what you do? What did you expect?"

What *did* I expect? I guess I figured that I'd go home, and my snake of a brother would have to step up and pay for his betrayal.

I realize now how foolish that was to believe.

Of course they can't let me go. An inside man is far more valuable than a hostage. If I go home, Mason's secret is out, and he's no longer useful to them.

So, where does that leave me?

My breath catches as the realization hits me. "You're going to kill me."

CHAPTER EIGHT

Elise

His silence is all the confirmation I need.

I stand, pushing the chair into the drawers behind me.

"You're such a sick bastard! What's the point of all of this, then?" I gesture to the medical equipment. "Why waste time patching me up if I'm a dead woman walking?" I don't think about what I'm saying. I just let the words spill out of my mouth.

I stride across the room, holding my arms out in a wide, dramatic gesture.

"Why wait at all? Just do it now and get it over with! Go ahead. Shoot me right here, you coward," I spit.

His loud huff is the signal that my temper tantrum is over.

I take hesitant steps back as he approaches me until I run into the dresser. My fight-or-flight instincts kick in, and as soon as he's close enough, I grab the red elephant statue and swing to hit him over the head with it.

Lightning reflexes grab my hand before I can make contact with his skull.

He grips my wrist and twists, turning me around and holding me tight against his front. My arms curve painfully behind me in his steel hold. The statue falls from my hand and lands on the floor mere inches from crushing my bare foot.

Thrashing against him, I wiggle an arm free and swing it back, elbow connecting with his cheekbone. He groans, and I feel victorious for all five seconds because that's when I hear the distinct *shing* of a blade. I freeze, feeling cool metal pressing against my throat.

He holds my wrists in one hand, and his lips find my ear. "You're really annoying, you know that?"

The blade digs in deeper. "If I didn't know any better, I'd say you *like* it when I hurt you since you insist on testing my patience every time we meet."

I shake my head in a small motion, too afraid to speak.

"No? That's not what you want?"

I whimper, and he moves the blade from my throat, quickly slicing it across my upper arm. I cry out, but the sting of pain never comes, and I realize he ran the dull end over my skin in warning. He returns the blade to my throat.

"I can't hear you, Princess."

"No," I manage in a trembling whisper.

"Good girl. Take a seat. *Now*," he commands, removing the blade and stepping away from me.

My movements are slow, giving him no reason to use the knife again as I take my place in the chair.

I wince but don't resist when he grabs my wrists and pulls them behind my back. I even hold them still as he removes his belt again to restrain me.

"And I just spent time treating your wrists," he mutters.

As he secures the binds, my body realizes just how tired it is. With the adrenaline rush wearing off, my muscles ache, and my eyelids grow heavy.

Clearing his throat, Moreno comes to stand in front of me, knife still in hand.

"Here's what's going to happen," he states. "You're going to keep that mouth shut. I'll treat your wounds and explain some of what's going on since you can't seem to put it together on your own. Do you understand?"

I nod sluggishly.

He narrows his eyes. "I asked you a question. Do. You. Understand?"

My brain tells me to curse him or spit on him, anything but obey him. However, my body's argument to comply is much more convincing. I can barely function as it is. I can't handle any more of his wrath.

"I understand."

He runs a hand through his dark hair, and for some reason, I get the feeling that he's just as much shaken by this situation as I am.

"Four years ago, Mason reached out for a meeting. It's not every day that your biggest rival's son wants to have a chat, so I was wary." He kneels as he talks, sorting through the first-aid kit and tending to the cuts on my legs.

"I was sure it was going to be an ambush, so I came prepared, but he really did just want to talk. He had some very bold opinions about your father and how he runs your family. Mason knew that even if he killed your dad, one of your older brothers would just take over. So, instead of killing his family to rise to power, he joined me here."

My stomach rolls at the idea of Mason debating killing our family. He is not the man I thought he was.

"I didn't believe him right away, but I was interested, so we made a deal. He'd feed me intel for as long as I deemed fit, and if he proved himself loyal, he'd join me."

Once I'm all bandaged up, Moreno takes a seat on the bed, resting his elbows on his knees. "A year passed, and your brother proved himself, but I decided he needed to stay with your father where he was most useful to me."

"Recently, I've been working to expand my territory, but your father has claims in areas that make my expansion impossible. Mason proposed the idea of blackmail, but you Consolis have a reputation for refusing to negotiate. That's when Mason told me about you. Had we taken one of your brothers, your father likely would've let them die. But you?" There's a dark yet admirable glint in his eyes as he regards me. "Your father would do *anything* to protect you, which makes you my golden hostage."

"What makes you think he won't just let me die, too?"

"I've spoken to him myself. He's quite anxious to get you back."

My heart clenches at the words. Of course, I want my father to save me, but at what cost? I open my mouth to ask more questions, but a stern glance stops me.

"No more interruptions, or I'm going to gag you." His words are matter-of-fact, but they still send a shiver down my spine.

"Everything was going perfectly. I had you, your father was desperate to get you back... and then you pulled that stunt in my office." His eyes narrow, but it's not in anger. If I didn't know any better, I'd say it's disappointment. "Well, that complicated things."

"As I said, I've worked toward this expansion for years. Those territories open up a lot of doors for me, and this is the closest I've ever been to getting them." He pauses, watching my guarded expression as he goes on.

"If I kill you now, I won't get my expansion. If I give you back, you tell your father what you've learned, and I lose my biggest asset. As of right now, I don't have a damn clue what I'm going to do with you."

I feel minimal relief at his words.

He scans my trembling body. "Go ahead."

"Why tell me at all? Why not just keep me in the dark until it's safe to put a bullet in my head?"

He shrugs. "I didn't originally intend to kill you. I figure the least I can do is be honest. It's nothing personal."

"Nothing personal? This is my *life* we're talking about. How can killing me not be personal?" My voice rises, but even I hear how broken it sounds.

He raises an eyebrow as if to ask *are you done?*, and I sigh. "What now? Are you just going to keep beating me and patching me up until it's time to kill me?"

"As of right now, I don't plan to hurt you unless you give me a reason to, but don't be mistaken. I *will* hurt you if you continue to push me like you have. I can make these cuts and bruises look like a spa day if necessary."

"So, you're just going to keep me here as bait for my father, and I'm just supposed to sit back, relax, and let you put a bullet in my head when I've served my purpose?"

Flashing me a humorless smile, he gestures to his cheek where, to my pleasant surprise, a light bruise is forming where my elbow made contact. "You've made it perfectly clear that you won't be doing any *sitting back and relaxing.*"

He crouches down in front of me.

"I don't blame you, but let's be realistic here. If you're going to die either way, why fight me? You can have nice food and a nice room, and I'll even allow you to visit the garden once a day if you'd like. You don't have to be miserable."

"Why do you care if I'm miserable?" My words are carefully curious, not rude. "So far, you've had no problem putting me through hell, and if you're just going to kill me anyway, why does it matter?"

It doesn't make sense. Obviously, I don't want to be left here and ignored until my death day, but his offer is almost worse. I can wrap my brain around an utter lack of care for my life. His concern, on the other hand, is too confusing, especially when it's only half-hearted.

He cares enough that he doesn't want me to be miserable, but not enough to save my life.

Slowly, he shakes his head and stands. With his back facing me, he walks the room leisurely, one hand pinching the spot between his eyes.

"One thing is for sure." He turns to meet my gaze. "We can't keep doing this. You can't handle any more abuse, and I can't fight you every time I step foot in this room. I have too much going on."

I keep my voice surprisingly calm. "I won't just roll over and die. I can't."

"Again, you've made that clear. However, if this is how you intend all our interactions to go, I'll be forced to leave you as you are now."

My wrists throb at the thought of remaining secured indefinitely.

"But I assume that's not too comfortable, so I'm willing to offer you a deal."

I raise a weary eyebrow. "What kind of deal?"

"Well, that's up for negotiation."

"I assume freedom is off the table."

He takes a deep breath and walks behind me, untying my wrists. As I massage each one, I can feel his breath skating over the sensitive skin behind my ear.

"Not all freedom."

CHAPTER NINE

Joshua

"I don't need to justify myself to you."

"Then an explanation would suffice."

Ryder knows damn well that I won't indulge him.

"What do you have to gain from making a deal with her? She doesn't have any leverage over you."

I already have an answer prepared for this question.

I stand from behind my desk and square my shoulders, daring him to challenge me. "It's not about leverage. I need her cooperation until we get this mess sorted out. The last thing I need right now is her temper tantrums."

My friend studies me for a long moment, but we both know he won't say what he's really thinking.

Smart man.

By the time I reach the door, Jay is waiting outside with the cart of the food I requested this afternoon. A nod is my only greeting.

I type in the code and push the door open.

She stands in front of the window that overlooks the garden and whips around the second I step through the door. Wide eyes assess me, but the usual apprehension isn't nearly as apparent as it had been earlier today.

There's not a trace of makeup on her face, but she doesn't need it. Her dark blonde hair falls over her shoulders, and if I didn't know that she doesn't have access to any styling products, I'd think she worked hard to achieve the flowing waves that come so naturally.

Her gaze drifts behind me to where Jay is setting the table, and her eyes double in size. She looks ready to drool as she takes in the assortment of food.

My chest clenches uncomfortably, and it takes me a second to realize what that feeling is.

Guilt.

She hasn't had a decent meal in a week, excluding her breakfast, but even that was cold. I hadn't noticed until I picked her up after her fall just how thin she'd become since coming here, and for some reason, that bothered me.

I've done far worse than deprive my prisoners of food and social interaction, so why the hell would I start caring now?

That very question has been bouncing around my head all day, but I refuse to give it any real thought. Instead, I suppress the emotion and fix a blank expression on my face.

"Shall we?" I take a seat just as Jay places the last dish on the small, nearly overflowing table and leaves the room.

Elise doesn't move right away and the urge to snap at her is strong, but as I study her expression, I realize her hesitation has more to do with surprise than defiance.

She's staring at the food like it'll disappear if she moves her eyes for even a moment. After going so long without a real meal, I'm sure the steak, potatoes, corn, salad, and wine are overwhelming.

"I wasn't sure how you liked your steak, so I had Jay cook it medium. I guessed on the wine as well, but this is one of my favorites."

After what feels like an eternity, she moves to the chair opposite mine, lowering herself and examining my expression warily.

"Last time I accepted wine from you, I woke up days later."

For some reason that I can't begin to comprehend, I want to put her at ease tonight.

I lift my glass to my lips and take a sip. "I can assure you this wine is drug-free."

Again, her response is delayed like she's engaged in some mental battle.

After a deep breath, Elise lifts her chin and raises her glass to her lips. "Lucky me."

We dig into our food, and I give her a few minutes to eat before getting to the point of this dinner.

"Have you given any thought to what you want in exchange for cooperation?"

It takes an intentional effort to stop myself from smiling when her jaw ticks, no doubt bothered by my choice of words. I wait for her to snap at me, but she sits up straighter and puts on her version of a poker face.

"I want to cook."

I'd been expecting her to ask for different forms of entertainment, but really I shouldn't be surprised. Cooking is Elise's whole life, so of course she'd choose this.

It's a reasonable enough request, but I can't help testing her limits. "No."

I study her face for any sign of disappointment, but there's nothing. I'm equal parts frustrated and impressed by that fact. What she doesn't realize, however, is that her lack of reaction tells me that she does have something to hide. I'm sure she plans to use it as an opportunity to escape.

Not that she'll be able to.

She arches an amused brow, and I admire her show of confidence.

"I'm no expert in negotiations, but I was under the impression this would be more of a compromise."

"The kitchen is fully staffed," I tell her. "And who's to say you won't try to poison us all?"

"Do you normally have poison lying around the kitchen?"

I scrutinize her under my cold glare, but she doesn't so much as blink.

"I suppose I could arrange it. There will be rules, of course."

Her well-composed exterior falters at this, and I catch sight of her clenched fists, but her voice doesn't waver.

"Such as?"

My head leans side to side as I contemplate the best course of action. It goes without saying that Ryder will be assigned as her personal guard. My men may respect and obey me, but I don't want any of them coming near her.

"For one, you'll have a guard with you at all times." I decide to push her just a little bit more. "The other men don't need to worry about babysitting."

Elise's jaw clenches, and I wonder if she's physically biting her tongue to keep from lashing out at me. It's a commendable effort.

"You'll take instructions from Tripp. He's the capo in charge of training new recruits and managing staff, but I'll have him stationed in the kitchen for the time being. You'll cooperate without complaint, and if there's even the slightest suspicion that you're planning something, you'll stay restrained in this room indefinitely."

She doesn't miss a beat. "On the days I don't cook, I'll spend a few hours in the garden."

I don't miss her careful wording. A statement, not a question.

My nod encourages her to continue.

"I want books that were written this century, music, and a TV."

I think back to the rows of classics lining her bookshelf in her apartment. So, collecting antiques had been her fascination.

"No TV," I say, and my firm tone brings her pause.

She visibly analyzes my mood before going on. "I can't use it to escape. I just get tired of reading or sleeping, and it would be nice to watch a movie for a change."

She thinks my rejection has to do with her ability to escape, which is almost laughable, but I don't bother correcting her. It's better that she believes I overestimate her than realize that I'm saving face with my men.

My authority is never questioned or challenged, but it will certainly be scrutinized when my men find out about the freedoms I'm allowing Elise. Books, music, and even cooking can be justified, but a TV is a luxury I don't even allow my soldiers living on base property.

"What about drawing? Or painting?"

I wonder if she realizes that her nose scrunches up at the suggestion.

"I suck at both," she explains. "But I suppose I'd appreciate the variety. All I'm asking for is a few DVDs or even VCR tapes. It can be as outdated as you want."

Again, I don't correct her.

For a moment, I find myself wondering how I'd justify the allowance to Ryder, but I catch myself before the thought is fully formed.

Still, I humor her because it's not like she could hate me any more than she already does. "I'll see what I can do."

She works to suppress a smile and, to my amusement, fails miserably to maintain her professional composure.

"There is one more thing."

I arch an eyebrow and sip my wine.

"A lock on the bathroom door. I don't want to worry about someone walking in on me."

My first instinct is to brush off her concern since none of my soldiers would be stupid enough to mess with her, but I stop myself.

Elise is horrible at hiding her emotions, and even though she's working hard to keep her expression perfectly neutral, I recognize the look from when she asked me what happened to her in the days she was unconscious. I hadn't liked the fear behind her eyes then, and I don't like it now. As it is, I've deprived her of every human right, and the least I can do is grant her minimal privacy.

"That I can do," I assure her.

What I cannot do is let her get too comfortable, so I add for both our benefits, "You should know that all of this is dependent on you. If you give me any reason to doubt your motives, I *will* keep you restrained in here. I expect full cooperation from this point on. If you can show me respect, I can allow you freedoms."

Her hair cascades over her shoulder as she tilts her head, curiosity glimmering in her brown eyes.

"What?"

She doesn't answer right away, and I'm sure she's worried about my reaction to whatever she wants to say. I steel my nerves, preparing for a potential fight.

"What's your name? Your *real* name?" she asks in a whisper.

The first time she asked me this, I used the switch on her. The second time was as a diversion to steal my phone.

I guess the third time's a charm because I find myself telling her, "Joshua. Joshua Moreno."

For the first time since I brought Elise here, a wide smile spreads across her lips. The expression is stunning, and my chest clenches uncomfortably.

She raises her glass, and I do the same.

"You have yourself a deal, Joshua Moreno."

CHAPTER TEN

Elise

A combination of dreams and memories results in a restless night of sleep. Fears and realities mix until I can't tell one from the other. Dark figures crowding me in a small room, a knife to my throat, a switch biting into my skin again and again.

I wake up in a cold sweat.

It's only 2:30 a.m.

I still have a lot of night left to go.

Laying here in the dark, it's harder to convince myself that I have things under control. I don't feel nearly as confident as I had after my dinner with Joshua.

A part of me wishes I paid more attention to how my family operates. Maybe there's a protocol for hostage situations that would give me some peace of mind. Then again, my ignorance has saved me in here.

A blessing and a curse.

My wishful thinking brings me back to the last time I saw my father and brothers, just a month ago.

Saturday, April 18: five weeks earlier

"Are you excited for graduation next week, Elise?" James's attempt to make this dinner less awkward is appreciated but ultimately ineffective.

My father, brothers, and I are seated in the grand dining room, attempting to enjoy a meal together, but it isn't going well.

Dad sits at the head of the table, choosing to ignore the glares between Logan and Mason, but it's too obvious for me to overlook. I have no idea what caused the tension, and since no one seems keen on filling me in, I have to assume it's about work.

Damon seems legitimately oblivious to the strain between his younger siblings. In fact, he looks ill with his shoulders hunched and his eyes drowsy. No one else seems concerned with his appearance, so I decide not to mention it.

James periodically shoots warning glances to Logan, no doubt silently begging his twin to get himself under control, as he simultaneously tries to distract me with trivial conversation.

For everyone's sake, I entertain the small talk. "Yeah, I am. At this point, I'm just filling out as many job applications as possible."

"You don't need to get a job," my father says, shoving a forkful of meatloaf into his mouth.

"I *want* to get a job. I mean, what else would I do all day?"

"Pick up some hobbies," he suggests. "Sewing, writing, piano. Do whatever you want."

"Cooking in a restaurant *is* what I want, Dad."

"I already told you that I'll be financially supporting you."

Before I get a chance to remind him that it isn't about the money, Damon waves a shaky hand. "Oh, just let her do it. She's already working at that bakery. Why does a restaurant matter?"

I shoot a grateful smile to my oldest brother, and I think he means to wink at me in return, but he just blinks.

Dad lifts a hand. "You can work if you want to, but I'm still financially supporting you."

"That's not necessary. I have plenty of savings from my years at the bakery."

"My mind is made up on this, Elise."

"If she wants to branch out on her own, there's no reason why she can't," Mason defends, but his glare is trained on Logan.

"The *reason* is that Dad has the means to provide for her, so there's no need to risk Elise being on her own," Logan counters, voice tight.

"She's been on her own for years and can take care of herself."

James tries to placate the situation. "As we've already said, both sides are perfectly valid, but it's been decided that Dad will provide for Elise."

I roll my eyes. "I'm not an idiot. You're clearly not talking about me."

Damon snickers, but the others don't look my way. They do, however, drop their poorly disguised codewords.

Mason's hand balls into a fist on the table. "Your reasoning is ridiculous. We both know I'm the most qualified candidate to establish the Austin base."

"It's my project to manage and my choice to make," Logan snaps. "A new base won't have a fraction of the security you'd require as a Consoli. It's not worth the risk to your safety."

"We risk our safety every day," Mason grates.

"Boys!" Dad's command silences the arguing, and we all look at him. "Logan, remember who's in charge here. Mason, the decision has been made. This is the last I will hear of this matter. Your sister is here. Let's try to have a pleasant evening. Understand?"

Both brothers begrudgingly nod and mumble their agreement.

The rest of our dinner is surprisingly enjoyable. Logan and Mason seem to forget their frustration with each other, and we spend the next few hours talking and laughing like a normal family.

And even though we're anything but a normal family, I wouldn't trade this for the world.

Present day

My heart squeezes at the memory, and there's a part of me that would give anything to go back to that moment and forget what I know now. Go back to my blissful oblivion where though my family wasn't normal, at least it was whole.

But there's an even bigger part of me that's glad I know what I do.

This is it—the Consoli family in all its dysfunctional glory. I've lived in my private bubble for so long that being with my family felt more like a second life altogether. Somehow, in being taken from my family, I'm closer to them than I have been in years.

Which I fully grasp the irony of.

Despite this grim realization, I have every intention to get out of here and make my snake of a brother pay for what he's done.

When morning comes, I'm not at all rested.

It's eight by the time I've finished getting ready and pick up *Pride and Prejudice*, taking it and a chair to the window for a morning of reading. I'm pleased to find that I'm actually able to get swept into the world of Elizabeth Bennet before being interrupted by the arrival of my breakfast. Thankfully, it's another tray of real food, and I'm hopeful that my days of bread and oatmeal are behind me.

It's nearly eleven o'clock when the door opens and Joshua steps inside. He wears his typical jeans, T-shirt, and unreadable expression.

"Ready to go to the garden?"

I set my book down without marking the page and follow him to the door, where he turns his body to hide the keypad from my view.

The lock clicks open, and he steps aside, but before I can step through the doorway, Joshua takes hold of my arm. I turn to face him, momentarily stunned to find we're only inches apart.

"Don't do anything stupid," he warns, dark eyes daring me to challenge him.

I'm not dumb enough to accept that dare, but I am prideful enough to taunt him.

"Wouldn't dream of it," I whisper, tilting my head upward to flash my doe eyes.

I expect him to snap at me or at least call me out, but he doesn't. He just holds me in place, eyes never leaving mine.

As the seconds pass, I become increasingly aware of our closeness and the heat radiating off his body. His intoxicating scent floods my senses as we share the same breath, and my heart doubles its pace in my chest.

By the time Joshua releases my arm, my head is spinning.

What just happened?

Commanding my legs to move, I step through the threshold and let Joshua lead the way. Though he's in front of me, he periodically checks to ensure I'm following him.

Obviously, I haven't gained much trust yet.

I pay close attention to my surroundings, though there's not much to take in since the stucco hallway is seemingly endless. We come to a staircase and walk down two flights leading straight to the garden entrance.

Joshua opens the door for me, and I walk into the most beautiful garden I have ever seen. The view from my room does no justice to the Eden-like space.

The sun's warmth soaks into my skin, and my bare feet curl into the soft grass.

I take my time wandering the grounds, observing each feature as I do.

Water glistens as it flows down a fountain, shimmering like fabric over a ballgown. Birdbaths fill the garden with the chattering of their multi-colored occupants. Benches are tucked into pockets of grass surrounded by vibrant flowers, and though the picture is stationary aside from the butterflies that flutter from flower to flower, it's a sight I could stare at for hours. There's even a small, stone-lined pond with a miniature waterfall spilling over the content koi fish that live there.

When I close my eyes, I can lose myself in the bliss of the floral scent, chirping birds, and flowing water. It's easy to trick myself into thinking I'm in paradise and not confinement.

A structure to my left catches my attention, and I explore it. As I approach an arrangement of blossom trees, I find a large stone gazebo resting in the center.

I step inside, and though goosebumps rise on my arms from the loss of the sun's warmth, I'm too intrigued to care.

A table of various foods lies before me. I step toward it, and my stomach growls at the sight of the sandwiches, wraps, salad, croissants, fruit, vegetables, and brownies.

"I had lunch brought out here today. I figured you'd appreciate the change in scenery." I jump at the sound of Joshua's voice from behind me.

Has he been following me this whole time?

He stands a few feet away, and I'm taken back by how light his eyes are in the sun, almost hazel.

Right now, with his black jeans slung casually around his waist, gray tee stretching over his muscular chest, and dark hair mussed to perfection, I can almost pretend Joshua is a normal guy. A guy who would take me out on a date. A guy I could take home to my father. A guy who would protect me. A guy who would love me.

Joshua is *not* that guy.

As I fill my plate, I notice Joshua doing the same as he claims the seat opposite me.

"What are you doing?"

His response comes with a small, playful grin. "Last I checked, this was *my* garden."

A blush spreads across my cheeks, and I resist the desire to roll my eyes. "I meant, why are you eating with me."

"I'm hungry," he says with a shrug, and I decide not to push him.

We dig into our lunch, and the urge to thank him for the food is strong, but I repress it... then again, I am trying to get on his good side. Does it really matter if I thank him as long as I don't let myself be fooled by his kindness?

Am I being fooled by his kindness?

"Everything okay?" I look up to see Joshua's raised brow. I must've looked as deep in thought as I was.

"Yeah. I, uh—Thank you… for the food, I mean."

"You're welcome?" he says, more like a question than a statement, and I take pleasure in the fact that he looks just as uncomfortable as I feel.

There's a beat of awkward silence, and Joshua clears his throat. "You'll start in the kitchen tomorrow and work every other day for lunch and dinner."

I nod, and he continues. "I'll come and get you at eleven, so be ready. As I said last night, you'll be taking directions from Tripp, and whatever he says, goes. All the other men have been instructed not to talk to you so you can work in peace."

I drop my eyes at his last statement. We both know that's not the reason they aren't allowed to talk to me.

"It's better than staying in that room," he defends.

"But just as isolated," I whisper and shake my head. "It's fine, I get it, whatever." Though my tone is less than respectful, his expression remains passive.

I finish my food and stand, ready to be back in the sun.

My shoulders relax the second the sunlight hits my skin. I'm about to walk to one of the various benches when I hear my name called from behind me.

"I have a meeting, but I'll be back to get you in a couple of hours. If you need anything or want to go back sooner, Ryder is over there," he gestures toward the door we came through, and sure enough, Ryder stands at attention.

"Thanks."

He smiles, and my breath catches at the sight. I've only seen Joshua's genuine smile a handful of times, but I'm not sure it's a sight you could get used to, no matter how many times you see it. His full lips tug upward, showing off perfectly straight, brilliantly white teeth.

It suits him.

Walking to a nearby bench, I lean back and will my skin to absorb as much vitamin D as possible.

It's hard to believe it's been so long since I've been in the sun—or outside at all, for that matter. It's such a basic human right to lose. I mean, even prisons let convicts go outside.

But me?

The only crime I committed was trusting an evil man, yet here I am, trapped in a beautiful prison.

But not for long.

Between my trips here and to the kitchen, I should be able to put together some sort of escape route. In the meantime, I need to gain as much trust with Joshua as possible. Maybe then he'll start to loosen up on his rules.

In my effort to think through every possible escape scenario, my mind spins itself into exhaustion, and I drift off to the sound of birds chirping and the feel of summer warmth on my skin.

"Morning, Princess." A husky voice draws me from my sleep. Blinking my eyes open, I jerk up when I see Joshua standing at the end of the bench, arms crossed.

"What the hell? How long have you been standing there?" I snap, and Joshua scowls at my language. "What? Watching me sleep is creepy."

I ignore his narrowing eyes and stand to stretch my limbs.

"I wasn't *watching you sleep*. I came to take you back to your room. Besides, if you slept any longer, you'd have a hard time sleeping tonight."

"Yeah, because I sleep *so* well at night," I mumble.

"What was that?"

"Nothing." I shake my head, unwilling to start a fight and risk my minimal freedoms. "I just don't sleep well."

I walk toward the door only to turn and find that Joshua hasn't moved. "Aren't we going inside?"

"Why aren't you sleeping well?"

I curse myself for not keeping my mouth shut. Apparently, he isn't going to let this go.

Meeting his calculating gaze, I decide to go with the simple truth. "Nightmares. Can we go now?"

Joshua's expression is unchanging, and after a long pause, he nods.

Once we reach my room, Joshua unlocks the door and holds it open for me. There's an anticipatory glint in his gaze that I don't understand until I step inside.

The statues on the dresser have been replaced with various art supplies—paper, pencils, pens, coloring books, paints, canvases, and an easel. A new table rests to the left of the bathroom door, holding a record player, and beneath it is a stack of a dozen records. There's a bookshelf, too, filled with modern books. I look at the bathroom door, and sure enough, a lock has been installed.

I spin on my heels to find Joshua leaning against the door frame, a ghost of a smile on his lips.

My first instinct is to thank him, but seeing as he's only upholding his end of the deal, I go a different route.

I point toward the empty space on the wall above the dresser. "I trust my flat screen will be installed soon?"

He rolls his eyes, but his lip quirks upward. "Goodnight, Elise."

"Goodnight, Joshua."

CHAPTER ELEVEN

Elise

I actually get to *do* something today.

I pry my body out of bed and make my way toward the dresser. Grabbing jeans, a T-shirt, and fresh undergarments, I go to the bathroom for a speedy shower.

Once my hair is dried and tied in a neat bun, a knock on the door signals that my breakfast has arrived.

I've just finished the food when Joshua enters, rendering me speechless as he does. He's not dressed in his usual T-shirt and jeans. Instead, he wears navy slacks and a matching jacket, and his hair is slicked back instead of its usual rustled mess.

The look is unreasonably attractive, but I'd rather shoot myself in the foot than admit that, so I'm careful to school my features into perfect neutrality.

His expressionless face studies mine intently, and I wonder if he'll call me out on the faint blush creeping up my cheeks.

"How did you sleep last night?" he asks without an ounce of mocking in his tone.

I silently curse myself again for mentioning my nightmares in the first place. For some reason, he can't seem to drop it.

"Fine," I say, avoiding his gaze.

He accepts my answer, though we both know it isn't the truth.

"I have something for you," he states, and before I can ask what it is, someone in the hallway hands him a box. He gives it to me, and I place it on the table and take the top off.

Inside is a pair of light blue tennis shoes.

I hadn't even considered the fact that I don't have shoes of my own. Up until now, it hasn't mattered, but working in the kitchen, these are a necessity.

There's a foreign flutter in my stomach at the thought that he recognized I'd need these and took it upon himself to get them for me. I've taken care of myself for as long as I can remember, so I'm not used to someone else noticing my needs and meeting them.

But, once again, I refuse to thank him.

I sit on the bed to try them on. They're a perfect fit.

"Ready to go?"

I nod and follow Joshua out the door, where Ryder is already waiting for us.

"Ryder will be your—"

"Babysitter," I finish. "I'm not sure if you've realized it yet, but I'm not much of a threat." I'm careful to keep my tone playful, though I mean the words.

Joshua's eyes narrow with a warning, and my chest tightens. Have I just started another fight?

"He's not here to protect my soldiers from you. He's here to protect *you* from my soldiers."

Goosebumps rise on my arms as I grasp the gravity of his warning. I know I'm the enemy—a prisoner—but no one would do anything to me, right?

Now I'm not so sure.

Joshua goes on. "If you need anything, just ask him. He'll bring you back for the night around six."

The three of us make our way down the hall in the opposite direction of the garden. This is good because I'll get to see more of the layout. We quickly come across a stairway and make our way down. The space we enter is so open that it takes me a second to process it all.

This building is much larger than I originally thought. High ceilings and tall windows are the first things I notice. Next, I see the hallways on all sides, doors lining them. I can see into a few, and from the looks of it, they are various offices.

The last thing my brain processes is the people. Well, not exactly *people*. Men. There are armed men from all directions, and they've all stopped to take note of our arrival. I survey their expressions: disinterest, confusion, disgust, hatred, and lust.

The last one makes me shudder.

He's not here to protect my soldiers from you. He's here to protect you from my soldiers.

Looking at the faces that surround me, I know he's right. Every one of these men would love to see my head on a stick or put it there themselves.

"Elise," Joshua calls, and I realize I've stopped moving.

Fear and uncertainty root me in place.

I meet his gaze, but I can't respond.

I can't move.

Maybe going to work in the kitchen is a mistake. How do I know Ryder isn't one of the men that wants me dead? Though I'm fairly certain no one would kill me without being given the order by Joshua, they'd hurt me in a heartbeat if given the opportunity.

For the first time, I see my room as a haven instead of a prison.

Irritation flares in Joshua's eyes, and my fear spikes. I want to take a step forward, but my muscles are frozen.

I know the second Joshua has lost his patience. His eyes flare, and he stomps toward me. Despite the danger radar blaring in my head, I don't resist when he grabs me by the shoulders and drags me to the side. My only protest is a whimper when he inadvertently digs his fingers into one of the bruises on my arm. He loosens his grip with a curse but continues to pull me.

"Out," Joshua barks, and I try to pull away, but his grasp on me is unmoving.

I realize then that his words aren't directed toward me but at two men in the small office that Joshua has taken us to.

Joshua slams the door and lets me go. "What the hell is your problem?"

My palms are sweaty, and it takes me a moment to find my words. Once I do, they shake with the nerves that wrack my body. "They're going to hurt me."

"Who?"

"*All* of them. Every single soldier in this building wants to see me dead, and nothing is stopping them from hurting me. I know I'm a dead girl walking, so why does it even matter? But—"

Joshua cuts me off with a step forward, closing the space between us and fixing me with his emotionless, analytic eyes. "No one is going to touch you. I warned you that people here don't like you, but that's why Ryder's here."

"How do you know *he* won't hurt me?"

"Because I told him not to, and when I give an order, it's obeyed," he huffs, checking his watch. "I don't have time for this. I need to leave so are you going or not?"

I close my eyes and take a steadying breath, willing my out-of-control nerves to cooperate.

A warm hand settles on the back of my neck, but I can't bring myself to open my eyes yet.

"No one is going to hurt you." The warm whisper caresses my ear, and I realize he's stepped even closer.

The words are so tender, so sincere, that for a second, I let myself believe that I'm safe. It's a ridiculous notion since I am quite literally surrounded by the enemy, but Joshua's gentle touch and firm reassurance are surprisingly convincing.

When I open my eyes, I'm struck by the softness I find staring back at me.

"Not as long as you keep up your end of the deal," he adds.

The reminder of our arrangement breaks me out of my wishful thinking, and I know he's done this for both of our benefits.

It's not right that we should feel so comfortable with each other.

"I want to go," I breathe, the shame from my panic attack settling in my stomach with a rush of blood to my cheeks.

Joshua was far kinder than I would've imagined him to be, and it's for this reason alone that I mutter a soft "Thank you."

His only response is to open the door and lead us the rest of the way to the kitchen.

We don't pass anything that appears to be an exit, but I don't let that bother me right now. I just focus on not having another panic attack.

We eventually approach a door that Ryder opens for Joshua and me. The kitchen is industrial and much larger than I expected.

Unsurprisingly, only men are bustling around—some working the grill, some chopping vegetables, some doing dishes. Only one person seems to notice our entrance, and the short, light-haired man approaches us. As he gets closer, I notice a large scar that reaches from his right eyebrow all the way to his chin, as if someone once attempted to cut out his face but only got halfway done.

He wears black slacks and a white button-up, but it doesn't suit him very well. He looks like the type to sport ripped jeans and old T-shirts.

I also note the mix of annoyance and disgust that make up the glare he directs at me.

He nods respectfully to the man at my side. "Boss."

Joshua accepts it with a nod of his own and looks at me. "Elise, this is Tripp Singleton. He'll tell you what to do."

"Today, you'll be on dish duty. Come, and I'll show you how it's done," Tripp orders, and his assumption that I don't know how to do dishes is, somehow, far more sexist than if he were to assume it's all I know how to do.

Joshua turns to go, and Tripp makes his way toward the sinks.

"Wait," I call.

Both men turn to me—neither happy.

"Joshua, our deal was that I get to cook. Dish duty doesn't count."

His eyes flash a warning, and I know this is pushing my luck after my hallway freak-out, but we have a deal.

Joshua steps closer, talking low so only I can hear him. "Don't forget that part of the deal was that you show me respect. Watch how you talk to me, or I'll call the whole deal off. Understand?"

I nod, and he raises an expectant eyebrow.

"I understand," I answer.

"Good." Joshua straightens, directing his next words to Tripp. "Have her on cooking."

I can almost feel the disdain rolling off of Tripp, but regardless, he replies, "Yes, sir."

Joshua faces me. "I'm leaving and won't be back until lunchtime tomorrow. If you need anything, ask Ryder."

"Where are you going?" I ask.

He gives me an incredulous look that tells me my question will go unanswered.

"See you tomorrow," he says, striding out the door.

When I turn to Tripp, his face twists with irritation the second Joshua is out of sight. "Come. I'll give you a tour."

The tour doesn't take long. Tripp quickly points out each station— grill, oven, prep, and dishes. He leads Ryder and me down a hallway with the pantry and storage on one side and a break room on the other.

"You'll be at the prep station," he tells me and walks me through the procedures, though it's pretty self-explanatory.

All I need to do is take food out of the freezer and prepare it to be cooked in the next few days, a task I could do in my sleep.

Tripp takes a step back to watch me for a few moments, assessing my work before leaving to do his own. I let myself get caught up in what I'm doing, rarely even remembering where I am or the fact that I have a giant shadow at all times. That's how cooking has always been for me—a way to relax and take my mind off the world.

It was also the only way I ever participated in my family's work. I cooked for every family dinner meeting from the time I was fifteen until I moved out. I even tried to go back with my security team once a month to cook for everyone, but my father wouldn't allow it.

I never did tell him how much that hurt. Instead, I went along with whatever he asked of me to pacify him.

I can hardly be mad, though, since the one time I openly disobeyed him ended with me being drugged and kidnapped.

I'm grateful to find that my time passes in a blur. Even though no one is talking to me, I still appreciate the normalcy of being surrounded by others. The chattering and bustling are comforting, which I recognize as both a good and dangerous fact.

Once I've finished the work Tripp gave me, I turn and search for Ryder, easily finding the large man leaning against the counter a few yards away. His eyes meet mine, and he comes my way.

"Where is the restroom?"

His response is to wordlessly lead me out of the kitchen and into the main hall.

Ryder takes a left, opposite of the direction that we came, and I'm on high alert for an exit strategy. The remaining hallway is short, with four doors lining the right side and two on the left. The four doors appear to be storage units, and the two are what I assume to be bathrooms. Ryder walks until he reaches the door farthest from the kitchen. Opening it, he gestures for me to enter.

It's embarrassing enough to have him follow me around, but opening the bathroom door is a new level of humiliation.

I rush past him and lock the door, enjoying the moment of privacy. I once again see my room as a haven instead of a prison.

I survey the one-stall bathroom. The sink and countertop are made of marble, and the walls are painted a dark red, which seems to be a common theme around the base.

A small curtain above the toilet catches my attention.

Within seconds, I'm standing on top of the toilet, peeling back the curtain to reveal a window.

I can barely believe my eyes. Not only am I looking at a window, but I'm looking at a window with a latch and no screen. The view from here doesn't face inside the complex like the garden window in my room. Instead, it shows a wall of trees.

This is it—my way out.

If I pick the right time, I can use *this* window to escape.

I close the curtain and climb down, not wanting to make Ryder suspicious of how long I take. I quickly do my business, wash my hands, and unlock the door. As Ryder and I walk back into the kitchen, I'm careful to keep my face neutral, but inside, I'm screaming with joy.

"Where the hell did you go?"

We've just reentered the kitchen when a glaring Tripp approaches me.

I gesture to the door. "Bathroom break. I finished the work you gave me."

"While you're in this kitchen, you report to me. Ask permission next time," he growls.

I'm all too aware that everyone has stopped what they're doing to watch our confrontation. I've become used to swallowing my pride when it comes to Joshua, but for some reason, the idea of doing the same with Tripp makes me sick. I'm about to come back at him with a witty remark when I imagine Joshua's face in my head. Making Tripp angry could result in me not working here anymore, which I can't afford.

Especially now that I have a way to escape.

I need to play nice.

Bile creeps up my throat as I speak the words he needs to hear. "I will be sure to ask next time. What would you like me to do now?"

Tripp's lips tilt in a smug grin, and I want to grimace at the sight, but my pride won't allow me to sacrifice more than I already have.

"You're going to unpack and organize the shelves." Tripp leads me toward the storage room and shows me where to put each item.

I'm tempted to mention—once again—that this isn't cooking, but without Joshua here, it seems silly to piss off Tripp. I follow his instructions, and after a few minutes, he decides that I'm ready to do it on my own.

The rest of the day passes in a blur of mixing, chopping, and organizing. I even made food for Ryder and myself during my lunch break and was surprised that we were able to sit in comfortable silence.

When Tripp informs me that my shift is over, I wash my hands and follow Ryder out.

The journey back to my room is uneventful. The hallways are a ghost town, and I'm too tired to calculate escape routes. Besides, the bathroom window is a solid plan for now.

When we get to my room, Ryder enters the code, and I don't even try to look. The door opens, and Ryder hands me the to-go box that I assume is my dinner. I barely eat before collapsing on the bed.

I'm thoroughly exhausted, but I don't mind the soreness that seems to resonate with every muscle in my body. It's refreshing after so long of doing nothing productive.

It's barely dark out by the time my eyelids are fluttering closed, and I don't fight the pull of sleep.

The nightmares are relentless, but instead of pocket knives and switches, there are meat grinders, pans, and utensils. It seems my mind can weaponize just about anything.

Unfortunately, this has opened up a whole new avenue of torture for my nightmares to explore, resulting in one more restless night.

CHAPTER TWELVE

Joshua

"You're sure you don't want me to come in? He brought one of his sons—one of the twins. I can't tell them apart."

"I'm sure," I tell Donovan for the third time.

I'm sure he's dying to get in on the action that is my meeting with Gabriel Consoli, but the only person I'd want to join me is currently on babysitting duty—likely sitting around the garden right about now.

"Well, if you need backup, we're a signal away."

I nod but know I won't need it. Consoli knows what will happen if he tries to hurt me.

I climb out of the car and walk to the door of the run-down bar. A row of motorcycles lines the front, and the burly man at the door eyes me expectantly.

"We're not going to have any issues, are we, Mr. Moreno?"

"I'll be on my best behavior, Catch," I answer with a broad smile that he answers with an eye roll.

"Don't get any smart ideas," he warns. "My guys don't care who the hell you are. If you cause trouble on our turf, you're all dead."

"Understood," I assure him. "I appreciate the hospitality."

"How much?"

I stop and lift a brow. "Well, I thought you'd wait a little while before calling in your favor."

"Why inconvenience you with a second trip?" he asks with a tilted smile.

"What do you need?"

"The DA's been cracking down on my guys, and recently, an

officer on my payroll flipped and sold us out. He's got guys watching mine, so I can't deal with it myself."

"Who am I handling?"

"The cop—I want him out of the picture."

"And the DA?" I ask.

Catch grins. "I've got that covered."

I shake my head. "You have the Consolis handling it for you."

"Two birds," he says with a shrug. "I expect you'll deal with this before you leave town?"

This pushes back when I'll be returning to the base—to Elise. I'm already a day later than I planned on being, but I don't exactly have a choice. My relationship with the MCs is a delicate one and one that I need to maintain.

I nod my agreement, and he opens the door.

Catch is a member of the Black Vipers—a motorcycle gang that runs this part of Wyoming. It's not uncommon that meetings like this one take place in motorcycle gang territory. They operate similarly to the mafia world but on a smaller, local scale that we can respect. Mafia families run most efficiently in big cities, but the rural areas tend to belong to gangs like this one.

Meeting here, instead of on Consoli's turf or mine, forces us to stay civil. If I were to go to Chicago, chances are I wouldn't make it two steps in the city before having my head blown off, but here we're on even footing with a host who won't hesitate to make good on his warning if either of us steps out of line.

But it means I have to work on their timeline. I wanted to have this meeting yesterday, but Catch wanted to be here to ensure our meeting is free of violence.

I step into the bar exactly an hour earlier than Consoli and I agreed, but I already knew he beat me to it.

He and his underboss, Logan, sit at a table with beers in hand.

Gabriel Consoli is an older man with greying hair and a permanent scowl stamped on his face. His green eyes are narrowed, identical to his son. The younger Consoli has dark hair that barely curls on the ends. He's built larger than Mason, with a broad frame that suits a family heir.

One day, he'll make a formidable foe.

I'm careful to keep my unbothered smile in place.

My once-perfect plan may currently be a mess of epic proportions, but Consoli doesn't need to know that. As far as he's aware, I have him exactly where I want him.

If only his daughter were better at doing what she's told, then I wouldn't have to stall with this stupid meeting in the first place.

In some ways, I can easily see how Elise fits into this family. Her anger, her strength, and her fire are pure Consoli. But the innocence and gentle spirit that has driven me crazy since I met her is unsurprisingly absent from these men.

"About time," Logan deadpans, leaning back in the booth like he's the one with leverage here.

Well, he isn't.

"You'll have to forgive me for not coming sooner. I've had my hands full these last few days," I say with a wink as I drop into the chair across from Consoli.

Logan's smile falls as mine grows.

"What's the point of this meeting?" he asks. "We know your demands."

"That's a relief. I was starting to wonder if you'd forgotten what was at stake. I thought you might benefit from a reminder." I punctuate my statement by reaching into my pocket and tossing a picture on the table.

It was taken the day I met Elise. She wears her ill-fitting bakery uniform, her hair pulled into a messy ponytail. Her cheeks are bright red as she smiles at me. Ryder had taken the picture from the street as I asked for her number.

"She's a pretty thing," I say absently, letting my eyes linger because it's less a taunt than the truth.

Elise is beautiful.

"Where is she?" Consoli asks in his toneless, gruff voice.

"Safe—for now." I lean forward, elbows resting on the table.

His expression is unchanging, but his son's glare intensifies.

"What have you done to her?" he asks.

I dig into my pocket, pull out the next photo, and toss it beside the first.

There's no trace of Elise's radiant smile in this photo. It was taken after she threw up all over my shoes. Her legs are bruised and streaked with blood. Her skin is a sickly pale. Her cheeks are hollow and gaunt, and her eyes have dark circles beneath them.

I'd taken the photo for this exact moment, but the sight brings me none of the pleasure I openly display. Consoli needs to know I'll do whatever it takes to get what I want from him—I can't afford for him to get the slightest whiff of my growing affinity for his firecracker of a daughter.

Consoli takes a long look at the photo, expression unchanging. Logan doesn't look at all, and I suspect he knows himself well enough to know it wouldn't benefit any of us if he killed me where I sit.

"I saw your proof of life video. What I'm asking is specifically what you have done to her."

Consoli could be talking about what he had for breakfast this morning for all the passion his tone implies, but when his eyes lift from the picture of his daughter, I see the first hint of fire behind his signature scowl.

Now we're talking.

I shrug again. "An introduction to my switch—hardly the *big guns*. You should be proud; she held up great for her first interrogation. I think she lasted"—I curl my lips thoughtfully—"half an hour before begging me to stop."

Logan's hands flatten against the table like he's about to flip it— then strangle me—but we're interrupted just then by a busty waitress who looks old enough to be Consoli's mother. She carries three beer bottles and wears an unimpressed look.

"I'm sure I don't need to remind you, gentleman, that civility is a requirement if you intend to walk out of this establishment alive." She doesn't wait for our answers before leaving the bottles on the table and walking away.

"It goes without saying that Elise's life is very much tied to my own. Should something happen to me, what happens to her will be a hell of a lot worse than a few marks from a switch." My smile is smug as I lean back in my chair, taking a long draw from the beer.

Logan's eyes light up, and it's identical to Elise's fiery anger.

He leans forward on the table, speaking in a deadly low tone. "And when she's home safe and sound, I'll revel in slowly severing your head from your body and mounting it on a spike outside my home to watch the birds pick at your decomposing skull until it's nothing but bone. Then I'll hang it on my wall."

My answering chuckle is just as deadly low. "I can see colorful threats are a family thing. They're a lot more convincing coming from you. Elise struggles to get the same intimidation factor when she's tied down to the bed."

Logan's face goes blank, and for a single second, I think I've pushed him far enough to get all of us shot, but Consoli slams a fist on the table, stopping his son and me from our verbal pissing match.

Which I won in a landslide.

"So far, you've done nothing but boast about abusing an innocent girl. What assurances can you give me that she's safe and, from this *second* on, untouched? I see no reason to trust she'll return safely to me when all is said and done."

That's because she won't, I think bitterly.

Though, it's no one's fault but her own.

I pull out my phone and call Ryder, all without taking my eyes off Consoli.

"Yes, sir?" he answers on the first ring.

"Show me the girl," I order, holding the screen to Consoli as the call switches to a live video.

Once it loads, the screen shows Elise lying on a bench in the garden, the same one she fell asleep on the last time she was there. Instead of sleeping, she holds the book above her head, flipping the page with an openly bored expression.

It's one of the older books that had been in her cell before I changed her room. She has a stack of the modern books she requested, yet she chooses to read one she already had. If I weren't with her brother and father right now, I'd probably antagonize her over it.

"As you can see, she's perfectly safe," I say, hanging up the phone before one of them tries to get her attention. "As for remaining *untouched*, that is completely up to her behavior. You'll be unsurprised to hear she's not exactly the most docile hostage."

It's fast, but for a moment, both men do look surprised to hear that Elise has been difficult for me.

Had they expected her to roll over and accept her fate?

I mean, I had, but that was before I spent any time with her. They've always known her argumentative personality.

"Your demands are too vague," Consoli says briskly, like he's eager to leave. "I need your detailed proposal on how this would work. You want the Houston base, but I can't just hand it over as it stands. Closing it down, relocating my men, and clearing the database aren't exactly overnight endeavors. You can't honestly expect me to give it up as is. I have soldier's lives to consider."

I don't expect him to hand it over as is. That would be suicide to his empire, and while I want his Houston base to establish my Austin base, I'm not looking to dismantle the entire Consoli family.

Not yet, anyway.

"I can't help but feel like I'm doing all the work here."

"Closing things down will take at least a week, and clearing out could be another few days," Logan says, sitting up straighter. "Until then, we're proposing a trade. You let Elise go and take me instead."

"You?" I deadpan.

He nods. "You've put her through enough. She won't last until this deal is over. Take me and let her go."

Something in the way he assumes his sister's weakness bothers me. I only need to study him for a moment to know that he's serious. He truly sees Elise as a helpless victim.

She is, but she sure as hell refuses to act like it.

"I'm supposed to believe you'd come as my willing hostage in her place?"

"You have my word," Consoli says, and Logan nods.

"Let's see,"—I tap the table thoughtfully—"I can either take you at your word or keep you by the balls... I think I'll stick with Elise." I gesture to Logan. "Something happens to you, and there are three brothers to take your place, but Elise? She's irreplaceable."

Getting what I want from Consoli fully relies on his belief that his daughter's life is on the line, but for some reason, it bothers me that they view Elise as weak.

It's for this reason that I add, "Besides, I'm getting used to the little spitfire." I gesture to my cheek, which is still lightly bruised. "She's got a wicked elbow."

"Elise did that?" Consoli asks with a raised brow.

After she failed to bash a statue over my head, I think wistfully.

"She won't again," I tell him instead.

Gabriel Consoli pulls in a deep breath, then levels me with a hard glare.

"The night the Venturi's murdered my wife, they threw a party to celebrate. One week later, they threw another. One week after that, every single member of that family was either dead or in hiding." He leans forward, and each word is said as a promise. "You may have my daughter now, but that will not always be the case. Enjoy your parties while you can, because when I decide to end your power trip, I will burn everything you and your father built to the ground."

I finish my drink and tilt my head. "Do you think Elise would enjoy a party? She seems more like the *stay in with a bottle of wine* type, but that could just be because you never let her do anything else." My smile is wide as I stand and fix my jacket. "Who knows, she might decide staying with me is better than the pretty cage she calls home."

"You've made your point," Logan snaps. "Leave Elise alone, and we'll handle this like real men—*without* torturing innocent girls."

The jab is fair enough. I don't make a habit of hurting anyone outside of our world. Unfortunately, I know what these two have been denying for twenty-three years—Elise *is* a part of our world. It's not my fault they hid her away instead of training and protecting her.

I drop my smile. "I'm done waiting. Have the proposal sent to me by tomorrow, or Elise pays the price."

As I walk out the door, my smile creeps back. All this talk about Elise has made me eager to get back to her.

CHAPTER THIRTEEN

Elise

Yesterday passed in a blur.

Ryder came to get me in the afternoon to spend the day in the garden and, despite the fact that art is not my first choice for a pastime, I spent hours sketching the exotic flowers there.

The sun was just beginning to set by the time Ryder took me back to my room for the night, where my dinner was already waiting for me.

Once again, my sleep was tainted with nightmares, and it feels like forever since I got through a night without them.

As I get ready, I wonder if Joshua will be here today. I haven't seen him since he dropped me off at the kitchen on Monday, and I could have sworn he told me that he'd be back yesterday. Though, I suppose, he could have returned and just hasn't come to see me, which would be a good thing.

Right?

Breakfast comes, and I eat it while I read the last chapters of *Pride and Prejudice*, which has turned out to be a surprisingly great book, even though I usually exclusively enjoy modern romance.

By the time eleven rolls around, there's a knock at the door, and I call for whoever it is to enter. I half-hope, half-expect Joshua to walk in, but it's Ryder.

He's dressed like he always is—black jeans and a T-shirt, which seems to be the go-to casual wear around here. In fact, I rarely see the men here in suits like Joshua was the other day, which is different from the endless slacks and blazers that roam the halls of my father's base.

We make our way to the kitchen, and as soon as I arrive, Tripp has me preparing a giant pot of potato soup.

I lose myself in my work, turning on autopilot and shutting out the world around me. I generally stick to the recipe he provided me, but I add a few spices here and there that I know will enhance the taste.

I'm chopping up celery to toss into the bowl when my mind wanders to my father, trying to picture what he's doing right now. I wonder if he's trying to save me, if he has a plan, if he-

The knife slips from my grasp, slicing my finger open.

I hiss, and Ryder appears at my side. I show him the cut as blood flows into my palm at a sickening rate. Ryder leaves, and I assume he's finding bandages and gauze.

My finger throbs, and I can't take my eyes off the blood. My stomach churns, and my vision blurs around the edges. I didn't think I was the squeamish type, but the nausea growing in my stomach says otherwise.

"Elise, this is Jay," Ryder says, and his smooth tenor pulls my eyes from the blood. He stands beside a heavy-set man with graying hair, dull green eyes, and countless laugh lines.

He reminds me of what my father would look like if he were a normal person.

I've seen Jay around before, and though no one has outright told me, I've figured out that he's the head chef. He spends more time teaching people how to do their jobs than he does actually cooking, but it never seems to bother him. Unlike Tripp and Ryder, Jay doesn't have a rough exterior.

But I've been fooled by a kind smile before, so I take a step back.

Jay doesn't let my hesitation bother him. Instead, he gestures to the injury. "May I take a look?"

For reasons beyond my understanding, I look to Ryder for some sort of assurance. He gives me a small smile, and it's the first time I've seen any emotion touch his face. His normally stony features soften. That alone eases a significant amount of my apprehension.

"Jay is ex-military. He used to be a combat medic. He can bandage it for you," Ryder explains.

"It's a shallow cut. It's not a big deal," I insist.

Jay tilts his head and lifts his brow. It's the kind of exasperated look a mother gives her child after they've misbehaved.

Somehow, it works.

I hold out the injured finger, blood splashing against the white tile floor as I do. The sight brings my nausea to the forefront of my mind, and bile crawls up my throat. I force myself to watch Ryder as he wipes the blood from the ground, focusing on his movements more than the task.

"You must have a high threshold for pain," Jay says absently.

I'm not used to conversing with anyone aside from Joshua, so I'm inclined to ignore him, but the statement holds too much irony.

"I've been through worse this week."

There's no awkward silence or tension like I'd expected. Jay surprises me by laughing lightly. "I suppose that's true."

When I drag my eyes to his work, my finger is securely bandaged.

"Thank you," I murmur, holding my hand to my chest.

Jay smiles so wide that I feel my lip tug upward by the contagious expression. "Of course, Miss Consoli."

He returns to work, and Ryder appears beside me with a wet rag. I use it to erase the last traces of evidence of my injury at my station since Ryder has already cleaned the blood off the floor. Tripp barges into the room the second I hand Ryder the rag, and I'm grateful for the miracle of his absence during the accident. I'm positive he would've made things more difficult had he been here.

By the time my lunch break rolls around, I still feel nauseous. I don't want Ryder to see just how sick I'm feeling because I don't want to go back to my room. So, I make the two of us lunch and force myself to scarf down as much of it as I can.

"Aren't you going to eat?" Ryder asks from beside me.

I stare at my plate, which is mostly full. "I'm not hungry right now."

"Want to save it for dinner?"

"That would be great. Thank you," I reply.

Ryder isn't nearly as bad as I expected. His quiet nature is intimidating at times but also strangely comforting. I'm glad Joshua has him with me all day instead of someone like Tripp.

I find myself, once again, wondering where Joshua is, and I almost ask Ryder that very question, but I stop myself. It shouldn't matter. If anything, life is significantly easier without him around.

By six, I'm ready to go back to my room. The nausea from earlier never fully subsided, and I need to lie down.

Ryder is at the door waiting for me, and I follow him out of the kitchen and down the hall.

We're halfway to my room when I remember my dinner is still in a to-go box in the fridge. "Wait! We forgot my food."

He deliberates for a moment and checks his watch. "I need to make a quick call. Come right back here when you're done." The words are said in the same measured tone as always, but his eyes send the real message: *don't run*.

I nod and make my way back to the kitchen. When I walk in, everyone is gone, but there's rustling in the break room.

I remember hearing that all the soldiers take a break after the dinner rush before closing up the kitchen, so I'm not surprised. I go right to the fridge but freeze when I hear them.

"I'm surprised the brat is still alive, not to mention working in *here*," one of them says, but I don't recognize any of their voices enough to place who it is.

There's a round of mumbled agreements.

"I couldn't believe it when she talked back to me the other day," Tripp says. "If Boss hadn't been there, I would've smacked her for it."

A few of the men laugh.

My palms get sweaty, and my head starts to spin, but I can't seem to make myself walk away.

"I almost lost it when she called him 'Joshua,'" Tripp mocks, mimicking a girlish voice.

"What did he do?" one of them asks.

Tripp scoffs. "*Nothing*, that's what. He whispered something in her ear, but then he took *her* side. I've seen this man kill in cold blood more times than I can count."

"I once watched him skin someone alive," one says.

"I saw him gouge a man's eye out," adds another.

"He burned his name on an enemy soldier's chest."

The list goes on, but my ears are ringing too loud to make out the words. I have to hold the counter to stop myself from falling over.

"See?" Tripp says. "This brat is just another prisoner, so why is she living in a capo suite instead of a cell? Then she comes in here to cook as if she isn't on death row," he huffs. "If I were him, I would've raped the brat the second she got here. That ought to put her in her place."

My stomach lurches, and I run to the door, leaving the laughs of the soldier behind me. As I throw myself into the hall, I see Ryder approaching, no doubt wondering what's taking so long.

I dart past him to the bathroom, not bothering to lock or even close the door behind me.

I get to the toilet and throw up everything I've eaten in the past twenty-four hours.

When I've emptied my stomach, the room is spinning, and I lie back on the cold floor.

Ryder's low voice fills the small space, but I can't hear what he's saying. I try to make out his words, then realize he's on the phone. I close my eyes in a feeble attempt to ease my pounding headache.

Suddenly, I'm not on the floor anymore. Strong arms hold me, and as I'm carried away, I can't stop replaying the words I overheard in the kitchen. The awful things the soldiers said play on a loop inside my brain until unconsciousness mercifully takes over.

The first thing I hear is an incessant beeping that acts as a jackhammer to my throbbing head. The second is the mumbling of two voices. I can't hear what they're saying, but they don't sound happy.

A jolt of terror runs through my veins as I remember the last time I woke up like this. My eyelids blink rapidly, and I look for the exposed brick of the basement, but there's only tasteful wallpaper lining the room.

I lay in a king-sized bed, surrounded by the softest pillows I've ever felt, and a thick comforter pulled up to my shoulders. The room is roughly the size of my entire apartment. A few feet beyond the bed is a sitting area complete with three black leather couches that look brand new. They face a flatscreen television hung on the wall across from them, above a gas-powered fireplace that's lit despite the fact that it's May.

A door beyond the couches is open, showing off the walk-in closet that looks to be the size of a bedroom. Double doors beside the closet lead to a bathroom that I can only partially see, but from what I can tell, it's as pristine as the rest.

My eyes stop on the men who have paused to watch as I absorb my surroundings, and my chest tightens.

It's Joshua and a man I've never seen before who is wearing a white lab coat.

Seeing Joshua brings it all back.

I know Joshua is a bad man—I've always known that—but hearing each cruel thing he's done...

I didn't realize just how vile he is.

But now it's all I see when I look at him.

Though we're easily fifteen feet apart, I back away from him as best I can on the lush bed, but something tugs on my arm, keeping me in place.

An IV.

I think I'm going to throw up again.

"Get this thing out of my arm." My voice is hoarse as I force the words out.

"Elise," Joshua says, but I'm flinching away from his voice before he can continue.

"Get this out of me now," I snap, and look at the man I assume is the base's doctor.

He looks to Joshua, and my blood boils.

"Don't look at him, look at me. It's *my* body, and I'm telling you to take it out *now*!" My shaky voice raises to a yell by the last word.

"Sir, I believe she's having a panic attack. I could give her a sedative if you'd like."

"No!"

Joshua's expression is a mix of so many emotions that I can't pinpoint any particular one.

He shakes his head. "You heard her. Take it out."

The doctor scurries over to get to work.

Joshua starts to follow, but my head shakes wildly. "Stay back!"

He does, raising his hands in surrender.

Queasiness sweeps through me as the doctor removes the IV. He bandages my arm and steps back, and I shuffle to the far side of the bed until I've put as much distance as I can between Joshua and me.

"You can go now," Joshua tells the man, eyes never leaving mine.

The doctor mutters a "thank you, sir" and quickly exits the room.

Joshua takes a step toward me, hands still raised.

It's strange to see such a powerful man show any sign of surrender, but it's not enough to ease my panic.

"Don't," I plead, voice strangled.

I shuffle off the bed and back into the corner of the room.

"Elise, tell me what's wrong."

Skinning, eye-gouging, murder, torture. It's *all* wrong.

One hand holds my chest, the other my throat, and all I can do is shake my head.

Concern is written all over his face, and it's worse than if he were angry with me. His concern is too confusing. It doesn't fit the evil image in my mind, and it only makes my head spin more.

I look out the window behind me and stare into the peaceful darkness that stretches for miles.

A full breath of air fills my lungs for the first time all night.

"Would you like to go to the garden?" Joshua asks, his expression as soft as his tone.

I nod spastically, and he holds the door open for me, but I stay where I am.

He reads my apprehension. "I'm not going to touch you. I'm just going to lead you to the garden from here."

It takes me a moment, but I force myself to put one foot in front of the other until I'm walking toward the door.

As I get closer, Joshua moves from where he holds the door open. "I'm going to step into the hall so you can follow me."

I feel a rush of relief as he goes.

He understands that I can't be near him right now, and instead of forcing me like he usually does, he's being respectful.

He's trying to help me, and although I'm fully aware that this could backfire, I follow him.

CHAPTER FOURTEEN

Joshua

Elise seems to forget my presence the second she steps foot in the garden.

She doesn't stop until she's reached the grass and her knees give out beneath her. My legs twitch to run and catch her, but the image of her horror-struck eyes is at the forefront of my mind, rooting me in place.

I lean back against the wall, careful to remain quiet as I watch each one of Elise's tightly wound muscles ease in the cool night breeze.

She holds her knees to her chest and lets her head fall back so she has a clear view of the star-filled sky. Her shoulders rise and fall at a slow, measured pace as she relaxes.

Now, I just need to figure out what the hell happened.

I'd been less than an hour from the base when Ryder called to give me an update, but when he found Elise throwing up, I doubled my speed back.

It wasn't until I finally laid eyes on her that I realized I'd barely been breathing since the call. I'm not sure what calmed me down more, seeing she was okay or seeing her in my bed.

But all the peace was sucked out of me the second our eyes met.

I thought we were on good terms when I left—as good as the terms could be considering our situation. Her chokehold of paralyzing fear completely blindsided me.

You'd think I woke her with a knife to the throat by her reaction.

"Does he know what you're going to do to me?" Elise's soft—and notably calmer—voice breaks through my thoughts.

"Who?"

"My conniving snake of a brother," she clarifies, never moving her eyes from the sky.

Her tone is even, and her breathing is steady, so I deem it safe to move forward. My steps are measured, careful not to spook her.

I reach a spot a few feet from her and lower to the grass. "Yes."

I expect her fiery anger at the news her brother knows I plan to kill her when all of this is over, but there's only a silent resignation.

It was only days ago that I tried to extinguish that fire. Why the hell do I find myself looking for it now?

Her head finally turns, and I face a painfully analytic gaze. She regards me like a child would a calculus book. There are a million questions in those deep brown eyes, and, for the first time, I find myself eager to answer them.

"Do you have any siblings?"

Except for that one.

The familiar stabs of guilt pierce my chest, but I manage to maintain my composure even as I strain for breath.

"No. I don't have any siblings."

Elise lifts her gaze to the sky. "My brothers were always so protective of me, especially after our mom died. I assume you already know about that?"

I nod in the darkness, but she's not looking at me to see it.

Everyone in our world knows what happened to Maya Consoli. It's not often that one of the patriarchs' wives is kidnapped and brutally murdered. The family responsible for the cruelty, the Venturis, weren't even one of the main American criminal families. They were reckless and thoughtless—an easy target for Consoli to destroy once he'd grieved the loss of his wife. It happened well before I entered the mafia world, but the story is common knowledge.

A sad smile forms on her lips. "After that, they all took on roles as my protectors, and they mostly did a good job. It's hard to wrap my head around the idea that Mason handed me over to you. I always thought we were the closest. To know that he put me here, that he's letting you kill me… I never really mattered to him."

Tears well in her eyes, and I instinctively recoil.

"It's not that simple," I tell her. "You weren't supposed to find out. Besides, Mason has no say in what happens to you now. He's not the one in charge."

"If he cared about me the way a brother should, he never would've let you near me in the first place. He'd do whatever it takes to stop you from hurting me." She shakes her head. "You don't understand. Siblings are supposed to protect each other."

Siblings are supposed to protect each other.

She has no idea just how right she is.

I should take her to her room—back to her confinement where she can't force the ghosts of my past into my present. I should stop visiting her and let Ryder deal with her from now on. I should end this conversation now before I make things more complicated than they already are.

But like everything with Elise, I don't do what I should.

"I do understand."

"You don't have siblings. You can't—"

"I had a sister."

I regret the words as soon as they leave my lips, but it's too late.

Elise's pupils dilate, and she studies my neutral expression before asking, "What happened?"

There's a tremor in her voice, and it hits me that she's afraid of my reaction to her question.

She's afraid I'll hurt her again.

But there's something else there, too, something softer. It's the first time all night that her gaze holds more than fear or apathy, and it takes me a second to identify what the new emotion is.

Hope.

She's looking for a way to understand me. She's looking for some deeper meaning for why I am the way I am. She's looking for the good in me.

She should know by now that it doesn't exist.

"Car crash," I explain, because, technically, it's the truth.

And way more than she has a right to know.

Those big, brown eyes overflow with undeserved sympathy. "Joshua, I'm so sorry. I had no idea."

A gentle touch on my shoulder startles us both. Elise pulls her comforting hand back, cowering away with the realization of her own action settling in. She hadn't meant to reach out to me, but, damn, it felt good.

Too good.

She clears her throat. "What happened to your sister is horrible, but you didn't choose that. Mason *chose* to do this to me. He didn't have to. Would you have done the same to your sister? Put her in the hands of someone who would kill her?"

Her blunt question drives a dull knife into my heart, and it's a moment before I can speak.

"No, I wouldn't have done what Mason did," I admit.

She nods like this was the answer she was expecting.

"But that doesn't mean he doesn't feel guilty. He was doing his duty and proving his loyalty."

"His duty was to protect *me*! Don't act like he's some man of honor." She barks a humorless laugh. "Hell, what would you know about honor?"

My fist clenches in a knee-jerk reaction to her disrespect. Elise lifts a hand before I can put her in her place.

"I'm sorry. I don't want to fight. I'm too tired." Her small voice is quiet like she's working to stop it from breaking, and the sound grates on my chest.

She looks tired, and I wonder if Tripp is overworking her or if her panic attack drained all of her energy. Probably a mixture of both.

"What happened tonight?"

I've given her plenty of time to calm down after... whatever it is that happened, and I'm ready for answers.

"Nothing."

"You and I both know that you're going to tell me whether I force you to or not," I remind her.

She must know I'm right because she doesn't object again. She pulls her legs to her chest and sighs, lifting a bandaged finger.

"I cut myself in the kitchen today, and the blood made me queasy. I still worked and forced myself to eat, even though I felt off. Ryder and I left for the night, but I forgot my dinner in the kitchen, so I went back to get it. That's when I threw up."

I wait a moment to allow her time to amend her story.

She doesn't.

"Anything else?"

Her eyes lift to the sky with the shake of her head, and even in the darkness, I can see the blush creeping onto her cheeks.

She can't lie to save her life.

"Elise, I know something happened in that kitchen. Ryder was on the phone with me, and when you didn't come right back to him, he went looking for you. It wasn't until he got to the kitchen that you ran to the bathroom. Something had to have happened during that time. So, I'll ask you one more time, and *only* one more time. What happened tonight?"

When her questioning eyes find mine, I know it's my tone that's caught her off guard. The words hold a real threat—and she knows it —but there isn't an ounce of malice in my tone.

I feel like an ass when her lip trembles, but I don't have a choice. I need to know what happened.

"They didn't know I could hear them," she whispers, the words barely audible. "The soldiers were in the break room when I came back for my food. They were talking about all of the horrible things they've seen you do. I was already nauseous, so I guess that was just the breaking point."

"What did they say?"

"A lot of things."

"Elise," I warn.

She huffs, and a flicker of fire burns in her eyes when she shoots me a glare. "That you've killed more people than you can count. That you skin them alive. That you cut their eyes out and burn your name onto their skin."

Damn it all.

It's no wonder she's afraid of me.

She's heard firsthand accounts of my cruelty, knowing her future rests in my hands. I can only imagine how she'd stood there, wondering which gruesome fate she'll face when she's served her purpose.

None of them.

And just like that, the decision is made.

But she can't know that.

"You know what I am," I remind her. "I haven't pretended to be a good guy."

"Except you *did* pretend to be a good guy! You came into that bakery and let me think you were some normal guy who wanted to take me out. You let me think I'd be safe inviting you over. Worst of all, you let me *genuinely enjoy* our date, knowing that you were about to ruin my life."

She swipes angrily at a few rouge tears.

"Why did you change my room? Why did you make a deal with me? Why didn't you let the doctor sedate me? It would be so much easier for you to tie me up and lock me away, so why don't you? All of your men seem to think it's weird, too, so I know it's not just me."

She takes a deep breath, squeezing her eyes closed.

"Why did you kiss me, Joshua? You could've drugged me either way. Why did you have to kiss me?"

I stand wordlessly, drawing her fearfully captivated gaze to my movements. She twitches to shift away, but I lift a halting hand, and she obliges. Her shoulders tense, shaking with each uneven breath she pulls in, and I can practically see the wheels turning behind her eyes as she tries to figure out how I'm going to retaliate for her burst of passion.

I crouch down, only inches away from her now. "Do you remember what I said that night after we kissed?"

It's a vague question, but she knows exactly what I mean.

She nods in a small, barely noticeable gesture, lips parting and uncertainty swimming in her gaze.

My skin pricks with anticipation, and the air around us is electric. My hand gently cups the side of her face, just as I had that night.

"I couldn't help myself then, just like I can't help myself now."

Her eyes widen more in confusion than fear—I move to erase both.

My lips meet hers in a gentle kiss.

I barely hold back my groan of appreciation because *damn* she tastes good. Her soft, full lips move hesitantly against mine, and I gladly take the lead.

For the first time since our date, the walls between Elise and me vanish, and we're no longer foes—no longer a captor and captive.

The animosity is eagerness.

The wariness is excitement.

The fear is passion.

I move from my crouched position and carefully push Elise's shoulders until she's laid back on her elbows, and I'm hovering above her, never breaking the kiss. One of my hands wanders to her hip, and the other finds the back of her neck. I pull her closer to me, deepening the kiss with the sweep of my tongue.

Gentle kisses bleed into desperation. I take her bottom lip between my teeth, eliciting a soft moan that sends a thrill through my entire body.

Seconds later, her shoulders tense, her lips slow, and I'm sure this is it. She's remembered who I am—what I've done—and she doesn't want to be anywhere near me.

I wait for the withdrawal, but it never comes.

Instead, she slips her arms out from under her and lays on her back, small hands cupping either side of my face to pull me closer.

She wants to touch me just as much as I want to touch her.

The realization is nothing short of complete satisfaction, and I let myself revel in the power she's willingly giving me. I plunge my tongue into her mouth and let myself explore every inch of her.

I'm high on the taste of her sweet lips and dizzy from the sound of her soft moans.

My decision becomes a vow: I will never hurt Elise again.

But it's more than that—I don't just want to keep her safe. The desire to make Elise *happy* is quickly climbing the list of my priorities.

Her hands move boldly across my skin, and my chest tightens as if I've never been touched before. My hand wanders up her delicate body and weaves into her thick hair.

Nothing has ever felt as good as Elise.

I'm imagining all the ways I could convince her to come back to my room when her head snaps to the side, breaking our kiss without warning. Her hands release me, and a brutal chill replaces the warmth of her touch.

Neither of us says a word. We stay there, each catching our breath.

I want, more than anything, to lean in and take her mouth with mine again—to hell with the consequences. But now that I'm sure of what I want, I'm not willing to risk facing those consequences after all.

"You should get to bed," I say as I climb to my feet. I turn to take a deep breath and clear my mind. "I'll take you to your room."

I hear her stand, and when I turn, I'm staring into the most hypnotizing brown eyes I have ever seen. Kissing Elise is incredible, but I could just look at her all day long.

The walk to her room is a blur, and I'm consumed with a million different things to say, but none of them seem right.

When we reach her door, I unlock and open it but block her path with my arm before she can enter.

"Elise—"

"What happened out there doesn't change how I feel about you." She doesn't try to mask her exhaustion and pain. It's on full display, and all I want is to replace it with one of her wide, easy smiles.

I see the irony, being the one who put her in this situation and now searching for a way to get her out of it. Though, if I could go back in time, I'm not sure there's anything I'd do differently. After all, she's here and, for the time being, mine.

"And how do you feel about me?"

Her chin quivers, and I catch a glisten in her eyes as she shakes her head. "Joshua…"

"What if I've changed how I feel about you?"

A single tear falls down her cheek. She brushes it away before looking up at me with resignation.

"Unless you've changed your mind about my freedom, your feelings don't matter."

CHAPTER FIFTEEN

Elise

Morning couldn't come soon enough. I breathe a sigh of relief when sunlight streams into my room, and I can finally escape my never-ending nightmares.

I stretch and stand from the bed, falling back onto the soft mattress when yesterday's events replay in my mind.

Throwing up, passing out, having a panic attack, kissing Joshua…

His words from last night still ring in my head.

What if I've changed how I feel about you?

I have no idea what he meant by that, and frankly, I'm not sure I want to.

Keeping with the current schedule, I'll be going to the garden today, so I pick out a pair of denim shorts and a white tank top, letting my hair fall freely over my shoulders. My natural dark roots are taking over, blending messily with the blonde.

The knock at the door pulls me from the mirror, and I call them in.

A tall, dark-haired man enters with my breakfast tray. He places it on the table and turns to leave. "I'll be back to get the plate."

I nod and watch him leave the room as quickly as he came in.

That was strange.

Joshua and Ryder are the only ones who have ever talked to me, but maybe after what happened in the garden last night, Joshua told his soldiers to ease up on me.

I push away from the table once I'm done eating, shifting the plates on the tray as I do. Before I can turn toward the dresser, I notice a white paper partially peeking out from beneath one of the plates.

For a moment, all I can do is stare at it.

When I can finally bring myself to move, I push the plate out of the way and inspect the square envelope. There's no writing on the outside, no way to be certain it's intended for me, but somehow, I know it is. The real mystery is who would try to give me a note, and why would they need to hide it?

There's only one way to find out.

I take the envelope with shaky hands and open it.

Elise,

I'm coming for you. Stay safe and stay quiet.

—Dad

My dad got a message to me.

A simple message, sure, but the implications change everything. First, my father knows where I am. Second, he's planning to save me. Third, and most importantly, he has a man on the inside.

A fresh wave of emotion brings on tears, but for the first time since I came here, they're tears of joy.

I tuck the note back in the envelope and shove it inside my pillowcase for safekeeping before moving to sit by the window.

I think back to how the dark-haired man talked to me today. Maybe that was a sign. I replay the words in my head.

I'll be back to get the plate.

Not tray, *plate.*

It has to be him.

So, what does this mean for my escape plan?

I picture the window in the bathroom and all the ways I imagined stalling Ryder to give myself the chance to use it. But now that I know my dad is working to free me, is trying to escape still a smart option?

If I try to escape, it might interfere with Dad's plan, but if I wait, Joshua might find a way to get what he wants without giving me back, and it'll be too late.

Heavy dread settles in the pit of my stomach as a chilling thought creeps into my mind.

What if that note wasn't from Dad at all?

It could be Joshua tricking me into thinking my father is coming for me, so I won't try to escape on my own. That would change everything. It would mean my dad doesn't know where I am, there is no inside man, and no one is coming to save me.

But what if it is real?

My heart is all but screaming at me to believe it was my dad, but my mind isn't so sure.

I rub my temples to soothe the headache forming there. The possibilities are endless, and there is no way to be sure I'm going to make it out of this alive.

It's almost noon when there's a knock at the door, and I realize I've done nothing all morning but stare out into the garden, letting my mind race with "*what ifs.*"

My heart leaps when the door opens, eager to talk to the dark-haired man, but it's Joshua who enters.

He's dressed in dark jeans and a navy tee that does nothing to conceal his hard muscles, and I flush, remembering how my hands roamed those muscles last night.

"Expecting someone else?" He tilts his head, and I want to kick myself for not composing my expression fast enough.

I narrow my eyes in what I hope resembles a playful look. "I wish I was."

He rolls his eyes. "How did you sleep last night?"

I inwardly groan but outwardly answer. "Not well."

The tension in the room is palpable, charged with the intensity from last night. I still haven't quite figured out how I feel about what happened. Honestly, I'm not sure that I even *understand* what happened.

"Would you like to join me for lunch in the garden?" he asks, and I recognize that he's not telling me what to do.

He's giving me a choice.

"I'd like that," I answer, slipping my shoes onto my feet.

I pick up the items I set aside for my time in the garden today, a small canvas, sketchbook, pencils, an easel, paints, and brushes.

Seeing my struggle, Joshua steps in.

"Let me," he says, taking everything but the sketchbook easily into his hands.

I mumble my thanks and walk the familiar path to the garden. Joshua silently follows, his eyes on me like a hawk, and I don't think it's because he's worried about me trying to run.

I feel as though a weight has been lifted off my shoulders the second I step into the sunshine.

Joshua sets my art supplies on a nearby bench. "Are you ready to eat now?"

I put my sketchbook down and turn to face him. I'd forgotten how striking his eyes can be in the light, captivating me where I stand. Even from this far, I notice the flecks of gold that only seem to be visible in the sun.

"Elise?" he asks, raising an eyebrow.

"Uh—yeah. I'm ready to eat."

I think I hear Joshua chuckle, but it's faint and gone before I can be sure.

The table is once again crowded with a buffet that the two of us could never finish alone, and I take a seat as I fill my plate and sip from the mimosa in front of me.

Joshua sits opposite me, and I'm glad that the sounds of nature can fill our awkward silence. It's nothing like the easy, content silence with Ryder when we eat during my lunch breaks.

It doesn't help that I can't get last night's events out of my head. It's difficult to make small talk with so many things unspoken.

Picking at my food, I sneak looks at Joshua, unsure if he's going to say something about last night. Should I? Do I even *want* to talk about it?

"Say it."

"Huh?"

"You look like you have something to say. So, say it."

I take another sip of my drink, untangling my jumbled thoughts. "I was just wondering... I mean." I clear my throat. "Last night..."

"Last night, we were exhausted. I think we can both agree we weren't quite ourselves. Maybe it's best if we forget what happened."

I'm filled with relief and nod enthusiastically. "I think that's for the best."

There's no change in Joshua's expression, and I realize his guard is up more than normal today, not that I blame him. Last night, he showed me a side of himself that I never knew existed. It's understandable that he'd regret his vulnerability and put up a wall.

I'm trying to build my walls up, too.

"Are you enjoying your time in the kitchen?" he asks, and I'm grateful for the change in topic.

"It's nice to get out of my room," I say with a small smile. "It makes me feel a little more normal."

"I haven't heard any complaints from Tripp, so that's a good sign."

His words are light—playful even—but my stomach drops at the mention of his name.

If I were him, I would've raped the brat the second she got here. That ought to put her in her place.

I compose my expression, but of course, it's too late.

"What was that?" he asks, playfulness long gone.

I look down.

"Elise," he says, and there's no mistaking the warning in his tone.

"It's nothing, just stuff that he said last night."

He waits for me to elaborate.

I don't.

"Damn it, Elise. I'm so tired of having to pull answers out of you. When I ask a question, you answer it, or have you forgotten how things work here?"

I sit up straight, a surge of white-hot rage running through my veins.

"Tripp said that if he were you, he would've raped me by now to put me in my place."

Joshua's face remains impassive.

"It's okay," I tell him, "you can laugh. All the other guys thought it was *hilarious*. So yeah, working in the kitchen is great aside from the fact that every man there would gladly take me against my will."

Joshua says nothing, and I scoff, standing to leave. I'm about to pass by when he stands, and we're flush against each other.

He looks down, and something passes between our gazes. His features remain hard, but the anger seems to leave him when he sees what's beneath the fury in my eyes.

Fear.

He lifts a hand, gently placing it on the side of my face. "No one else is going to touch you."

I don't miss his careful wording, but it's not a battle worth fighting.

I look at him through full lashes, nodding because what is there to say? Thanks for not letting people rape me?

The bar for gratitude is low.

He absentmindedly strokes my cheek, pulling me into a daze that draws my eyes to his full lips. They moved so effortlessly against mine last night, and I want to feel them again.

His hand lingers for half a second too long. My breath hitches. Then, just as quickly as he touched me, he pulls away.

"Back to our lunch?" His voice is unreadable.

I nod, breathless from yet another close encounter with him. I really ought to have better control over myself.

We take our seats, and I pick at my food, not nearly as hungry as I'd been a few moments ago.

"Where did you go the last few days?"

He studies me with his signature analytic gaze before saying, "I was with your father."

"Wait, really?" I picture the note hiding in my pillowcase right now. If Joshua was with my father yesterday, that would've given someone a chance to get the note from him here to me.

He nods, expression guarded.

I try to imagine Joshua and my father in the same room. That, alone, sounds like a horrible combination. Throw a hostage and desired territory in the mix, and I'm glad I wasn't anywhere near that interaction. I'm surprised Joshua even walked away alive.

"How is he?"

Joshua suppresses a cocky grin. "Not very happy with me."

I don't mean to, but I laugh at that.

"I really miss him," I mutter, more to myself than to Joshua.

"Would you like to call him?"

CHAPTER SIXTEEN

Joshua

If I had to write a book about my life, I'd title this chapter, "What the Hell Was I Thinking?"

I wish I could say that having Elise call her dad is some strategic play meant to give me the upper hand, but it's not. All I know is that her eyes—which are constantly plagued with sadness—lit up when I mentioned her father, and I didn't want that light to fade.

"I'll be there to monitor, of course, but Elise"—I leave no room for misunderstanding in my cold tone—"if you do something stupid, I'll take away every freedom and leave you restrained in your room, understand?"

"Yes! Yes, I understand!" She seems to have no qualms about submission now.

I stand and—for reasons I can't explain—hold out my hand to her. The most addictive thrill runs through me when she accepts it without hesitation—as if she trusts me.

Not that I've ever given her a reason to.

Once we're in my office, I lean against the front of my desk, and Elise sits in one of the chairs.

The phone I've designated for calls with Gabriel Consoli sits on the desk, and I pick it up, fixing Elise with a stern glare.

"*Anything* out of line and—"

"And you'll leave me restrained in my room, I know."

I press my lips together to suppress my amusement. Now isn't the time to let her think she can get comfortable.

"Watch it," I warn.

An enthusiastic nod replaces the witty retort I expect.

She must *really* want to call her dad.

This better not come back to bite me in the ass.

I dial the number, and the room buzzes with her excitement as we wait. Seeing Elise's smile and the anticipation in her eyes floods my chest with a satisfying warmth. It feels unbelievably gratifying to put a smile on her face after being the cause of its absence for so long.

She picks at the hem of her shirt, eyes never leaving the phone that I place on the desk beside me.

He answers after two rings, and Elise's eyes gloss over, though the harsh words of her father are meant for me.

"What do you want, you sick son of a—"

"Dad?" she says, her sweet voice starkly contrasting his gruff one.

"Elise? Elise, baby girl, tell me that's you."

Her lip wobbles, and she nods as if he could see her. "It's me."

"Are you okay? What has that bastard done to you? Is he there now?"

"I'm"—she pauses, eyes flitting to mine as she searches for the right words—"I'm alright. And yes, Joshua is here, but he's not hurting me, Dad. I'm okay."

My fist clenches when I realize my mistake, and judging by his pause, Consoli catches it, too. Even Elise's eyebrows pull together as understanding dawns on her.

She clears her throat. "How are the boys?"

My eyes narrow in a deadly warning to not mention anything about Mason, and Elise lowers her head submissively.

"Worried. We all are," he says with a sigh. "Baby girl, I'm so sorry. You were never meant to get caught up in this. I tried so hard to keep you safe."

When Elise lifts her head, a tear slides down her cheek.

"Dad." Her voice breaks on the word. "You did keep me safe. This is all my fault. I should've listened to you."

"It's okay. I love you so much, Elise. I'll see you soon, okay?"

More tears.

"I love you too, Dad. I'll see you soon."

"Now, let me talk to that bastard."

Elise walks to the window, burying her face in her hands, shoulders hunched forward. The sight sends a wave of guilt over me, but I repress the emotion.

I take the phone off speaker and lift it to my ear. "Consoli."

"Keep your hands *off* my daughter," he sneers, each word said as a lethal threat. "Do you understand me?"

I'm tempted to inform him that I've put more than my hands on his daughter, but for Elise's sake, my answer is a simple, "I understand."

He ends the call.

Elise's quiet sniffles are the only sound in the room, and after a few moments, I clear my throat. "Would you like to go back outside?"

Her only answer is the shake of her head.

"What's your problem? I thought you wanted to talk to him."

Her exhale is an exasperated sound. "Just take me back to my room."

Any satisfaction I felt from her joy dissipates in an instant.

Minutes ago, she'd been thrilled by the idea of talking to her father, but now that she has, she refuses to even look at me. I'm suddenly reminded why I've never attempted to make a woman happy.

They're too damn confusing.

"Turn and face me. Now."

She obliges with a vicious glare. "Just take me to my room."

Whatever patience I had dissipates.

"You want to go to your room? Fine by me."

I've taken one step toward her when her eyes widen with understanding, but it's too late. I effortlessly pick her up, throw her over my shoulder, and storm out of the office.

"Put me down!" She punctuates her request with a round of beatings to my back.

I roll my eyes at the wasted energy.

"Joshua! Put me down, or I swear—"

I squeeze her thigh just hard enough to get her to shut up.

"Another word, and I'm tying you to the bed again," I warn.

She groans dramatically but refrains from hitting me again.

When we get to her room, I type in the code with ease and toss her carelessly onto the bed. I cross my arms over my chest and tower over her.

"What the hell is your problem?"

She has the *nerve* to roll her eyes.

I reach to unbuckle my belt, and Elise brazenly shoves at my chest. "You! You're my problem! What did you expect? A thank you for letting me call my dad? You're the one keeping us separated in the first place! But you know what? *Thank you*. Thank you so much for letting me talk to my father one last time before you kill me. You're so *generous*, Joshua!"

I slip my belt out of the loops and squeeze the buckle until my knuckles turn white.

This is what I get?

This is what it looks like to try and make things easier for her?

A waste of time.

"You're right," I say, voice deadly low. "I am generous. Do you know what *normally* happens to my prisoners, Elise?"

She doesn't speak. She doesn't move. She doesn't breathe.

Her glare falters when I take a menacing step forward.

Good. She *should* be afraid.

"You've been here for what? A week and a half? By now, you'd be starved to the point of constant pain, but not enough to kill you. You'd have absolutely no forms of entertainment or human interaction. You'd be nothing but a shell of a human, and that's if I decided not to torture you within an inch of your life first."

Her eyes say what I know she never would—that she knows I'm right. She knows I'm capable of doing all of those things to her.

I wait for the begging, the groveling, the apologies, and promises to be more cooperative.

I get none of them.

Slowly, she rises to her knees on the bed, staring up at me with perfect sincerity.

"Then do it."

She must be out of her damn mind.

I close the distance between us until her hands are pressed to my chest, and I work to ignore how good that feels.

I firmly grip the back of her neck and force her gaze to remain locked on mine.

"You think I won't?" The question is practically a growl, but she doesn't so much as flinch.

"I think you could, hell, maybe you *should*," she whispers. "But no, I don't think you will."

The words cut deep, and I wish I could tell her she's wrong, but I'm not sure she is.

My grip on her neck tightens, but she doesn't resist me. In fact, her whole body seems to mold to mine, somehow relaxing despite my aggression.

112

The reaction both thrills and infuriates me.

For the second time today, I find myself bewildered by the level of trust she seems to have in me despite all I've done to her. Yet, here she is, leaning into me, staring into my cold glare with wide, hopeful eyes.

It forces me to imagine a world where I'm worthy of that trust—a world where I bring Elise comfort and peace.

But that's not how this ends.

I will break Elise long before I could ever make her mine.

The sobering thought draws me out of my head, and I release my hold on her.

"It doesn't matter," I whisper, taking a step back in an attempt to gain some clarity.

"Doesn't matter?" She scoffs. "Of course, it matters! Why am I different?"

I turn from her, taking measured breaths as I methodically slide my belt back into place.

The blankets on the bed are pushed aside, and light feet pad against the floor. "I deserve to know."

Can't she see how messed up this is? She should be cowering in fear when I walk into the room, not melting into my body and pleading with those big, innocent eyes to know why I do the things I do.

I should be in my office on a meeting with the capos at the Sacramento base—focusing on things that actually matter—not having garden lunches with the prisoner I can't stop thinking about, no matter how hard I try.

And I have no one to blame but myself.

I gave her a nicer room, I let her bargain freedom, I joined her for meals, and I let her call her father. I should've left her to rot in a cell like I do every other prisoner I have ever taken.

But that was never an option, not with Elise.

Even now, as furious with myself—and her—as I am, I know there's no world in which I treat her like any other prisoner.

She's *not* any other prisoner.

Elise is strong-willed but unashamed to shed tears. She's reserved but determined to stand her ground even when she knows she won't win. She's tender—both physically and emotionally—but absolutely resilient.

When her fingertips brush my arm, I recoil like her touch is a white-hot flame.

"I don't know, Elise! You're right, okay? There's no logical reason why you're different, but you are. For some reason, I don't *want* to hurt you!" I bark a laugh, and the sound is chilling. "But apparently, it doesn't matter anyway, so maybe I should just treat you like the rest."

"He thinks I'm coming home," she whispers, her voice as fragile as glass.

I don't answer, but my eyes open to find her arms wrapped around her midsection as if she's trying to hold herself together. Her anger melts away, leaving a hopelessness that I can practically feel radiating off her—the raw ache of losing her family, her freedom, and her life.

"I told him I'll see him soon, and I won't. The last thing I ever said to my father was a lie."

The urge to pull her into my arms is so overwhelming that I dig my fingernails into my palm to keep myself in place.

"I never disobeyed my father, ever. The *one* time I blatantly ignored him was when I had you over for dinner. If I'd just listened to him…"

"Don't give yourself too much credit. Your agreeing to dinner didn't make my plan possible, only easier."

"Oh yeah, that makes me feel *so* much better."

"All I'm saying is I would've taken you either way, so there's no point in dwelling over something that was inevitable to begin with."

"And why do you care what I dwell over?"

"Because I'm the one who has to hear you complain about it," I snap.

Her jaw drops. "You're kidding me, right?"

My fingers pinch the bridge of my nose. "I miss when I thought you were shy."

"I miss when I thought you were Hayden."

I breathe a laugh and let my lip twitch upward.

Just like that, the tension in the room breaks, and it's like a weight has fallen off my chest when I see that Elise, too, is sporting a faint grin.

A knock at the door steals my attention, and I move to open it, finding Ryder on the other side.

"It's time to go, Mr. Moreno."

"Go ahead. I'm right behind you."

He nods, and I let the door close.

"Why do I call you Joshua?"

I'd been expecting this question since the call with her father. It had been a rookie mistake on my part to leave that out of her instructions.

Since I don't want to kill the light mood we just achieved, I answer, "Well, it *is* my name."

I can see the desire to roll her eyes, but miraculously, she doesn't.

Not that I would've corrected her.

"I mean, how come you don't make me call you Mr. Moreno like everyone else? Tripp made a comment about it, and my father seemed thrown off, too."

I slowly close the distance between us, debating my answer. I could say that I wanted her father to see the influence I have over her or that she won't live long enough for it to matter.

I lift a hand, placing it gently against her cheek—a striking contrast to my rough grip on her only moments ago—and tell her the truth.

"I like my name on your lips."

Her pupils dilate, and my heart squeezes at the sight, but it doesn't feel so uncomfortable now.

Almost… pleasant.

Before she can respond, I tuck a loose strand of hair behind her ear and leave the room.

CHAPTER SEVENTEEN

Elise

"Ready to go?"

"Yeah, just a second." As I straighten from slipping my shoes on, I lose my balance and sway on my feet.

"Woah." Joshua puts a steady hand on my lower back. "Are you okay?"

My cheeks flush. "I'm fine. I just stood up too fast, is all."

I expect his hand to fall away once I'm balanced, but it doesn't. He keeps a possessive hold on me as we make our way to the kitchen.

Much like yesterday—when he held my face so tenderly—I can't bring myself to stop him. As unconventional as it may be, there's something comforting in his touch. Besides, it's not worth the fight it would likely start.

We're halfway to the kitchen when I sneak a side glance at Joshua.

Though he doesn't meet my gaze, he must feel it because he mutters, "What?"

"Can I ask a question?"

"You can ask, but I may not answer."

When I narrow my eyes, his only response is a *what did you expect?* look.

"How do you pick who works in the kitchen? Is it some rotation?"

When I first went to the kitchen, I figured that everyone in there would be a chef of some sort, but that's not the case. A few men seem to know exactly what they're doing, but most look completely lost and need detailed instructions from Tripp or Jay for each task.

"It's mostly a rotation of recruits. Some men work primarily in the kitchen because it's where they're most useful, but all of my soldiers are trained on the basics of every possible field of work within the base before they're placed."

Two parts of his answer surprise me.

The first is that he gave me an explanation when all I had expected was a simple *yes* or *no*. The second is that, though I'm no expert in the ways of mafia recruit training, I know enough to recognize that this isn't a traditional approach. Most bosses aren't concerned with having well-rounded soldiers—just functioning ones.

He chuckles at whatever expression my reaction created.

"Jay will be giving instructions today," he tells me when we get to the kitchen doors.

"Where's Tripp?"

Joshua shifts his gaze to Ryder, who, as always, is a few steps behind me. "He's out for a while."

"Does this have anything to do with the comment I told you about yesterday?" I try to sound casual, but I can't help shivering at the memory of Tripp's callous words.

Joshua doesn't answer—which is answer enough—and does something far stranger.

Leaning in, he presses a soft kiss to my forehead before turning to leave. It happens so fast I wonder if I imagined it, but the lingering warmth where his lips met my skin still tingles with electricity.

Joshua's halfway down the hall when he turns to flash me a rogue grin, leaving me reeling. What the hell just happened?

How does Joshua have the ability to affect me this strongly? I want to be mad at him for abusing his control, but after everything that's happened, I have to admit that I much prefer it when we're this way. I'll take playful and confusing over combative and suffering any day.

I can imagine that today is a more accurate representation of how the kitchen ran before I came to work here. Instead of Tripp roaming the room, barking orders, Jay takes a more subtle approach to leadership. He floats from one station to the next, teaching and assessing the work being done by each soldier, myself included.

Unlike Tripp, Jay treats me the same as everyone else. He doesn't single me out or shoot nasty looks my way every chance he gets.

It's unbelievably refreshing.

I'm not the only one who seems to notice the change in atmosphere. Usually, the only sounds filling the room are chopping knives, a sizzling stove, and running water in the sink, but today, it's accompanied by a pleasant chatter. I even catch some of the guys laughing among themselves in their private conversations.

Ryder stands a few feet away, watching as I mix the bowl of cherry pie filling that Jay assigned to me. I'd usually ignore him, but he's closer than normal and the lively setting has sparked my own desire for conversation.

"Are you normally a babysitter or does Joshua let you do actual work sometimes?"

I peek up and find Ryder caught off guard—which, with his stoicism, just means he lifts an eyebrow. Aside from asking him if he wants food, I've never tried to talk to him before.

"I go where I'm needed," is all he says.

I get the impression Ryder is a man of few words, but that doesn't stop me.

"Come on, this can't be fun for you. Shouldn't you be in the middle of a shoot-out or a car chase? Or anything more exciting than watching a twenty-three-year-old make cherry pie?"

He laughs for the first time since I've met him, and the sound is delightful. "You really have been sheltered, haven't you?"

I shrug. "By choice. Besides, I'm sure my theories are much more interesting than reality, so don't ruin it for me."

He shakes his head, though a small smile touches his handsome face. "Miss Consoli, you know we're not supposed to be talking, especially about work."

"First off, call me Elise. Second"—I scan the room dramatically—"I don't see Joshua anywhere. And third, I believe we were discussing my imagination, so unless car chases are a normal part of your workday, I think we're in the clear."

"Elise," he says slowly, like he's testing out my name. "Unfortunately, I'm more afraid of Mr. Moreno than I am of you."

I put down the bowl I'm holding. "Ryder, I'll handle Joshua. I'm pretty used to getting yelled at by him. Besides, I haven't talked to anyone but him since getting here, and I'm sure you can imagine how that could make a person lose their mind."

He just laughs.

The mesmerizing sound draws the attention of those around us and brings a genuine smile to my lips. "What's so funny?"

He tosses me a hand towel from the counter beside him. "You have cherry filling on your face. It's not exactly the most intimidating look."

Somehow, my pleas work, and I've convinced Ryder to indulge me. I expect to carry most of the conversation but am pleasantly surprised to find that words flow easily between us, requiring little effort on my part to keep things from being awkward. Though I do most of the talking, he always has a thoughtful comment or challenging question on the tip of his tongue, and the afternoon passes in a blur.

Jay tells me it's time to take my break, and he allows me time to make food before the thirty minutes begin. I throw together a bourbon and honey chicken salad for Ryder and myself, and we settle in the break room.

"I'm surprised you enjoy those movies at all. You don't exactly strike me as the graphic and gory type."

I shrug. "Movie violence doesn't bother me. Besides, it's good versus evil, and good always wins."

The real meaning of my words hangs heavy between us, but he says nothing.

I'm not under the impression that our situation is *good guys versus bad guys*, more like *bad guys versus worse guys*, but who's to say what title goes to what family? From my perspective, my father and brothers are the heroes, soon to save me from the clutches of the evil Joshua Moreno, but that's not exactly the case anymore.

Sure, Joshua is far from an upstanding citizen, but do I believe he's evil?

My hands twitch with the memory of how his body felt against them in the garden. Solid, capable, warm. His lips were soft and sure against mine, moving with confidence similar to that of putting the first pieces of a puzzle together when you still have no idea what the whole picture will look like, but you know this match is the start of figuring it out.

No, I don't believe Joshua is evil. In fact, I think there's a decent man beneath the rough exterior and instinctual need for power and obedience.

Ryder's analytic eyes don't leave my face, and I redden under the intensity of his gaze. "I'm surprised you even have time to watch movies. Don't you sell drugs at night or something equally as illegal?"

A hint of a smile replaces the seriousness. "No, no. We've already established that you have *no* idea what this job entails."

"And I'd like to keep it that way."

A beep from his phone steals Ryder's attention. Since we're done eating, I take our plates and clean our spots. I'm surprised the kitchen is so empty, but it's Friday, and my guess is that most men don't stay at the base over the weekend, so there isn't a need for many cooks today.

Ryder walks out behind me, his focus on his phone.

"Everything okay?"

"I need to step away for a bit." He turns to survey the kitchen, easily finding who he's looking for. "Jay, will you keep an eye on Miss Consoli? I'll be back soon."

His words instantly rub me the wrong way. After talking all day, I got used to Ryder acting like a friend, but that's not the case.

He's my babysitter, here to ensure I'm on my best behavior. It's dangerous for me to believe anything more than that.

A short silence makes me think Jay didn't hear Ryder, but then he yells, "Yeah!" Jay doesn't even bother to look in my direction, though, too busy digging through a cabinet.

Ryder nods, flashing me a small, apologetic smile before leaving.

I'm about to ask Jay what I can do next, but he talks before I can.

"Oh yes! Here it is! Thanks for your help." When he turns, I see the cell phone pressed to his ear.

Taking the bag of pecans that he just found, Jay walks back to the storage room without sparing me so much as a glance.

I take a moment to process what just happened.

He didn't hear Ryder's request to keep an eye on me.

I'm unsupervised.

I don't think. I just walk as casually as I can to the kitchen door.

I step out and scan the hall for witnesses but find none. My feet carry me to the bathroom of their own accord, and in the blink of an eye, I'm standing on the toilet seat, pushing the curtain aside and unlatching the flimsy lock. It takes a few shoves, but eventually, it slides open, and I'm staring into my literal window of opportunity. It's a narrow fit, and it'll be hard for me to maneuver through without any leverage on this side, but it's possible.

A breeze flows into the room, and with it, a slap of reality.

What the hell am I doing?

One hand reaches through the open window as if needing proof that nothing is stopping me from climbing to my freedom.

So then, why am I still standing here?

With every passing second, I risk someone noticing my absence, but I can't bring myself to move. My breathing shallows, and my head spins so fast that I press my palms against the wall to steady myself.

Is escaping really my best option?

If you don't leave now, they're going to kill you! one voice hisses in my head.

And if there's only wilderness for miles? You'd just die out there anyway! says another.

Better to die trying to escape than as a complacent hostage, my pride argues.

What about the note? my logic asks. *Dad could come any second now, and you could ruin his plan.*

My pride scoffs. *Every second you stay, Joshua gets one step closer to finding a loophole to kill you.*

And if he catches you, he'll make you wish you were dead!

I audibly groan, desperate for the warring voices to shut up and let me think clearly, but they've made their points. My palms dig into my eye sockets until indistinguishable shapes and colors dance through the oblivion.

Is this chance worth risking Joshua's wrath? Is it worth risking screwing up Dad's plan? Is it worth risking my life in the wilderness?

But can I afford to take the alternative risk of staying put?

The worst part is that I know the answer before I even ask, and it terrifies the hell out of me. I'm not sure there was ever a real choice, and I only told myself there was to help soothe the fear that never stops twisting in my gut.

I only pray I'm not making the biggest mistake of my life.

CHAPTER EIGHTEEN

Elise

Ryder returned less than an hour after he left and found me cleaning the last of the dishes from the various desserts I had spent the day making.

Normally I would've been touched by his concern when he asked me if everything was okay, but all my earlier lightness was sucked out of that damned window, and I'm left feeling unbelievably numb.

Usually, Ryder would ask if I'd like to make dinner or have it brought to my room, but he doesn't bother tonight, and I'm too drained to ask about it.

We walk silently back to my room, and I look at my feet to avoid eye contact when he holds the door for me.

I step through the threshold and close my eyes, taking a deep breath as the door's lock clicks behind me.

"Long day?"

I nearly jump out of my own skin at the sound of Joshua's voice.

My head snaps up to find him sitting on the bed, leaning against the wall like he doesn't have a care in the world. His hair is its usual tamed mess, and though he's lounging in gray sweatpants and a navy-blue tee, he looks ready to model for a magazine cover.

It's the most relaxed I've ever seen him, and I hate that—for the hundredth time—I wonder what things would be like if he were a normal guy. Would this be something I could come home to every night? That idea shouldn't wake the butterflies in my stomach, but here they are beating their hopeful wings.

What surprises me even more is that across from the bed, right in front of the dresser, is a large TV hung on a rolling stand.

"What's this?" I ask, breathless from both surprise and exhaustion.

"Well," he starts, and he seems almost... bashful. "Since we got through the week with minimal issues, I thought we deserved a bit of a break."

A series of events from this week flash through my head.

Freaking out on our way to the kitchen.

Throwing up when I overheard the soldiers.

Having a panic attack in Joshua's bedroom.

Yelling at each other after I called my father.

Minimal issues, my ass.

But I agree that we deserve this, so I don't correct him.

Joshua is my captor; that hasn't changed. But somehow, everything else has.

Though I don't understand why—or to what extent—Joshua cares about me.

It's a terrifying fact that I refuse to explore because I'm not sure I can handle the mental or emotional strain of knowing the truth. Maybe it's the coward's way out, but I decide to let myself enjoy this peace offering.

Haven't I earned this?

After a long moment of silence, he gestures to the space beside him on the bed. "Join me?"

An invitation, not a demand.

I slip into the bathroom to change into cotton shorts and a tank top, throwing my thick hair up in a ponytail. I probably need a shower, but the prospect of watching a movie is too good to delay, so I throw on another layer of deodorant and deem myself clean enough.

When I step into the room, Joshua's eyes heat with a familiar look that sends a wave of nerves through me. It dawns on me that it would've been smarter to wear sweatpants and a T-shirt, but there's no way I'm giving him the satisfaction of knowing he's flustered me, so I climb up into the bed and settle myself roughly a foot away from him.

He eyes the distance I've put between us with a knowing smile, and I clear my throat. "What are we watching?"

"Up to you," he tells me, holding out the remote.

I hesitate for a moment before taking it from his hand and flipping through dozens of titles. I'm overwhelmed by the options: action, comedy, science fiction, and romance—the last is definitely out of the question. It's only minutes later that I find the perfect movie.

"Really?" he asks, but he doesn't sound disappointed.

"Really."

The opening scenes of Die Hard begin, and I cuddle into the covers, keeping a safe distance between us.

"I didn't think you'd enjoy this kind of movie."

"Ryder said the same thing, but movie violence doesn't bother me." I catch my mistake too late and backtrack. "Don't be mad at him. I practically begged him to—" The lifting of his hand cuts me off.

"Ryder messaged me. I allowed it."

"Oh…"

Though I'm glad he's not mad, a frown still falls on my lips. I liked the idea that Ryder was talking to me because he wanted to, not because he had Joshua's permission.

Before he can see my disappointment, I direct my attention to the TV, losing myself in the mindless entertainment.

Dinner comes halfway through the movie, and we bring our bowls of chili to the table, turning the TV so we don't have to pause it and endure awkward silence. We finish our food, and Joshua hands our bowls to a man in the hallway while I readjust the TV.

Though their conversation is mostly hushed, I catch the last part.

"Have Jay send up a bowl of popcorn as soon as he gets the chance."

"Yes, sir," the man replies.

When he hops onto the bed beside me, I ask, "We just ate dinner. How can you be hungry for popcorn?"

His eyes spark playfully. "There's always room for popcorn."

I laugh, cuddling into the covers as Joshua resumes the movie.

The final scenes are playing when the popcorn arrives, and I shake my head as Joshua takes it at the door. "You're going to eat a whole bowl of popcorn before this movie ends?"

"No," he says, hopping onto the bed and tossing a piece of popcorn into his mouth. "We are going to eat this whole bowl of popcorn while we watch the second movie."

"Really?"

He nods, and we share a smile that floods my chest with warmth. I toss a handful of popcorn in my mouth before I can get carried away, and Joshua chuckles under his breath.

The movie ends, and Joshua stands, setting up the next movie and flipping the light switch off.

"What are you doing?" I ask, my body's exhaustion catching up to me in the darkness.

It takes a moment for my eyes to adjust, and I expect a rush of fear when his shadowed figure saunters toward me, but there's only anticipation.

"I prefer movie theater style," he says, and it's strange to think of Joshua Moreno, the big bad crime lord, as someone with simple preferences like having the lights off during a movie.

It's so very *human* of him.

Joshua climbs onto the bed, far closer than before, our arms separated by less than an inch, and I stiffen instinctively. It's weird to be so close to him. Though, this isn't the closest we've ever been...

The movie starts, and I yawn into the darkness, realizing that turning off the lights might not have been the best idea.

I'm fully engrossed in the movie when a gentle movement catches my attention, and Joshua's arm settles over my shoulder. His warmth encases me, and I'm suddenly overly aware of how tense I am.

Slowly, I lean back, glancing up to watch Joshua's expression as I lay into his body, tucking myself beneath his arm. He doesn't stop me.

It's difficult to read his expression in the dark, but it seems almost thoughtful.

I open my mouth to ask him if this is okay, but I'm silenced when, for the second time today, he presses a soft kiss on my forehead. His attention returns to the movie, and I blush furiously in the darkness.

What is up with him? And why am I letting it happen?

But I know the answer—I want this.

A part of me has wanted Joshua since the day he walked into the bakery. Of course, I didn't know then that he was a ruthless criminal, but our attraction was undeniable.

It still is.

Tucked into Joshua's side, the tension coiled tightly in every muscle in my body dissipates. His pine scent surrounds me, and though I'm literally lying in bed with the enemy, I feel safe.

I'm not stupid. I haven't forgotten where I am or the things that he's done, but I see that he's trying. He has no reason to treat me as anything other than a prisoner, yet here he is, holding me in his arms as we watch a movie and share a bowl of popcorn.

I know this isn't exactly a date. How could it be? But I'd be lying if I said that I was miserable right now.

"Joshua?"

"Yes, Princess?" The nickname doesn't sound so mocking now—more like a term of endearment.

"Thank you for tonight."

"Thank you for not picking a stupid movie."

I laugh and toss a piece of popcorn at him.

His chest rumbles with his breathless chuckle, and the sound is unbelievably soothing, like my own personal lullaby.

"Beats another night of poker."

"So, slumming it with the prisoner isn't all that bad?" I tease, but a yawn overtakes the end of the sentence, and another round of his laughter strengthens the call of sleep over my body.

He gazes down at me, and the sincerity there burns like wildfire—dangerous, destructive, unstoppable.

"I like spending time with you," he says.

His scent hits me, and my eyes close with a contented sigh. His arms tighten protectively around me, and my body melts into him like it's second nature. I want to open my eyes again but they're heavy with exhaustion, and I don't have the energy or will to fight it.

"It's a shame you have to kill me." My mumbled words morph into another yawn.

I expect him to stiffen at my words, but he doesn't. Of course, I'm only half kidding.

The world begins to fade as the need to sleep grows irresistible.

"Maybe I'll just have to keep you then," he whispers.

I want to ask him what he means, but all I can manage in my sleepy state is, "Hmm?"

Another soft kiss is placed on my forehead. "Don't worry about it tonight, Princess. You can sleep if you want," he says, and even though a violent fight scene is playing on the screen, I fall swiftly to sleep.

When I wake up, the TV is still in my room, prompting me to rerun last night's events in my head.

Once again, I have no idea what has happened between Joshua and me.

I notice then that the screen is on, showing the main menu. Why didn't Joshua turn it off before he left last night?

That's when I process the weight over my waist.

I suck in a breath as I turn around to see Joshua lying behind me, arm slung lazily over me.

I scramble out of bed as carefully as I can without waking him.

As soon as I'm standing, I check to make sure I'm fully clothed, breathing a sigh of relief when I realize that I am. I don't think we did anything beyond cuddling last night.

Taking a moment to steady my breathing, I place one hand over my racing heart.

"Morning."

I jump at the simple greeting and turn to see Joshua rubbing the sleep from his eyes. His husky morning voice spreads heat over my chest, but that's not what catches my immediate attention.

He's shirtless.

Joshua's chest is beautifully sculpted. Tight muscles ripple down his tan body, leading to a perfect V that I memorize with my eyes. I've touched that chest before, but always over his shirt, and I'm positive that touching him now would be infinitely better.

"Where's your shirt?" The words are out before I can stop them.

He smiles knowingly and sits up to reveal that, *thankfully*, his sweatpants are still in place. "I don't wear a shirt to sleep."

"And why did you sleep here?"

He shrugs. "I got tired and didn't want to go back to my room."

Shaking my head, I work diligently to avoid looking at his chest again.

"I'm going to shower," I say, shifting the TV to grab clothes before darting to the bathroom.

I lock the door, switch on the water, and set my clothes on the counter as I catch my breath.

I stare at my bright red cheeks in the mirror. The dark circles that are normally fixed below my eyes are missing, and I don't have my usual grogginess. For once, I actually feel well-rested, and I wonder how that can be with all my nightmares... only, I didn't have any last night.

The one night that I sleep in the arms of my captor, the nightmares don't come.

I picture Joshua fending off the nightmares to protect me, but that's not the right image. A more suitable picture is that all the other nightmares were too afraid of the monster that held me to try invading my sleep.

But the monster doesn't scare me, not anymore. All I feel right now is a desire to know him.

To touch him.

With that thought, I turn the water's temperature to *cold*.

After my shower, I towel off and throw on a light pink tee and black sweats. I brush and dry my hair, nearly forgetting to brush my teeth, and throw on deodorant before leaving the bathroom.

I'm not sure what I expected to see when I walked back into my room. Maybe I thought that Joshua would be gone. Maybe I thought he'd be seated at the table with breakfast. Maybe I thought he'd gone back to sleep.

I definitely did not expect to see him fuming beside my bed.

My eyes fall to the small paper in his hand.

The note from my father.

CHAPTER NINETEEN

Elise

"What. The hell. Is this?" Each of Joshua's words is concise with barely contained rage.

The blood drains from my face, pure fear shooting through my veins and leaving me paralyzed.

He's going to hurt me again.

Beyond the terror, I feel a warped sense of relief.

The note is real—that's all I can think.

My father really knows where I am, and he really has a man on the inside.

Unfortunately, that truth doesn't change the fact that I'm royally screwed right now.

I say exactly what's on my mind. "It's real?"

His brow furrows. "Elise, you have five seconds to explain before I drag you to the basement."

I blink to clear my eyes of the haziness threatening to take over and place a hand over my heart.

"Five."

I swallow, trying desperately to find my words.

"Four."

My hands ball into fists, fingernails digging into my skin in an attempt to pull myself from my fear-induced paralysis.

"Three."

"I—I don't know!"

His eyes narrow to thin slits. "Not good enough. Two."

My legs carry me backward until my back slams against the

bathroom door, and I hold my hands protectively in front of me. "I found it a few days ago underneath a plate when someone brought me food! I wasn't even sure if it was real until now!"

"I am going to ask you questions. You are going to answer them. Quickly and clearly. Do you understand me?"

I quickly nod but correct myself when his glare intensifies. "Yes! I understand!"

Still holding the note, Joshua folds his arms over his heaving chest. "When and where did you find the note?"

It's difficult to process his request in my current state. I think back through memories that might be able to give me the answer, but all the days here have become a blur.

It's only been a few seconds, but Joshua is low on patience.

"Elise," he warns.

"I'm thinking!" *What did I do after I found the note? The garden!* "Two days ago! Before you took me to the garden. It was on my breakfast tray that morning."

"Who brought your breakfast?"

"I don't know."

"Try harder," he says through gritted teeth.

I choke on a sob. "Joshua, I swear, I had never seen him before, and I haven't seen him since. I'm not even sure I could pick him out of a crowd. I wasn't paying attention when he brought me my food—I didn't have a reason to. I thought I could get a better look when he came back, but then you came to take me to the garden. Remember? You jokingly asked if I was expecting someone else. Well, I was. But I swear that I don't know who he was." I'm gasping for breath by the time I've finished rambling.

"What did you mean when you asked if it was real?"

"I thought, maybe, you faked the note," I admit.

"And why would I do that?"

"If I thought my dad was coming to get me, I wouldn't try to escape on my own."

He steps toward me, and I tense.

"Please," I squeak, but he hushes me with a hard glare.

Joshua doesn't stop until we're flush against one another. My hands, which were held out for my protection, are now pressing against his bare chest.

This isn't exactly what I meant when I so badly wanted to touch him this morning.

His whole demeanor overwhelms my senses, and I want to crumble into a ball, but I can't let my guard down—not again.

"What exactly was your plan?" His voice is a cruel whisper.

"I—I don't know."

"Did you really think your dad would just swoop in here and save you?" He scoffs. "Get it through your head, Elise. You're *never* seeing your father again."

His words cut like a knife, which I'm sure is exactly his intention, and I gasp for air as violent shudders take over my body.

Ryder swings the door open, not looking at all fazed by our closeness as he awaits instructions.

Joshua's fiery stare stays locked on me, but his words are aimed at Ryder. "Take her to the basement."

"No!" I yell, pushing Joshua's chest away from me, but he doesn't seem to notice my resistance.

Grabbing my shoulders, he spins me until I'm pressed face-first against the door. He holds my wrists together, taking a set of handcuffs from Ryder to secure me.

"Joshua, I promise I told you everything!"

Spinning me around to face him, he snarls, "Shut up, or I'll have him gag you too."

I'm unable to hide the intensity of the hurt, fear, and desperation that threaten to choke me, but it doesn't matter.

Joshua's eyes hold only unforgiving wrath.

"Joshua," I say, but the pathetic plea dies in my throat.

His only response is to push me into Ryder's arms.

Catching me before I stumble onto my ass, Ryder holds my shoulders tight, leading me out of the room. I throw one last desperate glance at Joshua, but he's staring at the floor.

Ryder takes me away.

Without a clock, I'm not sure how long I've been in here. Long enough that my arms, which are strung above my head, have gone numb.

This is all my fault. I should've destroyed the note as soon as I got it. I just wanted to keep the small token of home.

But that's not where I messed up.

I let myself trust Joshua, and I didn't realize just how deep that trust went until this morning.

He made it clear on day one that he was the villain, but his mask was so beautiful it made me forget the monster beneath it. His sweet words and gentle caresses were nothing more than tools for manipulation. Again and again, I've fallen for his charm only to find myself helpless.

A door opens from behind me, and I tense, though I don't have the energy to turn to see who it is. Footsteps echo off the concrete walls, and the hairs on the back of my neck stand up.

Something is wrong.

"Isn't this a lovely sight?" Just hearing his cocky voice is enough to make me nauseous.

"Tripp," I breathe.

"Did you miss me?" He steps around to face me, and though he's not nearly as tall as Joshua, he still towers over me.

He flashes a demented smile when I don't answer him. "I've missed you! Too bad I haven't been around lately. Any idea why that was?"

Even from this distance, I can smell the alcohol on his breath. I might not have a clock, but I know it's way too early for hard liquor.

Tripp grips my chin, forcing me to shake my head. "No? Well, I'll enlighten you. My title as capo was stripped because *someone* has loose lips."

Joshua demoted Tripp for what he said about me? I knew he was mad about the comment, I was too, but a demotion?

I try to cringe away, but that only makes him tighten his hold on me.

"I have some ideas on how to put these lips to better use. What do you think?"

My lips twist in disdain, and he drops his hand from my chin. I use the time to focus on taking a deep breath, but I'm interrupted by a sharp stinging that snaps my head to one side.

He slapped me.

"I don't like being ignored, brat," he slurs, stepping so close that our bodies are pressed together.

"Go to hell," I spit.

His laugh is maniacal. "Dirty mouth you got there. I've got just the thing for you."

I writhe in my bonds, and he chuckles, strolling to the table of tortures. He grabs a large whip, and my breath catches in my throat.

He wouldn't. He couldn't. Right?

"No," I rasp. "Joshua wouldn't let you."

He takes slow steps toward me, tapping the whip against his hand with a vile grin. "Who do you think sent me?"

With that, he rears his arm back and snaps the whip onto my back. I scream, but the pain is worse than I could've imagined. An agonizing sting ripples through my body, and I'm gasping for air, but it's so much more than that.

Joshua sent him here? To do *this*?

I don't want to believe it, but why shouldn't I? Joshua has made it abundantly clear that I am a prisoner, and this is what happens to prisoners.

The whip comes down again and again. Tripp's laughter, my cries, and the sharp crack of leather bounce off the walls like a warped symphony.

The lashes continue to meet my abused back until my throat burns, and I can't scream anymore. All I can do is focus on my breathing and take every white-hot lash that he delivers.

I've lost count of the hits by the time Tripp steps back, heaving as he admires his handiwork. Blood is dripping down my back, and I don't even have the will to lift my head.

"Not feeling so powerful now, huh?"

I don't answer, and he brings the whip down again, eliciting an animal-like groan from me.

"Don't make me repeat myself."

I clench my teeth so hard that I fear they'll break. No words leave my mouth.

"Stubborn girl, but that's okay. I'll break you."

The whip clatters to the floor, but I know better than to be relieved.

Nausea hits me right in the stomach when he reaches out, roughly groping my breasts in his calloused hands. "Relax, brat, we're just going to have some fun."

I open my mouth to tell him to get off of me, but before I can get the words out, Tripp shoves his hand into my mouth, fingers triggering my gag reflex.

"Bite down, and I swear I'll make this so much worse for you," he warns.

A muffled whimper is all I can manage when he emphasizes his point by pressing his free hand into my fresh wounds.

What's the point in fighting him? Regardless of what I do, he's not going to stop. I want to be able to say that I was strong, that I fought until the last minute, but that's not the truth. I'm not strong. I'm not able to fight anymore.

I have nothing left.

I sag in my chains, all the resistance leaving me.

Tripp releases my wound, returning his hand to my breast while his fingers continue to probe my throat.

"Good girl," he purrs. "There's no point in fighting me. Besides, you know you want it."

I've never felt so worthless.

Tripp finally removes his dirty hand from my mouth, and I gasp wildly for breath as he dries his wet palm on my face and hair.

The tears come easily now, spilling onto my cheeks to show Tripp just how weak I really am.

He roughly cups my face in his palm. "You like this, baby? Tell me you like it."

My silence inspires him to press a hand into my back again. "I can't hear you, brat."

There's no point in fighting him. My pride has done nothing but hurt me since I got here, and it isn't worth holding on to.

I squeeze my eyes shut, muttering the disgusting words in a hoarse, broken whisper, "I-I like it."

"There we go," he praises. "Now we can *really* start the fun."

I have no idea what that means, but he removes his hands from my body, and I relish the momentary break. His footsteps retreat, and I hear the sound of a lever being pulled. The chain that holds up my body is suddenly released, and though my hands are still bound, I fall to the floor.

I want to cry out as I collapse against the ground, but only a mangled groan leaves my trembling lips.

I don't try to stand. I only watch defenselessly as Tripp circles me like a predator playing with its food.

"You're going to be a good girl, right?"

Tripp lowers himself to his knees in front of me, laughing when I flinch away from his hand, which weaves itself in my hair, pulling my face to his.

His lips move cruelly against mine, and I want to gag when I taste the stale vodka on his lips. This is nothing like my kisses with Joshua. This isn't passionate or thrilling.

This is dark and perverse.

I don't fight him, but I also don't kiss him back, which only seems to fuel his malice. He bites down on my bottom lip and groans in appreciation at my helpless whimper.

Before he even pulls his lips from mine, Tripp's rough hands shove me back, and I hit the ground back-first. The blunt force to my open wounds sends a violent wave of pain over my entire body, and all the air is sucked out of my lungs. My vision blurs, and I wonder if I'm going to pass out.

I hope that I do.

I don't get a chance to steady my breath because, in an instant, Tripp is hovering over my lifeless form, pulling at the waistband of my sweatpants.

I feel a part of me break as I realize what's about to happen.

My brain screams at me to fight, run, or beg, but I can't. My body has reached a point of excruciation that makes functioning impossible.

So, I lay there, watching in horror as my clothing is dragged slowly down my legs. He stops at my ankles, not bothering to fully remove the fabric.

Tripp pushes to his feet, and bile rises in my throat as his eyes hungrily appraise my body, bound, beaten, bloody, partially stripped, and tear-stained.

A chilling sneer spreads across his lips as he slowly reaches for the buckle of his belt.

I can't take it anymore.

Squeezing my eyes shut, I hear Tripp's faint chuckle accompanied by the clinking and slide of his belt.

Please, let this be over quickly.

The deafening sound of a gunshot rings in the air, and my eyes spring open just in time to see Tripp collapse.

CHAPTER TWENTY

Elise

Joshua stands in the doorway, gun still raised though his target is hissing on the ground. I try to make out his expression, but I can't tell what emotion is most prominent—infuriation, disbelief, disgust, or horror.

Ryder and two men I don't recognize follow behind, none of them concealing their shock.

I want so badly to feel relieved, but for all I know, Joshua has only come to take Tripp's place.

Lowering his weapon, Joshua barks, "Get him out of here."

The soldiers grab Tripp and drag his writhing body out of the room.

Joshua takes in the scene before him—blood covering the floor, loose chains from the ceiling binding my wrists, and the bloodied whip lying on the ground. His eyes continue, now scanning my appearance—tear-stained face, torn clothing, and exposed legs.

He holsters his gun and rushes to me, but I scramble back as best I can.

"No!" I scream, but the sound is strangled. "Stay away from me!"

Just as he did the night of my panic attack, he lifts his hands in surrender and stops his advance toward me. "Elise, it's okay. You're just in shock right now."

I heave a sob. "Don't come near me, you sick bastard."

He doesn't even seem to notice my insults. "You're injured. Let me help you."

"Help me? You're the one that did this to me! He was only acting on your orders!"

"I gave him no orders, Elise. I swear, I never would've allowed this to happen to you."

He takes another step toward me.

"No!" I shriek, hurting my own ears. "I hate you, Joshua! Just kill me already and get it over with! Haven't you tortured me enough?"

I don't have the mental or emotional capacity to care when pain settles over his weary face. He has no right to hurt—not after what he's put me through.

"Elise," he calls gently, crouching down until we're at eye level. "I promise I'm not going to hurt you."

I only shake my head.

He gives me a look that I'm sure I've never seen on him before: regret.

"I told you everything," I cry, voice breaking pathetically on the words.

"I know."

"Then why did you do this to me?" I want to wipe my face, but the chains are heavy, and I'm too weak to raise my arms.

He opens his mouth but quickly closes it again. "Please, let me take care of you. We can talk once you're cleaned up. I promise no one else will touch you."

I've heard that lie before.

"Stay away from me!"

"I can't leave you here. You need to let me unchain you."

I look around, desperate for another option.

"Ryder?"

Ryder snaps out of his shock and composes his expression as he takes measured steps across the room to my crumpled body.

"Only to unchain me," I tell him when he's only a few feet away. "Nothing else."

He nods, crouching before me and reaching for my binds. I try to raise my arms to help, but my back throbs, and I drop them with a whimper. Ryder moves his hands gently over my wrists, unlocking the chains he secured not long ago.

Once I'm released, Ryder steps back.

I rub my wrists, though their pain is nothing compared to the wounds covering my back. Placing my hands on the cool concrete, I push myself to a sitting position. At first, the air connecting with the blood is cooling, but after a few seconds, there's a burning that forces another round of tears to fill my eyes.

My cheeks heat with shame as I tug my ripped clothing back into place.

After a strained breath, I work to get my feet beneath me, but every part of my body screams in agony, and I can't stop my pitiful whimpers. As hard as I try, my body is too weak, and I stumble over my own feet.

Right before I hit the ground, Ryder rushes to my side and takes hold of me under each arm.

But in saving me from the fall, his fingers dig into the open gashes on my back.

"Ahh!" I shriek, now dangerously close to passing out.

I can't bring myself to open my eyes and see their expressions, but I'm gently lowered back onto the floor. To relieve the burn, I roll onto my side.

Joshua curses under his breath in a strained whisper.

They've both just seen the *real* damage.

So, it's worse than I thought.

"*Please*, let me help you," Joshua pleads with a new urgency.

Turning my face to the ground, I shake my head. "You're about thirty lashes too late."

It's Ryder's smooth voice that speaks to me now. "Will you let me help you stand?"

I want to say no. I want nothing to do with either of these men, but what other choice do I have? Joshua's right, I can't stay here.

A weak nod is my consent.

Careful of my injuries this time, he takes hold of my waist and hand before pulling me to a standing position. I sway as soon as I'm on my feet, and black spots crowd my vision, but Ryder keeps a firm hold on me.

"Assist her in any way she needs," Joshua tells Ryder, but his eyes never stray from me.

We begin walking, and as we pass Joshua, I feel his eyes staring into my massacred back.

"Elise," he calls, and though we stop, I don't turn to look at him.

"I am so sorry. I know you hate me, and that's okay, but you need to know that I didn't mean for this to happen."

Tears stream down my pitiless face. "I won't ever forgive you for this."

* * *

It takes Ryder and me quite some time to get back to my room, and I'm deliriously tired by the time we get there.

The first thing I notice is that the TV is gone. As I look more closely at the room, I find that, though it's clean, everything is off, almost as if someone has been looking through my stuff.

Only, it isn't *my* stuff. The only thing here that really belonged to me was that stupid note, and there's no way I'll ever get that back.

Ryder takes a chair from the table and motions to it. "Sit with your stomach facing the back of the chair."

I nod, limping over and sitting as he told me to. He takes his time analyzing my back before he walks to my bed and pulls the sheets off.

He holds them out to me. "I need to get a better look at your back, so I'm going to cut off your shirt—"

"No!" I can still feel the ghost of Tripp's hands roaming my body, ripping my shirt down to touch me.

"Use the sheet to cover your front. I swear I won't touch you without your permission, but there's a chance that you'll need stitches, so I need to get a better look."

A shudder rocks my body, and more tears threaten to burst, so I only nod shakily. There's a rustling behind me, and a feather-light touch lifts the blood-soaked fabric from where it clings to me. Ryder is careful to avoid touching my raw, sensitive skin as he removes the shirt completely.

He mutters a curse, and I grip the sheet tighter, wishing it could hide my shame, too.

"That bad?" My voice is little more than a croak.

"He really did a number on you. You don't need stitches, but I'll need to clean these. I'm going to get the first aid kit. I'll be right back." I nod and hear his footsteps retreat, the door shutting behind him.

Ryder returns only minutes later, and I expect him to get right to work, but he circles in front of me first, holding out a bottle of water and two pills. I don't hesitate or even ask what they are. I just take them and gulp down half the bottle of water in one swig.

"Is it okay if I touch your back now? Just to clean it up, I promise."

I take a deep breath and reluctantly nod.

"This might sting, but it's going to help," he tells me. Though I fear I can't handle any more pain, his honey-smooth voice is reassuring enough to soothe me.

"Okay," I say, bracing myself for the worst.

I'm not sure if it's the pain meds kicking in or if my body is just numbing to the sensation of pain altogether, but the disinfecting process isn't nearly as bad as I expected.

"Would you like me to run a bath before I bandage your back?"

I nod, desperate to scrub my body clean. I feel filthy, and it has nothing to do with the fact that I'm covered in blood and sweat.

"I'll get the water running," he offers and goes into the bathroom.

I stand and limp to the dresser, holding the sheet over my still-naked front while I pick out a large T-shirt and loose shorts.

Ryder steps out of the bathroom. "I'll be right here if you need anything."

I shut the bathroom door behind me, leaving it unlocked on the off-chance I need him. Several more tears are shed while removing my remaining clothes, but I eventually get it done.

I know I shouldn't, but I turn my back toward the mirror and peer over my shoulder to see the damage.

Even after being cleaned up, there's not a single patch of unharmed skin. My whole back is blood red, either from open wounds, actual blood, or intense agitation.

This is my body. Marred and scarred.

Even if I happen to walk away from here alive, I'll never be the same. How could I be? I hoped I'd survive with only emotional damage, but that's impossible now.

I'll always have these marks.

I don't know how long I stare at myself in the mirror, but by the time I'm done, the tub is more than halfway full of lukewarm water.

I don't climb all the way inside, though my aching shoulders beg me to. Instead, I sit on the edge of the tub and use a washcloth to clean myself.

I take my time scrubbing every inch of my body, needing to erase the feel of groping hands. It's only when my skin is bright red that I deem myself clean and drain the tub.

Despite the soft towel, drying myself is a long and painful experience, so I'm still mostly wet when I pull my clothes on. I forgo a bra, stepping into my underwear and shorts before holding the bloody towel to my chest.

Half an hour later, my back is clean and bandaged, covered by a large T-shirt that rarely brushes against the raw skin.

"Can I get you anything?"

I shake my head, ready to be alone.

He nods, and I expect him to leave, but he doesn't.

"What?" I snap.

He meets my tired eyes with perfect sincerity. "Mr. Moreno doesn't apologize. Ever. He also doesn't do movie nights or garden lunches. I know he's done a lot of bad things, but—"

"Ryder." My throat burns, but I force the words out anyway. "I didn't ask for your help because we're friends. I asked for you because you're the only one who hasn't beaten and assaulted me. Don't be mistaken—I haven't forgotten that you're the one who chained me up in the first place. Patching me up doesn't actually *fix* anything, so you can give it a rest. I know what kind of man Joshua is, and nothing you say will change that."

CHAPTER TWENTY-ONE

Joshua

Blood covers the floor. *Her* blood.

All because of me.

I hate you, Joshua! Just kill me already and get it over with! Haven't you tortured me enough?

I hate myself, too.

The anger that had me seeing red this morning has hardened into a sickening ball of grief.

I want to leave, tell Donovan to have one of the soldiers clean this mess, and pretend this day never happened, but I can't.

Tripp may have held the whip, but Elise's blood is on my hands.

Moments later, I have everything I need, and I stand before the red-smeared floor. My chest heaves with ragged breaths, and the metallic smell that has never bothered me before is suddenly unbearable, but I force myself to take it in.

I lower to my knees.

The towel is soaked after the first swipe across the floor, and my stomach turns. I can't remember the last time I threw up, but I want to right now.

Every wipe of the towel brings with it a memory that stabs brutally at my chest.

Her stunning smile when she opened the door for me on our date.

Her lousy poker face during our dinner negotiations.

Her soft lips against mine under the starlit garden.

Her small, perfect body cradled against mine just last night.

She has no clue that I laid awake for hours wondering how I could keep her.

Make her stay.

Make her mine.

I drop the drenched towel into the bucket beside me and stare at my bloodstained hands that scream the truth I don't want to face.

It can never happen now.

Any chance I had at redeeming myself in her eyes is gone. My anger and pride stole the only thing I've ever needed, and I have no one to blame but myself.

What I *do* have, however, is a deserving culprit to direct every ounce of this anger at.

Tripp isn't just going to die for this. He is going to suffer in the cruelest ways imaginable until the whole world knows what will happen if they try to touch what's mine.

But she isn't mine.

And she never will be.

I stare at the floor, now absent of all evidence of today's events. If only I could do the same to my mind.

To hers.

"Sir, the other capos are ready in the conference room." Donovan's voice breaks through my grief-induced haze, and I realize that I have no idea how long I've been kneeling here.

Not long enough.

I rise to my feet, the hundred-pound weight on my chest taking my breath away momentarily before I'm able to turn and face him.

Perfect composure is one of my strong suits, but if Donovan's expression is any indication, I've lost my touch.

With a tight nod, I grab the cleaning supplies.

"I'll have someone come to get those, Mr. Moreno."

"Tell the others I'm on my way." I pass him, working hard to get myself under control.

And failing.

When I get to my office and fall into my chair, I can barely think straight. The plans to leave are all worked out, and my capos are making the necessary preparations now, but I'm having difficulty focusing on anything outside of Elise.

I need to see her.

I stand, planning to do just that when a knock at the door stops me in my tracks.

I'm on my feet the second Ryder steps into the room.

"How is she?"

"Traumatized," he practically spits the words in my direction.

"I meant physically," I say through gritted teeth. "Is she okay?"

"Okay?" Ryder scoffs. "Of course, she's not okay! She was tortured, assaulted, and almost raped!"

It's the first time the words have been said out loud, and it feels like a punch to the gut.

"She was never supposed to get hurt."

"Well, she was. Bad. She'll have scars for the rest of her life because of this. Because of you," he grates.

"Watch it," I warn.

He ignores me.

"It's not just her back, either. She has bruises on her face from where he slapped her, and her throat is raw from how much she screamed for help, but no one heard her because *you* banned everyone from the entire floor."

My vision blurs with the force of my guilt as the images from today flood my brain. What's worse is the mere *thought* of what I would've seen had I been only seconds later.

Ryder takes my silence for defeat. "You messed up."

I snap to attention, stepping up to my right-hand man until we're chest to chest and narrowing my eyes to dangerous slits.

"You think I don't know that?" I shove him in the chest, taking another step forward. "I made a bad call, but you still work for me, and I will *not* tolerate your disrespect. Your only job right now is to protect Elise until she lets *me* protect her because I *will* fix this."

My chest rises and falls with the force of my words, and for the first time since this morning, the hollow ache dulls, giving way to a fierce determination because I absolutely believe my words.

I will fix this.

I'll earn Elise's trust, but I won't stop there.

I want all of her.

Mind, body, and soul.

Mine.

I will protect her, I will cherish her, and I will spend the rest of my life trying to make her happy.

Though Ryder's anger is palpable, when he meets my eyes, the message there is clear—pull yourself together because Elise deserves that much.

I give Ryder a nod, and he clears his throat. "Yes, sir, it won't happen again."

This new sense of purpose eats away at the darkness that's plagued me for hours. I feel like I can move again—like I can breathe again.

And the urge to see Elise is stronger than ever.

I barely reach the door before he's calling after me, "Don't do it."

But I don't even slow.

I expect Ryder to follow me, but he doesn't. He must know that it'd be a wasted effort because nothing can stop me right now.

Even so, I know he's right. I know that I shouldn't go see her. I should give her space to think and heal after what happened, but I can't.

My strides are purposeful, and I'm across the base in record time, grabbing a warm tray of food from Jay before I make my way to her room. I stop in my tracks when I reach her door.

She's just inside, safe and sound. That should be enough to sate me.

But it isn't.

Warmth spreads through my body as I open the door and take in the sight of her like I need to be near her to finally breathe.

She sits in the middle of the room, straddling a chair backward and facing the window. Her hair falls over her shoulders in thick waves, and she wears an oversized shirt that fully conceals the evidence of her attack.

Elise doesn't move as I set the food tray on the table, and if it weren't for her shaky breaths, I'd think she'd fallen asleep there.

"You should eat something."

Nothing.

"How are you feeling?"

Nothing.

I can't blame her for ignoring me, but it brings the weight of guilt back to my chest with the force of a hurricane. My hands twitch to touch her—to soothe her pain in any way I can—but that would only make things worse.

"You were never supposed to get hurt."

The silence is expected this time, but it doesn't sting any less.

After a long moment of Elise's sniffles filling the room, I come to terms with the fact that she's not ready to talk to or even see me yet.

Ryder was right. I shouldn't have come.

"We're leaving in a few hours," I say as I approach the door.

Her head whips around at that, and my pathetic heart flutters at the idea of her wanting to see me, but her expression deflates my hopes.

"What? Why?" she croaks, and I painfully remember Ryder saying that her throat was sore from screaming. I'd hoped he was exaggerating, but he clearly wasn't.

Even now, she's breathtakingly beautiful. Her eyes are bloodshot and glossed over, her face splotchy and wet with tears.

A fallen angel.

But that's not what tears my heart to shreds.

Elise's lip trembles at the sight of me. She ever so slightly cowers into the chair, and her eyes plead with me to leave her alone.

I get lost in those watery eyes and completely forget that she asked me a question. I'm about to answer when she visibly sobers as the realization hits her.

We can't stay here if her father has a plan to come for her.

It's cruel of me to force this on her, too, but I don't have a choice. I still have a job to do.

When she turns to face the window again, it's as though the slow motion simultaneously rips my heart out of my chest, falling into the hands of its true owner.

For a moment, I wonder which one of us is the real prisoner.

I grip the door handle to stop myself from going to her and groveling for forgiveness. Only twenty-four hours ago, I would've thought I was above groveling, but I'd beg on my knees for hours if I thought it would make an ounce of difference.

I just know it won't.

"Elise, I know you're not ready to talk, but when you are, I'd really like the chance to explain."

Nothing.

"I'll have Ryder come and pack your things," I say, leaving before I can drown in the silence.

CHAPTER TWENTY-TWO

Elise

A cool breeze flows up my loose shirt and soothes my still-stinging back.

Sitting on the edge of a bench, I take in the beautiful flowers and let the sweet aroma calm me. Even in the darkness, the arrangements are breathtaking, and I appreciate them even more now that I know I have to leave.

When I asked Ryder if I could visit the garden before we go, I hadn't expected him to say yes, let alone open my bedroom door and tell me to come back up whenever I was finished.

Ryder gave me a small smile when he noticed my apprehension. "My instructions were to assist you in any way you need. You need some time in the garden? Go ahead. I'll come check on you when I'm done packing up."

I left before he could change his mind, resisting the urge to thank him. Getting down the staircase by myself was difficult, but I much preferred it to asking for help.

Now, I sit perched on my favorite bench, reveling in the nature surrounding me. It's so much easier to breathe out here.

I hope my next prison will have a garden, too.

I have no idea where Joshua plans to drag me to next, but it doesn't really matter. We could be traveling an hour away or an ocean away, and I still wouldn't know the difference. It's been proven repeatedly that I am helpless, so it's silly to worry as though I can do anything to change it.

I can't.

My mind and body are exhausted, but the idea of sleep is far from comforting. As it is, lying down comfortably will be a challenge, but that's not what concerns me most. I know that as soon as I close my eyes, I'll be met with relentless nightmares. Between the feeling of Tripp's hands on my body and the whip on my back... I'm not sure if I'm ever going to sleep peacefully again.

I can't stop imagining what would've happened had Joshua not come in when he did. Tripp had me at his mercy, helpless to do anything but obey his cruel demands.

He wouldn't have stopped.

Desperate to distract my mind, I stare at the stars splayed across the sky and recall the last time I was here at night. Joshua had been so considerate during my panic attack, so vulnerable when confiding in me about his sister, and so tender when kissing me. The memories seem so far away, though the events occurred only a few nights ago.

The same question plays on a loop in my head: *how did everything go so wrong?*

The sound of approaching footsteps pulls me from my thoughts, but I know without looking that it's Ryder.

He sits on the far side of the bench, placing a tray between us. "I noticed you didn't eat, so I got you some warm food."

I survey the tray, and my mouth waters. I haven't eaten anything all day, and the chicken noodle soup looks incredible.

Joshua brought me food when he came to see me a few hours ago, but I couldn't bring myself to look at the peace offering, let alone accept it.

Lifting the tray onto my lap, I bring the spoon to my mouth and taste it. The small movements elicit pain, but I hide it as best I can.

I must not be doing very well because Ryder gestures to the pills beside the bowl.

"You're due for another dose," he tells me. "They'll help."

Instead of responding, I simply toss the pills into my mouth and chase them with water. I don't have the energy to argue with him.

"It's almost time to go. All your things have been packed."

Though I'm not in the mood for conversation, my curiosity gets the better of me. "Why are we leaving tonight? Why not in the morning?"

I'm surprised when he answers me without hesitation. "We don't know what your dad has planned, so we want to be gone before he can make a move to get you."

There's not much I can say to that, so I stay silent.

"Traveling is going to be very uncomfortable with your injuries. You'll be able to lay on your stomach in the backseat, but it'll still be painful. If you want, I can give you something that will make you sleep for the ride." I can hear the reluctance in his voice.

He knows I won't like that option, and he's not wrong, but it doesn't really matter.

Either way, they're taking me away tonight, so why not let them knock me out? The alternative is enduring a who-knows-how-long car ride where every bump and turn intensifies my pain. Besides, maybe this way, I can get some dreamless sleep.

"I know you probably don't—"

"Give me the drugs."

Ryder studies my blank expression. "Are you sure?"

I nod and focus on eating.

The silence that settles between us is a comfortable one that reminds me of our lunches in the break room.

"Why did you have Jay bandage my finger when I cut it in the kitchen?" I angle my chin to my shoulder, looking over my back as much as possible. "Obviously, you're more than capable of administering first aid."

After several moments, I assume he won't answer me, but he nods to himself and meets my gaze.

"Mr. Moreno ordered that no one talk to you while you work. When you cut your finger, I used it as a loophole to introduce you to Jay."

"But why?"

Ryder shrugs. "Jay's a good man. I figure you haven't seen enough good lately."

He says the words like they're no big deal, but they knock the air from my lungs. Is it possible that I've misjudged Ryder?

I feel a sense of remorse when I think about how I spoke to him back in my room. He's not innocent in all of this, but it's not his fault either.

"I was harsh earlier, and I shouldn't have been. I know you're only trying to help." I say, careful not to apologize.

He frowns down at me. "Do you feel guilty?"

I avoid his gaze.

Ryder shakes his head. "You have every right to be pissed at me and everyone here. Don't feel guilty for your self-preservation."

Shouldn't he be encouraging me to comply and submit? Why would he give affirmation to my anger?

A yawn escapes me, and I decide that I'm too tired to figure it out. Seeing my exhaustion, Ryder holds out his arm for support, and I wordlessly accept it. Though I loathe needing help, I'm too weak to go far alone.

At first, I think we're returning to my room, but Ryder guides me down unfamiliar hallways.

My back is throbbing, and I'm ready to rest when we arrive at a thick metal door. Ryder opens it, and we enter the spacious garage. The concrete room holds several cars in various shapes and sizes, but my attention is drawn to four black SUVs that are being packed up by soldiers that I only vaguely recognize, though none of them acknowledge us.

We approach one of the vehicles, and Ryder opens the door to reveal that the back seat is covered in pillows and blankets.

Ryder opens his mouth to speak when the door we just walked through opens again. Joshua stands in the doorway holding a bottle of water.

His eyes find me and widen hopefully as if something has happened in the past few hours that erased the torture I endured because of him. What's worse is that he looks so tragically handsome that my heart's ache is briefly worse than my back, and I despise him and myself for the feeling.

"Elise," he says, coming closer.

I step behind Ryder, using him to shield me from the man I so desperately don't want to see.

"Ryder," I whisper, panic rising in my chest. "Please, I don't want to talk to him."

Though my words are quiet, they stop Joshua in his tracks.

My eyes are cast down, and Ryder leaves me, walking to Joshua. They speak too quietly for me to hear, and when they're finished, Joshua sighs.

I hear the phrase, "take care of her," before Ryder turns back to me. I lift my eyes but drop them again when I see Joshua's apologetic face.

I can't deal with his remorse.

He *should* feel bad.

His steps retreat, and Ryder returns to my side, holding two small pills and the bottle of water that Joshua must have given him.

"Here, take these."

I accept them. "How long will I be out?"

"It should last the six-hour drive."

"I don't want him near me," I tell Ryder with pleading eyes.

"He won't be," he assures me. "I'll be driving you myself."

I lower my eyes to my hands, which shake despite the fact that I'm willing them to stay still.

"Hey,"—Ryder lowers himself to find my eyes—"I promise nothing will happen to you. I won't let him come near you for as long as you need, okay?" His eyes are earnest, and I believe him.

"Why are you protecting me? He's your boss. Shouldn't you let him do whatever he wants?" I know that Joshua gave him orders to assist me in any way I need, but something about how he cares for me seems personal.

"You were right, saying we aren't friends, but I like to think we were starting to be. I'm sorry you got hurt."

For a moment, I'm stunned into silence. I never would have expected this man to offer me his apology and friendship. Yet, here he is, gaze filled with nothing less than perfect sincerity.

"Thank you," I mumble, unsure how else to respond.

I take a deep breath before popping the pills into my mouth.

Ryder helps me into the car, and I lie down on my stomach, turning my neck toward the windshield and curling my legs uncomfortably. Ryder barks orders at the men before he climbs into the front seat and starts the engine.

The car pulls away, and my eyelids grow heavy.

"Ryder?" I mutter before the darkness can pull me under.

"Yes?"

My words are slurred with exhaustion. "Where are we going?"

He hesitates before answering, "Mr. Moreno's private residence."

The lull of sleep is strong, but a new wave of panic hits me. "What?"

I can't see Ryder's face from here, but I imagine he's regretting telling me that when he hears the nerves shake my voice in that one simple word.

"I was serious, Elise. I won't let him near you until you're ready. I know you don't have a reason to, but I'm asking you to trust me." His ever-calming voice has my heart slowing to a normal rate.

Again, it's not like I have a choice.

So, I let the darkness take over.

* * *

I'm back in the basement.

Not only can I see every detail in vivid clarity—the cracks in the concrete floor, the row of light bulbs all lit aside from the fourth one to the left, and the hook-like knife that's so close to the edge of the table of tortures that I wait for it to slide off and clatter to the floor—but I smell, taste, and *feel* the room too.

The stomach-turning scent of blood mixes with the sweat pouring down my face as a result of the sheer will it takes to keep pulling air into my lungs.

The taste of bile as it creeps up my dry throat after I'm no longer able to scream.

The heaviness that comes from both fear and the realization that I am completely and utterly alone weighs down on me.

I can see myself in an out-of-body experience. My hands are chained above me, my clothes torn and disheveled, my head lowered in defeat.

I want to run toward the girl, unchain her bruised wrists, cover her beaten body, and wipe her never-ending tears, but I can't.

My feet are frozen to the ground, and there's nothing I can do as the door bursts open and Tripp storms toward the chained version of myself.

He takes the whip, savagely swinging it down on my back, and though I'm watching it happen several feet away, I can feel the agonizing burn of every lash.

I watch in silent horror as my body is dropped to the floor and my clothes are pulled aside.

My eyes flit between the door and Tripp, waiting for Joshua to burst in and save me from the torture like he did before.

Where is he?

It takes every fiber of my being to call out for Joshua, but even as I do, the sound is muffled and murky, like I'm trapped underwater.

Tripp, who had ignored me in favor of my chained body until now, turns at the sound of my weak call.

Only, it isn't Tripp at all.

Joshua's dark, wrathful gaze pierces me—harsher than the whip ever could.

He says nothing, but the message might as well blare like an alarm for the entire base to hear.

No one is coming to save you.

Joshua takes a step toward me, and I try desperately to force myself to run, hide, do anything at all, but I can't.

With each step, he calls my name, and I shake my head fervently, pleading with my eyes for him to stay back.

When he's only a few feet away, I can't stop him from reaching for me.

"Elise!" I startle awake to Ryder's firm but gentle hand on my shoulder.

I force myself to take a deep breath as I assess my surroundings. I'm still lying in the car, sunlight streaming through the windows that were pitch black when we began the drive.

I meet Ryder's worried gaze at the same moment I realize the car has stopped moving.

"We're here."

CHAPTER TWENTY-THREE

Elise

A soft knock on the door wakes me up.

My neck is killing me from sleeping on my stomach, and I rub it as I sit up, calling for the only person who comes here to enter.

Ryder opens the door, carrying a tray of breakfast food. He studies me warily, waiting to see my reaction, and I guess this means he's talked to Joshua.

I openly glare at him.

He sighs, setting the tray down on the table. "I'm sorry about last night. I thought your back would be able to handle getting up the stairs. I didn't mean for that to happen."

It's been three days since we arrived at Joshua's house.

The two-story log cabin could be mistaken for ordinary on the outside, but the interior is anything but. The dark knotty pine walls that cover every inch of the house are complemented by the river rock-lined fireplaces, deep green curtains, and brown leather furniture. Every room screams luxury in the most subtle way, like how the worn-looking stone tiles of each bathroom floor are heated, or how even the smallest throw pillows are still softer than anything I've ever owned.

I couldn't help but notice how the kitchen is in pristine condition, with countless appliances just begging for my attention. There's even a back porch with lounge chairs, couches, and a grill that I just had to admire.

My room here is twice the size of the one I had at the base. Floor-to-ceiling windows dominate the far wall, and I spend most of my time staring absently at the trees that span over the miles and miles of mountains. Each night, I watch the sunset from my bed, and the sight is breathtaking.

I have a glass table surrounded by four plush chairs and a fireplace that I haven't bothered to use. Even my art supplies are neatly organized, albeit untouched, in one of the corners.

These days, I live in self-imposed isolation, only broken by Ryder to bring me food and pills.

Since my tour when we first arrived, he reminds me at least five times a day that I'm free to go wherever I'd like in the house. Once, he even threatened me with starvation if I didn't join him downstairs for dinner, but he gave up when he realized I'd face that consequence before risking an encounter with Joshua.

So far, I've been successful in my efforts to avoid him, but my luck ran out last night.

I suppose it's my fault since I practically forced Ryder to take the evening to spend time with his daughter, who lives two hours away.

Yes, his daughter.

When he first told me about her, I'd been stunned into silence. It's not like Ryder is too *young* to have a child, but the idea of the Moreno family underboss fathering a smiley three-year-old girl named Lyla had caught me off guard.

It made me realize that his fierce determination to protect me must come from his hope that someone would do the same for his daughter. He hasn't said it outright, but in the few days we've spent together, I've gotten the sense that he never liked the idea of using me to blackmail my father to begin with.

He'd been reluctant to leave me yesterday, but I assured him I'd be okay for one night.

I was wrong.

Tuesday, May 26: one night earlier

"Okay," Ryder starts, gripping the overnight bag slung over his shoulder. "I'm going, but we're short on soldiers right now, so you'll need to go downstairs to get your own dinner."

I guess I'm skipping dinner tonight.

Ryder tracks my thoughts. "If Moreno hears you haven't eaten, he'll likely bring you food himself."

So much for that plan.

"I'll let him know you're going down around six and to stay out of the kitchen during that time. Unless you've changed your mind about me leaving?"

"No, of course not." I shake my head adamantly. Obviously, I'd rather have Ryder stay with me, but I hate knowing he misses his daughter and isn't spending time with her because of me.

He arches an eyebrow, unconvinced.

"I mean it," I tell him. "I'll get dinner at six."

Ryder finally leaves, but only after I assure him at least three more times that I'll be fine, and I even start to believe it myself.

I pull out a book that I don't have any particular interest in, but it beats another evening of staring aimlessly out the window.

My eyes drift to the clock, and my stomach drops when I see that it's almost seven.

Damn it.

It's a miracle that Joshua hasn't come here already, and since I don't want to give him a reason to, I throw down the book and climb out of bed.

I open the door, peering out to ensure that no one is there before I slip into the hall. I'm still walking with a limp, which makes it difficult to go unheard, but I try my best not to draw attention to myself.

Descending the stairs is just as uncomfortable as I thought it would be, but I manage to do it by myself. I hear rustling in the kitchen when I set foot on the main floor, but I can't see who it is from here.

During my tour with Ryder, he told me that several soldiers are staying here with us and even all of the capos from Moreno's main base, which is practically unheard of. When I asked Ryder why, he told me Joshua required his most trusted men to come with us, but I felt no comfort at that.

Only a few days ago, Tripp would've qualified.

According to Ryder, the only people staying in this house are the two of us and Joshua. The others stay in a guest house elsewhere on the property.

I'm about to turn around and go upstairs when the scent of food reaches me, and my stomach growls. It's not surprising since I've barely eaten all day, but it means there's no avoiding this interaction.

I breathe a sigh of relief when the only person in the kitchen is Jay.

I'd been surprisingly glad when Ryder told me Jay came with us to handle all the cooking while we're here. Jay is a familiar face that doesn't spark my anxiety—and these days, that's a win.

The burly man turns when I enter the room, and his face softens.

"Good evening, Miss Consoli. How are you?"

I'm exhausted, hurting, and hungry, so I bypass that question.

"Please, call me Elise."

He's made grilled chicken, baked potatoes, corn on the cob, and fresh rolls. My mouth waters at the sight, and I greedily breathe in the aroma.

"Can I make you a plate?"

I want to decline and do it myself, but it'll require a lot of arm and shoulder movements that will hurt my back, so I reluctantly nod.

He hands me a full plate, gesturing to a selection of wines on the counter. "Would you like a drink?"

"Uh, yeah, that would be nice." He turns and grabs a bottle, pouring a generous amount into a glass.

He holds out the glass, and I'm about to take it when a familiar, husky voice stops me.

"I don't think that's a good idea."

So much for avoiding him.

I would've been better off staying in my room. At least then, I could've told him to leave the food in the hall and avoided seeing him.

Placing my food on the counter, I turn to face him.

Joshua stands in the doorway, holding an empty plate he must be returning. He looks as handsome as ever, wearing casual sweats and a gray tee, similar to how he dressed for our movie night.

My heart squeezes painfully at the memory.

I instinctively step back when I see him, and I note a hint of anger in his eyes that doubles the speed of my heart. Only, he's not really looking at *me* but at my shirt.

No, it's *Ryder's* shirt.

Ryder gave me a few of his button-ups since pulling a shirt over my head isn't something I can do alone. They're way too big on me, falling well below my shorts, but the fabric is soft against my still-sensitive skin.

"Why can't I have wine?"

His gaze softens once fixated on my face. So, it *is* the shirt that bothers him.

"I'm not sure they'll mix well with the pain medication you're taking," he explains.

It's a fair enough point, so I'm not mad at the restriction, but I'm still anxious to get away from him.

I nod, slowly taking my food and looking to the floor as I pass him.

I half-expect him to stop me, but he steps aside to let me pass.

My relief lasts for all of two seconds as I stand at the base of the stairway and face my next obstacle. Getting down was hard enough, but going up with a full plate of food? I'm not sure how I'm going to do this.

Before I can find a solution, I feel his dominating presence behind me.

"I can help."

I grit my teeth. "No."

But I'm not sure how I plan to do this. Knowing that I look foolish, I bite my lip and think through every possibility, but nothing comes to mind.

"Elise, let me help."

"Don't come near me."

"Okay." I hear him step back. "How about I carry your food to the room?"

I consider my options, but there aren't many.

"Fine." I hold out the plate, refusing to meet his gaze.

He takes it from me and ascends the staircase. I don't want to be any closer to him than I have to be, so I wait here until he gets back. Moments later, I hear the padding of footsteps as he comes down.

He passes me, walking in the direction of his office but stopping in the archway. "I left two more pills up there for you to take in three hours. If you need me, I'll be in my office or my room."

"I won't need you."

He sighs. "Goodnight, Elise."

Present day

Ryder's worried gaze brings me back to our conversation, and I throw off my covers, stretching my neck as I do.

"Don't worry about it," I mutter because I'd rather just pretend it never happened.

I sit at the table and pick at the food he's brought me. "How was seeing your daughter?"

A rare smile touches his lips. "It was perfect."

"Maybe you'll join me for breakfast and tell me about it?"

"Unfortunately, I'm needed by Mr. Moreno for a few things today. Maybe tomorrow?"

"Tomorrow," I agree. "Can I ask you a question?"

He crosses his arms and nods.

"What happens now? With my dad, I mean." The question has plagued me for days, but I haven't had the courage to ask it until now. "Does he know I'm not at the base anymore?"

The question doesn't seem to come as a surprise to Ryder, and I wonder if he's been expecting this. "Mr. Moreno will be speaking with him soon about how things will proceed from here."

I nod, knowing he won't tell me anything more and realizing that I probably don't *want* to know more.

I finish my food and shower quickly, holding a towel over my chest as I do daily for Ryder to check my back.

"These are healing really well," he tells me as he finishes attaching the last bandage. "You might be able to sleep on your back by tomorrow."

"Hopefully," I sigh. "My neck is killing me from how I've been sleeping."

"Oh, and I almost forgot," he says, pointing to a bag that I hadn't noticed he brought in until now. "I bought some button-ups for you while I was out. Now you won't have to use mine."

My lip twitches at the gesture. "Thank you, Ryder. I really appreciate it."

The memory of Joshua's reaction to me wearing Ryder's shirt flashes through my mind. I don't even want to think about what that meant.

It's nearing two o'clock, and Ryder still hasn't come for his afternoon visit. I'd think it was another scheme to lure me out of my room, but after last night, he wouldn't pull something like that. If he isn't here, he must be doing something important.

My throat is parched, and my back is hurting since I'm due for more medicine. I loathe the idea of going to find him, but if I wait any longer, my pain will get out of hand.

I slip out of my room, and when I knock on Ryder's door, there's no answer.

Taking a deep breath, I decide it's worth the risk to go downstairs.

The kitchen is empty, and I head straight for the cabinet, quietly getting a glass and filling it with water from the filter.

My back throbs, and as much as I hate the idea of going to ask for pills, I hate being in pain even more. If Ryder isn't in his room, he must be in the office with Joshua. My only solace comes from the fact that I know he'll shield me if Joshua tries to pull something.

Before I can chicken out, I walk in the direction of the office.

During my house tour, Ryder pointed out Joshua's office and bedroom. I vowed to stay away from those rooms even after realizing that they're likely the only places in the house with any communication mediums.

I haven't given much thought to the idea of escaping since the attack. Maybe it's because I'm in no shape to run away or because, in addition to my sense of security, Tripp stole any hope I had left.

As I near the large doors, I can hear Joshua and Ryder's voices on the other side, and they suddenly go quiet. My heart drops, and I think they must sense me somehow, but then I hear the ringing of a phone behind the door.

I turn to leave, assuming this is a bad time to get their attention, but once the man answers the phone, I freeze.

"Go to hell, Moreno." His voice is gruff, as though he hasn't slept in days.

"It's nice to talk to you too, Mr. Consoli."

My heart leaps back up, lodging in my throat. I shouldn't listen to this, but how can I leave now? I need to know what's going on.

"Did you really think I wouldn't learn about your jailbreak plan?" Joshua asks when my father is silent. "I assume you're ready to talk business now?"

"No." My father's voice is deadly low. "We won't be making any deals."

Wait a minute, shouldn't he be negotiating?

Apparently, I'm not the only one confused because Joshua demands, "What the hell does that mean? Do I need to remind you what's at stake?"

Panic grips me by the throat, and my vision blurs around the edges. I have to hold onto the wall to stop myself from falling over.

Joshua wouldn't hurt me again, would he?

Of course he would.

"You don't need to remind me. However, I won't entertain your negotiations any longer. I am not a man who can be manipulated or swayed."

I don't understand what he means, but Joshua seems to.

"You only played along because you had a plan to break her out," Joshua states, voice tight with grim realization.

"As I said, I won't be manipulated. If others heard that I could be influenced by my daughter, she'd never be safe again, and my enemies would destroy me. I can't have that weakness."

"You do realize what I'm going to do to her, don't you?" Joshua practically growls.

"I do. Don't think you've gotten away with this, Moreno. I won't forget what you've done, and I swear I'll get you back for it."

The meaning of his words clicks, knocking the breath out of me like a punch to the gut.

My father just told Joshua to kill me.

CHAPTER TWENTY-FOUR

Joshua

"I won't forget what you've done, and I swear I'll get you back for it."

The line goes dead.

Ryder and I stand in stunned silence, both of us trying to process what the hell just happened.

Gabriel Consoli just told me to kill his only daughter.

My anger rises like billowing black smoke, filling my lungs and savagely choking me.

I squeeze the phone until it snaps in my fist, then throw it against the wall, leaving a hole in its place.

"Do you think it's a scheme?"

I shake my head and take a deep breath, but it does nothing to calm me. "I think Consoli cares more about his power than his daughter."

"What does this mean for us?"

"You think I have a damn clue what this means for us?" I snap.

Ryder is unfazed. "You never told her, did you?"

I know without any more context what he's referring to—my decision to give her back to her father for the territories after all and pull Mason from the field to work here.

"No, I didn't. But I can't tell her now. I need to figure out what my plan is."

"What options do we even have?"

I let out a sharp breath and pinch the bridge of my nose. "I don't know, which is why she can't know anything yet. It'll only make things worse."

"I agree that you can't tell her before you have a plan, but the longer you wait, the worse it'll be for her."

"I need to talk to her."

"No."

My teeth grind painfully. "Excuse me?"

He meets my glare head-on. "I told her I'd keep you away for as long as she needs. She isn't ready to see you. Besides, what could you possibly have to tell her?"

"You told her we'd be reaching out to her father, right?"

Ryder nods.

"Then I'm going to buy us some time and tell her the terms are being renegotiated."

"If that's all you have to say, then I'd be happy to deliver the message."

My fists curl into tight balls, just begging to connect with Ryder's jaw.

Though I spend most of my time with Ryder, we never talk about Elise aside from his assurances that she's okay. I've dutifully stayed away, giving her space no matter how much I hate it.

But that self-control was just stolen by her father.

"I'm going to see her."

"No, you're not."

I take two steps toward him. "I'd advise you to refrain from telling me no. I'm not asking permission. I'm *telling* you what I'm going to do."

After a long, deep breath, I know Ryder won't fight me on this.

"Fine, but I'll be upstairs, too. If she calls for me, I'm coming in."

I head for the door without another word. The idea of talking to Elise makes my heart race, but I suppress the excitement. I can't let myself expect anything more than her hatred.

When I reach her door, I bring my ear to the wood, but there's no sound on the other side. I knock lightly and listen for movement.

"Elise, it's me. We need to talk."

I don't expect a response, so I'm unsurprised when she doesn't give me one. My hand lifts to knock again, but I freeze when the handle twists from the other side.

I suck in a sharp breath when the door swings open, and I'm staring into the wide, brown eyes that I've missed so much.

She looks beautiful.

The bruise that covered her cheeks only days ago has disappeared, restored to its natural, flawless beauty. The waves of her messy blonde hair spill over her squared shoulders, resting on the new button-up that I forced Ryder to buy for her.

I nearly lost it when I saw her wearing his shirt last night. If Elise is going to wear a man's clothes, they're going to be mine. I hadn't noticed I'd been glaring at the piece of clothing until she cowered away from me.

She doesn't cower now.

In fact, she doesn't show any emotion whatsoever.

"Just do it. Get it over with."

"Do what?" I ask, taking in the dark circles under her eyes and wondering how she's been sleeping these last few days.

"Just kill me," she whispers.

The same broken sob that haunts my sleep resonates in my head.

I hate you, Joshua! Just kill me already and get it over with! Haven't you tortured me enough?

I'd hoped space would help assuage her anger and misery, but I can see now that it wasn't enough.

"Why would I do that?"

I expect her to snap at me with some smart comment or slam the door in my face.

I do not expect her to breathe out a laugh.

Turning away from me, Elise takes measured steps until she's overlooking the stretch of trees surrounding the house.

"My own father told you to," she mutters. "I'm nothing more than a *weakness* to him."

My blood runs cold with the realization.

"You heard the phone call."

"Just do it. I'm tired of fighting."

I close the door behind me and slowly step until I'm only a few feet away from her. It shouldn't please me so much that her entire body doesn't tense at my presence like it has since the attack.

I didn't come here prepared to have this conversation, but I also hadn't expected her to hear the phone call, so my original plan is out the window. I sort through my options, but there's really only one way to handle this situation.

The truth.

"I'm not going to kill you."

Her head snaps in my direction. "You're letting me go?"

The hope in her tone is unmistakable, and I loathe that I'm about to hurt her once again by squashing it.

"Not exactly."

"What does that mean?"

When I don't answer, she comes to her own conclusions.

Hope turns to confusion, which turns to horror.

Elise takes small steps back, frantically shaking her head. "You can't just keep me here."

"Calm down, Elise. I—" I take a deep breath to calm myself. Getting frustrated isn't going to help anything. "I can't let you go home, but I'm not going to kill you, either."

The words do nothing to reassure her, and I watch helplessly as her chest rises and falls with panicked breaths.

My efforts to comfort her are only making things worse, so I try another strategy. I lower my chin and fix her with a stern look. "Calm. Down."

That was the wrong thing to say.

Elise points to the door. "Get. Out."

"I'm not going anywhere. I—"

"Ryder!"

Damn it all.

"You do realize he works for *me*, right?" I remind her.

My oldest friend bursts into the room, and my hand briefly twitches for my gun when he steps protectively in front of Elise, blocking her from my view.

"Get out, Ryder."

"Mr. Moreno, I don't think this is the way to fix things—"

"You're right," I snap. "This isn't the way. The *'way'* is to sit and have a civilized conversation, but someone"—my icy eyes find hers— "won't calm down, so here we are. It's been days, Elise. I deserve the chance to talk to you."

My words seem to snap Elise out of her panic, and she steps out from behind Ryder.

"You *deserve* the chance to talk to me?" She laughs, but the sound is chilling.

Her hands go to the buttons of her shirt, and she begins undoing them.

Turning her back toward us, Elise lowers the fabric of her shirt, uncovering the extent of the damage done to her once unblemished skin.

Thick bandages cover almost every inch of her back. Bright red peeks out from beneath some of the gauze and the skin is scabbed over as it heals in jagged lines.

Elise's hoarse voice cuts through my thoughts. "Don't you dare, for a single second, think that I owe you *anything*. You have taken everything from me: my freedom, my family, my dignity."

She pulls the shirt back up and buttons it as she adds, "You're not my savior just because you've decided not to kill me. In fact, keeping me alive is so much worse. Death is better than any life you could offer me."

The words hang heavy around us.

I'm here.

I'm here and fighting for her, which is more than her father can say, yet she despises me. Even when everyone else has turned their back on her, she refuses to accept that I may actually be able to care for her.

"You'd rather just die, then?"

The answering silence drives me over the edge.

In one quick motion, my gun is secured in my hand and pointed directly at Elise's head.

"Woah!" Elise and I mutually ignore Ryder's exclamation, our eyes never leaving one another's.

She lifts a hand to halt Ryder's advance to protect her with his weapon. He freezes in his place, but his hand hovers over his gun, ready to spring at any moment.

As if he'd ever shoot me.

However, I hardly notice Ryder's movement when Elise's stoic expression registers. She doesn't so much as flinch or cringe away from the weapon in her face.

My eyes bore into hers, and a ball of dread settles in the pit of my stomach when I process the emotion there.

Peace.

With a long stride, Elise presses her forehead to the barrel of my gun. A deep breath relaxes her shoulders, and her eyes shut as she waits for me to pull the trigger that will end her life.

Elise genuinely believes that dying now is better than staying with me.

My dread is now all-consuming nausea, and I can't stand it.

I take her wrist and place the weapon in her hand.

Wide, enchanting eyes look up at mine, full of questions that I answer before she gets the chance to ask.

"I'm not going to hurt you," I mutter, furious at myself for needing to assure her of this *again*. "If it makes you feel better, you can hold the gun the whole time, but we *are* going to talk. Deal?"

There's only a moment of deliberation before she strengthens her hold on the gun and points it at my chest.

"What makes you think I won't kill you right now and get away?"

The thought of Elise killing anyone is laughable, but I humor her.

"I have a hunch."

"Care to share?" Her eyes flit from me to the gun, and the corner of her lip twitches.

She flips the safety off in one fluid motion and cocks the gun in another.

Well, damn it.

"I think you want answers more than you want me dead."

"I think you underestimate me."

"I think you're right," I admit with a small smile. "Now, Ryder is going to leave, and we're going to talk. You can keep the gun, but I'm not waiting any longer."

Her jaw ticks, but she must realize I'm not letting this go because she lets out a huff. "Ryder stays within calling distance."

I don't want Ryder anywhere near Elise right now, but this isn't the time to get possessive.

"Fine."

Ryder turns concerned eyes to Elise, and I fight to repress my jealousy when she gives him a nod and a small smile. "I'll be okay."

Ryder's cutting eyes pierce me as he moves to the door, and I return the glare tenfold, both of us sending the same message.

Back the hell off.

The door shuts behind him, and it's just Elise and me. This moment that I've waited days for and it's finally come at the price of a gun to my heart.

Though I can hardly complain because I'd take the damn bullet if it meant she'd forgive me for everything that's happened.

Elise does not share my eagerness to talk. The softness she directed at Ryder only seconds ago has vanished, replaced with a frostiness that drops the temperature in the room by a few degrees.

I'd almost believe she's angrier than scared if it weren't for the tell-tale wobble of her chin.

"You don't need to be afraid, Elise. I'm not going to hurt you." I emphasize my point by lifting my hands in a low surrender.

She doesn't acknowledge my assurance. "Why aren't you going to kill me? That was your plan all along."

"Killing you *was* my plan after you found out about Mason, but I changed my mind."

"Why?"

"Your panic attack in the garden," I tell her. "After what happened that night, I knew I couldn't kill you. I decided to return you to your dad and have Mason join my men at the base."

Her weary eyes grow distant. "But now my father doesn't want me."

My teeth grind in an attempt to hold back the anger boiling beneath the surface.

I don't speak until I'm sure I can keep my tone perfectly level. "I have to admit, I didn't see that one coming. Without getting the territories from your dad, I can't give you back and pull Mason from the field. It'll make me look weak, and Mason is the only advantage I have now."

The words are insensitive, but she deserves to hear the truth.

"What did you mean when you said that you knew you couldn't kill me? You've killed people before. How am I any different?"

I was expecting this question, but hell, if I know how to answer it.

"When we—that night at your apartment, I—damn it," I mutter, pinching the bridge of my nose. "I'm not good at this."

It's a few moments before I square my shoulders and lock my gaze with hers.

"I was supposed to drug you during dinner that night at your apartment, but I didn't. I told myself that I wanted to keep the conversation going to get as much information from you as I could, but that's a lie. I wanted you even then."

Nothing in her expression changes to tell me how she's taking this, but I'm in too deep to stop now.

"You said that kiss in the garden didn't change anything for you, but it changed *everything* for me. It made me realize that the territories weren't all I wanted anymore."

"What exactly is your plan?" she asks. "To keep me here like some trophy? That's not a life, Joshua."

"All I know is that I can't let you go, and I don't want to," I tell her because it's true. "Give me a chance, and we can figure this out."

"There is no *we*. I barely even know you."

"We can change that." I take a deep breath, wishing we could skip this next part and knowing we can't. "But there are other things we should talk about first."

Elise's eyes sober, but she doesn't object.

Her arms, extended to hold the gun in place, begin to tremble. The weight of the weapon is too much for her injured back.

I gesture to the table by the window. "Let's sit."

"I'd rather stand."

"I know your back is killing you right now. Let's sit, and you can prop the gun on the table."

I don't wait for her to agree. I move toward the table and take a seat, allowing myself to willingly turn my back on a gun pointed at me for the first time in my life. Luckily, I'm fairly certain she won't pull the trigger, no matter how much she claims to hate me.

She remains standing a few seconds longer before footsteps approach behind me. I pretend not to see her wince as she takes hold of the chair across from mine and flips it around. She straddles it, resting the gun against the table but never allowing it to veer from my direction.

"I assume you have questions for me."

She drops her gaze and tightens her grip on the gun. I don't react aside from watching her trigger finger like a hawk, but it's perfectly still.

"How did you find the note?"

I think back to that morning, and it's hard to believe it was only a few short days ago. "After you went to shower, I laid back down and heard it crinkle in the pillowcase."

She takes in the answer with a furrowed brow. "Why did you demote Tripp? Was it just because of what he said about me?"

In addition to sending her to the basement unprotected, this is another prime example of how I've let her down. Had I handled things differently with Tripp, she never would've been hurt.

"I didn't demote Tripp, not technically anyway."

I recall the conversation with him in my office after Elise told me what he said. I hadn't planned on taking action beyond a warning, but his eyes turned dead and emotionless—just as they do when he leads torturous interrogations—and the decision was made for me. When I called him out on his reaction, he had no problem sharing his opinions on the situation with Elise. He thought her privileges made me look weak, and she needed to be put in her place. All he accomplished was convincing me he needed to be sent far away from her.

"I transferred him to another base until the deal with your father went through. He didn't take it well, but I made it clear it was a temporary arrangement."

She nods absently, absorbing the information. I wait for her next question, which finally comes in a hesitant whisper.

"You said you knew I told you everything, so why did you have Ryder take me?"

The heavy guilt weighs on my chest.

"I needed you out of your room while I had it searched for anything else."

"The garden would've sufficed."

"But that wasn't the whole reason," I admit. "I was angry with you... well, with myself, but also with you. I let my guard down when I'm with you and because of that, the note slipped through the cracks. Seeing it made me realize just how distracted I'd become. I needed to make you respect me again."

"Respect you or fear you?"

I don't answer, and she scoffs.

"What would you have had me do? Give you the note as soon as I found it? Would it really have changed anything?"

I imagine coming into her room to take her to the garden that day, and instead of looking anxious to get outside, she looks anxious to tell me something. When I ask what's wrong she doesn't say anything, only hands over a small piece of paper. My eyes flit over the note, and a burning anger flares in my chest. Questions run through my head: Where did this come from? Who gave it to her? When did she get it? But none of them is the question that fuels my fury.

Why would she give this to me? She should hide it or destroy it. It has to be a trick.

And just like that, she's proven her point.

There's nothing she could've done with the note that would've changed the outcome.

She shakes her head with a sigh. "I told you from the beginning that I wasn't going to roll over and die."

"And I warned you what would happen if you tried anything," I counter.

"I *didn't* try anything! And even if I had, your threat was that you'd lock me away, not chain me up in the basement and send Tripp in to—"

"I never sent Tripp!"

"He *told* me you did."

"Elise, listen to me," I plead. "Tripp lied to you. He should've left the base two days before the attack. After I sent you to the basement, I reached out to Tripp for an update, and when there was radio silence, I got suspicious. By the time I realized he never left, I knew something was wrong, and I went to check on you." I drop my eyes from hers as I flashback to the exact moment I walked into the basement. "But I was too late."

A small droplet splashes against the wood under her eyes.

"You have to believe that I would *never* let anyone hurt you," I say.

"You hurt me in the basement yourself the first day I got there."

"That was different."

"Different? Different how? Because it was at your hand and not Tripp's? Or maybe it's different because you didn't rip my clothes off of me."

Her words turn the dagger in my chest.

"That's not what I meant."

"Enlighten me."

I open my mouth to defend myself but close it again.

What's there to defend? She's right. I hurt her, maybe not as severely as Tripp, but I'm the one who put her in his path. My goal is not to clear my name.

No, what I want is worth so much more than my innocence.

"I know I've hurt you before, but harm was never my intent. My only goal was to ensure your father knew I meant business."

"That's not better."

"I'm not saying it's better. I'm saying it's *different*." Despite the gun in her grasp, I slowly reach my hand across the table and cover hers. I feel a deep sense of relief when she doesn't pull away.

"Elise, I am so sorry."

Her chin trembles, and she looks down over her shoulder. "Your apology can't undo this."

"I know, but I mean it. I'm not a man known for apologizing, but I am truly sorry. You have to believe I never would've taken you there if I'd known you were in danger."

"Taking me there shouldn't have been an option in the first place." A light blush spreads across her cheeks, and she refuses to look at me. "I thought we'd moved past all of that. Especially after you stayed with me that night..."

"We were—*are* past all of that. It was a lapse in judgment—"

"It was a *lack* of judgment!"

My well-contained frustration begins to boil at her words. I'm not used to letting anyone talk to me this way. The need for her respect is almost irresistible, but I repress the knee-jerk reaction. I don't need her respect. All I want is her forgiveness and trust.

My eyes close, and I take a deep breath, but I'm interrupted by a bitter laugh.

"Even now, you can hardly control your temper. Tell me, Joshua, what would you like to do to me this time? Tie me to the bed again? Maybe pull out your knife and give me a few new scars. Or you could —"

I shoot to my feet. "Damn it, Elise! I don't want to hurt you. What about that don't you understand?"

She lifts an eyebrow.

Damn, she knows how to set me off.

I drop into my seat with a sigh. "I know that I have a lot of work to do. I'm not good at this, and I've never tried to be, but you? You make me want to try."

When I look up, her eyes are tortured with conflicting emotions.

Anger. Fear. Confusion. Hope.

"Why?" she whispers.

"You know why."

Elise shakes her head. "I need you to say it."

This is it, the only chance she's going to give me. I'm not going to screw it up.

I push myself out of my chair and round the table in two strides. Her body tenses as I get closer, and I'm careful to avoid any sudden movements.

I lower to my knees so we're at eye level.

"I want to try because I want *you*, Elise. Not as a prisoner, not as a pawn, as you. I want you to stay with me and give me a chance to make you happy."

"I can't spend the rest of my life stuck in this house."

One part of my plan falls into place, and the words fly out of my mouth.

"Give me one month."

CHAPTER TWENTY-FIVE

Elise

Could this day get any weirder? I keep waiting to wake up from this bizarre dream or for a camera crew to appear and tell me that I'm on some prank show.

Nope. This is my reality.

A father who doesn't want me. A captor who does.

"What?"

"Give me one month," Joshua says. "One month where you stay here, and we give this a try."

"What happens in a month?"

"Either you choose to stay here with me, or I'll let you go."

"You'll let me go home?" I expect hope to rise in my chest, but none comes. After my father's betrayal, the thought of home is bittersweet.

"Not exactly. You'd leave the country."

It wouldn't be the first time I've moved away with a new identity.

"What if I do go home?" I ask, fairly sure I don't want to hear the answer.

"You really want to go home to a father who told me to kill you?"

I don't answer.

He shakes his head. "If you went home, our families would go to war. Between Mason, your injuries, and the fact that I lied about killing you, it'd be unavoidable. Considering the size and strength of both families, it would be a bloodbath. Hundreds of people would die so that you could see your low-life dad."

I open my mouth to defend my father but close it because he's right.

"If, at the end of this month, you decide you want to leave, we'll pick somewhere for you to go, and I'll support you until you figure things out. The only catch is that you can't go home. You can have whatever life you want, wherever you want. You can start over."

I can picture it so clearly—overlooking an Italian vineyard as I sip exceptional wine and study under the most talented chefs in the world.

As much as I hate it, Joshua is right—my family has betrayed me, and there's nothing left for me at home.

I no longer have a home.

His warm palm cups my cheek, and I gaze into his softened eyes. "Give me one month, Elise."

Everything about this is crazy. Joshua can't expect me to forget everything he's put me through and play house with him. It's not that simple.

So then, why am I considering saying yes? And if I don't say yes, will it even matter? It's not like I have anywhere else to go.

Maybe it wouldn't be so bad. One month, and then it's all over. I'll be able to leave here and live a life far from Joshua, my father, and the criminal world they rule.

That's what I want, right?

"One month," I agree.

Joshua's lips pull into a dazzling smile.

"But I have a condition," I add, and he eyes me warily before nodding. "Transparency. You know everything about me, and I know nothing about you. If I stay for a month, I want to know the man I'm staying with."

He studies me for a long moment, but we both know he'll say yes. When I was his prisoner, it made sense that he wouldn't open up to me, but if he really wants me the way he claims he does, then I need to know him.

"Okay," he says, pushing to his feet.

Joshua removes his hand from my cheek and holds it out for me to take.

The gun is still in my hand, and I'm tempted to keep it with me, but deep down, I know I don't need it.

I release the weapon and place my hand in Joshua's.

As we pass Ryder's door, I stop to get the medicine that I originally went downstairs to get. The adrenaline from hearing the phone call and facing Joshua drowned out my pain, but it's making up for lost time now. Ryder apologizes for not coming up sooner, but we both realize that things are better now that I know the truth.

Joshua guides me downstairs, helping me only as much as I let him and not pushing for more. When we reach his office, he produces a key to unlock the double doors.

His office at the base was neat, simple, and generic, but not this room.

He hasn't even started telling me about himself, but this room screams more about him than I've learned in all our time together.

Sunlight from the two windows illuminates the walnut wood flooring. The desk in front of them is littered with stacks of paper and haphazardly placed folders. There's a desktop computer in one corner and a laptop sits directly in front of the dark leather chair that looks like it'd be more comfortable than the bed at my apartment.

Three walls are lined with black bookshelves, leaving the windowed wall painted a deep forest green that somehow perfectly matches Joshua's scent. The ceiling is stark white, reflecting the light of the caged chandelier from between the supportive beams where it's placed.

The room's furniture and coloring are stunning, but the objects on the bookshelves capture my attention.

Most of the space is occupied by actual books, though the collection has no rhyme or reason. There are classics, sci-fi, romance, thrillers, autobiographies, and self-help books lining the shelves, but that's not all. I can't make out the titles, but I recognize the languages French, German, Italian, and Russian. I judge their age by their spines —some look like ancient artifacts, while others seem brand new.

Then there are the objects that don't seem to have any particular purpose.

They look generic enough: an hourglass with sand settled on the bottom, three identical vases in different sizes, a brown candle with its wick unburned, and a pocket watch stuck on 3:14 resting against a stand that looks like it was meant for a small sign and not a watch.

I focus on the last object—a small horse resting in the space between the fantasy and sci-fi novels. It's not a statue like the elephant that had been on my dresser back at the base. In fact, it doesn't look like actual décor at all. It's cheap plastic, like a toy included in a kid's meal at McDonald's.

I want to ask who it belongs to, but I answer my own question when my eyes stop on the only framed picture in the arrangement.

None of the three people in this photo are looking at the camera, but the smiles are wide nonetheless. It's the kind of genuine happiness that can only be captured by a candid.

The woman in the middle looks a few years older than me. I can't make out the color of her eyes since they're squinted so tight with her smile, but they appear to be dark. Her sun-kissed, brunette locks are pulled half-up, with the other half falling just above her shoulders. She wears a red vest, with a white shirt peeking out from beneath it, and a child tucked under each of her outstretched arms.

The girl to her left can't be more than two years old. A pink shirt falls just above her knees, purple shorts barely showing from beneath it. Her curly hair matches the woman's, but I can see her striking blue eyes even from this distance. They nearly steal the attention of the whole picture with their brilliance, but I can't look away from the boy tucked under the woman's other arm.

He's smiling with the girls, hands clasped at his stomach as he leans over with a giggle. He wears bright blue basketball shorts, and the skin on his bare chest is tinted red with a splotchy sunburn. The unruly mess of hair on his head is far darker than either of the girls, but he undoubtedly has the woman's brown eyes that shine like hazel in the sunlight.

I'd know that boy anywhere.

My hand reaches for the photo before I know what I'm doing, and Joshua doesn't stop me from looking closer.

"Your mother," I state because there's no question about it. He's her spitting image.

Joshua nods. "She's twenty-six here, I would've been five, and Vanessa was two. It's the only picture that I have of all of us."

I glance at the photo, then back at him. How did this smiling family get torn apart? How did the pictured giggling child become the hardened man standing before me today?

"What happened?"

He stares past me to the picture, losing himself in the memories for several moments as if trying to decide where exactly to begin.

"My mother, Natalie Moreno, married Scott Perez when I was two. One year later, they had Vanessa, and we were a fairly normal family for a little while."

I put the picture back where I found it and look at Joshua. I expect to see a smile on his face, but Joshua doesn't seem lost in happy memories.

He looks disgusted.

"My stepfather was always an alcoholic, but it wasn't until Mom's accident that he became abusive. There was a gas leak at the restaurant she worked at, and the explosion killed three staff members and eight customers.

"She survived but landed on shards of glass, giving her severe nerve damage in her back. The recovery was long, and a lot of it's a blur to me, but by the time I was thirteen, she was addicted to her pain meds. Scott got violent after that."

I lay my hand on Joshua's shoulder, but he still won't look at me. I can't explain why, but I wish he would.

"I dropped out of school during freshman year and worked as a local gang's drug mule. The money was good—damn good for a kid. I was able to pay off Mom's medical bills and our rent. The only problem was I was rarely home. My parents didn't care, but I hated leaving Vanessa there."

I hate the picture he's painting in my head. The thirteen-year-old sacrificing his life to keep his family together. No child should have that kind of burden.

"I was sixteen when things got really bad. I was climbing the ranks within—what I learned was—the Marsollo crime family."

"Like, Marcus Marsollo?"

He smiles, but it doesn't reach his eyes. "You recognize the name."

Marcus Marsollo, the West Coast Conqueror, leads the biggest crime family in America.

Or, led anyway.

I don't know all the details of his ascent to power, but you don't have to be in the criminal world to know his name.

Marsollo started in Los Angeles, uniting the street gangs and creating a ring of power. He used that influence to claim cities across the coast from San Diego to Seattle.

At his peak, Marsollo had command over ten different cities, the most of any American crime family.

He goes on. "Scott was beating Mom, Mom was self-medicating, and Vanessa learned to stay at friends' houses as often as possible if I couldn't be home. One day, I came home to find that my mother was gone, along with ten grand from my stash."

My eyes bulge at both the news of his mother's actions and that a kid could be making that much money.

"No note, explanation, or goodbye. After she left, Scott started beating Vanessa. She did a good job hiding it from me because she knew how I'd react. Six months after Mom left, I got a panicked call from Vanessa. Scott was on a rampage, and she was scared."

My hand, still resting on his shoulder, glides until I'm cupping his cheek. The scuff prickles my skin, and a shiver runs down my spine.

When his eyes find mine, they're guarded, and I know why.

Joshua doesn't open up, ever. He's never been this vulnerable with another person, and it's killing him to tell me these things. I want to know his story, why he is the way he is, but I don't like seeing him like this.

"You don't have to do this, Joshua."

He studies me, gauging if I mean it. Though I'm sure he sees that I do, he slowly shakes his head.

"Transparency," he whispers.

I nod, and he takes a deep breath before going on.

"By the time I got there, she was covered in blood, unconscious on the floor, and Scott was lying on the couch with a beer," he practically spits the words. "I shot him three times in the chest without batting an eye, then got Vanessa in the car to take her to the emergency room."

Joshua visibly struggles to find the next words.

"We were almost there when a rival gang recognized my car and ran us off the road..." He trails off, but he doesn't need to say the words.

I know what happened next.

"Joshua, I'm so sorry."

He doesn't answer, probably because he realizes, just like I do, that the words are empty. Well intended but ultimately meaningless.

"I woke up the next day in the infirmary of Marsollo's main base in L.A. with the boss himself standing at the foot of my bed. I'd worked for the family for roughly three years by that point, but I'd never been to the main base. I knew who Marsollo was, but I'd never had a reason to meet him before then."

Joshua leans back to get a better look at my face before he says, "That's when I learned my rightful name is Joshua Marsollo."

My face must communicate my level of surprise because Joshua laughs. There's genuine amusement there, and the sound is enough to make my heart do a backflip in my chest.

"I'd never given much thought to who my father was, and my mother never bothered to tell me, so I just figured he was some deadbeat. I still have no idea if it was a relationship, an affair, or a one-time thing, but it doesn't really matter. All I know is that she didn't know who Marsollo was, and by the time she figured it out, she was pregnant with me."

He pauses like he's giving me a chance to say something, but absolutely no words come to mind.

Joshua laughs again, and I decide that there's nothing I wouldn't do to get that sound out of him. It's a deep, throaty laugh that touches parts of me that I never knew a laugh could.

"I would've told you this story weeks ago if I'd known that's all it takes to make you speechless."

I smack his bicep, ignoring the sting that reverberates up my hand as a result. "It's a lot to take in. You can't honestly tell me you weren't speechless when you found out Marcus was your father?"

"I guess I was," he admits, placing a kiss on my forehead before going on. "My mom moved to San Diego when she found out that she was pregnant, and that's where she met Scott."

"So, how did Marcus recognize you?"

"The soldiers I was working with the night I killed Scott had reported what happened to their capos since they had to deal with the body. When my name got to Marsollo, he recognized it as my mother's. It wasn't until years later that I found out that was a lie."

"What do you mean?"

He gives me an *I'll get to that part,* look and I nod.

"Marsollo didn't offer so much as a pleasantry before telling me that as soon as the doctors cleared me, I'd begin training to take over the family."

I'm unsure if he realizes it, but Joshua's arm wraps itself around my waist. The motion is so effortless that I don't think twice before relaxing into him.

"I trained with Marsollo for five years, learning everything there was to know about his empire and how to run it. When I was twenty-one, one of our raids went sideways, and Marsollo took a bullet to the gut. It was a miracle we got him out of there alive. At the same time, the FBI opened a large-scale investigation based on evidence they got from a convict looking for a reduced sentence. Marsollo was hanging on by a thread, and suddenly, all responsibility fell to me."

Joshua's tone is by no means upbeat, but the pained tightness from earlier is gone, and I'm glad we've moved to marginally easier topics.

"I took everything underground, cut all public ties, and temporarily called off any missions that could draw unwanted attention."

I rest a hand over Joshua's chest, feeling the steady thump of his heart as he brushes his thumb over my hip in lazy circles. Touching Joshua, having Joshua touch me, is the most natural feeling in the world, and I soak in the sensation as he continues.

"I was going through files in Marsollo's office that would help get the feds off my back when I found one with my name on it," he says, shaking his head. "Pictures, doctor visit summaries, school records, and more recently, a detailed description of every job I'd worked since joining the gang when I was thirteen. He had it all."

Joshua doesn't need to explain the implications. Marsollo knew about him all along. With all those records, he had to have known about Scott's abuse and Natalie's drug problem. If Marsollo had stepped in, would Joshua's mother have left? Would Vanessa still be alive?

"What did you do?"

"Confronted him," he tells me. "He didn't even deny it. I guess a deathbed is the best place for a confession."

His eyes find mine, dark and raw with honesty. "Let's just say I didn't wait for Marsollo's clock to run out naturally."

I suppose that admission should disgust or scare me.

It doesn't.

"Unfortunately, not everyone in the Marsollo family was thrilled with the idea of a twenty-one-year-old taking leadership, even though I was Marsollo's blood and had more than proven myself capable."

Joshua takes my hand and leads us to a map of the United States of America hanging between the windows.

There are colored pins across the whole surface, and he doesn't need to explain their meaning. They stand for the bases of criminal families across the country.

Green pins stagger from Chicago and Detroit all the way to Dallas and Houston, and it goes without saying that they stand for my father's territories. Blue pins color the West Coast, but they aren't the same. A darker blue claims Sacramento and below, while a lighter blue covers the northernmost cities.

Purple and light red split the eastern side of the country between the Diaz and the Rivera families. Dots of orange throughout the map must represent smaller, neutral gangs or families that have pledged their loyalty to whatever territory they reside in.

Joshua lifts his hand to point to somewhere on the map, and the motion brings the realization that this must mean *I'm* in California right now.

Joshua's finger hovers over the light blue dots covering Washington and Oregon on the map.

"Several of Marsollo's capos didn't want to follow me, but luckily, they weren't the majority. We were vulnerable between Marsollo's death and the FBI investigation, which had been dropped but was still too public for my liking. Normally, I would've shown force, but I didn't have that option, so I offered them a deal. They'd occupy the northern bases, and I'd have the rest of the coast. I even let them keep Marsollo's name when one of his cousins became their boss."

"Everyone was just okay with you changing the family name?"

He shrugs. "I didn't really care what they thought. Even seven years later, we're still making our public comeback since Marsollo's death, so it wasn't very difficult to make the change while we were still underground."

"You're twenty-eight?"

He nods, an amused smile growing on those taunting lips.

I always knew Joshua was older than me, but I assumed that since he was a boss, he'd at least be in his thirties.

I step away from him, trailing slowly back to the framed photo. I study the boy there and the longer I do, the more I see Joshua in him. The twinkle of his eyes in the sun, the charming smile when he's genuinely happy, and the love for his family that's visible in every feature of his young face.

Joshua comes up behind me, wrapping his arms around my waist, careful to avoid putting any pressure on my back. I gently lean into him, the warmth undeniably comforting.

"Who else knows?"

I feel him shrug. "Everyone knows bits and pieces of the story. Only Ryder knows it all, and that's just because he was there for most of it."

"He was?"

"Put the gun in my hand the night I shot my father. We've been inseparable ever since," he says, and his eyebrows pull together when his eyes bore into mine. "Until recently, that is."

The balls of my feet pivot, and we're chest to chest. "What's that supposed to mean?"

"He's protective of you, which makes him significantly more critical of how I handle things."

"That makes two of us," I mutter.

"Watch it, Princess," he says in a husky tone that sends a thrill through my body.

We stand frozen for several moments, and I'm grateful for the time to let everything sink in. He opened up to me more than he has for anyone before, and though I know we have a long way to go, I'm strangely looking forward to what the month has to offer.

"Jay should be done with dinner by now. Join me?"

My eyes jump to the window where the sun is setting over the miles of trees. I hadn't noticed how fast time was flying, but I shouldn't be surprised. That's how it always is when I'm with Joshua.

I nod, and he takes my hand, leading me through the hall. We reach the kitchen, where Jay is bustling around like a madman as he finishes the meal.

"I'll get us food. Wait here," Joshua tells me, brushing a lock of my hair behind my ear before he goes.

Muffled voices drift into the kitchen from the other room. As Joshua makes our plates, I peek into the living room, where Ryder and a few other guys are watching a movie I don't recognize.

I turn to leave before they notice me but freeze in my tracks when I hear the words.

"Come on, tell me you like it," the handsome actor purrs.

My blood runs cold.

Tell me you like it.

The words are no longer from the TV but from Tripp.

My hands shake, my chest tightens, and my vision tunnels as flashes from that night come rushing back to me.

From behind, I hear Joshua's voice, but his words don't register through the panic. All I can see is Tripp's malicious sneer. All I can hear is the whoosh of the whip and my own cries. All I can feel is my back burning and the shame that threatens to swallow me whole.

It's all coming back to me—the terror, the excruciating pain, the worthlessness.

A hand rests on my shoulder, and a wave of panic hits me so hard that I jump and scramble away from the touch.

"Elise, what the hell is going on?" I finally hear him say, but the lump in my throat makes it impossible to speak.

I force myself to turn and take in his wide, worried eyes as they assess my shivering body.

"Everyone, out." Joshua orders.

I hadn't even processed the other men that jumped to their feet, but they make an immediate exit at Joshua's demand.

"What just happened?" he asks, tone thick with worry.

I'm trying to collect myself, but it's difficult. The darkness from that day is overwhelming, and I'm afraid I won't be able to fight it off much longer.

Grabbing a glass of water from the counter beside him, Joshua takes a cautious step toward me, carefully watching my reaction.

I don't stop him from approaching.

When he's about six feet away from me, he holds out the water, which I immediately take and sip. The liquid is refreshing, slowly bringing me back to reality.

He steps back, giving me more than enough space. "What just happened?"

I drop my gaze when an overwhelming sense of shame drowns me. "I—I'm sorry. I didn't—"

"I'm not mad, Elise. Just talk to me."

"The attack," is all I can manage to say, but I know he understands what I'm trying to say.

I wrap my arms around myself as if I can stop from falling apart this way.

He steps toward me once again, but I don't feel the fear. In fact, it's as though his body is calling to mine.

Right now, it's the only place I want to be.

Surprising us both, I walk into Joshua's open arms.

CHAPTER TWENTY-SIX

Joshua

Elise doesn't turn around when I step onto the porch, and I'm relieved to see that her shoulders aren't tense and her breathing has finally evened out.

I brought her out here after her panic attack for some fresh air, but I might need it more than she does.

Anger twists my gut when I recall her fearful eyes and pale face only minutes ago. My hand twitches with the urge to make Tripp pay for everything he's done, and I will—soon enough.

But I need to do this first.

I sit beside her on the couch, and she accepts the Chamomile tea I offer. "That was my sister's favorite tea, you know."

"Can you tell me more about Vanessa?"

I take in the stretch of trees and think of my sister for what feels like the hundredth time today. I normally avoid thoughts of her at all costs, but at Elise's request, I push past the grief to reach the happier memories that I keep locked away.

For most people, it's the happy memories that give them peace after they've lost a loved one, but not me. When I recall my sister's glowing smile or snorting laughter, it feels like a white-hot blade slicing through my chest.

I'm the reason she'll never smile again.

Still, when Elise looks at me like this—like there's a human hidden beneath the monster—I can't deny her anything.

"You remind me of her sometimes," I tell her.

"She was unbelievably charismatic?"

I roll my eyes, and my low laugh echoes against the trees. When I look down to see Elise's small smile, it knocks the air out of my lungs. Her smile is a rarity these days, but I plan to change that.

"She was stubborn and irritating."

"Hey!" Her hand smacks my arm for the second time tonight, and I'm sure it hurt her more than it did me.

I lean into the couch and sling an arm around Elise, gently pulling her closer.

"She was quiet around most people, but not me. *Damn,* she had a mouth on her when she was pissed." I raise my eyebrows. "And I pissed her off a lot."

Elise leans in closer as I talk.

"I'd put empty milk cartons back in the fridge or leave the toilet seat up, and she would *freak out.* She kept saying she'd let me starve, but there was always food ready for me when I got home."

"Sounds like we would've gotten along," she says and places her small hand on my knee, which I reach out to take in my own.

Elise curls into my side, and I wonder which screwed-up situation she's thinking about now.

Her father's abandonment.

Tripp's attack.

Mason's betrayal.

Elise's life has been turned upside down in the span of a few weeks.

All I want is to take that pain away from her, which is why I hate what I need to do next.

"We need to talk."

"Wow, I thought we'd last at least twenty-four hours before this conversation," she quips, but there's a nervousness to her small smile.

I kiss her forehead again and breathe in her scent, relishing how she feels curled into me. I have a feeling it won't last much longer.

"You'll have to work harder to scare me off," I tell her.

"Trust me, I've been trying for weeks."

I want to laugh, but I can't bring myself to.

It feels like a punch to the gut when Elise's smile drops from her face, and she pulls her knees to her chest. "What do we need to talk about?"

"I know this is going to be difficult for you, but I wouldn't ask if it wasn't necessary."

"Joshua, what is it?" she snaps.

"I need you to tell me exactly what happened in the basement with Tripp."

She recoils on instinct. "What? No, Joshua, I can't—you know that I can't—"

I rest a hand on the nape of her neck. "It's okay—"

She pushes me away. "You can't ask me to relive that."

"I know what I'm asking is a lot, but it's important."

"Why? Don't you have security cameras to see for yourself?"

"There aren't cameras in there, sensitive content and all," I explain, and I hate how she cringes away from me. "I just need you to trust me on this one."

My hands itch to pull her into my embrace and soothe her, but I force myself to give her space instead.

After a few moments, her breathing evens out, and I'm about to gently coax her into telling me about that day when she whispers, "What happened to Tripp after you shot him?"

My expression is perfectly composed when I answer. "That's not something you need to worry about."

"Then it doesn't matter. You know enough of what happened."

"I understand it's a lot to ask, but I need you to trust me."

"Trust *me*, Joshua. I have a right to know what happened to Tripp."

"Just trust—"

She abruptly stands and walks to the door.

"Where are you going?"

"To bed," she calls without looking back.

I'm in front of her in two long strides, and she glares up at me. "I'm not doing this with you. You can't ask me to relive that day when you won't even tell me what happened after."

I place my hands on either of her shoulders. "You really want to know?"

She nods slowly, and I know it's because her voice would shake with uncertainty if she spoke, but I grant her wish anyway.

"Do you remember what I told you happens to my prisoners?"

She nods, and it feels like only yesterday that I'd threatened her with that very fate.

"He's been starved, isolated, and thoroughly beaten. He's also being kept awake by electrical shocks. I need to know everything that happened so I know exactly how much he needs to suffer before I kill him and ensure that no one ever touches you again."

I mutter a curse when she tenses beneath my touch.

My hands move to cup her cheeks, and I soften my tone. "I also need to know so we can avoid triggering another panic attack."

"You're going to kill him?" she asks, and the worry in her tone makes me sick.

She should want him to suffer just as much as I do.

"What did you expect? The fact that he disobeyed my order to leave the base was enough to put a bullet in his head, but after what he did to you? He signed his death sentence."

She swallows but stays silent.

"Elise, I can't let people think they can get away with hurting you. I need to do this to protect you."

After a long moment, she finally nods, and I drop my hands from her face.

"Will you take me to my room?"

"Elise—"

"I'm not mad. I've had a long day; my back hurts, and I'm exhausted. Will you please take me to my room?"

This isn't how I wanted our night to end, but the fatigue in her voice is too evident to ignore, so I oblige.

We reach the door to her room, and I hold it open for her, but she doesn't step through it.

Instead, she closes her eyes, takes a deep breath, and tells me everything that happened in the basement, from the moment Ryder chained her wrists to the moment I shot Tripp.

Her voice is brittle, focused, and shaky, like she's trying to tell the story while avoiding stepping on shards of glass. It makes me miss being yelled at by her. At least then, I'd get the fire that makes her cheeks flame with passion, and her eyes blaze in indignation. Right now, her shoulders curl inward, her chin lowers submissively, and her skin turns sickly pale.

I knew when I asked her to tell me about what happened that it would be hard for me to control my temper—but the fury that I experience when I hear what she endured is unlike anything I've ever felt.

The need to hold her close rivals so violently with the need to make Tripp suffer.

My mind doesn't only process the information she gives me, but paints the picture in perfect clarity.

She tells me that he shoved his fingers down her throat, and I can practically see it happening right in front of me, which does nothing to calm my bloodlust.

Whether she sees it or not, Elise doesn't acknowledge my reaction. Every bit of energy goes into her story, like it's taking everything in her to get through it.

She tells me how he kissed her before shoving her back to pull off her pants, and I see red.

She stops there. We both know what happened next.

"Happy now?" she asks, brown eyes narrowing to slits as she folds her trembling arms over her chest.

I engulf Elise in a hug before she has the chance to object. After a moment of hesitation, she relaxes in my arms, tears soaking the fabric of my shirt.

I don't try to console or calm her. I only hold her close. My lips rest against her forehead, and I place soft kisses there.

"Nothing about this makes me happy," I whisper, pulling away just enough to look into her puffy eyes. "I won't let anyone hurt you ever again."

"Don't make promises you can't keep."

"Then I promise to always protect you," I amend.

I can see in her eyes that she believes me before she nods. "You're really going to kill him?"

I tuck a lock of hair behind her ear. "I need to."

I can tell she still doesn't like the idea, but she doesn't object again.

With a step back, she pushes the door to her room open. "Can you get Ryder?"

My stomach twists with what can only be jealousy. "Why?"

Elise must pick up on my thoughts because she rolls her eyes. "To change the bandages before I sleep."

"I'll be right back."

I'm out of her room and knocking on Ryder's door only a minute later.

"Is Elise okay?" he asks as the door swings open.

I push past him. "She's fine, but I need new bandages for her back."

"I can—" His offer dies when I cut my eyes at him. "They're over here."

Ryder walks into his bathroom, and I hear him rustling through the cabinets before coming back out with a small box.

"Everything you need is inside."

I take the box, but Ryder doesn't let go right away. "You need to be careful. Her back isn't the only thing that's still healing."

I glance down at my tear-stained shirt. "Yeah, I know."

Ryder releases the box, and by the time I walk into Elise's room, she's already seated backward in a chair.

"Where's Ryder?" she asks, but we both know I didn't ask for his help.

"I can do it."

I set the items out on the table, and when I turn to face Elise, she's shrugging the button-up off her shoulders.

I watch, mesmerized as the thin material slides down, leaving her upper body bare except for the bandages. I take in her smooth, tan shoulders and the few small freckles that decorate her skin.

I'd noticed those spots the night she fell asleep in my arms, and it had taken all my restraint to stop from brushing my fingertips over them. I can so clearly recall that steady rise and fall of her chest and how she'd held small fistfuls of my shirt as if asking me to stay with her, so I did.

I'm pulled back to the present when she clutches the shirt protectively to her front and squares her shoulders.

I survey the bandages. "Are you ready?"

She nods.

My hands move gently over her skin, peeling away the bandages with the utmost care. When they're all free, I pull them away from her back, seeing the damage in its entirety for the very first time.

I'd seen it in the basement, but it had been covered by her shredded shirt and blood. Even today, when she pulled her shirt down, I only saw the bandages.

But now, I see it all.

Dozens of raised lash marks decorate her skin like a morbid canvas. The areas that Tripp hit multiple times have morphed into singular injuries, which are still bright red. Scabbing covers the majority of the marks that were once open wounds.

When I first met Elise, she was pure, innocent, and unblemished. Then, I took what was good and twisted—tainted it.

But I didn't ruin it.

Earlier, Elise said I'd taken everything from her, but she was wrong. Her strength, her fire, and her heart remain perfectly intact, and there's not a thing in the world that could take that away from her.

Here she sits, after everything she's had to endure, as graceful as ever.

As beautiful as ever.

So beautiful.

I lean in, and my lips gently brush the marred skin. I barely make contact as I place feather-light kisses across her back.

Elise sucks in a sharp breath, and I wonder if I'm hurting her, but as my kisses trace along her back, the tense muscles relax under my lips. That assurance sends a thrill through my body, and I slide off the chair and onto my knees.

When she gasps, the soft sound is enough to drive me mad. I've never felt so satisfied, so content in my life.

My kisses travel up her shoulders, and my lips trail along her collarbone as I circle the chair without breaking contact. I'm kneeling in front of her when I finally pull away and meet her leveled gaze.

Neither of us says a word. We just share one breath, completely intoxicated by one another.

She has to see how badly I want her.

How badly I *need* her.

I'm about to open my mouth to tell her just that when she leans forward, and her soft lips meet mine. When my momentary surprise has passed, I'm kissing her back with the need of a starving animal. Just like with our other kisses, she lets me dominate her mouth, but her passion is just as furious as mine.

Elise slides out of the chair, her lips never leaving mine. The fabric of her discarded shirt presses to my chest, holding it in place. Her arms wrap around my neck, anchoring me to her, and the feeling is euphoric.

She wants me just as much as I want her.

This fact is a hit from the most addictive drug, and I wrap my arms around her body to pull her closer.

I realize my mistake at the same moment Elise cries out.

I mutter a slew of curses as I withdraw my hands from her back immediately. "I'm so sorry! I didn't mean to—I didn't—*damn it*, are you okay?"

To my surprise, she chuckles breathlessly. My eyebrows knit together as she shakes her head, still wincing.

"It's okay. I've just never seen you so flustered before," she explains with a ghost of a smile.

I breathe a sigh of relief before holding my hand out to her. "Let's get you ready for bed."

I take extra care while bandaging her back to avoid hurting her again. When I'm finally done, I turn to pack up the supplies, giving her a chance to put her shirt back on with some level of privacy.

She sits on the bed when she's done, and I sit beside her.

"I leave in the morning, but I'll be back in a few days."

"Where are you—" The words die in her throat.

She knows where I'm going.

"Going to miss me?" I quip in an attempt to lighten the mood.

It must work because a faint blush colors her cheeks. "I didn't say that."

"Didn't have to. Don't worry, I'll be back soon. Ryder will be here the whole time. If you need anything, just ask him."

She nods but doesn't answer as she climbs into bed, lying on her stomach.

I run a hand over her hair. "I'm just going to straighten some things out so I can work from here for the month. I'll be back before you know it. Now get some sleep."

"Goodnight, Joshua," she murmurs as her eyes flutter to a close.

"Goodnight, Elise. I'll be back soon," I promise, kissing her temple gently.

When I reach the door and look back at the beautiful girl whose hair is splayed across the pillow and whose face is resting in an expression of complete and utter peace, the realization hits me like a punch to the gut. It sucks the air from my lungs and nearly brings me to my knees.

I'm in love with Elise Consoli.

CHAPTER TWENTY-SEVEN

Elise

"Why am I hearing from Ryder that you're not eating?"

I glare at Ryder, who gives me a halfhearted, apologetic smile.

Joshua has been gone for two days, and this is the first time I've heard from him in that time. It's been a boring two days since I don't have the motivation to do much more than sit in the upstairs lounge and watch TV. It's a simple luxury that I've missed these past few weeks, and I like to think I'm making up for lost time.

I was watching a Harry Potter marathon when Ryder approached me, holding out his phone. I figured it would be Joshua checking in, not questioning my dietary habits.

I pause the movie and tuck my legs beneath me. "I'm eating plenty."

"Oh yeah? What have you eaten today?"

It's just past two in the afternoon, and I haven't been hungry enough to eat yet. I want to lie and say I've had two full meals already, but Ryder would rat me out.

"I'm building up an appetite," I say instead.

"By watching TV?"

My glare toward Ryder intensifies, but he doesn't seem bothered.

"I'm a grown-ass woman fully capable of taking care of myself. I'll eat when I'm hungry. Did you need anything else?" My tone is snappier than I intend, but I have a right to it.

He declares his feelings for me, leaves for days, and finally reaches out—but only to let me know he doesn't like what I've been doing in his absence. Deep down, I know he's genuinely worried about me, but if I'm being honest, I want him to come back. The time I've had to sit around and do nothing has made me realize that I enjoy being with Joshua, and I'm angry that he hasn't reached out until now.

"A grown-ass woman knows it's not healthy to go without eating." His tone matches my aggression.

"Why don't you mind your own business?"

"You are my business."

"I'm not your anything."

We're silent for a moment, and a part of me wishes I hadn't snapped.

Joshua sighs, and I can imagine that he's pinching the bridge of his nose like he always does when he's frustrated. "Just promise me you'll eat soon?"

"I will," I agree. Letting my guard down, I ask what I really want to know. "When will you be back? You only have twenty-seven more days, you know."

I hear the smile in his voice. "Trust me, I know. I should be back tomorrow."

My stomach knots at the reminder of what tomorrow is. I'd almost forgotten, and I *wanted* to forget.

"I'll see you tomorrow," I tell him.

"Can't wait." And with that, he hangs up.

I set my icy scowl in place before turning to Ryder. "You told on me?"

He shrugs. "He asked about it, so I told him. I'm more afraid of him than I am of you, Elli."

Elli—the nickname that Ryder insists on calling me.

Though I've missed Joshua these last two days, I've enjoyed getting to know Ryder. We've had plenty of time to talk, and I've learned quite a bit about him.

Four years ago, Joshua and Ryder moved to Sacramento for a few weeks to get some properties in order. Ryder admitted that they spent equal parts enjoying the clubs as they did managing them, and it was one of these nights that Ryder met Rachel, the mother of his child.

When I asked how much Rachel knew about Ryder's work, he only laughed and assured me she was well-informed.

I've even seen pictures of Lyla, who looks *just* like her father. She has the dark skin of both her parents, but the wide, thoughtful eyes are all Ryder. She has long, unruly curls that are pulled into a ponytail in all the pictures he shows me. I also notice that she only ever wears big

T-shirts with leggings beneath them, none of the frilly, colorful dresses that other three-year-old girls seem to favor.

Apparently, throughout Rachel's pregnancy, the other capos referred to Ryder as *Ride-her*. I mentioned then that I've never had a nickname, and Ryder quickly rectified that situation and has been calling me *Elli* ever since.

"You had to have known he was going to react that way. Couldn't you have just lied? I thought you were on my side." I press play on my movie, cuddling into the fleece blanket.

I'm finally able to lean my back against the couch, though not for long periods of time before the pressure brings on waves of tingles that morph into throbs if I'm not careful.

Still, it's progress.

He shakes his head, dropping down next to me. "There are no sides, but he's right. You need to eat. When was the last time you had a full meal?"

I imagine he won't count the bowl of carrots I had last night as a *full meal*.

"I had a sandwich and chips yesterday for lunch."

"That was two days ago. You slept through lunch yesterday."

I search my memories only to realize he's right. We had lunch together the day Joshua left, but I slept through most of yesterday, having had relentless nightmares the night before.

"Okay, so maybe it's not the healthiest thing, but I can't help it if I'm not hungry."

He searches my face. "Are you feeling okay?"

"I'm fine, Ryder," I assure him. "I'm just adjusting to being here, is all."

I hope he'll drop the conversation, and after a few moments of silence, I think I'm in the clear, but then he declares, "You're depressed."

"Wow, you should be a doctor or something."

He ignores the jab.

"Why? You're not a prisoner here, and in a month, you'll get to choose what you do next. Shouldn't that make you happy?"

I turn off the movie and adjust to face Ryder.

"Just because I'll leave in a month doesn't mean I'm not trapped now. I might be free to walk around the house, but we both know I can't actually *go* anywhere. Even after this month, it's not like I can go home. Sure, I have the choice to leave, but I can never go back to normal. My life, as I've always known it, is over. That's not something I can easily accept and move on from."

Speaking the words out loud lifts a weight that I didn't realize has been crushing my chest since Joshua and I made this deal. I'll live through this, but I still lost my life.

"You sound so sure about leaving in a month."

I laugh, but the sound is dry. "Come on, it's not like staying here is a real option. I've spent my whole life trying to get *away* from your work."

"Have you considered that it's not something you *can* get away from?"

"What do you mean?"

"Well, you've spent your whole life trying to run away, but have you ever actually done that?"

"Of course I have. I lived on my own for six years."

"Sure, under constant security, with a fake name, unable to see your own family without extensive arrangements. Let's say you leave here and go to Europe, the same will apply there, too. Moreno will ensure you have security and a fake identity, and you won't be able to come back to America. I'm not saying that you actively participate in what we do, but you've never gotten *away* from it—not really. Even after being in hiding for years, you're still valuable enough to kidnap. All I'm suggesting is that maybe you should try and embrace it for once."

His words hit me like a truck.

I thought I was free from my family's work, but I've never truly escaped.

The simple fact that I couldn't leave my home whenever my dad held family dinner is evidence that I've never been free. I've given up traveling the world, having real friends, going on dates, and engaging in countless other completely mundane life activities all because of my father's job.

All the time I thought I was being strong and independent, I've been anything but.

Have I *ever* been free?

"Come on," he calls, standing up from the couch and pulling me from my thoughts. "Let's go get some food."

A commotion from the kitchen drifts up the stairs, followed by hearty laughs.

"Could you bring something up here? I'm not feeling great."

He doesn't believe me for a second. "Elli, there's nothing to be afraid of. No one here is going to touch you."

"That hasn't been my experience."

He opens his mouth to protest but closes it quickly.

"That's what I thought," I mutter.

Shaking his head, he holds his hand out to me. "At least let me introduce you. It's only the L.A. base's capos. Maybe you'll feel better after getting to know them, and if you don't, you can hide up here all you want. Deal?"

"Aren't they under instruction from Joshua not to talk to me?"

"They were told not to bother you, but I think it'll help for you to meet them. Elli, trust me. I won't let anyone hurt you." His soothing voice works its magic, and I find myself reaching to take his hand.

The sounds of teasing and laughter travel through the house as Ryder and I enter the kitchen. None of the three men see us right away, and I use the opportunity to size them up.

The first thing I notice is how young they are.

None of them look older than thirty. In my—admittedly minimal —experience, the only time a capo is under the age of thirty is when they're blood-related to the boss. My brothers are my father's main capos, and the only other capo even remotely close to their age is our cousin, Matteo, who works at the Detroit base.

I know without their confirmation that none of these men are related to Joshua.

The first man has light brown hair pulled back in a man bun. The scruff on his jaw is short, and the rugged look suits him well. Dark jeans and a red flannel are his outfit of choice, giving him the look of a hipster rather than a mafia capo. He laughs as he puts peanut butter on his sandwich, and I must admit that he doesn't seem very intimidating.

The second man—who looks more like a boy—holds an orange in his raised hand, aimed at the first man. By the looks of it, he's no older than twenty and dressed similarly to the first man, though he wears a light blue shirt instead of the flannel. His tanned skin, wavy dark hair, and green eyes look vaguely familiar, though I'm sure I've never met him before.

The third man sits on a barstool, watching the other two with a smile that shows off his perfectly straight, white teeth. His dark buzz-cut and cleanly shaven face give him a professional look, which is accentuated by his navy slacks and white collared shirt. His rounded face and blue eyes can only be described as *cold*, though he looks friendly enough.

Ryder clears his throat, effectively getting each man's attention.

They turn to face us, excited to see Ryder, then confused once their eyes drop to me. The first man stops making his sandwich, the second lowers the orange in his hand, and the third straightens his back.

"Boys," Ryder greets. "Meet Elli."

I'm not sure what I thought they'd do, but for some reason, I'm caught off guard when each man smiles kindly at me, mumbling greetings.

Ryder points to the first man. "This is Donovan Riley." His hand moves to the second man, "Alec Tonis," then to the third man, "and Kade Manning."

"It's nice to meet you all," I say, and the words sound just as awkward as I feel.

Ryder continues his introductions. "Donovan is the head of security—"

"So, I'm the guy you need to kill if you want to break out of here," Donovan says, a playful smile plastered on his face.

"What the hell, Don?" Ryder's voice is sharp, and Donovan's expression immediately sobers.

Despite my initial apprehension about coming downstairs, I can't help but laugh at the reaction.

All four men turn to me.

"It's okay, Ryder," I assure him, grateful to Donovan for breaking the ice. "Thanks for the tip. I'll have to keep it in mind when I'm planning my big escape."

Donovan grins spiritedly.

Ryder shakes his head, but there's a small grin on his face as he points to the next man.

"Kade runs all of our cybersecurity." Ryder turns to the last capo. "And Alec runs the day-to-day life of the base. He's in charge of all the boring stuff no one else wants to do, but we give him a capo title to make him feel like he's doing something important."

Alec flips him off, but his smile is unmoving. "I might just accidentally forget to have your kitchen stocked next month."

"As if I actually eat the crap you've been stocking lately. Not all of us are twenty-one."

In one fluid motion, Alec throws the orange at Ryder, who ducks with lightning-fast reflexes, causing the fruit to fly into the hallway.

"Hey!" another voice calls, and we all turn to see a pissed-off Jay enter the room, holding the fruit and rubbing a red spot on his head. "What the hell was that for?"

"Sorry, Uncle Jay!" Alec makes a face, his hand cupping the back of his neck in a gesture that only makes him look younger.

Uncle Jay?

That's why Alec looks so familiar. He and Jay have the exact same dark hair and dull green eyes. In fact, if someone told me Jay was Alec's father, I'd believe them in a heartbeat.

The room is filled with laughter, and Jay rolls his eyes, muttering something about how he'd let them all starve.

The guys start talking among themselves, and I look at Ryder. "Thank you."

He gives me a half-smile. "Anytime, Elli."

CHAPTER TWENTY-EIGHT

Elise

"That's not fair! I called dibs on playing with Elli next round," Alec says, pointing an accusing finger at Donovan, who smiles like he's won the lottery and not a game of cards.

"No way. We're on a winning streak."

I roll my eyes, but a flattered blush rises in my cheeks. "Don, we've won four games in a row. I think your ego can handle playing with another partner."

He frowns, surveying his options around the table—Kade, Ryder, and Jay.

We're playing Kemps—a personal favorite of mine that I've always had a particular knack for.

Jay raises his whiskey glass. "I'll be your partner if I don't have to play with Kade again. He *never* wins."

Kade flips him off. "I don't want to play with a drunk anyway. What's that, your third glass in the last hour?"

"And I *still* played better than you," Jay mutters.

Today has been exactly what I needed to get out of my self-pity.

Jay made potato soup for dinner, which I had intended on taking to my room, but the guys insisted that I join them. It was awkward at first since I didn't fit into their conversations, but once Jay served the second round of drinks, we all started to loosen up.

After dinner, Kade suggested we play cards, which is how we've spent most of the night. Their first choice had been poker, but I convinced them to try Kemps, though none of them had played it before. Of course, they all picked up on it ridiculously fast.

I finish off my drink and raise the empty glass. "Maybe you should all team up, then you might actually have a chance at beating me."

"Woah!"

"Uncalled for!"

"She's not wrong..."

Their laughter is contagious, and I can't help but join in.

Suddenly, all laughter and taunting are silenced.

I open my mouth to ask what's happening but close it when I follow their gazes to the door behind me.

A figure stands in the open doorway to the porch.

Joshua.

I sit up, anticipation coursing through me at just the sight of him. I knew that I missed him, but now that he stands in front of me, I feel the weight of just how strong that longing was as it slides off my shoulders. It should scare me just how much my body reacts to being near him.

Of course, that's when I notice his expression and why everyone else went dead silent.

He's livid. Even with the minimal light from the dim bulbs, I can see his lips are pressed in a hard line.

"Joshua, you're back early," I say, stating the obvious just to break the silence.

Raising his chin, he meets my eyes, and I'm relieved to see that his expression softens.

So, he's not mad at *me* then.

"Ryder, Elise." Though all he says are our names, we get the message.

Clearing his throat, Ryder smiles tightly at the men around the table and stands. I follow suit, and we make our way toward Joshua, who curtly steps aside to let us by. As we go into the house, I hear the guys behind us packing up the cards for the night, and I hate that the light-heartedness is gone.

Ryder and I follow Joshua past the kitchen and to the steps.

Joshua faces me. "Go upstairs. I'll be up in a minute."

"What? Why?"

"Just go. I'll be there after I talk to Ryder."

I scoff, not moving an inch. "I'm not some toddler you're about to tuck in for bed. What's going on?"

Joshua closes his eyes and takes a deep breath as though he's counting to ten in an attempt to calm himself.

That's when I finally put it together.

"Is this about me hanging out with the guys? That's not Ryder's fault. I—"

His narrowed eyes snap open. "Elise, do not push me right now."

"You're acting insane."

"Do not make me ask you again."

I take a daring step forward. "Or what?"

Joshua glares at me with enough fury to send an army running, but before he can say anything, Ryder steps forward, effectively shifting my attention to him.

"Elli, it's okay. Just go, and I'll see you tomorrow." His damned soothing tone eases the frustration growing from Joshua's demands.

As much as I want to defend Ryder, I know he's fully capable of handling himself. I nod and turn to go, glancing at Joshua's expression as I do.

He looks murderously at Ryder.

I begin to ascend the staircase, and when I'm halfway up, the two men walk silently down the hall to Joshua's office.

On a dangerous whim, I walk back down, tiptoeing after them. I stand sideways at the double doors, allowing my ear to pick up the conversation.

"What the hell were you thinking?" The deadly words come from Joshua.

"That she'd be more comfortable getting to know the strangers surrounding her, and I was right." Ryder sounds as level-headed as ever.

"That wasn't your call to make. She was perfectly fine," Joshua snaps.

"Perfectly fine? She hadn't moved from that couch or eaten in days until I stepped in. She was not *perfectly fine*."

"I know she was struggling, but that's why I came back early. Imagine my surprise when I come home to see that she's out there with the capos when I specifically told you to keep them away from her."

"Have *you* seen her laugh like that before? Because I haven't. All I ever see her do is cry or yell at you." Ryder's voice climbs to a shout, and it's the first time I've heard him yell at anyone.

When Joshua speaks, the words are ice cold. "You'll leave first thing in the morning for the base. You can stop to see Lyla on your way back to L.A., but you're not staying here."

Ryder laughs, but the sound is far from humored. "Are you going to take away everything that makes her happy aside from you? That'll only make her resent you, Joshua."

The words hang in the air, and both Joshua and I realize the weight of their truth.

"I should've called to ask you," Ryder says, tone softened. "I was just worried you'd react… like this."

"Yes, you should've called. And, *Elli*?"

"A harmless nickname. She's never had one. Are you seriously jealous right now?"

"I'm pissed that my second in command is blatantly disregarding my orders and acting overly friendly with *my* girl."

"I won't go behind your back again—"

"Damn straight you won't. Just because I've known you forever doesn't mean you get to disrespect me." Joshua takes a deep breath. "I don't want her around the others without one of us. I will *not* put her in danger again."

"Yes, sir."

I decide now is a good time to leave so neither man walks out and sees me.

I've taken a total of two steps before I hear my name. "Elise, come in. I know you're listening." Joshua sounds more tired than frustrated.

I guess I wasn't as stealthy as I thought.

I enter the room with flushed cheeks and find Joshua standing behind his desk, arms folded. Ryder stands similarly, and neither of them looks happy with the other.

Ryder gives me a forced smile before nodding to Joshua, and leaving the office.

The door shuts, and thankfully, the tension leaves with Ryder.

I open my mouth to break the silence, but before I can say anything, he's making his way around the desk. Every nerve in my body senses his presence, longing for the electricity his touch brings. I don't have to wait very long because, within seconds, he's cupping my face, bringing his lips to mine.

The moment is wordless, but we're communicating perfectly.

The tenderness of his touch says *I missed you*. The parting of my lips says, *welcome home*.

I revel in this kiss, forgetting his anger and my annoyance, focusing only on how our bodies react to each other.

We're both panting by the time he pulls away. "That's how I

should've greeted you tonight."

"I would have preferred that," I say breathlessly. "How did you know I was listening?"

He smiles, turning the computer monitor so I can see it. The screen shows the feed from surveillance cameras that seem to cover the whole property. He points to the small box that shows the outside of his office.

I was impossible to miss.

"After you overheard the call with your father, I decided it would be best to watch the feed."

I'm not surprised that Joshua has cameras around the house, but I feel silly for never noticing them before.

"I should've known you'd be curious," he says as he wraps an arm around my waist and tugs me to his side. "Come on, let's get you ready for bed."

I let Joshua lead me upstairs, loving how he keeps a possessive hold on me the whole way. I remember how he did this back at the base and how it felt like I was doing something wrong by letting him touch me.

It doesn't feel wrong now.

He stops us at the threshold of my door. "Are you still wearing bandages?"

"No, Ryder's just been putting some cream on the scars."

"I'll go get it."

By the time he returns, I've set up the chairs and am sitting shirtless, covering my chest with the large button-up I've chosen to wear to sleep.

With my arms crossed over the back of the chair, I lay my head on them and close my eyes. After days of nothing but watching TV, hanging out with the capos tonight has drained my energy.

"Tired?" Joshua asks, closing the door and walking to the chair behind me.

"Mmm."

His low chuckle fills the room as he gets to work, and the sound, mixed with his delicate touch, makes the pull of sleep even stronger.

I fight against my exhaustion and ask, "Joshua?"

"Yes, Princess?"

"Are you really making Ryder leave?"

"No, I'm not, *Elli*," he says slowly, testing the nickname on his lips. "Don't call me that."

"Why not?"

I turn my head until I find his mesmerizing eyes that look down on me with all the care in the world. "I like my name on your lips."

His dashing smile sends my heart racing, and I have trouble remembering what we'd been talking about.

"How come Ryder called you Joshua? I've only ever heard him call you *'Mr. Moreno'*."

"It's a respect thing. He'll only call me by my first name if we're in private. Someone's inquisitive tonight."

"A little," I admit. "I have one more question."

"And what's that?" He puts the supplies away, and I button up my shirt.

"Is he right? Are you jealous?"

Joshua freezes, and I can't see his face to read if it's due to anger or surprise.

After a long moment, he places the first aid kit down and turns to face me.

When his searing eyes meet mine, I'm only partially relieved to find that there's no anger there, but the look of pure, dominant possession scares me just as much.

Slowly—too slowly—he lowers himself to his knees until we're face to face.

"Do I strike you as the type of man that likes to share?" The huskiness of his voice causes my heart to flutter.

"No," I whisper.

"I don't want anyone to touch what's mine, and you, Elise, are *mine*."

I should tell him he's wrong. I don't belong to him. I don't belong to *anyone*.

But I'm not so sure that's true.

Our lips meet, and the familiar energy sparks to life, igniting an all-consuming desire for him.

I lean forward in the chair, wrapping my arms around his neck and pulling him close to me. He keeps a firm hold on me as he rises, and I instinctively wrap my legs around his waist. With one hand circled beneath my bottom and the other weaved into my hair, Joshua carries me to the bed.

He turns before laying us down so his back is against the bed, and I'm flush against his hard chest. Deepening the kiss, I gasp as he takes my bottom lip in his mouth, tugging deliciously on it.

I move one hand down to his waist, splaying my fingers beneath his shirt and slowly trailing my hand up. His skin is warm, and every ridge of his stomach and chest is meticulously defined muscle.

Joshua groans, pulling away just enough to say, "You're going to kill me, you know that?"

"Sounds like I should've tried this method weeks ago," I murmur against his lips.

His soft laugh is addictive. "If kissing you is what finally takes me out, I'll die a very happy man."

I hum against his mouth. "I'll just have to keep trying, then."

His response is to nip at my ear, tugging lightly as I laugh. After another quick kiss, he sits up, pulling me with him.

"How have you been sleeping?" he asks, stroking my cheek affectionately.

I almost tell him I haven't been sleeping well but pause when I remember the night he slept beside me—the only night when there were no nightmares at all.

"What?" he asks.

I bite my lip absentmindedly and scold myself. I really need to get a handle on my facial expressions around him. Joshua doesn't miss a thing.

"It's nothing."

"Elise, tell me."

"No, I haven't been sleeping well."

"And?"

Blood rushes to my cheeks. "There was one night that I didn't have any nightmares…"

"When?"

I avert my eyes, sure he's already guessed the answer.

"Elise." My name is a command on his lips.

My voice is barely a whisper. "The night you slept with me, back at the base."

A gentle finger raises my chin until I stare into his adoring eyes. An intensity burns there that would bring me to my knees if I wasn't already sitting.

"Then I'll sleep beside you," he says simply.

I'm speechless, which is okay because he doesn't give me the chance to say anything. Pressing a short but sweet kiss to my lips, Joshua stands and takes off his shirt and shoes.

He's stunning, muscles flexing across his tanned and toned body.

If I didn't know that he spends most of his time locked away in his office, I'd think all he does is work out and sunbathe.

Joshua turns the lights off and climbs into bed behind me.

"Thank you," I whisper.

"Anything for you, Princess," he says, kissing my temple. "You should sleep. You have a big day tomorrow."

"I do?"

"Mmm-hmm." Raising his head, Joshua glances at the clock that reads midnight. "Happy birthday, Elise."

CHAPTER TWENTY-NINE

Joshua

Before I even open my eyes, I feel her beside me.

Elise moved away from me in the night but subconsciously placed her hand on my chest, and I'm glad she's not awake to feel how fast my heart is beating. Her thick hair is splayed across the pillow, and her usually expressive features are peaceful.

It had always been my plan to return in time for her birthday, but getting everything in order so I could work from here took longer than I'd hoped.

I'm sure Elise wasn't expecting me to know about her birthday, or maybe in the craziness that her life has become, she forgot about it altogether. Either way, I intend to use the occasion as an opportunity to show her that I can make her happy.

She stirs beside me, and after a glance at the clock, I decide it's time to start the day.

I press a light kiss on her forehead. "Time to wake up, Princess."

She groans, turning away from me.

"Come on, we have a big day."

"Let me sleep," she grumbles.

"You've slept long enough. It's almost nine," I say, sitting up against the headboard.

When she looks at me, it's the same expression she wore the morning we woke up together at the base, like she's memorizing my every feature as if I'll disappear at any moment.

Well, I'm not going anywhere.

"How did you sleep last night?"

Her lips pull into a small smile. "No nightmares."

She sleeps better with me. After everything that's happened between us, I have the power to give her peaceful sleep.

Damn. That feels good.

"Guess I'm sleeping here from now on."

"If I don't kick you out for waking me up too early."

"Don't be dramatic. You're going to want to get up and get ready. We're going out today," I tell her, awaiting her reaction.

"Outside?"

I shake my head. "Out in public."

Her eyes double in size, and she rises to sit. "Like public, public? With real people?"

I nod. "We leave at ten-thirty."

"To go where?"

"You'll see," I say and wait for the question.

"You're not afraid I'll run away?"

There it is.

"Well"—my hand falls to her waist, and I rub lazy circles there—"the way I see it, we made a deal. You stay for a month, and I let you choose what you do from there. If, for some reason, you did decide to run, you'd be breaking your end of the deal, which would entitle me to break mine. As long as you intend to uphold your end of the bargain, I see no reason why we can't enjoy a day out."

A small hand rests over mine. "I'm not going to run."

My chest tightens at her words, and I wish it were as easy as believing them, but I can't—not after what I've seen.

Elise is a horrible liar, so I know she means what she says, but words don't mean much in the face of opportunity. Still, I can't keep her trapped in here forever.

Ryder's words from last night still ring as clear as a bell.

Are you going to take away everything that makes her happy aside from you? That'll only make her resent you.

I hate it when he's right.

Forty-five minutes later, I walk into my office, where Ryder and the capos are already seated.

I take the seat behind my desk. "Is everything at the warehouse in place?"

Alec nods. "We're the only ones with access to that area."

"Good. That stays top-level security only." I turn to Donovan. "I'll be out with Elise today, and I want our four best guys on security. Definitely Finn and Luke, but you can pick the others."

"Yes, sir."

"Kade, any word on who gave Elise the note?"

He shakes his head. "I'm still working on it. The footage is gone, so I've just been taking testimonies."

"Don't stop until you find something."

"Sir, the best place to start would be talking to Elise."

"She stays out of this."

Kade lifts a placating hand. "I'm just saying, she may recognize one of our men—"

"She stays out of this," I repeat. "End of conversation."

He nods, knowing better than to push.

Of course, he's right. Elise is the best person to help us locate the traitor, but after her panic attacks and breakdowns, I've decided to leave her out of it completely. She needs more time to heal.

"That's all for now. We'll be back late afternoon. Don, have the guys you're sending come to my office in twenty minutes." Don nods, and everyone stands from their chairs.

"Ryder, stay."

The door swings shut, leaving Ryder and me alone. His posture is rigid, and I'm sure he's still mad about last night.

Well, I am too.

"You're staying here today. I want a list of candidates for the vacant capo position, but put Warren in charge of the recruits for the time being."

"I take it this means you're not sending me back to the base?"

"Take it as a warning. I respect that you're protective of Elise, but she's mine. When I give an order, I need to be able to trust that you're going to follow it. Otherwise, I won't let you near her. Don't let what happened last night happen again, understood?"

"Yes, sir."

Half an hour later, the men running security for our outing leave my office, and I hear Elise's soft voice among the guys. Though I can't make out what she's saying, she doesn't sound happy, and I wonder what she's found to be upset about now.

Lucky me.

As expected, it's only moments later that I watch her approach the office door through the security camera. When she reaches out, she hesitates before knocking, second-guessing whatever it is she wants to talk to me about.

She must decide it's worth it because, after a deep breath, she knocks on the door.

"Come in," I call.

She enters the room, and any sign of her wariness is gone. If it weren't for the fact that I watched her demeanor change from the footage, I wouldn't know that she's definitely up to something.

Her eyes wander up and down my body, and I don't hide my satisfied smile as I let my eyes do the same to her. Her light jeans and a gray tank top cling to her body perfectly, but it makes me look overdressed in my black slacks and white button-up. Her limited clothing options are certainly less than ideal.

"Ready to leave?" I ask her.

"Can we talk first?"

"About?"

She approaches the desk. "I want Ryder to come with us today."

So, that's what this is about.

My jaw ticks, but that's the only sign of my frustration. "Ryder has work to do here."

Elise takes one slow step after the other around my desk, trailing her hand along the oak wood as she does. The motion is mesmerizing, almost... seductive.

"Surely he can do it later, right?"

I eye her warily. "Unfortunately not."

She looks up at me through thick lashes. "Come on, Joshua. It's my birthday."

"I've already selected the men who are joining us today. Ryder is staying here."

She takes the final step so she's directly in front of me and places one hand on my chest. "Would it be so difficult to make the arrangements?"

"You're playing with fire, Princess," I warn. "Careful, or you'll get burned."

She feigns innocence. "I'm only asking for my friend to come along, that's all."

She reaches her other hand to my chest, but I grab hold of her wrists in one hand before it makes contact and use my other to wrap around her waist, lifting her to the desk. Once she's situated between my legs, I place my arms on either side of her, effectively trapping her there.

"I think I've made my decision clear, have I not?"

She lifts her arms, and I think she's about to push me away, but her arms wrap around my neck as she absentmindedly plays with my hair.

Damn, that feels good.

"I think I've made my preference clear, have I not?"

I hold her taunting glare for a long moment, equally annoyed and proud that she doesn't cower or flinch away.

"Ryder can come but only as security," I relent, straightening when she drops her arms.

"Thank you!" she says, face lighting up as she leans in and kisses me.

I deepen the kiss, taking her bottom lip between my teeth and biting down just hard enough that Elise squeaks in surprise.

When I pull back, her face is bright red with a growing blush. "What was that for?"

"Teasing me," I tell her. "And it was generous. It wouldn't be wise for you to do it again, understood?"

She curls her lip in, poorly suppressing a smile. "Understood."

"Could you send Ryder in?" I ask as she hops off the desk.

"Sure," she chimes, closing the door behind her.

Ryder walks in only a minute later. "What can I do for you?"

I curse myself for being unable to deny Elise anything.

"You're coming as security today."

He nods. "She's almost as stubborn as her father."

He's damn right about that.

I take a deep breath, knowing before I even open my mouth that Ryder isn't going to like what I'm about to tell him.

"I just met with the soldiers coming today, and there are a few things you need to know before we go."

We're twenty minutes into our drive, and Elise hasn't said a single word. At first, I thought she was just tired, but as we approach civilization, she begins fiddling with the hem of her shirt.

I rest one hand on her thigh. "You okay?"

"Overwhelmed."

There's a twinge of guilt at the fact that something as mundane as driving through town overwhelms her after so long in isolation. Fortunately for me, my guilt is greatly outweighed by the satisfaction of having her here with me.

"Where are we?" she asks suddenly.

"Where do you think we are?"

"California," she says without missing a beat. "I just can't figure out which part."

Perceptive little Elise.

"The house is a few miles outside Redding," I tell her.

"Why do you have a place this far north? Your closest base is in Sacramento."

I'm starting to realize that I haven't given Elise enough credit. She continues to surprise me.

"I bought the house a few months after Marsollo's death when I was negotiating terms with the capos who kept his name. It made a good halfway point, so I come up now and then to meet with them."

"So, when you told me you'd come to Milwaukee from California, you weren't lying."

"I also told the truth when I said I was coming back on Monday." I throw her a wink and she laughs, relaxing in her seat for the first time since getting in the car.

We pull into the parking lot, and her jaw drops when she surveys our surroundings. "A mall? What are we doing here?"

"I figured it's time you pick out your own wardrobe."

"Are you serious?"

My answer is to climb out of the driver's seat and round the car to open her door. My hand hovers, and she takes it without a second glance.

Ryder's car pulls up beside us, and the four men climb out, immediately dispersing to blend in with the crowd. I watch Elise, but her eyes wander to every person as she inspects them, fascinated by the normality after so long.

I gently squeeze her hand. "Lead the way, Princess."

"What's my budget?" Of course, she'd ask something like that.

"There isn't one."

"No budget?"

"None."

When her lighthearted smile turns mischievous, I know I've made a mistake.

She pulls me alongside her, and we walk into the building. With a glance around, she spots a directory and studies it. She must find whatever it is she's looking for because before I know it, we're off again.

When we approach the storefront, I know exactly what her plan is. "Are you sure about this?"

She nods. "No point in hiding anymore."

With that, she walks to the front counter of the hair salon, and I trail behind her.

"I'd like a cut and color," Elise informs the receptionist.

The pale girl looks to be in her early thirties with a platinum blonde pixie cut and mousy features. Her face screws up into a bitter smile. "We're all booked for the day. Besides, we schedule weeks in advance for something that time-consuming."

I take a step forward, and Elise must sense my presence because her hand reaches back to halt my approach.

"I'll give every employee in your salon a five-hundred-dollar tip in addition to the fee if you can get me in right now."

Next time, I'm giving her a budget.

The woman's eyes double in size, and she wordlessly opens and closes her mouth like a fish out of water. When her disbelieving gaze trails to mine, I give a tight nod, confirming the validity of Elise's offer.

"Um, let me see what I can do for you," she squeaks and nearly jogs to the back.

"Five hundred dollars each? Are you insane?"

"I thought I didn't have a budget," she says with an innocent head tilt.

"My mistake."

The receptionist is back within minutes. "Right this way, ma'am. Your boyfriend can come back with you if you'd like."

Elise hesitates, and it wouldn't take a mind-reader to know she was about to correct the woman on our titles. I have no interest in being Elise's boyfriend, but I suppose for the sake of convenience, it's the best term. Elise must agree because she doesn't comment.

"That's okay, he can wait—"

"I'd love to. Thank you," I interject, unwilling to leave Elise's side.

She gives me her *are you serious* look, but I don't dignify it with a response.

Two hours later, we're walking out of the salon with a significant amount of money taken from my bank account and Elise's new look. I'd been skeptical when she told the stylist what she wanted, but, damn, she's beautiful.

All traces of blonde are gone, replaced by a dark chestnut color that already makes her look more like her family. Her hair, which used to fall to her mid-back, is cut just below her shoulders. Before we left, the stylist insisted on curling her hair, a look I've never seen on Elise, but it suits her.

She's gorgeous.

The next three hours are spent walking in and out of stores, each time with more and more bags that I make my men carry out to the car. I'd underestimated Elise's ability to shop. She hadn't struck me as the type who likes to buy clothes, but I suppose after everything she's endured, retail therapy is the least she deserves.

My phone buzzes in my pocket, and I glance down to see the message from Ryder.

Ryder: The guys are ready whenever you give the signal. I still don't think this is a good idea, but we're all in place.

Ryder made his opinion perfectly clear, but that doesn't change the fact that I have to do this.

"Which one?" Elise asks, pulling me from my thoughts. She holds up the same pair of shoes in two different colors.

"Does it matter?"

She rolls her eyes. "Of course, it matters. If I wear a white top, the brown will match better, but if I—"

"Just get them both," I exclaim, and she laughs.

Glad *someone's* amused.

We walk around the store, and the next section we stop at is bras and underwear.

"Now, this is something I'm happy to share my opinion on." I arch a suggestive brow.

Elise brushes her dark locks over her shoulder, though they fall back almost immediately. "I think I can handle this on my own."

Looking back at my phone, I decide to use this as my chance.

"Actually, I'm stepping outside to make a call," I say, and dig into my wallet to hand her my card. "Come out whenever you're done."

She nods, and I place a gentle kiss on her forehead before turning to go. My chest is tight with nerves, and I hope I'm not about to screw up all the progress we've made.

Time to see how Elise's words fare in the face of opportunity.

CHAPTER THIRTY

Elise

My blood boils. Did he really think this was a good idea? Did he think that I wouldn't know what he was doing?

I'll admit, there was a moment when I imagined what it'd be like to run, but I wouldn't have done it.

I don't want to.

So, why Joshua felt the need to do this is beyond me.

When I'd left the store with my new purchases, Joshua, Ryder, and the other soldiers were gone. My eyes fell to the exit immediately, so close and completely unguarded, but this isn't an opportunity to run.

It's a test.

Well, if he wants to play games, that's fine.

Game on.

Thinking fast, I turn a confused gaze downward to the bag I hold in my hand. I take out the receipt and study it, shaking my head. I turn on my heels and walk back into the store.

Hopefully, Joshua buys the act from wherever he's hiding and assumes I'm going in to fix something with my purchase.

I walk far enough into the store that no one from the outside can see me and cast a glance around. An employee in the back section catches my eye—a short teenager trying to hide the fact that she's texting on her phone.

She's perfect for what I have in mind.

"Excuse me," I timidly greet.

The girl, Taylor, according to her name tag, jumps at the sound of my voice. Her cheeks turn a bright shade of red, and she tucks her phone into her pocket. "Oh my goodness, I'm so sorry! How can I help you, ma'am?"

My warm laugh seems to calm her.

"Don't worry about it. Actually, I have a favor to ask." I make a show of looking behind me and lower my voice. "My ex-boyfriend is right outside, and I think he's stalking me."

Her eyes go wide, and I work hard to maintain my composure.

"I'm pretty sure he's going to come in here looking for me. Is there a back exit I could use?"

"Yes!" Her whisper-shout draws the attention of a few customers, but we ignore them. "Come with me. It's right over here."

"Thank you so much."

Walking to the back, she takes me to a door that reads 'Employees Only' and we step inside.

"Past the storage room is the exit. It leads right out to the parking lot." Taylor points behind me before turning to go.

"Taylor," I call before she walks away. "My ex can be really… aggressive. If he comes in here looking for me, there's a chance he'll become hostile."

Taylor's mouth gapes.

"You should probably call security now, just in case. He's wearing black slacks and a white button-up. He has really dark hair, and he'll probably have two or three other guys with him. I'm really sorry about this."

Her head shakes furiously. "No need to be sorry. Don't worry about a thing. I'll call security right now."

I place my hand over my heart. "You're a lifesaver."

After sharing a warm smile, Taylor and I part ways. When I open the door and step outside, I don't even try to hold back my laughter.

As she said, the door leads to the parking lot, but to my right, there's another row of stores with entrances on the outside of the building. Compared to the inside of the mall, not many people roam this area.

There's no telling how much time I have before Joshua starts to freak out, but I figure it'll be just long enough for a much-needed manicure. I slip into the nail salon tucked between the comic book store and sandwich shop, and there are only two other customers inside.

The woman at the front counter gives me a welcoming smile. She looks old enough to be my mom, but her smile is youthful, and her silky black hair is pulled into a stylish low ponytail.

She introduces herself as Clara, helps me pick my color, then takes me to a seat and tends to me herself.

"You're not from around here, are you?" she asks.

"That obvious?"

She laughs, and it sounds like bells. "What brings you to Cali?"

I consider my answer before giving it to her. "A boy."

Her thin eyebrows shoot up. "Oh no. Everyone knows following a boy always leads to heartbreak."

I breathe a laugh. "Well, I didn't have much choice in the matter."

"I suppose the heart wants what the heart wants," she says with a dreamy sigh. "Oh, to be young and in love."

Love? I'm not in love, right? Wouldn't I know if I was? My stomach twists with uncertainty, and I spend the rest of the manicure debating the term and its relevance to my relationship.

What Joshua and I have is strong, so if it isn't love, what is it?

I know as soon as I swipe the card—leaving a 500% tip—that Joshua will track the purchase, but I figure I've taunted him enough.

I sign the receipt and head out the door, strutting to the car just around the corner. It's a miracle that I make it there without a single one of Joshua's soldiers in sight, but it just means my plan was effective.

The cars are both locked, so I lean back against one and wait for the inevitable.

I'd forgotten how relaxing people-watching could be. Or maybe it's just the fact that I haven't been out in public for weeks. Either way, it makes me feel unbelievably normal to see these people going about their days.

A large, familiar figure bursts through the door and jogs in my direction.

Ryder.

When he sees me leaning against the car, he stops, lifting his phone to his ear and saying a few words before stalking the rest of the way toward me. I can see from here that he's irritated, but I still flash him a cheeky grin.

"What took so long?"

Ryder shakes his head. "He's going to kill you."

He's probably right, but I still laugh.

"Where the hell were you?"

I wiggle my cherry red nails. "Made a pit stop."

He rubs his temple like he's fighting a major headache. "You are unbelievable."

"He started it by wanting to test me in the first place."

"I knew you wouldn't like it, but I didn't think you'd do *this*. You two are infuriating."

I'm about to throw back a reminder that I haven't given anyone a reason to test me in the first place when I catch sight of Joshua storming out of the mall.

His glare is visible from here, but it doesn't scare me like it used to. I square my shoulders and match his stare head-on.

When he's only a few yards away, my lip turns up. "Thank goodness you got out of there," I say, and cup my hand around my mouth. "I hear there's a stalker ex-boyfriend inside."

"You've *got* to be kidding me," Ryder mutters.

My taunt is the last straw, and in an instant, Joshua is pinning me to the car. His body is hard against mine, and when I look up into his fiery eyes, my heart flips in my chest.

"Go." Joshua barks, and the men get in their car. Ryder shoots me a warning glance before he climbs in and drives away.

I turn my attention to the seething man caging me between his muscular arms.

"Mall security? Are you kidding me?"

I stifle a laugh.

"You think this is funny?"

He's making it seem like *I'm* the one who started this.

"What right do you have to be mad? I'm the one being tested like a child! Might as well put a tracker on me if you're so worried about me running away."

Just when I think he's going to snap at me again, Joshua pushes off the door and takes a step back. I stay still, giving him a moment to cool off.

A hand runs through his hair, and his muscles flex under the white button-up. The few buttons are undone at the top, giving me a perfect view of his hard chest.

"Get in the car," he says, voice deadly low.

His demand snaps me out of my staring, and I cross my arms over my chest. "Not until you tell me why you're mad."

His fists curl into tight balls, and his voice carries over the parking lot. "Get in the car, Elise."

"Tell me why—"

"Because I thought you left!" he snaps. "I needed to see for myself what you would do if you had another chance to get away, and I thought you took it. I thought you were gone."

For a second, I'm speechless. His eyes, so ablaze with fury, work to conceal what he's really feeling.

Fear.

When I still don't say anything, he rakes another hand through his hair.

"Please, get in the car." His voice is softer now, and I don't even think of arguing.

I climb in and patiently wait for him to settle beside me. He starts the car but makes no move to drive away.

"What did you mean by '*another chance to get away*'?"

"You know what I mean."

My mind races, but I come up empty-handed. I've never been given a chance to escape, and I know because I probably would've taken it.

Joshua shakes his head, exasperated. "The window in the bathroom by the kitchen, Elise."

My heart nearly stops. I thought I was in the clear, that no one would ever know what I nearly attempted to do.

"How do you know about that?"

"While I was at the base, I had some guys go back through security footage by the kitchen. They were looking to see where Tripp went after he was supposed to leave the base, but they found this." He turns his phone toward me.

The video was taken from right above the kitchen door, able to capture the whole scene. It shows me coming out of the kitchen, scanning the area for watchful eyes, then running to the bathroom.

"I thought it was strange, so I checked the cameras outside that bathroom." He swipes to the next video. This one clearly shows the window opening, and my thoughtful face is barely visible through it. My heart sinks as I realize the key information that this video has given me.

There's no barrier in sight.

If I had climbed through that window, I would've been free.

If I had taken that opportunity, I wouldn't have been slapped, whipped, and nearly raped by Tripp. I wouldn't have been dragged away to Joshua's house to learn that my father didn't want me anymore. I would be free.

But if I had taken that opportunity, I also wouldn't have been held by Joshua during our movie night. I wouldn't have learned so much about his family and his past. I wouldn't know how desperately I crave his touch and his kiss. I wouldn't know that he wants me the way I want him.

Is it possible to feel regret and content at the same time?

"Why did you stay?" he asks in a whisper.

I recall the mental battle that had taken place that day. Two voices warring in my brain—one telling me to run far away and never look back, the other pleading with me to stay.

"I'm not completely sure. A part of me wanted to stay in case my dad was coming for me, but…"

A gentle finger lifts my chin. "But?"

If I was still looking down at my hands, I might be able to tell him that it was only about my father and planning the perfect escape, but when those deep brown eyes bore into mine like I'm the only person in the entire world who matters, I can't do anything but tell the truth.

"But the other part of me wanted to stay with you."

The words drain all tension from the car.

Suddenly, Joshua has me out of my seat and on his lap. Our lips mold to one another as we work out the remaining aggression.

There's an urgency to the kiss. His relief that I stayed, and my surprise that he thinks I *could* leave.

Can't he tell by the way my body melts into his that I am just as helpless as he is?

When Joshua finally pulls away, his eyes burn into mine. "Don't doubt for one second that I'm above putting a tracker on you. If I had it my way, you would, but I'm working very hard to control myself."

"You're such a caveman," I say, and scramble back to my seat as Joshua pulls the car out of the lot.

We drive for a half hour before Joshua pulls onto an unmarked road.

"Where are we going?"

He taps his finger against the steering wheel in time with the music. "Lunch."

"Here?" I ask.

There's no building, car, or person in sight, only trees.

"Yes, here."

When Joshua stops the car, I don't notice anything particularly special about where we are. It's just the end of a dirt road surrounded by tall trees and wildflowers.

"You better not be planning to murder me in the woods on my birthday." I climb out of the car and give him a playful side-glare.

His light laughter echoes around us. "And let all those clothes go to waste? No, I think I'll save murder for another day."

Joshua opens the trunk and takes out a large basket and a jacket that he slides on. When I raise my eyebrow, he only holds out his hand. I take it and let him lead me to the tree line.

The path he takes us on is obscure, and I probably wouldn't have noticed it if he hadn't shown me. Neither of us is dressed for a hike, so I don't expect us to go far, and I'm right.

Stepping out from behind a wall of trees, I'm faced with the most incredible view I have ever seen.

Miles of land lay beneath us, covered in a sea of green leaves that rustle in the wind like waves rolling onto shore. What I assume is the Sacramento River winds through the trees. I can make just barely out people near the water, as small as ants from here, taking their tourist photos and enjoying the beauty same as Joshua and me. A mountain rests in the distance, so tall that white snow drapes gracefully over its peak.

"This is beautiful," I murmur. "How did you find this place?"

"I can't take the credit," he admits, resting a hand on my waist. I tear my eyes from the view to gaze at him which is just as captivating. "Donovan grew up in Redding, so he knew about this spot. He told me about it when I needed a quiet place."

"If he grew up in Redding, how did he get to be one of your capos?"

"Donovan joined the Marsollo family a few years after I did to make enough money to pay off his dad's gambling debt. At first, he made drug runs between some of the bases, but word of his talent for strategic planning made its way to Marsollo and me, so he was promoted and moved to Sacramento. When a drug deal got busted, Don became the fall guy and was facing twenty years in prison."

"Isn't that excessive?"

Joshua shrugs. "He'd been on their radar long enough to justify it and they wanted to make an example out of him. When I heard about it, I pulled some strings to get him off the hook, and I brought him to L.A. to work with me. He's talented and now more loyal than ever. Once Marsollo died, making Donovan a capo was a no-brainer."

He says the words like they're no big deal like he didn't save

Donovan from wasting away in a cell for twenty years. In most mafia families, loyalty comes from blood and reputation.

Joshua earned the loyalty of his men through friendship and respect.

It puts Joshua in a light that I've never seen him in before, as a savior instead of a monster that hides under the bed.

I gesture to the basket he places on the ground. "What's that?"

"I had Jay pack us a picnic for lunch," he explains, laying out a blanket that must have been inside.

"Where are the others?"

Joshua takes out containers of food, placing them down between us, along with two wine glasses.

"They went back to the house," he says, pouring us each a generous amount of wine.

"No security then?"

"I think we're safe out here."

Sipping from my glass, I raise an eyebrow. "So, all I need to do is incapacitate you to make my escape?"

He sits up so he's towering over me. "Hit me with your best shot, Princess."

I place my hands on his chest as if to push him away, but instead, I take fistfuls of his shirt and pull him closer, bringing my lips to his. The taste of wine mixes with him, and it's the sweetest thing I've ever tasted.

We eat in peace, enjoying the stunning view and listening to the gentle rustling of leaves and the singing birds as they fly overhead. The entire scene is like something out of a fairytale, right down to the villain-turned-prince.

It makes me think of my family and how today would be going if I was home.

My birthday hasn't *always* been a bittersweet occasion.

When I was younger, my father and brothers would take me to an authentic Italian restaurant, where we'd all share massive plates of spaghetti. Afterward, we'd go home, have cookie cake, open presents, and watch the original Jumanji.

For years, I adored the simple traditions, but in my adult years, they've become redundant.

When I moved out, it was like my relationship with my family froze. Instead of growing and changing as I did, it was as though my brothers only ever saw the seventeen-year-old version of me, never getting to know the woman I became.

The dinner outing, cookie cake, and movie seemed more like tasks on an old checklist than a celebration. I stopped looking forward to my birthday years ago.

"What are you thinking about?"

"My family." I look at Joshua, smiling half-heartedly. "I wonder what they're doing today."

Deliberation wages behind his eyes.

"What?"

He takes a deep breath. "They're having a memorial service."

I almost laugh, but it's not funny at all.

For the second time in less than a decade, my family is standing over my empty grave. My chest hurts as I picture it. At least the first time, they all knew it was fake. This time, their grief is real.

"So, they really think I'm dead..." I muse. "Does Mason know that I'm alive?"

"No, he doesn't."

"Why not?"

"Elise," he warns, "it's family business."

"And it concerns *my* family." I place my palm against his cheek. "Please, Joshua?"

Our silent standoff lasts only a few seconds before he shakes his head. "You really will be the death of me. This isn't information you're meant to have."

Nodding, I cuddle closer to him.

"I haven't spoken with your brother in a while. Things have become... *complicated*. The fact that I had no idea your father was going to cancel our negotiations means one of two things: either Mason knew and didn't tell me, or your father deliberately never told *him*. I don't know if your father chose to keep his intentions secret because he knew your brothers wouldn't allow him to give you up or if he's suspicious of Mason. Regardless, it's not safe to communicate with him right now."

"You think my dad lied to my brothers about my death?"

He nods. "I can't be sure, but I assume your father told them I murdered you. I can't imagine he would've admitted to telling me to do it."

I process his words, trying to contain the bitterness I still feel toward my traitorous father and snake of a brother.

As I think about my deceptive sibling, I remember he isn't the only inside man involved in our situation.

"Did you ever find who left me the note?"

He tenses around me. "Have you ever heard the saying 'ignorance is bliss'?"

"I just… I was wondering if you killed him… like Tripp."

"No, I haven't found him yet. The footage of who brought you food that day has disappeared. Right now, I have no leads. As for what happens when I do find him, well, that's nothing you need to worry about, Princess."

Joshua places a soothing kiss on my forehead, and a warm feeling spreads through me.

I'm not sure if it's the wine or the complicated situation life has put me in, but my throat is thick with emotion, so I do the only thing that feels natural—I lean into Joshua.

Being held by him has quickly become my favorite feeling in the world.

Closing my eyes, I imagine an alternate universe—one where my family is normal. My dad is a banker or maybe a doctor, and we'd all come together for a *real* family dinner.

My brothers enter one by one, their wives and children joining them. They'd tease one another and compare stories about work. Then the doorbell would ring, and I'd open the door to reveal my handsome boyfriend.

In my mind, Joshua is a businessman, innocent of criminal activity but still ruthless. He'd come inside, and I'd introduce him to my family. At first, they'd give him a hard time, maybe some smart comments and cold looks, but as the night went on, they'd warm up to him and welcome him into the family.

The fantasy is so sweet, but it's just that, a fantasy. As much as I'd love to be normal, that's not who we are.

"What's on your mind?" he asks, and his husky voice calls me from my daydream.

"It's silly."

"And?"

I relent with a heavy sigh. "I was thinking about what it'd be like to have it all. My brothers, my father… and you."

Having expected him to laugh or offer some sarcastic comment, I'm surprised when Joshua's expression is guarded. It's a look that usually means he has something to say, and I won't like it.

"Joshua, what is it?"

He scoops me up and sets me on his lap, holding me so close I wonder if he's worried I'll try to run away.

"I need you to hear me out."

"Hear what out? You're starting to scare me."

"There is a way."

"What do you mean?"

"There is a way to have it all—your family and me."

"How?"

"Marry me."

CHAPTER THIRTY-ONE

Elise

There's no way I heard him correctly because if I did, that means Joshua has officially lost his mind.

"Excuse me?"

"Marry me, Elise."

Yeah, he's insane.

I try to scramble off his lap, but his grip on me tightens.

"Let me go!" I struggle against his chest to no avail.

"Just listen to me."

But I can't breathe.

Joshua finally loosens his hold with a huff, and I clamber off him.

"Calm down, you—"

"Calm down? You just asked me to marry you, and now you're telling me to *calm down*? I know you're new to relationships, but you're skipping a few steps. I barely know you."

He opens his mouth to speak, but I don't let him. "This is insane, Joshua. You can't expect me to just—"

"Would you shut up for five seconds and let me explain?"

It's a tone I know all too well from our fights, and though it doesn't scare me, it does effectively silence my objections.

"Better. Now, I'm going to explain, and you're going to listen," he informs me.

I cross my arms over my chest but nod.

"I am fully aware that this is unorthodox, but to be fair, that's how things have been for us from the start."

He has a point.

"You said you want to have it all—your family, your life, and me, right?"

I nod again.

"Then this is the only way. If you and I were to be married, it would act as a sort of…treaty with your father. A union like that would bring our families into an alliance that could benefit everyone. As allies, you'd be free to see your family, and more than that, Mason wouldn't exactly be a traitor."

The words bounce around my head, and I try to make sense of what he's telling me.

"Elise," he says, and his tone softens at the conflict in my expression. "This could be really good for our families."

There it is. The real reason he's doing all of this.

"So, nothing's changed."

"What?"

"You don't want me."

Genuine confusion twists his face. "What are you talking about?"

"You only said you were falling in love with me because your original blackmail plan didn't work. But if I marry you, you get what you want anyway. This was all just another way to use me as a pawn against my father."

Joshua gapes like I've slapped him across the face.

"Are you out of your damn mind?"

The intensity in his tone has me taking a step back, but he's not having that. Striding toward me, Joshua grips my shoulders before I can get very far.

"Do you *honestly* believe that?"

I can't bring myself to do anything but stare wide-eyed into his fiery gaze.

"Dammit, Elise, answer me! Do you honestly believe I'm using you right now?"

"I—I don't know!"

His lips crash violently against mine, devouring me with every ounce of the aggression his tone carried. My reaction is the same as it always is when his lips meet mine—I give myself to him.

My arms wrap around his neck, and that familiar warmth seeps through my clothes, soothing the very core of my being. The same peace I always feel from his touch eases the uncertainty waging in my heart.

Joshua breaks the kiss. "Tell me you believe it now."

I'm gasping for breath, unable to do anything but stare helplessly at him.

"Don't question my feelings for you again, understand?"

My head nods on its own as though my body knows what my mind is still learning—Joshua's feelings for me are genuine.

"I'm not using you to get to your father. I have no intention of taking the territories that I was originally after. My *only* intention is to have you."

"Really?"

"Really."

Joshua lets go of my shoulders and takes my hand, leading me back to the blanket. We sit and he lies me down so my head rests in his lap. His fingers run absentmindedly through my hair, and the gesture calms my still-racing heart.

"If an alliance would benefit both families, then why wasn't that your original plan?"

"I wasn't trying to benefit both families. I was trying to benefit *my* family. I wanted power, not a partnership." His hand lightly brushes my cheek. "But now I want you, and the only way to do that without starting a war is an alliance."

"Why marriage? Can't you just negotiate an agreement?"

His lip turns up. "Your father wants to kill me. After everything that's happened, he won't agree to anything I have to offer. Marriage, however, is a union strong enough to persuade him. He'd be forced to legitimately consider making a deal."

"Are you saying there's a chance he'll ignore it and try to kill you anyway?"

"A chance I'm willing to take for you."

Well, I asked for a way to have it all, and Joshua is offering me just that. So then, why do I feel so conflicted?

"You don't have to decide right now," he tells me.

"How long do I have?"

"Well, you promised me a month. At the end of that time, you can choose to go, but if you stay—"

"If I stay, we get married," I finish, and he nods. "How long have you known it would come to this?"

"Since I asked you to stay," he admits. "I was waiting for the right time to talk to you about it. And I was waiting for this—"

He reaches into his jacket pocket and I sit up at the same time Joshua pulls out a small box.

My heart leaps in my chest when he opens it to reveal the most beautiful ring I have ever seen. The round diamond is the size of a pea. Its intricate cuts catch the sun's light and cast rainbows onto the forest floor. The band is shining silver, with smaller diamond studs lining it all the way around.

"I know this is a lot to take in, but you should know what's waiting for you at the end of this month."

He takes my hand in his, pulling my attention from the stunning ring to his earnest gaze.

I've never seen this look on Joshua before, this pure, raw need. Like he'll burn down cities and slaughter anyone standing in his way —and it would scare me if I wasn't absolutely positive that every ounce of this intensity is dedicated to wanting me.

"Elise, I am in love with you. You're not a pawn in a game. You're the woman I love and the woman I intend to marry."

"I—I don't—" The words trip over themselves, but he only smiles, lifting my hand to kiss the very finger where that ring belongs.

"Like I said, you don't have to decide right now." He closes the ring box and slips it back into his jacket pocket.

Before I can awkwardly stumble over my words again, he leans in, taking my lips with his.

The kiss is passionate, and I can't stop the singular thought from playing on repeat in my head.

Joshua Moreno is in love with me.

We've been driving for half an hour in complete silence. Our conversation bounces around in my head, and I attempt to make sense of it.

Over the last month, Joshua Moreno has been many things to me— a crush, a captor, even a suitor. But a husband? I never let my imagination drift far enough into the future to consider whether we might have any long-term connection. Even the fact that he wanted me to stay after this month never prompted me to contemplate what life with him would be like.

Yet, here I am, seated beside the only man I've ever wanted, a ring in his pocket.

We're pulling into the driveway when Joshua finally speaks. "I have a few things I need to do, but I'll come find you around dinner time."

As much as I enjoy being with Joshua, I'm grateful for the space.

He's given me a lot to think about, and I need time to process everything.

Joshua and I enter the house, and he places a breathtaking kiss on my lips before turning in the direction of his office. Not wanting to go to my room quite yet, I make my way to the back porch and take a seat on the couch.

I replay our conversation over and over again. Could Joshua truly go from being my captor to my husband?

Do I even want that?

The sun moves across the sky as I lose myself in my thoughts, but I'm interrupted by the opening of the back door.

"Hey, birthday girl."

I turn to scowl at Ryder. "You knew what he was going to ask me, didn't you?"

He sighs, coming to sit beside me. "Yes."

"A warning would've been nice."

"Do you honestly believe it would've been better received from me?"

"No," I admit. "I feel like every day I'm faced with a new life-changing twist. It's exhausting."

He nods.

"Ryder, I don't know what to do." It's surprisingly easy to admit this to him, not because I feel persuaded to, but because I really do view him as a friend.

He leans back, crossing his arms over his broad chest. "Well, you have a month to figure it out."

"I guess... I just can't see it, Joshua, as my *husband*." The word sounds foreign on my tongue. "This isn't how I thought getting married would go. I always thought I'd meet a nice guy. We'd go out, he'd meet my family and get my father's approval, then pop the question. You know, like *normal* people."

"We're not normal people."

"No kidding."

"Isn't this what you wanted? Moreno and your family?"

"Hypothetically, yes. It's just not what I imagined."

Ryder shakes his head. "Moreno is no Prince Charming. He's not a romantic, and he has no interest in giving you a normal life."

"Not the best sales pitch," I mutter.

"Let me finish," he says, and I dramatically gesture for him to go on. "He's not going to give you a fairytale, but he'll give you something better—authenticity. It won't be what you imagined, but it'll be *real*. Moreno isn't perfect, but he's loyal, and he'll protect you. He'll make a good husband."

Nodding is the only response I can give him.

I think of my family for the hundredth time today and picture what things would be like if my father hadn't left me to Joshua.

"Ryder?"

"Yes?"

"Don't ever give up on your daughter like my dad gave up on me." When I turn to meet his eyes, I'm unashamed by the tears that fill mine.

Let him see how bad it hurts. Let him resolve never to do what my father did.

My friend gives me a rare, genuine smile. "I won't."

No sooner has the back door opened than I hear Donovan's silvery voice. "Hey, we're all waiting for you!"

Ryder stands, holding out a hand that I take without hesitation. "Come on, your birthday isn't over yet."

I smile, not just because my birthday has turned out to be so much better than I could've imagined, but because as I walk into the house, it very nearly feels like *coming home*.

CHAPTER THIRTY-TWO

Joshua

"So, you're telling me that none of the *fifteen* soldiers I sent on this assignment could locate an *entire* shipping crate?" My tone is calm, but I've been doing this long enough to know that's more intimidating than yelling.

There's a shake in Jackson's voice. "Yes, sir. But we aren't done looking yet. I'm sure we'll find it."

"You better, or it's your ass."

I slam the phone down and pinch the bridge of my nose.

Dealing with business from here is a headache, but I don't exactly have a choice. I can't take Elise back to the base. It isn't that I think anyone will touch her—I know they won't after what happened to Tripp—but she's not ready to go back there.

I'll just have to suck it up and do what I can from here. If it weren't for the fact that Elise trusts Ryder, I'd have him back at the base running things. Instead, I have to trust that my second-tier officers can handle everything.

Even with the door shut, I can hear the faint laughter in the kitchen, and I wonder if Elise is out there now.

All things considered, she took my proposition well. She didn't give me a yes, but I hadn't expected one. The reasons I gave her are all legitimate points—she doesn't need to know that I figured them out well after I decided she was going to be my wife.

Still, it is the best option for everyone, which is why she'll choose it at the end of the month.

A knock on the door sounds, and I check the camera feed.

Elise.

Her newly short hair is partially pulled back on either side, and she's changed into a pair of leggings and a sweatshirt she bought today.

"Come in."

She walks in, carrying a bowl of something I can't see, but the room fills with the scent of marinara.

"You haven't eaten yet, have you?"

I shake my head, and she hands the bowl to me. "Spaghetti? You know you could've had Jay make anything you want, right?"

Her lip tugs up in a bashful smile. "Actually, I made it. Spaghetti on my birthday was always a tradition."

I expect the mention of family traditions to dampen her mood, but it doesn't. If anything, she looks excited to share this with me.

Placing the bowl on my desk, I lean in for a kiss, and she happily obliges.

"We could make our own traditions."

"Oh?" She smiles, lips still pressed to mine. "What do you have in mind?"

"Anything but shopping," I grumble and decide that there's no better feeling than Elise's soft laugh against my lips. "Maybe we'll take a trip."

"Really?"

I answer by taking hold of her hips, lifting her onto the desk, and planting kisses along her cheek and jawline. "Where would you want to go?"

"Italy," she says without hesitation.

"Italy it is, then."

She shakes her head. "Don't make promises you can't keep."

When I lean back, it's to stare earnestly into her beautiful eyes. "Elise, if you let me, I'll take you anywhere you want to go."

I'd spend every penny I have traveling the world with Elise if it meant she'd keep looking at me the way she is now—like I hung the moon and splayed the stars across the night.

"What would you like to do tonight?" I ask.

"Well, I suggested a movie night, but Ryder refuses to watch a chick flick," she says with an eye roll. "So, we're going to play cards instead. Are you done working?"

"Not quite, but I should be able to join you soon."

She shrugs. "All the same to me. I'm undefeated."

She's pretty confident for someone who has only played cards with these guys once, but I think I can capitalize on it.

"What game?"

"Kemps."

The name is familiar, but I've never played it myself. All I need is twenty minutes of research, and I'm fairly certain I can hold my own.

"How confident are you?"

If the question catches her off guard, she doesn't show it. "Very."

"Enough to make a bet?"

The slight narrowing of her eyes gives away her wariness. "Depends."

"On?"

"What you have in mind."

"Whoever wins more games tonight wins." I cross my arms over my chest. "Name your terms."

She doesn't hesitate. "If I win, you have to watch chick flicks with me *and* apologize to Ryder for yelling at him last night."

I grimace at the last part, which only feeds her satisfaction. I don't like her terms, but I don't plan on losing.

"If I win, you move into my room. Starting tonight."

She looks at me like I'm crazy. "You can't ask me to marry you *and* move into your room before we've even had a *real* date."

I open my mouth, but she covers it with her hand.

"A date that doesn't end with me being drugged or loyalty tested."

I kiss her palm, and she blushes as she drops her hand to her side.

"If you're so sure you're going to win, then it shouldn't be a problem."

Elise draws in a deep breath. "Why do you want me in your room? I thought you *weren't the sharing type.*"

"Sharing *with* you is not the same as sharing you."

"But—"

"Do you sleep better with me?"

She nods, expression still unsure.

"Then, worst-case scenario, you get a bigger closet *and* a good night's sleep."

Her narrowed eyes study me for a moment longer before she squares her shoulders and lifts her chin. "You're on."

By the time we're sitting around the table on the back porch, everyone is nursing their second drink. I didn't put up a fight when Elise downed her wine within a minute of having it because she looked like she needed it. For all the courage she had earlier, she sure looks nervous now, and I enjoy sending winks her way from across the table.

I only needed one YouTube tutorial to give me the confidence I need to win.

The game is simple: collect four cards of the same rank, then signal your partner to announce *Kemps*. With Ryder as my partner, this will hardly be a challenge.

Elise teams up with Donovan—a fact he's a little too pleased about. I cut my eyes at him when Elise isn't looking, and he nods in solemn understanding.

Kade and Alec are the last pairing since Jay opted for an early night and went inside.

Elise studies me, and I know she's still thrown off by the fact that Ryder and I refused to come up with a sign for the game. The other pairs decided to use their signs from the night before, but Ryder and I didn't need to talk about it.

Our sign was established years ago.

The game begins, and it's silent, aside from the switching of cards and birds chirping in the night. Despite the fact that it's my first time playing, Ryder and I operate effortlessly. I barely need to look at him to know we're on the same page. The cards that he drops and picks up tell me exactly what I need to know about his hand.

We're on the third round of cards and an eight of spades away from victory when Donovan declares, "Kemps!"

I toss my cards down, and Elise shoots me a triumphant smile that solidifies my absolute *need* to win.

I can't wait to take her to bed tonight.

Round two starts, and I'm glad to see that Ryder's picked up on my urgency. He doesn't know why I want to win so badly, but he ups his game regardless.

My brain works overtime to memorize every card that's switched and analyze what that tells me about my opponents' hands.

Alec moves without haste and switches cards randomly, and I'm sure he has nothing good. Kade seems to be onto something, but he moves slowly, overthinking every move too much to play effectively.

Donovan is skilled in thinking on his feet, giving him an edge in this game that I'm wary of. He switches cards almost too fast for me to believe he's processing all of them, but I don't let myself underestimate him.

Elise is the most fascinating to watch, and I need to stop myself from getting distracted. I wait for her face to give her away, but it never does. Her usually overly expressive features are frozen, eyes narrowed, lips parted, and eyebrows drawn together.

And she's watching everyone almost as intently as I am.

The last card I need hits the table, and I snatch it up, silently signaling to Ryder as I do.

"Kemps," he announces.

Elise clenches her teeth, and I send another wink her way.

The games pass in a blur of cards and signs. By the fourth game, I've figured out both pairs' signs. Elise and Donovan lift an eyebrow, and Kade and Alec scrunch their noses. As far as I can tell, neither pair has learned Ryder's and my sign. I catch Elise staring at us on more than one occasion, and I'm sure that's exactly what she's trying to figure out.

Games start and end, and finally, we're tied three-three with Elise and Donovan. Alec and Kade managed to win once in there, but they never stood a chance.

"We're out. Next point wins," Alec says, throwing down his cards and finishing his drink in a single gulp.

Kade grumbles to himself, but we don't pay him any mind.

Donovan leans back in his chair, a relaxed grin in place. To him, this is a friendly game with no stakes. Elise, on the other hand, is on the edge of her seat, and her fingers tap against the table.

By the time Kade deals the cards, we're all back in game mode.

We have our cards, and it takes intentional effort to keep from laughing.

I only need two more cards to win right off the bat.

A quick look at Ryder is all I need for him to know that I'm on to something.

I'm fully consumed in the game as I switch my cards and analyze the moves of my opponents. I'm once again amazed by Elise's poker face. She's never been particularly gifted at hiding her emotions, but she does it effortlessly when focused on the game.

We're on the fourth round of cards this game when it happens.

Donovan places the last card I need.

Ryder's hand was already extended as he placed down one of his other cards so he didn't waste a moment in picking it up. Now, he just has to get it to me.

Elise's eyes light up as she reaches for another card in the deck, and it's a look I recognize.

She's about to win.

Ryder catches this, too, because he snatches the card she reaches for and sets down the one I need in its place. Instead of reaching for a new card, Elise pauses, confirming my suspicion.

I let my guard down and wear a big smile as I pick up the final card I need.

"Kemps," Ryder announces.

"Damn it," Donovan exclaims, but Elise is silent.

Her face turns a deep shade of red, and she glares at me.

I stand and round the table, holding out my hand to her. "It's time for Miss Consoli and me to retire for the evening."

The men bid their goodnights, and Elise begrudgingly places her hand in mine. Before we leave, she smiles at Donovan. "We'll get them next time."

His answer is a small smile, and I lead her inside.

She doesn't say a word, and her hand tightens in mine when we step into my room. I notice—for the first time since coming inside—that her posture has gone rigid.

She fiddles with the hem of her shirt and doesn't meet my eye.

"What's wrong?"

She shakes her head, still refusing to look at me.

"Elise, talk to me."

Several seconds pass, and when it's clear I'm not letting her off the hook without an answer, she sighs.

"You know that I've never... *been* with anyone before, but you've never told me..." she drifts off, lifting her reluctantly curious gaze to mine.

I'm fairly sure there's no good answer to this question, so I might as well go with the truth.

"Yes, I've been with other women."

"How many?"

I *know* there's no good answer to this question.

"Enough," I say with a dispassionate shrug.

Her head drops, and I wonder why the hell she asked in the first place when she knew she wouldn't like the answer.

"Elise," I coax, using a hand to lift her chin.

She swats my hand away and walks toward the couch in my room. She doesn't make it two steps before I take hold of her arm.

"Don't do that," I say, holding her firmly in place.

She glares at me. "Do what?"

"Close yourself off because you don't like where the conversation is going."

She shakes my arm off, and I let her since she doesn't attempt to walk away again.

"Excuse me for not liking the idea of being another notch in your bedpost."

I bark a laugh. "You've *got* to be kidding me."

Her expression indicates that she is, in fact, *not* kidding me.

I roll my eyes and hold out my arms to either side. "You think I work this hard just to get laid?"

"I think you talk about sex like it doesn't mean anything," she snaps.

"It didn't mean anything," I answer simply. "None of it meant *anything*. Not until you. You think I go around kidnapping just anyone?"

A short laugh breaks through her anger, which I suspect is a cover for what she's actually feeling right now.

"What's really wrong?" I ask.

Her eyes soften, though they take on an edge of insecurity as they flick briefly to the bed.

She swallows. "You're used to women with experience, and I don't want to be a—"

"Don't you dare finish that sentence," I say, though it sounds more like an order.

I don't know what's more absurd, that she thinks I expect her to have sex with me tonight or that she thinks she could disappoint me.

I take Elise's face between my hands. "My one and *only* expectation for tonight is that you sleep by my side. That is it. And even if I were asking for more"—I shake my head—"I can't begin to explain how insignificant every woman in the world is next to you."

This relaxes her, but only marginally.

"So, you don't want to..." she drifts off again.

"If you're asking if I want to have sex with you, the answer is yes, but only when you're ready. That particular aspect of our relationship is yours to dictate," I tell her and level her with an honest sincerity. "But you should know, Elise, once I have you, I am never letting you go. Remember that."

She lifts her eyebrows, and her reservations seem to wane as an attitude edges her tone. "So, you won't touch me?"

I laugh again. "I won't cross a line we haven't already crossed."

"Good," she says, taking a step to close what little distance there is between us. She presses her hands to my chest, and her cheeks tint red. "I don't want you to stop touching me."

I answer by taking her lips with mine, holding her face between my hands.

Like all our kisses, Elise comes alive when our lips meet. The tension in her muscles eases as my hands wander down her body, and the feeling is thrilling. She throws her arms around my neck, and I sweep her into my arms. I carry her to the bed and fall on the mattress first, wrapping my arms around her so she's trapped against me, but I'm careful to avoid putting pressure on her back.

If the card game was intense, then kissing Elise is all-consuming. It doesn't feel like time is flying—it feels as though time simply doesn't *exist*. When her lips move against mine, nothing else matters.

Her hands slowly trail down the front of my body, like she's taking care to memorize every inch of me, and damn, it feels good. When one hand reaches my waistband, Elise splays her fingers over my skin, just barely reaching up my shirt. It's a hesitant motion like she's unsure how I'll react.

To answer her unspoken question, I sit up just enough to tug my shirt over my head and toss it to the floor.

She pauses, taking in the gesture—as well as the view—and the expression on her face is enough to make my chest tight with every feeling I would've suppressed before she came into my life.

She looks at me with the same awe that I feel for her. When she looks at me like that, I swear I could move mountains.

I reach up, cupping her face in my hands, and gently pulling her lips back to mine. She obliges, blush creeping back up her cheeks as she does. When her body is flat against mine, her hand returns to my waist. She spreads her fingers over my skin, gently digging them in like she's trying to leave her fingerprints indented on me.

Her hand slowly moves up my body, tracing over my stomach, chest, and biceps. The feeling of Elise's lips on mine while her small, delicate hands wander over my body is unlike anything I have ever felt before. It makes her earlier worry of disappointing me beyond laughable.

There is no one like Elise.

And if she chooses to leave me after this month, I can't say with certainty that I will be able to honor that decision.

CHAPTER THIRTY-THREE

Elise

"You're kidding me, right?"

"Moreno said to tell you he's sorry and that he'll—uh, '*make it up to you later.*'" Ryder looks uncomfortable repeating what I'm sure is a direct quote.

It's been a week since my birthday, and I don't remember the last time I was this happy.

I've started cooking again, which takes up most of my time, but I don't mind. I've missed it. Jay and I alternate between who cooks breakfast and lunch, but we normally make dinner together.

I've had the opportunity to get to know everyone better, too, even going so far as to spend time with each of the capos without Joshua or Ryder as a buffer.

Ryder had been right in saying I'd feel better knowing the guys who live here. It's given me a sense of comfort that I thought would be impossible after Tripp's attack.

Ryder typically joins me for lunch on the days Joshua is caught up in work. It's easy to talk to him, like I've known him all my life, and not merely a month of it.

My relationship with Joshua has grown the most.

Since losing the bet on my birthday, I've officially moved into Joshua's room. All the clothes I bought at the mall were moved into Joshua's oversized closet, and just like that, it became *our* room.

I love waking beside him after a dreamless sleep, even if he quickly leaves me to go to work each morning. He tries to take a break during lunch to eat with me, but it always depends on the calls he gets tangled up in. Most days, he's done around dinner time, and we spend the whole evening together.

I always insist that Joshua and I spend time with the capos, playing cards, watching movies, or talking over drinks. At first, he objected, preferring our alone time, but I think he's realized that I enjoy hanging out with them. Even before my kidnapping, I never had a group of friends like this, and these guys give me the small sense of normalcy that I crave—even if they do talk about things like their body count.

And I wish I meant sexually.

Things between Joshua and me have been great over the past week, aside from the occasional argument. I never considered myself a hot-headed person, but Joshua brings out a side of me I hadn't realized existed.

The characteristics that have defined me for so long are shifting and changing the core of my being, or perhaps Joshua is just revealing what has been inside me all along.

But no matter how well things have been going, it doesn't give him the right to blow me off *again*.

Going out for my birthday meant so much to me that Joshua promised we could do it more often. First, we made plans to go out for lunch, which was canceled for a last-minute meeting. Next, we'd scheduled time to go hiking, which was postponed because of a shipment delivery error. Today, we're going out for lunch and hiking to make up for the other dates, but now he's canceling on me for the third time.

He'd better have a damn good reason.

"What's his excuse this time?"

"He has a lot to get done. I didn't get specifics."

Turning on my heels, I stalk out of the kitchen and down the hall.

"Where are you going?" Ryder calls from behind me.

I don't spare him a glance. "To find out what's *so* important."

"He's not in his office," he says slowly.

I stop in my tracks. If Joshua isn't in his office, there's only one other place Joshua would be.

The warehouse.

Last week, Joshua and I went for a walk around the estate. Until then, I hadn't realized just how vast the property was. I knew the main road led to a parking garage and a guest house where most of the men stay, but I didn't know that it also leads to the warehouse.

We walked to the parking garage and guest house, but Joshua made us turn around after that. He's made it abundantly clear that I'm not allowed to go anywhere near the warehouse—though he spends most of his time there.

Instead of responding, I push past Ryder and make my way to the front door.

"Don't do it."

I ignore him and slam the door behind me.

It's opened a moment later. "Elise!"

I stop dead in my tracks.

Ryder's voice is a rose—alluring and pleasant, but it's got the bite of a poisoned thorn. I can imagine it comes in handy in this line of work, but I hate when it's directed at me.

"Why is he blowing me off?" The anger seeps out of my voice, giving way to my disappointment.

"I'm sure he'd rather be with you."

I close my eyes, soaking in the sun's warmth. It's a beautiful day, and the idea of sunbathing is tempting, but when another idea hits me, I decide it's worth forgoing my day in the sun.

"There are only three bedrooms in the house, right?" I ask, head tilting toward the sky.

I don't open my eyes to watch Ryder, but his pause gives away his wariness. "Right. Why?"

"No reason," I say, turning on my heels to go back inside.

"What are you about to do?"

"I have no idea what you mean." I close the front door, barely hearing Ryder muttering to himself about cleaning up my messes.

This one shouldn't get him in trouble.

I haven't been to the bedroom upstairs since the morning of my birthday. None of the things put here were actually mine, so I didn't bother having them moved to Joshua's room. It's untouched from the last time I was here, bed unmade, bathroom door ajar, and two dresser drawers half open.

Fifteen minutes later, I'm walking back down the steps, surprised that Ryder never came after me. He's not in an official *babysitter* role, but he still acts like it sometimes. In fact, none of the guys seem to be hanging around the house today, which is fine by me.

I spend the next hour making food.

I have years of practice making just enough food for one, and I put those skills to use now. By the time I'm done, I have a club sandwich with a side of chips, broccoli cheddar soup stored in a large thermos, and a small platter of all the cheeses and meats Jay insists on having on hand at all times—including prosciutto, capicola, goat cheese, and an aged cheddar which has recently become a favorite of mine. I add crackers, wrap the platter in cellophane, and grab the last few items I need—a bag of caramel-filled chocolates, two bottles of wine, and the biggest wine glass I can find.

Then, I write two notes and leave the first one on the kitchen counter.

With my lunch, dinner, snack, dessert, and drink of choice all ready, it's time to settle in. It takes three trips from the kitchen to the bedroom to get it all in there, but once it is, I stick the second note on the door, promptly lock it, and then spend a tedious ten minutes pushing the heavy oak dresser in front of it.

My final touch is to close the curtains overlooking the backyard.

If Joshua wants to blow me off, that's fine, but I won't be at his beck and call whenever he decides he has the time.

I haven't had the chance to try out the projector screen in our room, and now is the perfect time. Joshua isn't logged in to any streaming apps, but his credit card is attached to the digital store profile so I buy all the movies I want to watch.

The Proposal, How to Lose a Guy in 10 Days, The Devil Wears Prada, and *Pretty Woman* are my first round of purchases.

I turn on the first one and pop open the bottle of wine. My first glass is gone before I get halfway through the movie, and when that thought makes me giggle, I make myself eat the club sandwich I made.

Four hours, two movies, half a cheese plate, and an entire bottle of wine later, I hear clamoring coming from the back door. I have no idea if it's Joshua or a few of the capos, and I don't care.

And to show just how much I don't care, I turn the volume up as high as it will go.

It's absurdly loud, and if I'd thought to bring bottles of water in here, I might've turned it back down. Instead, I kick my feet up on the couch and toss a piece of aged cheddar in my mouth. I miss and spend the next several moments fishing the cheese out of my shirt.

Not my sexiest moment.

I jump when I hear pounding on the door. Really, I'm just surprised I'm able to hear it over the movie.

I promptly ignore it.

I can tell when the pounding turns to kicking because the dresser starts to rattle, but it doesn't budge. Joshua can only blame himself for getting top-of-the-line doors, locks, and furniture.

By the time Pretty Woman ends, Joshua has been beating at the door for almost an hour. When I click out of the movie, my ears are ringing from the sudden quiet. That *quiet* lasts less than three seconds before Joshua furiously pounds at the door again.

"Open the door, Elise!"

"Joshua?" I call in my sweetest voice. "I had no idea you were back! Didn't you get my note?"

My note, which I left stuck to the door, states:

Girls only.

It wasn't as nice as the note I left for Jay, which explained that I wouldn't be able to help with dinner tonight because I'd be busy teaching his boss that I don't appreciate being blown off three times in a row.

"Open the door, or I'm breaking it down," Joshua yells.

"Let me know how that goes for you!"

"I'm going to kill you, Elise. I swear if you don't open this door—"

"Not making a strong case, sweetheart," I say, then add, "I'm going to take a bath while you keep at it."

"Elise! Don't you dare ignore me again!" he shouts, but I'm already grabbing the second bottle of wine—I don't bother with a glass this time.

Joshua must have had the bathroom stocked with me in mind because I refuse to think he would ever use lavender bath bombs and Epsom salt. In any case, I'm grateful for them as I run a steaming bath.

I don't climb out of the tub until my toes and fingers are pruny. I have no idea how much time has passed—only that it's been approximately half a bottle of wine and seven chocolates since I left Joshua at the door.

It's quiet when I open the bathroom door, and I wonder if Joshua is still waiting in the hall. My answer comes when I take three steps—which he must hear—because he calls in a raspy voice, 'Elise, please, open the door."

I'm sure my alcohol intake, combined with not having seen him since early this morning, is the reason I'm tempted to let him in, but honestly, I'm not sure I even could. It took a heck of a lot of strength to move the dresser into place, and that was when I was sober and running on anger.

Now, I'm very drunk and very tired.

"I'm going to bed, Joshua. We can talk in the morning."

"You're not sleeping until you've opened this door."

"Watch me," I say, then erupt in giggles. "Oh wait, you can't."

His pause is brief. "Are you drunk?"

"Yes, yes I am," I tell him, climbing into bed. "Damn, these sheets are cold."

Something hits the door—probably his head. "I'm sorry I canceled our date today. I couldn't step away from work. Just let me in, and I'll make it up to you."

The anger that drove me to lock Joshua out in the first place has mostly worn off, and I want nothing more than to let him in and fall asleep in his warm embrace—especially when I know that without him, my sleep will be plagued with nightmares.

But I can't let him in. Not yet.

I'm not new to loneliness—I've spent most of my life alone.

And I hated it.

Here, with Joshua and the capos, I finally have people surrounding me. People I genuinely enjoy being around. When Joshua blows me off, it takes me back to the dozens of times my brothers and father did the same.

I'm not spending the rest of my life hoping people make time for me.

"You'll have to find somewhere else to sleep tonight," I tell him.

"You know I can't do that," he says in a low, tightly controlled tone.

Oh right.

I'd almost forgotten about that.

I left Ryder's room untouched, but the only other bedroom in the house no longer has a functioning mattress.

It had been surprisingly therapeutic to cut several four-foot-long slashes into the mattress.

I smile, then turn off the lamp at my bedside.

"Goodnight, Joshua," I say and burrow into our bed, shivering between the cold sheets while I breathe in Joshua's scent.

It's nothing like having him here, holding me as I fall asleep, but I hope it's enough to keep the nightmares at bay for a night.

Joshua doesn't answer, but I have a feeling I'm not the only one who falls asleep staring at the door.

I'm walking down the long hallway toward a muffled sound that I can't make out. Shouting? Crying? All I know is that my stomach lurches with every echo.

With each step I take, the door at the end—which I am somehow sure is where the noise is coming from—gets further away. I walk faster, then switch to a jog when that doesn't work either. I'm full-on sprinting when I look down to find that I've made it to the end of the hallway, and the door knob is in my hand.

Suddenly, I have no desire to open the door. The muffled cries are loud, and I think I'm going to be sick.

I try to force my legs to get me the hell out of here, but they might as well be cemented in place. I watch in suspended dread as my hand —which I have no control over—turns the knob and pushes the door open.

I realize then that I already knew what I'd find behind the door.

Of course, my eyes refuse to close, so I'm forced to witness my lifeless body hanging by my wrists in the basement.

I try shaking my head, stepping back, closing my eyes, and screaming for it to stop, but nothing works.

I'm shaken to wakefulness by strong hands wrapped around my arms.

"You're safe," Joshua whispers, pulling me into his chest. "It's okay, Elise. You're safe."

My mouth feels like it's full of cotton, and my heart races from the adrenaline. Deep breaths calm me down, but not as much as the smell and feel of Joshua.

Little things begin to register as I come to full consciousness. Joshua is wearing a shirt—he never wears a shirt to bed—and chilled air raises goosebumps on my arms—though I never turn on the fan. The rest of the night comes back to me, and I think to actually take in Joshua's appearance.

Not only is he wearing a shirt, but he's wearing the faded blue jeans that he left the house in this morning. One look at the door—or rather, the oak dresser blocking it—returns the rest of my memories.

"Are you okay?" he asks, brushing his lips over the shell of my ear and placing a light kiss there.

I nod. "How did you get in here?" I whisper and cough through my dry throat.

Joshua leans over, grabbing a bottle of water that was not on the nightstand when I went to bed. I take it from him and drink most of it.

Joshua nods toward the windows, which I can only see because the back porch lights have been turned on. The curtains on either side of the window are pulled open.

"How did you—"

"I had a ladder set up last night in case, well, *this* happened," he explains.

I rest my head against his chest. "So much for keeping you out."

His laugh is light and beyond comforting. "I'm surprised you didn't lock the windows."

"Not as surprised as I am that you own a ladder."

I'd bet money he's rolling his eyes at me.

He lays us down—not bothering to remove his jeans or shirt—and covers us with the duvet.

"I'm still mad at you," I mumble through a yawn.

"I've spent the last four hours sleeping on the hallway floor," he deadpans. "You're not my favorite person either."

Smiling, I curl into Joshua's chest and fall into a deep, dreamless sleep.

CHAPTER THIRTY-FOUR

Elise

A typical morning consists of Joshua waking up at seven, placing a kiss on my cheek, and getting ready for the day. I wake up an hour later, when he brings me a coffee, another kiss, and tells me that he can't wait to see me later.

This is not a typical morning.

When I open my eyes, I wince at the sunlight streaming in and squeeze them shut again with a hiss as a throb resonates in my skull. When the pain subsides, I squint to check the clock on the nightstand. It's nine o'clock, and strong arms are still firmly wrapped around me.

I must have woken Joshua because he's suddenly hovering over me, mercifully blocking me from the sunlight.

He pulls his phone from his pocket, presses a few buttons, then brings it to his ear.

I wince as soon as he starts talking and bring my hands up to cover my ears.

"Jay, I need Tylenol, a large glass of water, and a greasy breakfast brought to my room immediately."

Jay must agree because Joshua hangs up and puts the phone back.

"My head is killing me," I say, only then realizing how dry my throat is.

Man, I'm thirsty.

"That's what happens when you drink two bottles of wine," he says, guiding me to sit up with him.

I do, then close my eyes as I lean my head on my knees.

"It was only a bottle and a half," I murmur, and his light laugh makes me wince.

I open my eyes to glare at him, which is when I notice the dark circles under his and remember that Joshua spent most of the night sleeping on the hardwood hallway floor.

I also remember why.

"You blew me off—*again*."

He points to the door. "I spent ten hours outside that door, four of which I was sleeping on the floor. I think we're even."

"It's not about getting even." I lift my head, working very hard to ignore the dull pulsing that comes with the motion. "It's about making me a priority."

"You're my *main* priority," he corrects. "Keeping you safe is all I care about, Elise. I would love to spend every second of every day with you, but if I ignore my responsibilities to this family, I won't be able to keep you safe."

"I'm not asking you to ignore your responsibilities. I'm asking you to keep your word if you say you're going to spend time with me."

"I can't control if something comes up that I have to deal with," he says, but his tone isn't defensive. He sounds genuinely at a loss. "I've never had to balance my work with a personal life."

I know that Joshua didn't want to cancel our dates. When he returns to the house each night, it's obvious that he's excited to spend time with me.

But that makes me feel like a puppy sitting at the window while their owner goes off to work.

I nod, then immediately stop when my head throbs. "I know you can't control when important things come up. I also know your work will keep you from me sometimes, but you can't cancel three dates in a week and expect me to happily stay put and wait for you to have time for me."

"I know," he agrees. "I won't do it again."

"And if you do have to cancel, come tell me yourself instead of sending Ryder to do it."

"Would it help if I said I sent Ryder because I knew that if I came myself, I wouldn't be able to force myself to return to work?"

"No, not at all," I answer, laying a hand on his hard chest. "But I do recall Ryder saying you'd make it up to me."

Joshua's smile is enough to melt any remaining anger.

"But you'll have to do it later," I tell him, just as he starts to lean in to kiss me. "I need to sleep off this hangover."

"Oh no, you don't," Joshua says, pulling the covers off of me. Goosebumps break out across my entire body. I sit up to grab the duvet so fast my head spins, and I briefly wonder if I'm about to throw up.

"What the hell?" I hiss, all my anger returning tenfold.

He pushes the duvet off the bed. "You wanted time with me—you got it. You have me all day long, Princess, and I'm not going to let you sleep it away."

I glare at him, but he ignores it, dipping his head down to take my lips in a sweet kiss. "Come on, beautiful. We've got big plans for the day."

"Like what?"

"For starters, mattress shopping."

After taking Tylenol, drinking two bottles of water, and forcing myself to eat a plate of sausage, bacon, and eggs, I don't feel so miserable. After a shower, I almost feel human.

Despite the hangover that isn't gone until well into the afternoon, my day out with Joshua is perfect—which seems only fair for all the hell it took to get it.

He hadn't been joking about mattress shopping. We spent over an hour buying a new one for the bed I ruined upstairs, but Joshua didn't seem bothered by the fact that I cost him a few thousand dollars.

After that, we went to lunch at a local sports bar, to hike at a park, and had dinner at a small winery almost an hour from the house. We were supposed to do a wine tasting before dinner, but I vetoed that. The idea of having wine today could not be less appealing.

Conversation with Joshua flows naturally, as if we've known each other all our lives. The ruthless mafia boss who drugged and kidnapped me to blackmail my father made me laugh so hard I almost spit my drink out with a story from his early days when he and Ryder showed up at the wrong location for a drop-off and nearly sold a duffle bag of cocaine to a very confused elderly woman at a bus station.

The car ride back to the house is the longest stretch of silence we've had all day, but I'm okay with that. It's a comfortable, easy silence that still feels as if we're getting to know each other.

Joshua has one hand on my thigh, and I'm working hard not to show him how much the simple touch affects me. He taps a finger on the steering wheel to a song on a local station I've never heard, and I hope he doesn't notice that I keep glancing at him.

On days like today, Joshua doesn't seem like a mafia boss at all. He seems like my...boyfriend? That term feels juvenile compared to the feelings I have for him, but I'm not sure what else he is.

If it were up to Joshua, he'd be my husband.

By the time Joshua parks the car in the driveway, the sun is just starting to set. Neither of us moves to get out.

I place my hand over his. "Are you sure your boss won't give you the day off tomorrow, too?"

Joshua shakes his head. "No way. That guy's an asshole."

I smile as he intertwines our fingers, bringing them to his lips to kiss my hand.

"Thank you for today," I tell him. He didn't have to take an entire day to spend with me, and I'm sure it wasn't as easy as moving meetings around to make it happen, but he did it anyway. "It meant the world to me."

"Well, it's not over yet," he reminds me. "What would you like to do tonight? I'm sure the capos would be in for a few rounds of Kemps."

Joshua lowers our hands to the middle console, and, once again, I try to imagine this man as my husband.

The thought is slowly starting to seem less crazy.

"Can I see the ring?"

The question catches him off guard, and it's a moment before a wide—and hopeful—smile touches his lips.

We walk inside, hand in hand, and the hollers from the capos in the kitchen echo through the house, but we don't stop on the way to our room.

Joshua pulls me to the couch, and I sit, watching as he retreats to the closet.

I note that someone has cleaned up my mess from yesterday. Any traces from my girl's night in are erased.

He returns only seconds later, sitting on the couch beside me, and my eyes drop to the small box.

When Joshua opens it, I feel the same overwhelming admiration I did the first time I saw it. I've never given any thought to the kind of ring I want, but if I had, this is what I would've chosen. Its design is simple yet breathtaking.

I'm not sure how long I've been staring at it, but I'm pulled back to reality when Joshua removes it from the box. He lifts my hand and slides the ring into place.

A perfect fit.

And more than that, it feels *right*.

I already know that Joshua's feelings for me are genuine, but the fact that I'm starting to doubt that I could be without him makes me realize just how strong *my* feelings have become.

"I love it," I whisper.

"It suits you."

Before I can get carried away, I work the ring down my finger to return it to the box, but Joshua's hand over mine halts the action.

"Keep it."

The implication makes my heart race with excitement, but there's panic there, too. As right as it feels to wear this ring, I'm not ready to say yes to him.

"Joshua, I'm not—"

"I know this isn't a yes." He lifts my hand to his lips, placing a gentle kiss there. "But will you wear it while you're here?"

His lips against my skin ignite the now-familiar electricity, and there's no way I could deny him.

"Okay," I breathe and bring my lips to his for a long, adoring kiss.

"What would you like to do tonight?" he asks.

I'm about to tell him he can pick, but I'm interrupted by a yawn.

"Tired?"

I nod. "I never feel rested after nightmare nights."

"*Nightmare nights*? You have a name for it?"

My cheeks heat, and for the first time today, it's out of embarrassment. "That's just what I started calling them in my head," I admit.

"Have you always had nightmares? Or did they start when I brought you to the base?"

My heart sinks with this particular topic. I'm tempted to tell him I don't want to talk about it, but I don't. Joshua is the only person who's been able to chase my nightmares away. The least I can do is explain where they come from.

I pull my knees to my chest, wrapping my arms around them. "They started when I was thirteen."

It takes me a moment to find the words as I recall the day that I've worked so hard to erase from my memory.

"I'd only known about my dad's work for a few months, so I was still wrapping my head around the whole idea. I'd been going to our family's base my whole life, but up until then, I'd always thought of it as Dad's office. One day, I was looking for my dad, but I couldn't find him anywhere. I wandered down a hallway I probably shouldn't have, but I heard his voice, so I followed it. He sounded angry, but that wasn't what scared me. There was this animal wailing."

I can't stop the shiver that runs down my spine as I remember the day that scarred my child self.

"I'm not sure why, but I couldn't help myself, and I opened the door. Needless to say, it wasn't an animal, but the man didn't look all that human after what my dad had done to him. There was blood covering almost every inch of his body, bone was visible where my father had carved out part of his leg, and one of his eyes had been cut out along with his tongue. It didn't take long for my dad to notice I'd walked in, but it was long enough."

Joshua places a comforting hand on my thigh. "I could barely look at him for months afterward. I understand that sometimes you guys need to do stuff like that, but it was unnecessarily cruel. It's not like my dad was getting information out of him if he cut his tongue out. He was doing it for fun, and it made me sick to think that he was entertained by that."

It occurs to me that I've never told anyone this before. By that point, my brothers had all inflicted that sort of cruelty themselves, so they wouldn't have understood anyway.

"The nightmares started that night, and they've never gone away for more than a few months at a time," I explain.

After the long stretch of silence, I look at Joshua, but his focus is on the floor.

"Are you okay?" I ask, feeling exposed and vulnerable.

It's like my question flips a switch.

Joshua's shoulders relax, and his eyes soften. "I'm sorry you witnessed that, Elise."

Nodding is my only response and my gut twists at his guarded expression.

I'm about to ask him what's wrong when he kisses my forehead and stands. "I am so sorry for this, but I completely forgot about a few things I need to get done before tomorrow. If I go to the warehouse for an hour, will I need a ladder when I get back?"

I breathe a laugh, and his carefree smile puts me at ease—mostly.

"Depends on what time you come back," I taunt. "Don't keep me waiting all night."

He dips down and places a long kiss on my lips.

My smile falls the second Joshua closes the door behind him. I don't mind that he has work to do. He spent the entire day giving me his full attention, not so much as taking a phone call or answering an email.

What bothers me is the little voice in the back of my head that tells me Joshua is keeping something from me. I know that there are plenty of things that he hides because it's *family business*, but this feels different.

I walk to the window, watching Joshua and Ryder make their way down the gravel path. By the time they disappear behind the trees, I've made my decision.

I'm going to follow them.

I quickly throw on my tennis shoes and leave our room. The house is quiet, but I still tiptoe to the front door. Miraculously, I don't encounter a single person as I open it and walk into the warm evening.

I pass the extra garage and the vast guest house, being extra careful to conceal myself along the tree line as I do.

The sun is on the brink of setting by the time the large metal building comes into view. I've never seen it before, but it's exactly what I expected—bare metal aside from the big set of doors that dominate the wall facing me.

Unable to hear or see anything from where I am, I go around the back and try my luck there. Surely, there's a window somewhere.

Ensuring the coast is clear, I creep close to the building, looking for anything that might give me a clue about what's going on.

My heart jumps to my throat when I hear the sound of a racing car coming down the gravel path, and I'm thankful that I decided to move to the back since I undoubtedly would've been caught.

I nearly laugh at my good fortune, but the joy is short-lived because that's when I hear the unmistakable sound of gunshots.

CHAPTER THIRTY-FIVE

Elise

A million thoughts race through my head, but only one of them has my total attention.

Joshua.

I briefly wonder if there's a shooting range inside, but the panicked shouts that accompany the shots confirm this isn't a routine drill. All I know is that Joshua is inside that building, and he's in trouble.

Without the knowledge of the warehouse's layout, I'm not exactly sure what to do, but staying here isn't going to help anyone. As stealthily as possible, I race along the back of the warehouse toward an area with several abandoned crates that make for good cover.

Peering around the corner, I spot a garage door entrance that seems to be unoccupied. As I make my way through the various shipping crates, I work to ignore the deafening gunshots and listen closely to the words being shouted.

"South exit! Dammit, Alec, stay down!" Joshua's commands carry over all the other noise.

His voice brings with it a slap of reality.

What the hell am I doing?

Joshua has control of the situation. Running in there without a plan or weapon won't do anything but distract him and put everyone at a greater risk.

Turning back the way I came, I stumble into a large metal crate, and pain shoots up my leg.

"Did you hear that?" an unfamiliar voice asks.

My heartbeat doubles in speed as footsteps head in my direction. I want to run, but I'm too afraid of making noise again, so I stand frozen in plain sight.

I stare wide-eyed at the entrance, seconds away from being discovered, when a large hand clamps down over my mouth and an arm as strong as steel wraps around my waist.

I'm dragged backward.

Thrashing in the arms of my captor, I think through every self-defense move I know, but my frazzled mind can't pinpoint a particularly useful one. We stop behind the cover of several crates.

I'm about to work up a scream when his arms squeeze me tighter.

"Don't make a noise," the familiar voice growls.

Sagging with relief, I stop struggling, and Donovan eases his grip on me, though his hand remains over my mouth. I want to pull away, but the sound of shuffling a few feet from us freezes me in place once again.

From behind the crates, I don't have a clear view of the door. Still, I can see the figure of a man running out of the building. I wonder if he's one of Joshua's soldiers or if he's an attacker. It doesn't matter for long because a gun fires nearby, and he falls to the ground, yelping in pain for only a moment before going silent.

My stomach rolls at the sight, and I wish I hadn't left the house.

How could I have been so stupid?

When the action moves away from us, Donovan loosens his hold and turns me to face him. His normally easygoing expression is replaced with a fury I didn't know he possessed.

"What the hell are you doing here?"

"I followed Joshua," I say in a choked whisper.

And here I thought he couldn't look any angrier.

I was wrong.

"Why would you do that?"

I open my mouth to answer, but another round of gunfire interrupts me, and Donovan tenses.

"Forget it," he mutters, pulling a gun from his holster. "We need better cover."

Taking my hand, Donovan leads me back the way I came. His strides are much longer than mine, so I'm running to keep up with him.

We reach the back corner of the building, and when he points to my left—toward a blocked-off doorway that provides minimal cover—

I don't hesitate to enter the space. Don steps in beside me, using his body to shield mine.

I feel a deep sense of guilt when I realize that if I hadn't been stupid enough to come here, Donovan would be one more person inside protecting Joshua.

The sounds of gunshots and shouting fill the air, and I don't notice the tears rolling down my cheeks until Don looks back at me.

"It's okay," he whispers. "I won't let them hurt you."

He thinks I've worried about myself?

I shake my head. "Joshua is inside."

Don's jaw goes slack. "That's what you're worried about?"

I nod.

"Mr. Moreno is perfectly capable of taking care of himself. He'll be fine." Donovan's eyebrows draw together. "Wait a minute, were you about to go inside when I got to you?"

My eyes fall to the floor.

Donovan mutters a slew of curses.

We're silent for a few moments, listening for approaching footsteps. Minutes pass without a sign of unwanted visitors before Donovan steps out of the doorway.

"Stay here, and do not make a sound," he instructs.

I nod, and he makes his way around the building.

He returns a few minutes later, silently gesturing for me to follow him. I do, and we make our way in the direction he investigated. Neither of us bothers to quiet our footsteps, and I figure Donovan is focused solely on getting me out of here as fast as possible.

I expect us to stay close to the warehouse wall, but Donovan leads me toward the trees.

"The road is too exposed. We'll go through the woods for better cover," he whispers in explanation.

As we enter the tree line, the shouts and shots seem to grow louder. Closer.

Don pushes me in front of him, shielding my body, but my feet falter, and I twist my ankle, falling into the rough foliage.

"Dammit," he spits.

My entire body aches and blood seeps through my jeans in several spots where the fabric has ripped.

Once I'm back on my feet, I wince at the pain that shoots through my foot. Donovan must notice because, in an instant, I'm in his arms, and we're racing through the trees. I have no idea how he manages to jog through the woods while holding me, but I'm immensely grateful.

Don stops running only after we can no longer hear the gunfire and shouts. He sets me gently down on a moss-covered log and turns his back to me. His long hair falls into his face, and he doesn't bother brushing it away as he controls his breathing.

"Why didn't we go back to the house?"

He doesn't look at me when he answers. "I don't know if the house was attacked, too, and I'm not willing to risk taking you there yet."

"So, what now?"

"I don't know, Elli!" Don's shout carries through the trees, and I cringe, not because it could draw attention this far away but because I've never seen him look so angry.

Dropping his eyes, Don takes in my huddled figure. "I'm sorry. It's just—I'm screwed."

"What do you mean?"

"Well, based on your experience, how do you think Mr. Moreno is going to react when he finds out that you left to follow him to the warehouse?"

I stand, ignoring the pain in my foot, and place my hand on his arm. "That's not your fault. He'll be mad at *me*."

"I was in charge of watching you at the house. Mr. Moreno said you were in your room, but when I went to check in, you were gone. I was outside searching when I heard shots. I was lucky to find you before you got yourself killed."

My face turns a deep shade of red, and I'm swallowed by guilt. "I had no idea you would get in trouble if I left. I'm so sorry, Don."

He rubs his hand down his face with an exhale. "Take a seat, Elli. We aren't going anywhere for a while in case things didn't go our way."

I suck in a sharp breath, pain slicing my chest at the mere thought of something happening to Joshua. I know I wouldn't have been much help, but running away isn't any better.

I just left him there.

"Is there any way to see if they're alright?"

Donovan shakes his head. "I left my phone at the house."

I fall onto the log once again, overwhelmed with the weight of my guilt and worry.

I'm glad I didn't change out of the jeans I wore to dinner tonight because when the sun sets, and the cool breeze blows through the trees, it's nice only to have to worry about my exposed arms. I hug myself tightly, trying to contain my shivering since I know Donovan has it worse.

He wears a pair of gray basketball shorts and a black shirt with the outline of a mountain over his heart. Still, he doesn't mention the cold, and I don't see a single goosebump on him.

I remember Joshua telling me that Donovan grew up in this area and isn't a stranger to the woods of California, but that doesn't ease the anxiety that simmers just below the surface every time a twig snaps in the distance, concealed by the growing darkness.

We've been here for roughly an hour when Donovan finally takes a seat, but even then, it's not to relax. He wraps a strong arm around my shoulders and pulls me closer for warmth.

I don't realize I've been spinning the engagement ring on my finger until his gaze falls to it with the tilt of his head.

"So, are you going to tell me about that?" he asks, breaking the tense silence.

I inspect the ring myself, turning it side to side in the minimal light that remains. The overwhelming sense of belonging it had given me only an hour ago is replaced by the thick knots of dread as I think about what could've happened to Joshua. My mind threatens to spiral with dark theories, so I distract myself by indulging Donovan.

"I'm not sure there's much to tell."

He gives a light laugh, and it's the first time he's seemed like himself since he found me at the warehouse. "Not much to tell? It looks to me like you're engaged."

I never agreed to marry Joshua, but I did agree to wear the ring while I stay here. I'm not exactly sure what that makes us.

"It's complicated," I whisper before grinding my teeth to stop them from chattering.

"That's the understatement of the year. I swear things were never this interesting before you came around."

"That's high praise from someone who once faced twenty years in prison."

Donovan pulls back to look at me. "How do you know about that?"

"Joshua told me. I think it's great how he stepped in to help you."

"Then I'm sure you loved hearing about how he saved Kade's life."

"Wait, what?"

Amusement dances in his gaze, and I forget all about how cold I am as Donovan fills me in on how each of the capos came into their power.

Kade, whose parents are surgeons in the L.A. area, never supported his interest in cybersecurity. They wanted him to follow in their footsteps and go to medical school. He would often hack into the hospital his parents worked at to see what they were up to, which is how he started to notice that some patients and procedures would disappear from the records with no explanation. After more investigating, Kade discovered that his parents worked for the Marsollo family, often doing surgeries off the books. One of the Marsollo capos discovered Kade's digging, and a hit was ordered on him. Joshua stepped in, having noticed Kade's talent and taken an interest in him. He was hired and quickly worked his way through the ranks.

Next, Donovan tells me about Alec, who went to live with his Uncle Jay after his mother—Jay's sister—overdosed when he was only ten years old. Jay, a veteran who was abandoned by the system, had been working for the Marsollo family for years by that point and decided against hiding his work from his nephew. Alec grew up seeing all of the good parts of mafia families—the camaraderie, the loyalty, and the luxury. He took on jobs around the base at a young age, and as time passed, no one knew the base better than he did. Joshua made Alec the youngest capo in the country, at only nineteen years old.

Donovan even tells me Tripp's story, which I'd been reluctant to hear but agreed out of sheer need for a distraction. Tripp was thrown into the foster care system when he was seven. He was kicked out of several homes because of fights he would instigate with the other kids. He started working with the Marsollo mafia family in his teen years, where his sadistic tendencies were not only appreciated but encouraged. He thrived in an environment where his cruelty was admired and his particular skill set was noticed by Joshua, who utilized it in interrogations and recruitment training.

The common thread through each story is Joshua's ability to not only see the potential in someone but use their skills to give them purpose while also strengthening his family. It's a win-win situation that builds loyalty and respect. It's why Joshua has such a strong family, even though it isn't built on a long bloodline.

It gives me a sense of pride that the man I'm falling for is the kind of man who sees value in others and actively embraces it, not only for his benefit but for theirs, too.

And I am, without a doubt, falling for Joshua Moreno.

As Donovan finishes his storytelling, I let my eyes fall to my ring once again. I try to pull in a full breath of air, but I can't, not when there's a chance that Joshua isn't okay right now.

The sun has long since fallen by the time Donovan finally stands from the log, gently taking my hand to bring me with him.

"We should head back now. Do you think you can walk?"

I put pressure on the ankle I twisted. It throbs, but I grit my teeth. "Yeah, as long as we're not running."

"Good," he says and pulls his gun out. "I want to be ready, just in case."

We make our way through the woods in silence, both of us listening for any indication that we might be in danger. My ankle is aching, and I'm grateful that Donovan travels at my speed.

I hadn't realized just how far we'd gone into the woods, and I nearly collapse in relief when I finally see the faint light of the house ahead.

We're about to break the tree line when Donovan holds out his arm to halt me. I follow his gaze, and we watch the soldiers bustling around inside, looking for anything out of place.

Ryder is barely in view, talking furiously into his phone. Kade is typing away on his computer, a look of defeat on his normally expressionless face. Other soldiers I don't recognize buzz around, everyone seeming to have a mission to accomplish. Alec and Jay are nowhere in view, but I imagine they're running around, too.

Of course, none of them hold my attention.

Joshua sits on the couch, elbows on his knees, head in his hands. My heart breaks at the sight of his slumped shoulders and tousled hair.

I want nothing more than to comfort him right now.

I don't waste another second.

I push Donovan's arm out of my way and force my ankle to move as fast as it can, with Don following close behind me. None of the men seem to notice our approach, and soon enough, we're making our way up the staircase of the back porch.

I reach the door and slide it open.

CHAPTER THIRTY-SIX

Joshua

I've never been anything but perfectly composed in front of my soldiers, but here I sit with my head buried in my hands like a child.

She's gone.

One minute, she was in my arms, and the next, she was gone.

Her father must've found us and planned another escape. But then, why would he attack the warehouse and not the main house? Perhaps to draw my attention away, but then he wouldn't have needed to take anything like he did.

I picture the shock she would have shown when she saw her father. Did he have to convince her to go? Or was she all too eager to get away from me? Did she ever want me at all, or was she just biding her time?

I might never know.

The shouts and curses of my injured men in the warehouse echo in my head, and I know that I need to pull myself together for their sake. Elise's father needed extensive knowledge of my private security system and layout to pull this off, which shouldn't be possible. I need to figure out how he obtained that information and ensure it never happens again.

Even as I make the list of things that need to get done, I can't pull myself out of this chair.

The sliding of the backdoor blends into the chaos of the room, but that's when I hear it.

"Joshua?"

Every head in the room snaps in the direction of the back door, and I can barely believe the sight before me.

Her dark locks are a tangled mess, and there's dried mud streaked across her cheeks, hands, and arms. The same clothes she'd worn earlier tonight are torn in a few places, blood dripping down one of her legs, and she looks utterly exhausted.

I'm across the room in a second, pulling her into my arms.

"Elise," I rasp, lifting her and crushing her to my chest.

She clings to me just as tightly, and I forget all about the audience we have.

"I thought they took you, too," I mumble into her hair.

She pulls back just enough to see my face. "Who? What happened?"

My gaze flicks to Ryder, and I know he's thinking the same thing I am. If the Consolis didn't attack us, then who did?

And why would they have stolen what they did?

"There was an attack at the warehouse. When no one could find you, I assumed it was your father taking you home."

With the reminder of her absence, my eyes snap to the man behind her, who I'd charged with her safety.

Donovan stands at attention, back straight and hands behind his back. He's in a slightly better condition than Elise but still looks rough, and he knows he's screwed.

"You'd better have a damn good explanation for why she wasn't safely inside this house."

My grief has given way to fury, and I'm seconds away from putting Don in the ground with the men who lost their lives tonight actually doing their jobs.

Elise places a hand on my chest, and I reluctantly look away from my head of security.

"It's not his fault."

My jaw ticks, but my words are perfectly controlled. "Where the hell were you?"

My question opens a floodgate, and Elise cries into my chest. As furious as I am, I hold her closer as she cries.

With a deep breath, I soften my tone before asking again. "Baby, where were you?"

She chokes back the tears and looks at me through wet lashes.

"You were acting so strange after dinner, and I couldn't shake the feeling that something was wrong, so I followed you to the warehouse."

She followed me to the warehouse.

The one place she knows she's not supposed to go.

The one time it was attacked.

She could've gotten herself killed.

I thought I wouldn't be able to handle her father taking her back, but at least then she'd be alive. I had no idea how close I was to *actually* losing her tonight.

"You did *what*?" I say through tightly gritted teeth.

The words pour out of her mouth in one breath. "I wanted to know what you were doing, so I followed you down there. I went around back when I heard a car pull up, but then I heard gunshots, and I didn't know what to do. I tried to come in and help, but I heard voices coming closer and froze up. That's when Donovan found me, and we went into the woods until it was safe to come back."

I can barely breathe through my rage.

Squeezing my eyes shut, I take long, deep breaths in an effort to stop myself from strangling the very girl I'm trying to keep alive.

"Joshua, I'm so sorry," she says. "You were right. I shouldn't have gone. I promise I'll trust you from now on."

When my eyes snap open, Donovan is the target of my glare. "My office. Now."

"Wait," Elise interjects. "He didn't do anything wrong! It was my fault that—"

"Not another word from you," I say, voice deadly low and eerily calm. She curls into me but says nothing.

Donovan disappears down the hall, and Elise looks after him with another round of tears threatening to spill. My eyes fall over her tattered clothes and marred skin.

"You're hurt?"

She nods.

I sweep her into my arms and carry her out of the crowded room. She fists my shirt in her small hands, and it feels damn good to hold her despite the fact that I'm barely holding on to my sanity by a thread.

When we reach our room, I place her on the bed and disappear into the bathroom. I flip the nozzles to start a bath and grab the first-aid kit.

When I step back into the room, she's fiddling with the hem of her shirt and biting her bottom lip, waiting for me to say something.

I don't.

I'm so furious that I don't trust I won't say something I'll regret later. I need to cool down before we have this conversation.

With the curl of my finger, she scoots obediently to the edge of the bed, and I kneel to tend to the various cuts.

"Maybe it'd be easier to get me a personal nurse with how often I need medical attention," she murmurs.

I grind my teeth to stop from snapping at her.

Thankfully, she abandons her attempt to lighten the mood. "Why are you running a bath?"

"It'll ease your muscles," I explain curtly and assess her swollen ankle. Only a sprain, so she'll be just fine.

She must realize that I'm not in a talking mood because she finally gives up and remains quiet as I finish taking care of her.

"Go take a bath and elevate your ankle. You should be fine." I stand to leave, but she catches my arm before I can.

Her eyes glisten with another round of tears. "Joshua, please. I said I'm sorry."

"Don't do that," I bite out.

"Do what?"

"Use your tears against me. What you did tonight was so remarkably stupid, and I have every right to be pissed at you."

She pulls her hand back like I've burned her, but before she can respond, my phone buzzes with an incoming call.

I don't even check to see who it is before answering. "Moreno."

Kade's voice comes through the line. "Sir, some of these injuries are worse than we thought. We're going to need to call in professional help."

Damn it.

It's been over a year since I vetted doctors here that I could pay off to stay quiet about the injuries they treat for us. I hope those doctors are still around and morally gray.

"How many do we need?"

"Two or three, minimum. We could use a surgeon or two if possible. Jay's doing all he can, but I'm not sure it'll be enough."

"Have Ryder reach out to the local hospitals. He'll know who to ask for."

"Yes, sir."

I hang up without another word and squeeze my eyes shut.

"Is everyone okay?"

I almost laugh at how ridiculous the question is.

"No," I say.

"Who?"

Normally, there's no way I'd tell her, but I want her to understand the gravity of the situation and just how close she was to getting herself killed.

"Everyone at the main gate is dead. Half a dozen more were hit at the warehouse—Alec included." Her shoulders slump, but I go on. "No telling how many will survive the night."

Elise pushes off the bed to stand and winces when her foot hits the ground.

"What are you doing?"

"Coming with you."

She can't be serious.

"Absolutely not. You're staying here."

"Joshua, let me help—"

"Like how you *helped* at the warehouse? How did that go?" I shake my head. "I don't have time to deal with you right now."

Her lip wobbles, but I don't relent. "Elise, *do not* leave this room. Understand?"

"Yes," her voice breaks in a whisper.

I turn my back and walk out the door.

The door to my office is open, and I slam it shut before rounding the desk. Donovan stands in the center of the room, unmoving at my entrance. With his back straight and chin held high, I admire that he refuses to let his nerves show.

"Explain."

He doesn't waste my time. "I went to check on Elise when you left for the warehouse, but she wasn't in your room. I searched the whole house before going outside and was halfway to the warehouse when the shooting started. Thankfully, I got to her before they did and took her into the woods. I didn't want to take her back to the house in case it was attacked, too."

"Let me get this straight: my capo—who is charged *specifically* with security—lost track of the *one* person he was supposed to protect *and* allowed an attack to get past the gates and hit the warehouse?"

He knows better than to give me excuses. "Yes, sir."

I take my time rounding my desk and let venom drip from my tone. "The only reason I'm not killing you where you stand is that Elise is here and safe. She knew better than to leave, but you should've caught her before she did. If anything like this happens again, you're

266

out. Are we clear?"

"Yes, sir. Thank you, sir."

"For now, you're on strict probation."

"I understand, sir."

"Get out of my office," I demand, and he's out the door.

I fall back into my chair and bury my head in my hands.

I was so close to losing her tonight, all because of her curiosity.

A curiosity that would've ruined everything if her mission hadn't been interrupted by the attack.

Not that she'll ever know that.

CHAPTER THIRTY-SEVEN

Elise

As exhausting as tonight has been, it's easy to avoid sleep. If I were to drift off without Joshua beside me, the nightmares would be relentless.

So, I rest on the couch, only half reading a book, waiting for Joshua to return.

It's nearing three in the morning by the time the bedroom door finally opens, and he trudges in.

His eyebrows pull together when he takes in the empty bed, so I clear my throat to grab his attention.

When he sees me, his shoulders relax. "Why are you still awake?"

"I'm not tired," I lie, because he doesn't need to know that I didn't want to sleep without him.

Joshua sits on the couch beside me.

"How is everyone?"

"We lost seven soldiers, and several more are injured but in stable condition. Alec is going to be fine," he assures me.

A relieved sigh leaves my lungs, but it's hardly fair that I should feel so glad since so many others lost their lives tonight.

I place my hand on Joshua's leg. "Do you have any idea who it was?"

He shakes his head, and I mentally note that he probably wouldn't tell me even if he did, and that bothers me.

I open my mouth to suggest we sleep, but I'm interrupted by the growl of my stomach.

"When was the last time you ate?" His tone is almost accusatory.

"Dinner," I answer sheepishly.

He squeezes his eyes shut. "That was eight hours ago. Why haven't you gone to get food?"

"You told me not to leave this room…"

By the time he opens his eyes, I see how truly tired he looks and feel a stab of guilt. I should've assumed I could go to the kitchen to eat, but I didn't want to make him angrier than he already was.

"Come on," he says, holding his hand out as he stands.

"Where are we going?"

"To get you some food."

"I can get it myself. You should sleep."

"I'm not tired," he says, repeating my lie. I want to object, but his tone leaves no room for negotiation, so I let him lead me to the kitchen.

Though we both know I'm perfectly capable of working my way around the kitchen, I don't protest as he sits me at a barstool and makes me a sandwich.

When he's finished, he walks to the liquor cabinet and pours himself a glass of whiskey. He downs it in one gulp, then pours another serving before sitting beside me.

It's only when I've scarfed down the food that I look over and see that he's avoiding meeting my eye.

"Are you still mad at me?" I ask in a whisper.

"Yes."

I figured as much, but hearing it still makes my heart ache.

"And Donovan?"

If I wasn't watching him like a hawk, I might've missed the white on his knuckles from how hard he's clenching his fist. "He's been dealt with."

"What does that mean?"

"It means you don't need to worry about it. He messed up, and he'll face the consequences. That's how things work around here."

"But we both know this was *my* fault, not his."

"He was in charge of watching you, and he failed to do that. That's on him."

I open my mouth to object, but his sharp glare silences me. "But I agree, it's also your fault. You *knew* you weren't supposed to go to the warehouse."

My eyes plead with him to see my sincerity. "Joshua, I'm sorry. I should've listened to you."

"I'm not mad because you didn't listen to me. Hell, I'm used to that." I appreciate the minimal humor in his tone, but it's short-lived.

"First, I'm mad that you put yourself in danger. I mean, coming in to help? What was your plan?"

"I—I'm not sure. I just knew that you were inside, and I needed to do *something*."

"It was stupid. You have no training or experience! You would've gotten yourself killed."

"I know," I say, as if he needs to remind me how helpless I was.

Joshua places a hand on my thigh, and I lift my gaze to see my own hurt reflected in his dark eyes. "And I'm mad because you didn't trust me."

"I do trust you!"

"You clearly don't. I don't know what else to do, Elise."

"It's going to take time," I tell him. "Even normal couples struggle with trust issues, and we're *not* a normal couple."

When he doesn't respond, I feel the need to explain. "You seemed off after our conversation, and I couldn't figure out why. I just had this feeling that you were keeping something from me."

"Of course I'm keeping something from you! I'm keeping lots of things from you, Elise! But it's for your protection. Why can't you see that?" Though he's not shouting, the words bounce off the walls of the quiet kitchen.

I place my hand over his, feeling a sense of relief and pride when his muscles relax at my touch.

"I know you're trying to protect me, but I don't like being kept in the dark."

"You never minded being in the dark with your father's work. How is this different?"

I wondered the same thing in the hours I sat in this room waiting for Joshua to come back, and the answer surprised even me.

"I never wanted to know what my father was doing because I was never going to stay there. But now I have you, and everything's changed. I don't want to be in the dark anymore."

The conversation I had with Ryder only a week ago has weighed heavily on me. I'm tired of running from something inescapable.

Whether I like it or not, this is my world, too.

The twisted features of his face soften all at once. "And what do you want?"

My eyes fall to my newly decorated finger, and I almost laugh because, isn't it obvious?

"You," I whisper.

The distance between us disappears, and our lips meet in a blaze of passion. The whiskey on his tongue and the scent of him overwhelm my every sense until there's nothing left but my desperation for him.

Joshua lifts me from my barstool and onto his lap, all without breaking our kiss. My arms wrap around his neck, and I hold him close to me, knowing with every fiber of my being that this is where I am meant to be.

Nothing has ever felt so right.

An overwhelming flood of emotion hits me, and I pull away from the kiss.

Without fear, hesitation, or doubt, I say the words that I mean with every ounce of my being.

"I love you, Joshua."

He sucks in a breath, brow furrowing like he's afraid to believe me. I let him search my eyes because he'll see it there, the unabashed love shining for him alone.

A heart-stopping smile spreads across his face. "I love you, too."

Joshua scoops me into his arms, and I instinctively wrap my legs around his waist as he carries us to our room. The familiar electricity is amplified by tonight's events, filling the room with thick tension that threatens to choke us.

And we let it.

With one arm anchored around his neck, I run a hand through Joshua's hair, gently gripping it and holding his lips to mine. His fingers dig into me in response, and I revel in the feel of it.

Joshua starts walking, but I don't bother to look where he's taking us until he tosses me to the bed with an ease that suggests I weigh no more than a decorative pillow. He kicks off his shoes and joins me.

With one arm braced on either side of me, Joshua towers over me, and for a moment, all we do is soak in the sight of each other.

Tonight, we were forced to confront the possibility that the other was dead.

We both imagined a world where we were robbed of a future together, where we had to return to what life looked like before we met and turned each other's lives upside down.

Before we fell in love.

I could never go back to the way things were before. I don't want to. I wasn't happy. My brothers and father tried to placate me, but it was never going to be enough. Anything less than a life with Joshua isn't going to be enough for me. Not anymore.

I know what I want.

Joshua's lips dip to take mine, but I shake my head.

"No," I whisper.

He pulls back just enough to look at me. "You want me to stop?"

I laugh because the mere thought of him stopping is the last thing I want.

"I *want* you."

His lip turns up in a dashing half-smile. "You have me."

"No, I mean, I want *all* of you."

Whether by my words or expression, Joshua finally understands my meaning.

"I told you, once I have you—"

"You're never letting me go," I finish with a dreamy smile. "Don't let me go, Joshua."

Seconds feel like years as the deliberation wages behind his eyes.

I let every ounce of my love and desire pour into my words. "I love you, Joshua Moreno. I love you, and I *want* you."

"I love you, too," he answers without a moment of hesitation, but his face still makes me think he isn't sure.

To convince him, I wrap my arms around his neck, pulling him back to me. Our lips meet and move like they were made for each other. Hell, I'm starting to think Joshua and I *were* made for each other.

What we have is rare. It's the kind of chemistry that can survive anything—and it's survived some pretty messed up stuff so far. We tried to ignore it because it was unconventional and complicated, but it was always a wasted effort. This was always meant to happen.

"Promise me that you're sure about this," Joshua whispers against my lips.

With a hand on either side of his face, I say, "I promise, I want you more than I have ever wanted anything in the world."

His lips meet mine in a searing kiss that I never want to end.

With my head resting on Joshua's chest, I feel his heartbeat slow to its normal pace. His arms are still wrapped around me, and I've never felt so content.

I have no idea how long we've been lying here, and I don't care to find out. I wish I could stay in this moment forever—safe and warm in the arms of the man I love.

Joshua runs his hand absentmindedly up and down my back, and I find myself being lulled to sleep by the motion, but there are things we need to talk about.

"So, what does this mean?"

"What does what mean?" His words are heavy with exhaustion.

My eyes fall to the sparkling diamond on my finger. "I mean, what does this mean for us? Our future."

"Well"—he shifts to his side so we face each other—"we'll wait until the month is up before making plans."

"What happened to, 'once I have you, I'm not letting you go'?"

Joshua takes hold of my chin. "You're mine, Elise. There's no question about it, but after everything that happened today, I have a lot to sort through. Besides, it'll give you a chance to get more comfortable."

His sentence ends with a yawn, and I realize that the day's events are probably made that much worse by the fact that he barely slept the night before on the hallway floor.

My bad.

I turn to switch off the lamp before cuddling into his warmth. "Okay, the end of the month then."

There, held in the arms of the man I love—the man I belong to heart, body, and soul—I let sleep take me.

CHAPTER THIRTY-EIGHT

Joshua

When I walk into the kitchen two days later, Elise and Ryder are sitting at the counter eating a late breakfast. Neither one notices me at first, and I take the opportunity to watch them.

Elise is leaning back in the chair, laughing at something Ryder says, and his shoulders shake with a chuckle. Her hair is pulled back in a short ponytail, and even from behind, I can see the pieces that frame her smiling face.

I hope that smile will still be there after this conversation.

"Morning, Princess." I stride into the room and wrap my arms around her.

She leans into me, and her glowing smile tilts upward. "Well, good morning to you, too."

When Ryder meets my eye, he knows what's about to happen.

"I should go," he says, taking his and Elise's dishes to the sink.

"No, stay! I feel like I haven't hung out with you in days."

"Actually, I was hoping to talk to you," I tell her. "Alone."

Her eyes flicker between Ryder and me, but he doesn't look her way.

"About what?" Her muscles tense in my arms, and I sigh. This is not how I wanted to start this conversation.

I reluctantly remove my arms from around her and take the seat Ryder was occupying. He leaves the room without another word but sends me a *good luck with this* look before going.

"Joshua, what's going on?"

My hand falls to her knee, and I rub reassuring circles there.

274

"Nothing's going on. It's just—" I take a deep breath. "We need to go back to the base."

She doesn't say anything at first, only stares at me like she's waiting for me to crack a smile and tell her that I'm joking. When I don't, the pink that colors her cheeks drains along with her once-radiant smile.

I'm about to say something when she shoves my hand off and turns away from me.

I've dealt with a panicked Elise on more than one occasion, and damn if I haven't learned a thing or two.

Despite my instincts, I don't reach out to touch her again or try to reassure her with my explanations. Instead, I sit still and wait for her to get a hold of her breathing.

She covers her face with her hands, resting her elbows on the countertop, and I can just barely see her lip wobbling. I briefly wonder if I should've pulled her into our room for this conversation but decide it doesn't matter.

Everyone else is already packing.

After two excruciatingly long minutes, she lifts her wary eyes to mine. "Why?"

"Between the fact that so many soldiers were injured in the attack and that we have no idea how the attackers got around our security, we're not safe here anymore. I don't have half of the resources here as I do at the base to figure out who did it and why."

She tugs at the hem of her shirt. "Please, don't make me go back."

"This isn't like before. No one is going to touch you."

"No one was supposed to touch me before."

"I know," I admit. "But this really is different."

Elise slides out of her chair with a shake of her head and strides out of the room. "I'm not going."

I knew she wasn't going to like this, and she has a good reason to be apprehensive, but that doesn't change the fact that I need to go, and I refuse to leave her behind.

The slam of our bedroom door echoes through the house, and I make my way toward it. I reach for the door handle, and my composure starts slipping when I find the door locked.

"Open the door," I clip.

Nothing.

Damn it.

"Open the door, or I'm kicking it down."

"Be my guest. We won't be here much longer anyway." Her humorless chuckle steals the last of my sanity.

I kick the damn door down.

I'd already damaged the hinges trying to get into the room earlier this week, so it didn't take much force.

Elise screams as the giant wooden door crashes to the ground—scratching the hell out of the floor—and she drops the stack of pants she was carrying out of the closet.

"Are you crazy?"

"I wasn't before I met you," I snap, kicking a piece of wood out of my way as I walk inside. "What's your problem?"

"My problem?" She scoffs. "You're kidding me, right?"

"Do I look like I'm kidding?"

"You look like you've forgotten what I went through there!"

I let out a long breath, the anger draining from each muscle as I relax them.

"Trust me when I say I will never forget what happened." My long strides close the gap between us, and she doesn't stop me from placing my hands on either of her shoulders. "I can't change the past, but I can swear to you that it'll never happen again."

"How do you know?"

"Do you remember why I went back to the base two weeks ago?"

She finally looks up at me. "You went back to kill Tripp."

"Yes, and I made it abundantly clear that anyone who even *thinks* about messing with you will suffer the same fate. This is nothing like last time."

She doesn't say anything, and her features remain hard, unconvinced.

"You'll stay with me in *our* room. You'll have security instead of a *'babysitter,'* and you'll be able to go wherever you want, whenever you want. I know you only have bad memories of the base, but give me a chance, and we can make some better ones."

She steps into me, burying her face in my chest, and I revel in the pleasure of holding her.

"I don't want to take steps backward," she whispers after a few minutes of silence. "We've come so far."

I step back and take her hand in mine. "Come on."

She doesn't question me as we head to my office. When we get there, I round the desk, grabbing the rectangular box and praying that this doesn't come back to bite me in the ass.

"You're right. We have come a long way, which is why I'm giving you this." I hand her the box.

"You're giving me a cell phone?" Her wide eyes inspect the object like it's alien technology, but I can hardly blame her. She's been without one for weeks now.

"I want you to be able to reach me without needing to go through someone else," I confirm and take her face between my hands. "And I want you to understand that this is nothing like last time. You're my fiancée now."

She freezes, looking up at me like I've spoken another language. "Your what?"

Absolutely nothing on planet Earth can stop the smile that breaks across my lips.

I release her face only to take hold of her hand and kiss the ring there. "You, Elise Consoli, are my fiancée."

"But—but I never agreed to marry you," she says in a weak protest.

"Not yet, but you're wearing my ring, and I have every intention of making you my wife, so we might as well adopt the term."

Elise's cheeks turn my favorite shade of pink, and she bites her lip to hold back a smile. "Okay."

"Okay?"

"We'll go back to the base," she agrees, and the look of complete and utter trust in her gaze nearly brings me to my knees. "If you say things are going to be different, then they're going to be different."

I pull her in for a long, adoring kiss. "They will be, I promise."

I place a hand on Elise's thigh for the fourth time to stop her leg from shaking. I don't bother reassuring her that everything will be okay because she swears she already knows. If only her body were as sure.

We're approaching the gate when I get a message from Ryder, who left half an hour before us to ensure they'd be ready for our arrival.

Ryder: All good here. Gate's opening.

We pull up to the eight-foot gates swung open to welcome us in. I watch Elise from the corner of my eye as we drive through them. It's the first time she's seen the outside of the base.

She takes in the scenery with wide eyes, and I suppose this would be quite a shock to someone who has never seen more than a few rooms of the entire facility. I take this as a good sign.

I *want* her to see this place through fresh eyes.

"It's… beautiful," she says, evidently surprised.

She's not wrong. The Spanish-style architecture mixed with the modern security measures makes the place look more like a castle than the fortress it is.

"Just wait until you get a tour of the inside. You've only seen a fraction of this place."

Ryder, Donovan, Kade, and Alec—who sports a thickly casted leg and a crutch under each arm—wait at the main entrance for us, a sight that seems to calm Elise even more. I hoped the familiar faces would have that effect.

I throw the car in park and walk to open the door on Elise's side. She takes my hand, holding tight even after she's out of the car.

The guys form a perimeter around us as we walk inside, and I'm pleased to see that they've followed my instructions down to the letter.

Every soldier in the building, not currently on security, lines the hallways. They stand at attention as we walk past and do a good job maintaining their composure, though I'm sure it's strange for them to see their leader holding the hand of a girl he took as a hostage only weeks ago.

Hell, I'm still getting used to it.

The overwhelming number of men here has Elise squeezing my hand almost to the point of pain, but this is necessary. My soldiers need to see that I'm serious about this, about her. I won't let rumors spread through the base and have anyone question the validity of my affections. I want every one of them to see that this is real.

Elise is mine.

Surprised or not, the only emotion visible on any of their faces is fear. Good.

They've all seen firsthand what happens if they step out of line, so I'm confident they won't.

I'm brought out of my thoughts when Elise suddenly stops walking. One glance, and I know what's going on—this isn't the first time this has happened.

Ryder and the others halt, and I take Elise's hands in mine, drawing her attention away from the soldiers.

"You okay, Princess?"

She looks up like she's just broken out of a spell, and I doubt she realized she'd stopped walking until now.

"I know this is overwhelming after—"

"I'm okay," she whispers. "It's just weird being back here, that's all."

Instead of reassuring her with my words, I pull her to me and place a possessive kiss on her lips. The action does exactly what I hoped, and she relaxes in my arms.

When we pull away, I take her hand and continue down the hall. I wonder if she notices how the men's eyes fill with reverent admiration as she passes them.

We reach our bedroom, and I've barely shut the door before she's on me again. Whether it's her nerves wearing off or her relief at finally having privacy, I don't care.

I scoop her into my arms and carry her to the bed.

My mind wanders to all the things I'd like to do to her now that we're alone when the door swings open.

"Seriously? We *just* got here." Ryder's voice bursts through my fantasies.

"Ever heard of knocking?"

He's unfazed by the hostility in my tone. "Ever heard of a lock?"

I move to get up, but Elise's gentle hand on my chest stops me from kicking my best friend's ass.

"What's up, Ryder?" she asks.

"Ready to train?"

"Train?"

"You didn't tell her?" Ryder asks, and Elise sits up.

"Tell me what?"

I stand, and this time, Elise lets me. "I was going to tell her. I just didn't think you'd start now since we just finished a six-hour drive."

"Didn't stop you from other physical activities."

"Is anyone going to tell me what's happening here?" Elise slides off the bed, crossing her arms over her chest.

"You're going to learn self-defense with Ryder."

Most of the time, I can predict Elise's reactions, but I have no idea how she'll feel about this. She's made her disdain for violence clear in the past, but a lot has changed since then. She's not in hiding anymore, and she's always going to be a target. I'd feel better knowing that she has the ability to protect herself.

"Really?" Her eyes glint with interest, and I breathe a sigh of relief.

"You're okay with that?"

She nods, a small smile touching her lips. "I don't like feeling helpless. Besides, maybe then I can convince you that I don't need security watching me all the time."

"We'll see," I say, pulling her closer to place a kiss on her forehead.

"You ready to go now?" Ryder asks.

"Let me change, then we can go."

She rolls one of her suitcases into the closet and shuts the door behind her.

"You're not actually going to let her go without security, are you?"

"Absolutely not, but there's no need to tell her that now."

He chuckles at that.

"I'm picking security for her today, but I'm not having them start until tomorrow, so you'll be staying with her until then."

"Not a problem."

"Ready to go?" Elise asks as she steps out of the closet.

I step into her path, blocking her from Ryder's view as I assess the workout set she picked—skintight leggings that cling to her *every* curve and a matching top that's cropped to show a few inches of her toned stomach.

"Absolutely not. Go change."

She crosses her arms over her chest—which only further proves that she should change. "I like this outfit."

"Outfit? It's lingerie. Change. Now."

"Excuse me?"

"Ryder," I call, not bothering to look away from Elise. "I'll escort Elise to the main gym to meet you."

"Yes, sir." I hear him walking to the door and watch Elise's confidence slip.

"No need for that," she says. "I'll go with you now."

Elise tries to walk past me, but I grab her arm and whisper so only she can hear me. "If you walk out of this room wearing that, I'll have to shoot every single man who looks at you, and since I'd rather not murder half of my soldiers, you need to change."

She laughs, and I'm sure she thinks I'm exaggerating. I'm not.

The idea of anyone seeing her like this makes me downright *murderous*. She's lucky I'm here to block her from Ryder's view; otherwise, I'd have to shoot him where he stands.

After a moment, she seems to grasp my sincerity, but, of course, she takes it as a challenge.

"I'll meet you in the hall in just a moment, Ryder," she says.

We both ignore his muttering as he shuts the door behind him.

"I'm not changing."

"Fine by me," I say, stepping back to sit on the bed. I run my eyes down her perfect body. "I love the view. You're just not leaving this room until you put on actual clothes."

She rolls her eyes. "You're the one who bought this for me."

"And I think you look incredible, but so will every *single* one of my soldiers. So, unless you're okay with me murdering all of them, you're going to change."

Elise rubs her face with both hands, shaking her head. "You're threatening to murder your own soldiers because I'm wearing athleticwear. Athleticwear which *barely* shows any skin."

"It might as well *be* skin."

"If I were at a gym, I'd be the most conservatively dressed woman there."

"But you're not at a gym," I remind her. "You're at my base, and I'm telling you to change."

She makes a show of taking a deep breath and releasing it before walking into the closet and slamming the door behind her.

I know my fiancée well enough to know she isn't about to walk out of that closet wearing something sensible. I'm already bracing myself to force her to change again.

When the closet door opens, I break out in a laugh.

I was right. She has not chosen a sensible outfit at all.

Elise has chosen to wear *my* clothes. She's taken a blue hoodie—which she looks like she's drowning in—and a pair of gray sweatpants rolled at least three times at the waist and once at each ankle.

She looks absolutely ridiculous.

"Now, *this* is perfect," I say, taking a step toward her. I wrap my arms around her waist, bunching up the fabric as I do, and dip down to kiss her. "You should wear my clothes all the time."

She rolls her eyes. "Am I free to go, Your Majesty?"

"Almost," I tell her, then lift her into my arms. She wraps her legs around my waist and meets my lips. The extra fabric makes it harder to get a good hold on her, but I manage.

Only after she's out of breath do I pull back and set her down. "Now you're free to go."

She does a dramatic curtsy, then turns to the door, giving me the middle finger right before she closes it behind her.

Damn, that girl makes me laugh.

I can hear Ryder's laugh from the hall before their voices carry as they go to the gym.

Since I don't have anything else I have to do today, I decide to make room in the closet for Elise's things. It won't take long since I was only taking up half the storage to begin with. Once I condense it, there will be plenty of room for Elise's wardrobe.

I'm ten minutes into the project when my phone buzzes.

Elise: Left you a present at the door<3.

I take a deep breath and grind my teeth.

It better not be what I think it is.

I leave the closet and go to the door of my room, throwing it open to find *exactly* what I thought I would.

My hoodie and sweatpants discarded on the ground.

Joshua: I am going to kill you.

CHAPTER THIRTY-NINE

Elise

"Are you sure about this?"

Ryder doesn't hesitate. "Positive. You're picking up on the techniques really fast. There's no reason why we can't start sparring today."

I nod, sliding my fingers into the gloves and stepping into the ring behind him. I don't feel nearly as confident as he says I should, but I'll trust his judgment anyway.

My eyes flicker to the clock hanging on the far wall. There's another hour left in this training session and two hours before I'm expected in the kitchen, where I spend most of my time these days.

When we moved back to the base a week ago, Joshua had me join Jay as the base's head chef. I was caught off guard by the news and even more surprised to find it was Joshua's idea.

He told me it's a win-win since it frees up Jay to do other jobs around the base and puts me in a position of power. I don't fully understand his reasoning, but I enjoy the job.

So, after my training sessions with Ryder, I work in the kitchen until late evening and spend the night with Joshua.

Ryder and I get in our fighting stances, and when he doesn't move an inch, I come at him with a kick to the knee.

That is a mistake.

Ryder catches my foot effortlessly, twisting it just enough for me to lose my balance and fall on my ass.

"What the hell?" I brush my legs off and get back on my feet.

"Did you think I would make it easy for you?"

I narrow my eyes at him and get back in my fighting stance.

This time, I opt for a punch instead of a kick. As I feared, he knocks my arm out of the way, but I follow it up with a quick jab to his stomach. As he arches over, I swing my elbow back, hoping to catch him in the face, but my legs give out when his arm hits the back of my knees.

"Damn it! You're so much bigger than me!"

"Most people you're up against will be, but you can use it to your advantage."

"How?"

"You'll see." I wait for him to elaborate, but he doesn't. Instead, he makes the first move this time.

The hook punch misses me by an inch when I duck out of the way, but when Ryder's weight carries the motion through, I have the perfect opportunity to knee him in the gut. Bringing my elbow up, I come down on his back with all the force I can muster. The motion elicits a throbbing up my arm, but I ignore it.

Ryder grunts, but he's still on his feet. I sidestep the swing of his arm, taking a stance behind him. I'm about to knock his legs out from under him when his hand snakes back and grabs hold of my wrist. On a dangerous whim, I let him swing me around toward his front and use that momentum to drive my fist into the side of his face. His grip on me loosens, and I kick him square in the gut, driving him to the ground.

Sweat pours down my face, but my smile is wide.

Ryder stands, reaching to touch the quickly forming bruise on his face with an expression that looks a lot like pride. "See how it's an advantage now?"

"I can use my opponent's weight against them."

"Exactly," he praises. "Ready to go again?"

By the time we're done, I'm covered in bruises that I'm sure Joshua won't be pleased about, but it's worth it. Though Ryder kicked my ass far more times than I did his, I'm feeling optimistic about how far I've come in my training.

When I exit the gym, Finn and Luke—my security detail—are nowhere to be found. My heart kicks into high gear, but I'm put at ease when I check the message on my phone.

Joshua: Needed Finn and Luke for a job. Have Ryder walk you back to the room. Love you.

At first, I was worried that bodyguards would make me feel like a prisoner again, but that isn't the case at all. If anything, I'm treated like royalty by every man here.

"Ready to go?" Ryder asks when he exits the gym, and I'm sure he got a message from Joshua, too.

We go over notes from our session as we walk and make plans for tomorrow's session. When we get to my room, we go our separate ways, and I waste no time hopping in a hot shower.

To complement my badass mood, I pick out black jeans, a low V-neck, boots, and a black leather jacket. It's not the most practical outfit for cooking, but a shipment of supplies just came in, so that should occupy most of my time anyway.

I complete my look with winged eyeliner and a slick ponytail, wanting to look as confident as I feel.

By the time I step into the hall, Ryder is just ending a call on his phone.

"You clean up nice," he tells me.

"I could say the same to you."

Ryder has traded his shorts and shirt for slacks and a navy button-up, looking more like a CEO than a criminal.

"Mr. Moreno needs Finn and Luke indefinitely. He's bringing in a new security team for you, but they won't be ready until tomorrow. In the meantime, you're stuck with me."

"Just like old times," I muse.

When we get to the kitchen, everyone is at their stations, poised and ready for my directions.

Ryder stands back, allowing me to grab the men's focus as I explain the schedule and who will be assisting me in organizing today's shipment.

Everyone gets to work, and the hours fly by. I've just stepped back into the kitchen from using the bathroom when I notice a few of my men aren't at their stations. It wouldn't be a big deal if it weren't for the fact that dinner starts in half an hour, and we need everything done by then.

I'm on my way to the break room to look for them when I hear voices in the storage room.

"I was handling things just fine before they came back. Life here is so much easier when Mr. Moreno isn't around."

I know the voice's owner right away—Elijah Frey.

Elijah stepped into Jay's role as head chef when we went to Joshua's house. He's always been frosty toward me but never rude or aggressive, so I've learned to ignore him.

"I couldn't give a damn either way," the other voice answers, and the scratchy tenor belongs to Caleb.

Caleb is a recruit in the last phase of his training. He has a few more weeks of job-switching before he'll be assigned an official position, and it's no secret that cooking is not his strength, so it's unlikely he'll be put here long-term.

"Just wait," Elijah tells him. "It doesn't matter where you're placed. You'll see it eventually. He's an asshole."

I'm teleported back to nearly a month ago when hearing vile words made me sick to my stomach.

A lot has changed since then.

I cross my arms over my chest and lean back on one leg in the middle of the hallway, unfazed when Elijah and Caleb leave the storage room and come face-to-face with me.

The color drains from Caleb's already pale face, and I almost feel bad for the kid.

Elijah, on the other hand—a buff man standing over six feet tall—meets my stare head-on. There was a time when the scruffy-faced soldier would've intimidated me, but after sharing a bed with his much more intimidating boss, I barely notice his bravado.

Though neither of us says a word, our stances catch the attention of the men in the kitchen directly behind me, and the whole room goes quiet.

I smile sweetly. "Were you saying something, Elijah?"

He doesn't answer aside from a glare that's laughable next to the ones I've received from my fiancé.

"I asked you a question. I expect an answer," I say.

Though I have my back to the room, the change in atmosphere is not lost on me. The air is thick with anticipation, and everyone is holding their breath as they watch the standoff.

"I didn't say anything."

My mouth turns up in a smile, and I take two slow steps toward him, letting my head lull to the side.

"Well, that's good because if you *did* have something to say, I would expect you to have the balls to speak up, or does Joshua know that he has cowards on his payroll?"

Snickers and gasps fill the room as Elijah's face turns a deep shade of red.

It takes him a moment to answer, and when he does, it's through tightly gritted teeth. "It won't happen again, ma'am."

I smile and place my left hand on his chest. "I should hope not because if it does, my fiancé isn't the one you'll have to worry about. Got it?"

Elijah nods tightly, and I decide I've embarrassed him enough. With the approving nod of my head, he and all the other soldiers scurry back to their work.

"That was interesting."

My cheeks flush when I turn to face a thoroughly amused Ryder. I completely forgot that he was my security today and witnessed the whole exchange with Elijah.

"Too much?"

"What do you think?" It's not sarcastic but a genuine question.

"I think that asking nicely doesn't earn respect around here."

His lip tugs up. "I think you're going to fit in just fine."

My phone buzzes in my pocket.

Joshua: My office.

What are the odds...

I turn skeptical eyes to my friend. "What did you do?"

The lack of confusion on Ryder's face gives him away before his answer does. "I might've told him to check the security footage in here."

"I thought there weren't cameras in here."

"Did you think he'd let you work in here without them?"

That's exactly what I thought.

"He was going to hear about it sooner or later. Better through the feed than rumors."

"You better hope this doesn't start a fight because if it does, I'll keep him up all night, and you can deal with his grumpy ass tomorrow," I threaten with complete legitimacy.

His eyes narrow only slightly, but I take satisfaction in the fact that I got a reaction at all.

Minutes later, I'm knocking on the oak door to Joshua's office, trying to ignore the butterflies swarming in my stomach.

"Come in."

Joshua doesn't look up as I enter the room, opting to finish whatever he's reading instead. I take the moment to assess his demeanor and get a reading on his mood. He's leaning back in his chair, finger tapping against the desk, and lips silently mouthing the words he reads.

He shows no physical signs of anger, so why would he call me to his office?

I take slow steps to the center of the room. "Is everything okay?"

"Everything's fine," he answers, still not looking up. "Can't a man just want to see his fiancée?"

I breathe a laugh that too closely resembles a sigh of relief. "You don't normally summon me mid-day."

His eyes finally flicker up to mine, and his brow lifts. "Are you okay?"

"Yeah, I'm fine," I say, and smile to emphasize my point.

"Oh good, because if something was wrong, *I would expect you to have the balls to speak up.*"

Blood rushes to my cheeks, and he stands, rounding the desk.

"So, you saw..."

"I saw," he confirms, placing possessive hands on my waist.

"Then you know how disrespectful he was being. I can't just stand by and do nothing when he talks about you like that."

His eyelids fall to half-mast. "Elise, I am fully capable of fighting my own battles."

"Well, yes, but—"

"And I couldn't care less what Elijah or any of my men think of me. So long as they're loyal and obedient, they can have whatever opinions they want."

I feel my cheeks heating when Joshua lowers his lips to my ear. "But it was very sexy."

My eyes snap to his. "You're not mad?"

"I'm not mad, but from now on, let me be the one who pisses people off, deal?"

"Deal."

I lift onto my tip toes to kiss him, then turn to go, but Joshua doesn't release his hold on my hips.

"Where do you think you're going?"

"Back to work," I answer. "Disappearing after telling off a soldier probably looks like I'm getting in trouble for it. I should get back before people start talking."

"Let them talk," he says. "I'm going to spend some *quality time* with my fiancee."

Without warning, Joshua sweeps me into his arms. I laugh, and my cheeks are burning bright red before he even sets me down on his desk.

His fingers have just begun to tug up the hem of my shirt when there's a loud knock at the door.

I sag in disappointment—prompting a light laugh from Joshua.

"To be continued," he promises, helping me stand and kissing my forehead.

He opens the door, swinging it just enough to hide the visitor from my still-flushed face.

I catch only a few mumbled words before Joshua turns to me with a smile. "Elise, come here."

I meet him at the door, and he snakes an arm around my waist.

Joshua gestures to the two men standing in the hall. "Meet Nate and Quincy. They'll be your new security team."

I open my mouth to greet them, but no words come out.

Because the dark-haired man that Joshua has introduced as Nate is, unmistakably, the man who left me the note from my father.

CHAPTER FORTY

Elise

"You know I'm fully capable of putting on a tie, right?" Joshua says, watching me intently in the mirror as I secure his tie.

"Don't interrupt my concentration," I hiss.

I step back to admire my handiwork, and Joshua raises an impressed brow. "Where did you even learn to tie a tie?"

I hop on the bathroom counter to sit while Joshua fixes his hair. "My dad taught me when I was young so I could feel like I was helping him get ready for the day."

"I think I'd like to see you all dressed up," he muses, coming to stand between my legs.

I wrap my arms around his neck. "Take me out, and I will."

Joshua kisses my forehead. "I have a video conference at 8:30 tonight, and, unfortunately for me, it won't be over until late. How about we go out tomorrow night?"

"Tomorrow it is." I try to hide my disappointment with a smile because I hate the idea of falling asleep without him beside me.

Picking me up, Joshua carries me into our bedroom. "What are your plans for the day?"

"I was thinking about reading in the garden after my shift in the kitchen."

He sets me down but keeps his arm snaked around my waist.

"I'll wake you up when I come back to the room tonight."

"Can't wait." I reach up to meet his lips one last time before he walks out the door.

Halfway through my session with Ryder, he receives a phone call summoning him elsewhere, so we have to end early.

When I exit the gym, Quincy is waiting for me in the hall, but Nate is nowhere in sight.

It's been almost a week since I came face to face with my father's inside man. The initial shock had hit me so hard that I went a sickly shade of white, prompting Joshua to have Dr. Hanes come check me out.

After the doctor cleared me, I had all day to lay in bed and consider how to handle the situation. Contrary to what my conscience is still screaming at me, I've chosen not to tell Joshua who Nate is.

I know it's wrong, but I can't shake the guilt at the thought of Nate being tortured because I ratted him out. At the same time, I can't betray Joshua by approaching Nate myself.

So, I decided to do nothing at all.

If Nate wants to talk, he can approach me, but I won't make the first move.

Only, after six days, he still hasn't.

I was thankful when my new security duo decided Quincy would stay near me at all times and Nate would keep an eye on the general surroundings from afar. Luke and Finn were great guys but stifling security. It also means I only interact with Quincy, a bulky, bald man with fascinating knife-throwing abilities that he's promised to teach me.

Nate rarely says a word to me.

Sometimes, I wonder if I have it all wrong. Maybe Nate brought me my food that morning with no idea that the note was there. After all, he never approached me after that morning, and he didn't do anything to help me when Joshua found the note. Wouldn't my father's inside man have protected me at all costs?

But then something will happen—Joshua will kiss me, or I'll laugh with some of the capos—and I'll catch Nate's disapproving eye. The look lasts only a moment, but it's long enough to assure me that I'm right.

Regardless, I plan to let him come to me if he wishes to speak. Until that happens, I'll go about my life as normal.

I consider asking where he is now, but both my security guards take breaks throughout the day, and I'm not usually out of training this early.

I'm showered and heading to the kitchen within forty-five minutes despite not being needed for another two hours.

The sound of shattering glass echoes in the busy room as soon as I walk in, and I don't need to look to know who it is.

"Again?" I ask, drawing attention to my entrance. Chuckles sound from around the kitchen as I make my way to the sink.

"Elliot, I swear, if you break any more glasses, we'll run out."

Elliot's face turns the same shade of red as his hair, encouraging the laughter behind us.

"I'll be more careful, I promise."

I wave my hand at the boy who's even newer around here than I am. "Don't cut yourself cleaning it up."

"Thanks, Elli."

I'm surveying the job board of the day when a buff brunet comes into view.

"He's lucky you walked in when you did," Elijah mutters. "I was about to rip him a new asshole."

"Oh, come on. He's a kid. Cut him some slack."

Contrary to what I'd feared, things are smoother than ever since my standoff with Elijah. The men around here take my leadership more seriously, which has made my job far more enjoyable.

Elijah and I have even developed a surprisingly pleasant friendship. After I saw Nate and was too nauseous to work the rest of the day, I asked Joshua to put him in charge to help recover his wounded ego. By the time I came back the next day, there wasn't an ounce of frostiness.

His brows pull together. "I'm not training *kids*. He needs to toughen up if he's going to survive here. Besides, dealing with me is nothing compared to dealing with Moreno. Slack is the last thing these recruits need."

"Fair enough," I say with a shrug because he's got a point. "He's all yours next time. Just don't make him cry."

Elijah flashes a mischievous grin that makes me think that's exactly his goal.

Just like every other day, my time in the kitchen passes in a blur, but not for the reasons it used to. Losing myself in recipes has been my go-to form of therapy for as long as I can remember, but I rarely have the chance to lose myself these days. I'm constantly working with the other guys, whether that means teaching them how to operate the appliances or bantering over lunch break.

For the first time in my life, I'm never alone.

When the clock hits six, I do one last round to ensure no one needs me before I head back to my room for a shower.

I throw on a pair of black sweatpants and a gray tank top, letting my hair fall in wet strands around my shoulders to air dry.

My security team dutifully follows me through the halls until we reach the garden.

I've just opened my book to the chapter I last left off when Quincy comes to my side. "I'm going to take my dinner break, but I'll be back in an hour."

"What? I thought you took a break when I was in the kitchen."

Every day, Quincy takes his break early, usually while I'm still cooking, which means I never have to be alone with Nate.

"Nate took his break then instead. Is that okay?" He seems to pick up on my anxiety, but I don't want him to ask any questions, so I wave a dismissive hand.

"Yeah, yeah, of course. I'll see you later." I smile, and Quincy gives me a long look before finally turning to leave.

I can feel Nate's eyes on me as I stare at the words on the page, not reading a single one of them. The air has become stifling in the mere ten minutes that it's been since Quincy left us.

Something in me knows, without a doubt, that this is it—the moment Nate has been waiting for.

His footsteps announce his approach, but I don't turn around.

"I was beginning to think I was crazy," I say. "Why did you wait so long?"

"I've been watching." His voice is a low rumble that brings me back to the day he left that note for me to find.

"And?"

"And I think it's real."

I turn to face him, crossing my arms over my chest. "What's that supposed to mean?"

"I think you *actually* love him."

"Of course, I love Joshua. You thought I was pretending?"

Nate takes a step forward. "I hoped and prayed you were pretending. That all of this is a strategy you're using to escape. But no, you actually care about that bastard."

"Joshua is a good man."

He laughs. "You're delusional."

"You know, I could tell him who you are, and it's game-over for you."

"Then why haven't you?"

293

I narrow my eyes but don't answer.

"And you don't think Moreno would wonder why his loyal fiancée waited so long to tell him that her security guard is a traitor?"

My expression is unchanging. "Joshua would listen to me."

"Oh yes, he does have a reputation for being understanding. How did that go when he found the note I left?"

It takes me a second to push away the bile creeping up my throat at the reminder.

"Things were different then," I say, hating the hesitancy that rattles my voice. "He trusts me now."

"So, he tells you everything?"

"Yes."

"Then you know what happened that night at the warehouse?"

I give him a smug smile. "There was a raid. I was there."

The victory I feel is short-lived because Nate's smile grows. "That's all he told you?"

I don't answer because we both know it is.

"Word gets around quick here. I know that you went to the warehouse before the raid even started because you didn't trust that Moreno was telling you everything."

I open my mouth to ask how he could possibly know that but close it just as quickly. I painfully remember how I confessed that very truth to Joshua while sobbing into his chest, surrounded by his men who heard everything.

"It's no secret that Joshua and I have had our issues. He asked me to trust him, and I do. He only wants to protect me."

I briefly wonder which one of us I'm trying to convince.

"What if I told you that you were right? That there was something Moreno was hiding from you that night?" His words add a hundred-pound weight to my heart.

"You're just trying to get in my head."

"On the contrary, I'm the only one being honest with you."

"Then what is it?" I snap. "What am I missing?"

He raises his hands in surrender. "I think we've established that you don't trust me, and that's okay because I'm not asking you to. You can see it for yourself."

"How?" I ask, knowingly taking the bait.

"Moreno's office is unlocked. All you need to do is look at his computer. It's all there."

"What if I don't want to know?" Living in ignorance is a coward's solution, but it sounds so much better than potentially shattering the slice of happiness I've managed to find despite everything I've been through.

Nate shrugs. "I think we both know you do."

I don't move a muscle as Nate turns to leave.

He's only a few steps away when he calls, "Oh, and Elise? Meet me back here at eight when you're ready to get the hell out of here."

I want to say that I've been standing here for the past half hour debating whether or not I should go to Joshua's office, but there is no debate.

I'm going to go.

The real problem comes with all the questions I have bouncing around my head. What will I find? Why did Joshua hide it? Will it have the power to ruin what we have?

I'm sure I can give Joshua the chance to explain, no matter what I find.

A quick look at my phone tells me I have fifteen minutes before Quincy gets off break, and he'll come looking for me. If I'm going to get to Joshua's office without raising suspicion, I need to go now.

Steeling my nerves, I abandon my book and leave the garden.

I keep my face composed and smile at the men I pass on my way, as I normally would.

Before I'm mentally prepared, I'm at the door to Joshua's office.

When I step inside, everything is so normal that I almost turn around and leave, but I don't. Instead, I force my legs to carry me around the desk.

The computer is open to a video clip, and my heart is in my throat as I process the frozen scene before me. The footage was taken from one of the security cameras in the gym.

In the very same ring that Ryder and I spar in daily stands Joshua and Tripp. A shiver runs down my spine at the sight of my attacker. I haven't seen him since Joshua shot him in the basement that day.

Now, the man who inflicted such cruelty on me is hunched over on his knees with his arms bound behind his back. He's shirtless, covered only by a bandage over the bullet wound on his shoulder. Though the image is grimy, I can see how frail and skinny he is, and I recall Joshua telling me that Tripp was starved and kept awake for days after my assault.

It certainly shows.

Soldiers surround the ring from all sides, reminding me of how they lined the halls for our arrival. They even wear the same somber expressions.

I press play.

Joshua's voice booms through the room as he circles the ring, slowly addressing the crowd.

"For those of you that don't know who this is, meet Tripp." Joshua kicks the crumpled man as he says his name.

A man whose face I can't see hands Joshua a whip, and I recognize it as the same one that was used on me.

"Tripp ignored a direct order to work from the San Diego base," Joshua says as he brings the whip down on Tripp's back.

"He got trashed when he should've been working." Another lash.

"But his biggest mistake? He hurt Elise Consoli. He put his hands on what's *mine*."

The lashes come down nonstop, one after the next at full force, and my own back stings with phantom pains at every snap of the whip.

Groans from Tripp are the only sounds that fill the deadly silence. Not a single one of the somber-faced soldiers says a word.

Once Tripp's back is a mess of blood and marred skin, Joshua tosses the whip aside. "Did you really think you could touch her and get away with it?"

When Tripp doesn't answer, Joshua kicks him again, this time with enough force to tip his crumpled body over.

"Answer the question," he yells.

Even in our most intense fights, I've never heard Joshua yell like that. The sound makes goosebumps rise on my arms.

Tripp looks up, staring daggers at Joshua as he whispers, "She wanted it."

If looks could kill, Tripp would've died mercifully.

With a flick of Joshua's wrist, two men approach and untie Tripp's hands, but he doesn't make an effort to escape or fight. Someone hands Joshua a small device that resembles a cigar cutter.

Joshua crouches beside the bloodied man, a sadistic smile on his face as he takes hold of one of Tripp's hands, which is already cut up from being caught in the crossfire of the whip.

Taking the device, Joshua slips one of Tripp's fingers into the circular section, and bile rises in my throat as I realize what's about to happen.

"You shoved these filthy fingers down her throat."

I watch in utter horror as Joshua clamps the device, and Tripp roars in pain as his amputated finger falls to the floor.

One by one, Joshua cuts off every finger on Tripp's right hand.

By the time he's finished, the floor around them is painted red, but Joshua isn't done yet. Another flick of his wrist cues Dr. Hanes, who wraps the hand as Joshua addresses the crowd once again.

"I am going to make this abundantly clear because there will be no mercy if I am disobeyed—Elise is *off limits*. If anyone so much as lays a hand on her, I will make Tripp's treatment look charitable."

Dr. Hanes leaves the ring just as Joshua pulls out his gun and points it directly at Tripp's head.

The seconds drag as I await Tripp's final moments. His expression is peaceful, ready to be put out of his misery.

Just when I think he's about to pull the trigger, Joshua smiles, lowering the weapon. "I'm not even close to done with you."

The video ends and tears are running down my cheeks. I want to walk away, but as the video automatically closes, a file of pictures takes its place.

My hand flies to my mouth as the images register.

Screenshots from security footage show Joshua, Ryder, and the other capos torturing Tripp in various ways.

Joshua holding Tripp's head underwater.

Ryder etching what seems to be words into the skin of Tripp's arms.

Joshua and Donovan ripping out Tripp's toenails.

Joshua pressing hot metal against Tripp's feet.

All the capos taking turns beating Tripp with whips.

Picture after picture—all different, but all the same.

My eyes fall to the dates attached to each picture, showing me exactly what I feared it would.

Joshua didn't kill Tripp when he went back to the base—he took him.

Tripp was in the warehouse all along.

CHAPTER FORTY-ONE

Elise

My stomach is in knots, but I can't bring myself to look away from the horrific images.

Joshua—*my* Joshua—did this. The same man who holds me every night. The same man who wakes me up every morning with a gentle kiss. The same man whose engagement ring is on my finger.

I'm so caught up in the shock that I don't hear the door open.

"Elise? How did you get in here? What are you—" Joshua pauses when my horrified eyes snap to his. "What's wrong?"

My heart jumps to my throat. This man standing before me bears so little resemblance to the monster on the screen, and I want to convince myself it's all fake.

"Elise, what's wrong?"

I want to answer him, but I can't find my words. All I can do is look between Joshua and the man in the pictures. Surely, they aren't the same person.

He takes a step forward, and I instinctively step back.

Joshua's eyebrows pull together in a warning.

"Elise." He takes another step.

"Don't," I whisper, stepping back into the bookcase behind me.

"What's going on?"

When I don't answer, Joshua huffs and stalks toward me. My brain processes the danger as he rounds the desk, and I clumsily dart around the other side, reaching one of the chairs and holding it for support.

Joshua is about to follow me when he sees his computer. Stony neutrality replaces his confusion, and it's a look that I haven't seen in weeks.

His mask of indifference.

"You lied to me," I say, my voice more than a whisper. I dig my nails into the wooden chair and let anger replace fear. "You *lied* to me. You told me you came here to kill him, but instead, you brought him to the house."

"You weren't supposed to see this."

"That's all you have to say?"

"What do you want me to say? That I'm sorry? I'm not."

As the shock of what I've witnessed starts to fade, I begin to understand what I was too blind to see before.

"The raid. They took Tripp, didn't they? He's out there, alive."

One sharp nod is his answer.

"How could you do that?" Tears spill onto my cheeks. "That was pure cruelty, and for what? I was safe!"

Joshua sighs, but it's exasperation, not regret. "I went there to kill him the night of the raid. You had just told me how your nightmares began. I was going to stop for you."

"For me?" I scoff. "I never asked you to do *anything* for me. I didn't even like the idea of you killing him, but I accepted it because I know that's how things work around here. But the things you did to him for weeks…"

"He deserved it all and more."

"No, he didn't! Joshua that"—I gesture to the computer—"wasn't justice!"

"I wasn't after justice. I was protecting what's mine."

He rounds the desk, but this time, I stand my ground.

"I am *not* yours."

Joshua pulls my hips to his and lowers his lips to my ear. "We can play this game if you want, but I can tell you right now that it ends with you sprawled out on my desk, screaming—"

I act on instinct.

I swing my arm as hard as I can, but before my hand can make contact with his cheek, Joshua catches my wrist. A sound like a growl breaks from his lips, and he pushes me until I'm pinned against the wall, his chest flush against mine.

His eyes glint with possessive darkness. "Want to try that again, Princess?"

His words send heat through my body, but I keep my glare firmly in place. "What I want is for you to let me go."

"Liar," he whispers.

Joshua buries his face in my neck, placing rough kisses there that make my head spin. The most primal part of me wants to wrap myself up in him because he's right.

I want him.

I'm his, and we both know it.

But that doesn't change the fact that he lied to me.

It takes all of my mental and physical strength to push him away. "Dammit, Joshua! Get off of me!"

To my surprise, he actually lets go, and I clutch desperately at my pounding heart. "I need to get out of here."

"Fine. We can go to the garden."

"No." I gesture around us. "I need to get away from this base. I need to get away from *you*."

"You're not going anywhere, Elise."

"Then I'll wait four days until this stupid deal is over, and then I'll get the hell away from you!"

Joshua laughs, the sound bitter.

"What?"

The cold look on his face makes him look identical to the man in the video, and a shiver runs down my spine as he takes one step forward.

"Did you really think I was ever going to let you go?"

"But the deal—"

"Was to buy enough time for you to realize, on your own, that you wanted to stay with me."

I feel like I've been slapped in the face.

How could I have fallen for his tricks *again*?

"You were never going to let me go," I murmur.

Joshua shrugs. "Doesn't matter. You were going to choose to stay. You love me."

You love me, not *we love each other.*

The words are blades slicing through my chest, stealing my breath and inflicting the deepest pain possible.

I want to hurt him back. I want him to experience the same pain that I feel now.

"And what if none of it was real? Maybe I've just been biding my time until I could get away from you."

He laughs, but I know him well enough to catch the flicker of uncertainty, as brief as it is. "That's just a lie."

The sound of his laughter is another stab to my heart, but I suddenly know exactly how to make him feel the same way.

I let the malicious words fall from my lips with ease.

"Is it? You're a cruel man who ruins everything he touches. Your own parents didn't even love you. How could I?"

He freezes, expression stoic and unfeeling.

Slowly, I slide the engagement ring off my finger and toss it carelessly to the side. "I hate you, Joshua. You can keep me here as long as you want, but I will *never* love a monster like you."

Making my way toward the door, I turn to see that Joshua hasn't moved a single inch.

I deliver the final blow.

"Vanessa is better off dead than seeing the man you grew up to be," I say and slam the door behind me.

My legs carry me down several hallways, and I don't know what my destination is until I'm standing outside of the bedroom that used to be my prison. The lock is gone now, so I open the door and step inside.

It looks just like it did when I was first brought to it. Back then, it had seemed so luxurious, but now it just looks empty.

I fall onto the bed, and tears run freely down my cheeks.

It's not surprising that my heart twists with the pain of betrayal, but what does surprise me is the regret I feel for saying those things to Joshua.

But why should I feel bad? Doesn't he deserve it? Hasn't he put me through enough to justify my revenge?

Then why don't I feel better?

My head rests on the pillow as I recall the things that I saw Joshua do in those pictures.

Weeks ago, when I overheard Tripp and other soldiers discussing things they've seen Joshua do, it was enough to make me throw up. Yet, when I saw the cruel acts myself, it didn't have nearly as strong of an effect on me.

In fact, my anger didn't come from Joshua's ruthless actions but from his dishonesty.

Though I can't say I encourage the barbaric behavior, it would be foolish of me to believe that this is unexpected of Joshua. I knew when I fell in love with him what kind of man he was.

He never claimed to change, and I never asked him to.

Maybe, deep down, the savage part of me believes that Tripp

deserved it, too.

The girl I was a few weeks ago never would've let herself think such a thing. She'd be too repulsed by what Joshua's done to ever consider forgiveness. She'd be packing her things right now to meet Nate in the garden.

But I'm not that girl anymore.

It's time to get off my high horse and stop pretending I have some moral high ground. The truth is, if someone hurt Joshua the way Tripp hurt me, I'd want to make them suffer, too.

It's eight on the dot when I stand to leave the room, but it's not to meet Nate.

I need to talk to my fiancé.

My tear-streaked face draws attention as I make my way down the hall toward Joshua's office, but I barely notice. A part of my heart feels like it's missing, and the only thing that will fix it is mending things with Joshua.

If my time here has taught me anything, it's that even when I can't stand Joshua, I can't be away from him either. He is easily the most infuriating human I have ever met in my life, but there is no me without him.

Not anymore.

And I need to apologize for the horrible things I said.

I'm rounding the last corner when I nearly run into a broad chest.

"Elise, are you okay?" Ryder asks, inspecting my splotchy face.

"I need to talk to Joshua," I say in a voice that's hoarse from crying.

"What happened?"

"We got in a big fight, and I need to talk to him right now."

"Elise," Ryder says, lowering his voice. "Mr. Moreno left."

"What? Why?" My heart drops at the thought that I've driven him away. "This is important."

He takes a deep breath. "I can take you to him."

The knots in my stomach loosen the closer we get to the garage. I follow Ryder's lead to a black SUV, and we wordlessly climb inside.

The car pulls out of the base, and we speed past the wall of trees lining either side of us, illuminated only by the headlights. In the minutes it's been since I left my old bedroom, I've imagined countless ways our conversation could go. Will we yell at each other again? Will he ignore me? Will we forgive each other and fall into bed?

I'm ready to find out.

We drive in silence, which is odd for Ryder and me these days, but not unpleasant.

Besides, I'm so anxious that I wouldn't be much fun to chat with. So, I settle for staring out the window and focusing on evening out my breathing.

I glance at the clock, which reads 8:30 p.m.

Time for Joshua's video conference, I mentally note.

The air freezes in my lungs.

I completely forgot about the conference that Joshua told me he has tonight. So then, why would he leave the base?

Joshua doesn't take time off work, ever. He wouldn't abandon a meeting just because we fought.

For the first time tonight, I stop thinking about Joshua and evaluate the man sitting beside me.

If I hadn't been so caught up in my own problems, I might've noticed the stiffness in Ryder's posture. I might've noticed that he called me *Elise*, not *Elli*. I might've noticed his knuckles turning white from how hard he's squeezing the wheel. I might've sensed the chill in the air surrounding him. And I might've noticed that the silence between us is far from natural.

Something is wrong, and though I don't know what it is, I'm sure of one thing.

Ryder isn't taking me to Joshua.

I try to convince myself that Joshua had to go somewhere else for the conference, but I can't. This instinct is the same one I felt when I followed Joshua to the warehouse, and I had been right then.

Just the idea of Ryder being a traitor is enough to make me spiral, so I can't dwell on my emotions. There will be plenty of time for that later.

Right now, I need a plan.

As inconspicuously as possible, I scan Ryder up and down. As predicted, his gun is strapped to his right hip, and there's a good chance he has a knife in a holster on his left.

The gun is my best bet.

The plan forms quickly in my head, and I pray it works.

"I'm going to puke," I abruptly announce as one hand flies to my stomach and the other covers my mouth.

When Ryder turns to look at me, I see sincere concern in his eyes and wonder if I'm making a mistake.

"There isn't a gas station anywhere near here," he huffs.

"Pull over!" My shout is louder than necessary, but I need to sell it. He grunts but obliges.

As soon as the car pulls to a stop, I swing the door open and climb out. Leaning over, I dry heave in a performance that truly deserves an Oscar.

As expected, Ryder appears at my side. "Uh, should I hold back your hair?"

I nod, and when he's only a foot away, I make my move.

Ryder once told me that my biggest advantage in a fight is that I can use my opponent's weight against them, but he was wrong.

My biggest advantage is that my opponent will underestimate me every time.

Right before he grabs my hair, I swing an elbow back into his gut. He doubles over, but I don't stop there. I jerk my knee into his chest and bring my elbow down on his back. Before he has a chance to recover, I grab a hold of the gun and scramble toward the thick woods.

Within ten seconds, I've bested the very man who trained me.

"What the hell, Elise?"

"You never call me *Elise*."

"And that warrants an assault? Put that gun down before you hurt someone." His wide eyes are disbelieving, but there's a darkness there that keeps my gun firmly in place.

"Where were you taking me?"

"To Mr. Moreno! What the hell is going on?"

"Joshua is back at the base, isn't he? He has a conference call that he wouldn't have rescheduled just because of our fight. So, I'll ask you again," I say as I casually flip the gun's safety off. "Where the hell were you taking me?"

Lifting his chin, Ryder lets the act fall away. "Put the gun down, and we can have a conversation."

"We are having a conversation, and I suggest you start talking because I'm getting impatient."

He lifts his hands defensively. "You're making a mistake."

I laugh at that. "I'm not the dumbass betraying Joshua. I saw what he did to Tripp, and what he does to you will be *so* much worse."

He ignores my threat. "Put the gun down, Elise."

It's obvious that he's not going to tell me what I want to know, so I try a new approach.

"Give me your phone," I demand, cursing myself for leaving mine in the garden.

"I'm not going to do that."

Shifting the gun just slightly to the left, I cock it back and pull the trigger. The boom pierces the quiet night, but I don't let it rattle me.

"You sure about that?" I ask sweetly.

"Dammit, Elise! Are you insane?"

"I'm not messing around, Ryder. Toss your phone over here before I blow your head off."

Ryder glares, but slowly reaches into his back pocket, and I prepare to catch the small device, but it never comes.

In a flash, Ryder's arm snaps out, and a metallic shard flies through the air. Before I know what's happened, the knife slices my upper arm.

My scream echoes against the trees. The searing pain is immediate, and my grip on the gun falters.

In my dazed state, I barely notice Ryder darting forward, knocking the gun from my hand and dragging me toward the car.

Blood flows down my arm, but it doesn't stop me from thrashing in his hold.

"Get off me! Ryder, get off! Let me go! I'll kill you, you bastard!"

Streams of insults pour from my mouth, but Ryder doesn't acknowledge a single one.

He slams me roughly against the car, pulling my arms behind my back and securing them with duct tape. He does the same to my legs, rendering me powerless to escape him.

"Shut your mouth before I have to do it for you," Ryder snarls in my ear.

I'm shoved carelessly in the back seat and he settles in behind the wheel, pulling onto the road.

Despite his threat, I rattle off every insult that comes to mind. If nothing else, I want to get under his skin. But when all my spiteful words have no effect, I try a crueler tactic.

"Your daughter should be ashamed to have a traitorous bastard like you for a father," I spit.

The car jerks to the side of the road so fast that I slam painfully against the door. When Ryder whirls around in his seat to face me, true fear grips my heart at the fury in his eyes.

"That's it," he mutters as he grabs a handful of my hair and drags me toward him.

I writhe against him, but it doesn't matter. He silences me with two layers of duct tape and tosses me back into the seat before driving off again.

Instead of struggling, I lay idly in the back to conserve my strength as much as possible.

We drive for another twenty minutes or so when the car finally pulls to a stop.

"Don't make me regret this," he warns as he pulls me from the car, but I have no idea what he means until the tape is ripped from my mouth.

It burns, but all I can do is glare daggers at him.

He uses his knife to cut my legs free, but my wrists remain bound. When I can walk, Ryder drags me up the cracked sidewalk that leads to the building that I finally take in.

An abandoned factory.

When we enter the worn doorway, I don't have time to take in my surroundings because I'm pushed into another man's arms.

Nate.

My mind works unsuccessfully to put the pieces together. I look to Ryder. "Wait, you work for my dad, too?"

Why would Ryder treat me so harshly if he was taking me back to my father?

"No. They work for me," a new but familiar voice announces.

My heart nearly stops as the voice's owner enters the room.

"Mason."

CHAPTER FORTY-TWO

Joshua

Vanessa is better off dead than seeing the man you grew up to be.

The words echo in my head for the hundredth time in the last half hour. I haven't moved from this spot since she slammed the door, and I wish I could hear that slam on repeat, but I'm not so lucky.

Vanessa is better off dead than seeing the man you grew up to be.

The worst part is that I know she's right. It's why I've never once given legitimate thought to what Vanessa would see in me if she were alive today.

She'd probably be ashamed to call me her brother, disgusted by what I'm capable of. But maybe she'd understand that I've fought like hell to get where I am, and she'd be proud of what I've built.

Yeah, right.

Most likely, she'd think I was no better than the sadistic drunkard who fathered her.

The comparison feels like a punch to the gut.

At no point have I been under the impression that I'm a good—or even decent—man. Still, I always thought I was better than Scott.

But how could I be?

I've hurt far more people than he ever did without an ounce of regret. I even *enjoyed* inflicting the pain—same as him.

But that's not completely true. I never wanted to hurt Elise.

So, why did I?

Seeing her face deflate at my callous words felt like a knife sliding across my heart, but it came so naturally. I don't know how to love her. I never have. My first instinct is to lash out, to hurt, to kill.

Being with her means denying everything I've ever known, and I thought I could do it.

Maybe I can't.

It takes all my willpower to drag my eyes to the ring she so easily threw aside before she left me.

I move to pick it up and fall into my chair, inspecting the only gift I've ever given someone.

Her eyes filled with wonder the first time she saw it. She had forgotten all about our argument when I told her I wanted to marry her, and for a moment, I could imagine her saying yes to a life with me.

When she finally decided to wear the ring, I didn't think anything would beat that. Then I saw how happy she was here at the base—taking on responsibilities, gaining respect, and getting to know the other soldiers. I swear it was like she was made for this life.

Like she was made for me.

Yes, I lied, but it was to protect her. She was so at ease knowing Tripp was gone and could never hurt her again. I couldn't bring myself to tell her he wasn't, but I also couldn't bring myself to finish the job.

Every time I saw him, I was taken back to that day in the basement. He'd stood over her beaten and stripped body, ready to break her.

He loved hurting her, so I let myself love hurting him, and I did.

Too much to stop.

Now he's gone, and I have no idea who took him or why. All I know is that I should've killed him when I had the chance.

I wish I'd told Elise the truth. I wish I hadn't lashed out at her. I wish I hadn't let her leave.

I wish she was here now.

Loving Elise doesn't come naturally to me, but I was learning. I was getting better.

And I just screwed up big time.

I clutch the ring in my fist, hating that it isn't on her finger now, but I'll fix that. I have to—because all I can think about is how much I need her.

My eyes flit to the clock, and I curse when I see my conference call starts in five minutes.

It can't hurt to call real quick and hear her voice—even if it is just to have her yell at me again. I'll take Elise's anger over her silence any day.

My phone is in my hand, and I dial before another second passes. I guess it shouldn't surprise me that she doesn't answer. I'd ignore me, too, after how I acted, but that doesn't change how badly I need to talk to her.

I try a different tactic and dial the next number. The phone rings for so long that I worry no one will pick up, but finally, Quincy's voice comes through the line.

"Wha—what happened?" His words are slurred, and I jump to my feet.

"Are you drunk right now when you should be watching Elise?"

"Elise…" he mutters like he's testing the name on his lips.

Something is wrong.

"Quincy, where are you?"

"My room," he says the words like they're one.

I'm running down the hall when I make my third call, and when this one goes to voicemail, I know, without a doubt, that something is very, very wrong.

The next call—Nate—goes to voicemail, too.

My fifth call goes to Donovan, who answers on the first ring. "Mr. More—"

"Where the hell is Elise? And why isn't Ryder picking up his phone?"

"I'll have Kade run through security footage," he says without missing a beat.

"Order every soldier in this building to look for Elise, and come to Quincy's room now."

"On my way."

I hang up and fire off an email canceling the conference call, all without breaking my pace. When I get to Quincy's room, I throw the door open and curse under my breath at the scene.

Quincy lies sprawled across the floor in the middle of the room. His head rocks side-to-side as if he's trying to shake it clear but can't muster the energy to. His phone rests in his limp arm, and it's a wonder he was able to answer it when I called.

"What the hell happened?" I ask, getting down to help him to an upright position.

He says nothing but points to the table on the far side of the room, where a half-empty beer bottle sits.

I go to it, and even though I find nothing out of the ordinary, it doesn't take a genius to know what happened here.

Just then, Donovan reaches the door. "What's going on? Quincy, are you okay?"

"Get Dr. Hanes to take Quincy to the infirmary. I need him to run tests to figure out what drug was put in here," I say as I lift the bottle.

He pulls out his phone, and I do the same. After two rings, I already know he won't answer.

Where the hell is Ryder?

"Hanes is on his way. What the hell is going on?"

"I don't know. Elise is gone, Nate and Ryder won't pick up their phones, and Quincy was drugged."

He nods and looks like he has more questions, but I'm already out of the room and racing down the hall. The room I'm heading to is well across the base, but I barely break a sweat as I run there at full speed. When I reach the door and see it's open, I sag with relief.

That is until I step inside to find it empty.

But I can tell by how the covers are bunched together that she *was* here.

This is where she went after our fight.

I have no idea why she'd find comfort here. Maybe it's because it reminds her of how far we've come since she was confined in this very room, or maybe it's because she didn't think I'd look here.

But if Elise isn't here, then where the hell is she?

An hour later, I still have no idea where Elise is.

All we have so far is the security footage of Elise and Ryder leaving the base earlier tonight, but there's absolutely no context to go off of.

The small voice in the back of my head has drawn its own conclusions, and I've done a good job of ignoring them, but with every minute that passes, it gets more difficult to fight it off.

She really left me.

Elise convinced Ryder to help her leave me, and he did.

I've always feared that all this time, she was only pretending to want me as a way to bide her time—then she said as much in my office tonight. My instincts tell me she was only trying to hurt me like I hurt her, but there's a part of me that's inclined to believe it.

Though, even that part of me has to admit that something about this doesn't seem right. Why would they drug Quincy, and why has Nate disappeared completely?

Then there's the fact that, though we can't trace it, there's definitely security footage missing. There's an entire hour before my fight with Elise that was replaced with a loop.

Kade sits beside me in his office, relentlessly searching for the missing footage or anything that could help us. His team occupies the other half dozen computers, all reviewing footage from the day.

"Mr. Moreno," one of the newest recruits, Daniel, calls. "I'm not sure if this is out of the ordinary, but you should check it out."

I stand over him and watch the screen, which depicts the events that occurred in this very room when Elise and I would've been in my office.

The room is empty, and there's no movement on the screen. After several seconds, I ball my fist to stop myself from hurting this kid. "What the hell am I looking at right now?"

His eyes snap up at the bite in my tone, and his voice wavers as he answers, "Nothing yet, Mr. Moreno, but keep watching."

I repress the urge to snap again as I watch the screen.

That's when I see it.

It's barely noticeable, and I'm surprised that Daniel was able to catch it at all, but it's there.

To anyone else, the person in question would be indistinguishable, but I know, without a doubt, who it is.

"Play it again," I demand, and Daniel obliges.

The motionless room on the screen has my complete attention now, and I see the second his shoulder comes into focus. He knew just where to stand so that none of the security cameras would catch his face, and there's only one man with that level of skill and intimate knowledge of this base.

It's Ryder.

"Can you trace the activity on the server to see what he was looking for?"

The kid nods, and it's another excruciating ten minutes before he looks nervously over his shoulder, and I come to stand behind him.

"Sir, he wasn't *looking* for anything," Daniel says, breaking into a sweat. "He took everything."

"What does that mean?"

"It means *literally* every file on our entire database was copied onto an external hard drive today at the same time that security footage was taken."

It takes everything in me to stop from throwing my fist through a wall.

"I mean, that shouldn't be possible in the first place, and this was done in the span of a few minutes. A download that size should've taken most of the day."

Kade and I share a look over Daniel's head because we know exactly how he did it.

After all, the idea had been mine.

When I came into power, it was during an FBI investigation, and in an effort to wipe any incriminating evidence, most of our digital records had to be purged. We didn't have time to securely transfer the data onto an external hard drive first, forcing us to erase it outright. It's the main reason it took me so long to rebuild the empire—we were digitally starting from scratch.

To prevent that from happening again, Ryder, Kade, and I devised a plan for quick data extraction. Only the three of us knew about the project since it could be disastrous if it fell into the wrong hands.

Just like this.

Ryder—my oldest and best friend—stole every file on our database, then left with the only girl I've ever loved.

I'm not sure how much more I can handle, but when Kade's eyes widen in horror, I know things are only going to get worse.

"Sir," Kade says, voice tight with urgency, "we just got a message."

CHAPTER FORTY-THREE

Elise

"What the hell is going on?"

Mason turns to me. "Nice to see you too, Elise."

I open my mouth to respond, but Ryder steps forward, stealing my brother's attention.

Lifting his hand to his ear, Ryder pulls out a small object and tosses it to the floor. "I did what you asked. Now, let her go."

What the hell? Why would Ryder kidnap me and bring me here just to demand my release?

Unless he's not talking about me.

"Lyla," I breathe.

Ryder cuts his eyes at me, and white-hot guilt courses through my veins as I recall what I said in the car.

Mason shakes his head. "I'm not done with you yet. Your daughter will be released when I get what I want and not a second sooner."

"What does that mean? What's going on?"

Mason doesn't answer my question but looks to Nate. "Take Ryder downstairs to see the kid, then bring him to my office in twenty minutes."

Nate nods and takes hold of Ryder's upper arm, which he rips away immediately. Still, Ryder doesn't argue as he follows Nate around the corner.

It's just Mason and me now.

"What have you done?"

He grabs my shoulder and pulls me in the opposite direction that

Nate and Ryder go. "We've got some catching up to do."

I get my first good look around the space as we walk, and I'm surprised to see how well-kept it is. The factory is rundown on the outside, the kind of place thrill-seeking teens would make their playground, but it's only a front for this hiding spot.

The inside looks like it was recently renovated by a two-star construction company that volunteered to do the job for free. The floors are an uneven concrete but shine like they've been scrubbed clean in the last hour. The cracked drywall has a coat of light gray paint covering most of its divots, which makes me wonder who decided that painted walls were a priority in the midst of what seems to be a hostile takeover.

We turn down a series of hallways, footsteps echoing against the concrete floors. Neither of us speaks as we finally stop to enter a set of grand double doors. A giant desk occupies one side of the room, while two lounge chairs and a couch fill the rest of the space.

Mason takes his place behind the desk, not bothering to untie my wrists as he gestures to one of the chairs across from him. "Take a seat."

I contemplate whether or not to obey him, but much like with Joshua, I decide cooperation will get me further than resistance.

I study my brother's face as I lower into my seat, but he gives nothing away. It's different from Joshua's stony mask, more neutral and pleasant.

Completely unreadable.

"What are you doing, Mason?"

"You really do look just like her." His eyes fall to a small picture lying on his desk and though I can't make it out from here, I can guess who it's of. "Do you remember what she looked like?"

"I was seven," I answer. "I don't remember much of anything."

"Thought so," he says and slides the image across the desk.

He's right. I'm my mother's spitting image.

The picture is an old one, and she looks to be around my age now. Her thick, dark hair and brown eyes are just like my own. I even have her small nose and high cheekbones.

"I started noticing inconsistencies about her death when I was fifteen, but it was six years later when I began looking into it. By that point, she'd been dead more than a decade, and the family that killed her—the Venturis—had already fallen apart."

"What does this have to do with holding Lyla hostage?"

Mason doesn't acknowledge my question.

"There was one cousin, Marty Venturi, who skipped town a few months before the family collapsed, so I went to pay him a visit. He knew exactly who I was as soon as he saw me. He said he'd never forget her eyes."

My chest squeezes. "Mason, stop."

"He said he'd never forget her scream."

"Stop," I croak again.

"He said he'd never forget her begging for her life."

"Stop!"

"He said he'd never forget the look in her eyes when she heard her husband tell them to kill her."

The air is sucked from my lungs—the life from my soul.

He wouldn't, right?

Of course he would. He did it to me.

"He let her die to protect his empire, just like he did to you."

I squeeze my eyes shut. "Why are you doing this?"

"Because my mother is the least of what he's taken from me."

My eyes meet his, and the pain there hides just beneath the surface.

"You have *no* idea how lucky you are," Mason says as he stands from his chair. "Dad just let you go off to live whatever life you wanted, but us? Damon, Logan, James, and I were damned to this life from the minute we were born. We had no say in how the rest of our lives would play out."

"He would've let you go, too! Mason, you don't have to do this—"

"But even then, with my mother and future taken from me, I still followed him. I didn't know any better."

He stares out the window, lost in his memories. "A few months after I found out about Mom, Dad had me going to the docks a few times a week to monitor our shipments. That's where I met Mary Anderson."

He says her name with such reverence.

"She worked security there, so I saw her every time I went." Mason looks at me, and for a moment, he looks just like the sweet brother I grew up with. "I was in love with her, Elise."

None of my brothers have ever dated or seemed even remotely interested in the concept, so I know these words are said with utter sincerity.

"We kept it a secret for a year, and then we found out she was pregnant."

My mouth falls open.

"I had no choice but to tell Dad, though I knew he wouldn't approve. He has this idea that relationships of any kind are a distraction unless it's time to produce heirs, and even then, it'd be through marriages arranged by him."

This is the first I've heard of this, and I'm furious. I'm furious at Mason for all the horrible things he's done, and I'm furious that of all my family, he's the only one telling me the truth.

"I went to see her the night before I planned to talk to Dad, but she was gone. There was only a note that said she left and wasn't coming back. She told me not to look for her, to let her and our child live a peaceful life, but I knew it was a lie."

"What do you mean?"

The look he gives me is so cold, so patronizing, that I flinch.

"He killed them, Elise. Dad found out before I could tell him, and he killed them, then made it look like she left me."

I'm careful to speak softly, like I'm talking to a child and not my estranged brother. "You don't know that. She could be—"

"Don't be stupid. He wouldn't save his own wife or daughter. Do you honestly believe he's above killing the woman I love?"

I hate that I can't say a single word in our father's defense.

"He took my mother, my future, the woman I loved, and my unborn child."

"Mason, why didn't you tell—"

"Our brothers?" he laughs, but the sound is bitter. "They wouldn't have done anything. They worship the ground our father walks on. Even if they did believe me—which is doubtful—they would still side with him."

"No, they would've defended you."

"You're so naïve." He steps forward, pushing me back into the chair, and I gasp, surprised by the physical aggression.

"I'm sure you'd love to believe that our brothers are honorable men, but they're not. Damon's been an alcoholic most of his life—"

"What?"

"Logan became an egotistical ass when he was named heir to the family, and James will always be Logan's mindless follower. None of them would've attempted to fight Dad, and why would they? Dad doesn't lose."

I'm momentarily stunned by the overload of information. Damon's an alcoholic? Logan's the family heir? Why didn't anybody tell me?

I thought Mason was the only one with something to hide, but it turns out that my whole family has been keeping secrets from me.

"I know Dad has made mistakes, but that doesn't mean—"

Mason towers over me. "Mistakes? You think killing our mother was a *mistake*? A momentary lapse in judgment?"

He only shakes his head when I don't answer. "Dad's not stupid. He doesn't do anything without thinking of every possible angle. He knew exactly what the consequences would be, but he didn't care. He doesn't care about anything except his own power."

I straighten in the chair. "Then why did you give me to Joshua? If you knew he wouldn't save me, then why would you do it?"

"After Dad took everything from me, I still didn't have a way out. The only way to really be rid of Dad was to destroy him and everything he's built, but I couldn't do it on my own."

"You started working for Joshua."

"I wasn't surprised when Moreno had me working undercover for a year, but when it became clear that he intended to keep me there and take over our father's empire for himself, I got to thinking. What if *I* took over both families? What better way to make Dad pay for everything he's done than to take him down while simultaneously growing more powerful than he's ever been?"

The wild desperation in his eyes sends a shiver down my spine like a caged animal desperately clawing its way to freedom.

I don't like where this is going.

"With one foot in both families, I started pulling men from either side who were fed up with how things were run. It was pathetically easy to recruit soldiers."

"Do you want to skip to the part where you sell out your only sister?"

"I'm getting to that," he assures me. "A few months ago, Logan started noticing problems with the shipments and other deals that I've been sabotaging, and they figured out that there was a mole. When Moreno proposed expanding his territories, I knew it was time to make my move."

"You mean it was time to hand me over?"

He, unsurprisingly, ignores me.

"Moreno would take you expecting a negotiation, and after Dad refused, our brothers would force him to go in, guns blazing, to save you. We were all too young when Mom was taken, but we're not kids anymore. The fight would take out our father, brothers, and Moreno, leaving me to pick up the pieces," he says with an easy grin.

"At first, everything was going perfectly. Dad was pissed, Moreno was overconfident, and I was so sure I had it all figured out. That is until you found out about my compromised loyalties."

"Betrayal," I mutter under my breath.

"My plan still could've worked. Dad would attack, but Moreno would kill you before you got the chance to spill my secret to anyone else."

I shouldn't be surprised by his easy acceptance of my death, but I am.

"But then, Dad started dragging his feet, which is when I learned that he and Logan met up with Moreno without telling anyone else."

"Dad was going along with the negotiations," I fill in.

He nods. "I hadn't been expecting that. When we all confronted him, he told us that he was planning an extraction, and the negotiations were for show to buy time. To his credit, it was a smart move, but it screwed up my plan. If Dad set you free, you'd tell him about me, and I wouldn't get the fight I needed to take him out. I needed something that would tip off Moreno as well as piss him off enough to force Dad into aggression."

The realization comes with bile crawling up my throat.

"The note was from you," I breathe. "Nate never worked for Dad. You had him plant the note in hopes Joshua would find it."

Mason shrugs. "Dad would never be stupid enough to leave evidence of his plan in enemy territory. After a few days, I was worried it wouldn't work, but then I got the call that Moreno found it. I'm not sure I could've asked for a better reaction."

I'm momentarily grateful that my hands are bound so Mason can't see them shaking. I wonder if he has any idea what that note cost me.

"I was *so* sure that Dad would be ready to fight then. But the next thing I know, he calls us into his office to tell us you're dead."

"Which you should've expected if you knew he'd done the same to Mom," I snap.

"And I did. I planned to expose our father for the selfish asshole that he is, but words weren't going to be enough. I needed proof that Dad gave Moreno the order to do it. They'd turn on him and then come for you, which still would've accomplished my goal. The only problem was that Moreno stopped talking to me."

I remember Joshua telling me that he cut off communication with

Mason.

"I thought my plan couldn't get any more screwed up. You knew my secret. Dad gave you up with no traceable evidence. Our brothers believe wholeheartedly that you were dead, and Moreno wouldn't talk to me."

He smiles so wide and genuine that it sends shudders through my body. "That's when I started hearing rumors so crazy that I didn't believe them at first."

I narrow my eyes at him because I know exactly where this is going.

"My sister let Joshua Moreno seduce her."

"It wasn't like that," I bite.

"Oh yes, I'm sure it was such a beautiful love story. The cruel captor and the helpless prisoner. What a tale to tell your kids one day," he deadpans.

I open my mouth to tell him off, but his raised hand silences me. "Now *that* was enough to save my plan. Suddenly, I had bait that would lure both families here. Though Dad didn't want to fight Moreno for you, he did want revenge which is how I got him to agree to let me fly out here to do some reconnaissance, and what do you know? I found our lost sister."

Mason checks his phone. "Our family is set to land any minute now, and they'll be on their way here. Of course, you won't be waiting for them when they get here, but your boyfriend and his men will be stationed at the packing warehouse, ready to greet them with gunfire."

There's a pounding in my ears with the growing realization that things are so much worse than I thought.

"Joshua won't fire," I assure him. "He wouldn't attack our family without reason."

A knock interrupts my defense, and Mason calls the visitor in.

Nate opens the door and pushes Ryder inside. My heart squeezes at the hollow look in his eyes.

He's shoved into the chair beside mine.

"Welcome back, Ryder," Mason says. "How is she?"

Ryder's answering glare is chilling.

Nate takes his place beside the desk, standing at attention as my brother clears his throat.

"You're right, Elise. Moreno won't come here ready to attack Dad unless he has a sufficient reason." Mason looks between Ryder and me, a cruel smile playing on his lips. "That's where you two come in."

"What's that supposed to mean?" I ask.

Instead of answering, Mason steps around the desk, holding his hand out to Ryder, who digs into his pocket and hands over a black flash drive.

"What the hell is that?"

Mason holds up the small device. "This is every file on Moreno's database. It's his shipment plans, employment records, safe codes, and an inventory of every weapon and substance he has, along with their location."

My breath catches.

If that flash drive holds everything that Mason claims, it would destroy Joshua.

I'm careful to maintain my bravado. "And how exactly is this supposed to convince Joshua to murder our family?"

Mason's lip quirks upward. "I think Moreno will be more than trigger-happy when he finds out his fiancée and best friend—who have been sleeping together behind his back for weeks—are going to give the flash drive to Dad unless he brings a million dollars here."

"Joshua won't believe it," I say with more confidence than I feel.

"I agree. A written confession won't be enough to sell it. That's why you two are going to seal the deal and convince him on camera that the affair is real. You'll tell him that unless he brings the money here tonight, you're handing the information over to Dad."

"And why would we do that?"

Mason's smile spreads into a demented grimace as he nods to Ryder. "Because if you don't, it'll be his daughter who pays the price."

My cheeks burn with rage. "How could you threaten his child after what Dad did to yours?"

It's a low blow, but it catches him off guard.

My brother moves in front of me once again, crouching down until we're at eye level. "I'm going to give you a chance to do the right thing here, Elise."

"What does that mean?"

"It means that we can work *together*. You're more capable than all our brothers combined, and together, we could make them pay for what they've done. All you need to do is say yes."

There's no way this is happening.

He's asking me to turn my back on my family, on Joshua, and for what? Power? Revenge?

"And if I don't?"

Mason's jaw ticks, but he doesn't look surprised. "If you're not with me, you're against me. Sister or not, you'll be as dead to me as the rest of our family."

Goosebumps rise on my arms from his ice-cold threats, and I know he means every word.

But we both know my answer before I open my mouth.

"I can't," I say in a whisper.

Mason's hands tighten into fists at his sides, and I momentarily wonder if he's going to hit me, but he stands and makes his way around his desk.

"Well, now that lines have been drawn." He reaches into a drawer, pulls out a video camera, and sets it on the desk. "Let's get to business."

CHAPTER FORTY-FOUR

Joshua

I sit at the head of the conference table with Donovan, Alec, and Kade filling the other chairs. I can't shake the dread churning in my stomach.

The screen before us is paused, but I already despise the scene it depicts. Elise is sitting on Ryder's lap, arms wrapped securely around his neck in the same way she's done to me a dozen times. She doesn't look nervous or afraid. In fact, she's perfectly composed, staring straight into the camera.

Despite knowing I'm going to hate every second of this, I nod for Kade to press play.

"Joshua," she draws out my name, the sound full of pity. "By now you've seen some questionable security footage, so allow me to clear up any confusion."

She turns her head away from the camera until her lips are pressed firmly to Ryder's. Bile rises in my throat when one of his hands rests on the small of her back, and the other weaves itself into her hair, pulling her in closer.

I know her so well that I can practically feel her moving against me now. Her full lips pressed to mine, her possessive arms locked around my neck, her hips pushing into me like she can't get close enough.

For the second time since Elise came into my life, I show weakness in front of my men. I stand, turning to look out the window so I don't have to see it.

It's too damn long by the time she speaks again.

"After you let Tripp assault me, it was Ryder who nursed me back

322

to health, and we couldn't stay away from each other after that."

"Unfortunately, we still had to deal with you," Ryder says.

"You had this delusion that I could somehow fall in love with you." Elise breathes a laugh. "So, Ryder and I decided our best option was to bide our time. I'd play the loving girlfriend, and he'd play the loyal friend."

There's a brief silence, but I don't let myself turn to see it.

"Tonight, while I was distracting you with our argument, Ryder was gathering every file from your database. So, I'll make this simple —bring one million dollars to the address attached to this video, or I'll hand the drive over to my father before Ryder and I skip town."

I'd laugh at the ridiculous request but can barely breathe.

"Maybe if you didn't have your head so far up your own ass, you might've seen this coming. Did you really think I could love an egotistical, maniacal snake like you?"

It's like the word flips a switch, forcing air back into my lungs as I whirl around to face the screen.

Elise looks down at Ryder like he holds the entire world in the palm of his hand, but it's the slight tremble of her lip that catches my attention.

"We'll see you soon," Ryder bids, and the screen goes black.

"Play it again," I demand.

"Sir, I think we should—"

"Play the damn video!" My shout reverberates off the walls, and the video starts again.

It's just as difficult to watch them kiss the second time, but I force myself to keep my eyes focused.

"So, Ryder and I decided our best option was to bide our time. I'd play the loving girlfriend, and he'd play the loyal friend."

A relief like I've never known before washes over me when I see it.

The pause is brief—practically imperceptible—but it's everything. Ryder's shoulder slides downward ever so slightly, but he knew it'd be enough for me to notice.

Our sign.

When you work with someone as long as I've worked with Ryder, you don't need to communicate with words or looks. That subtle change in posture is all I need to see to know that something is wrong.

And if the narrowing of Elise's eyes tells me anything, it's that she's figured it out, too.

The whole thing happens in two seconds, too fast for anyone else to notice.

As the rest of the video plays, nothing is out of the ordinary until the very end.

"Maybe if you didn't have your head so far up your own ass, you might've seen this coming. Did you really think I could love an egotistical, maniacal snake like you?"

The move is undetectable if you don't know what you're looking for, but I do. Her eyebrow lifts at the word *snake*.

Donovan sits up straighter. "That's our Kemps sign."

"It's Mason," I say.

We watch the video one last time, and I point out the evidence.

"Why the hell would Mason make this? And how?" Alec asks.

I pull out my phone and dial a number, putting it on speaker. It rings twice before she answers.

"Moreno? Is everything okay?" The velvety tone that compliments Ryder's so perfectly doesn't sound distressed in the slightest.

The genuine confusion gives me pause, and I wonder if I have this all wrong.

"Rachel, where are you and Lyla?"

"Home. Why?"

I share a look with the capos. Donovan glares, brows tightly knit and jaw ticking. Kade sits utterly frozen aside from his steady breaths. Alec chews on the end of his fingernail, and his chair moves with the incessant shaking of his leg.

They're just as perplexed as I am.

"Some family business—nothing to worry about. I just wanted to make sure you guys were okay."

"All good here. Thanks for calling, Moreno."

Kade straightens his back. "Ryder," he mouths.

Rachel didn't ask about Ryder.

If family business drove me to call Rachel, she'd have to guess Ryder was involved somehow, so why didn't she ask if he was okay? Ryder and Rachel may have a complicated past, but there's no denying that they care about each other.

Something is off.

"Call me if you need anything," I tell her.

"Of course," she says, ending the call.

My capos and I are on our feet in an instant. "Alec, send someone from the Sacramento base to Rachel's house to check on her and Lyla."

"Yes, sir." And he's out the door.

"Kade, prepare eight cars and as many escape routes as possible from the address on the video. Don, get twenty-five of the best soldiers we have ready to go within the hour."

They don't hesitate for a second, and I very dangerously allow myself one moment to believe that we may be onto something.

"Mr. Moreno!" Alec bursts into the garage, sweat dripping down his face with his heavy breaths. It's been only twenty minutes since our meeting, and Kade, Don, and I are almost done prepping the cars we need to transport all the men coming with us.

"The house was empty. Rachel and Lyla are nowhere to be found."

Damn it.

As great as it is to have found Ryder's motive, this is far from good news. This means that Mason not only has Ryder and Elise at his disposal but Rachel and Lyla as leverage.

The list of things I want to do to Mason spans well beyond anything I did to Tripp.

No one takes my girl.

And I will do whatever it takes to get her back.

CHAPTER FORTY-FIVE

Elise

The red light on the camera goes out.

"Well, damn. You almost had me convinced," Mason says.

I want to sigh with relief that he didn't seem to catch either of our signals, but I refrain. It had been a risk to Lyla's life, but when I caught Ryder's shoulder sliding downward, I immediately recognized the motion—it was the sign I'd spent weeks trying to figure out.

We need to hope it was enough for Joshua to notice.

I scramble off Ryder's lap and glare at Mason. "Let Lyla go. You have what you want. She has nothing to do with this anymore."

He almost smiles. "That's not going to happen."

Ryder jumps to his feet. "You motherf—"

He doesn't get to finish because Nate presses a taser to his neck, and he falls to the ground.

"Stop! Don't hurt him!" I shout, tears pricking my eyes as I run to my friend.

Before I can reach him, I'm grabbed around the waist and throat from behind. I struggle against Nate… only I'm watching Nate restrain Ryder's arms behind his back.

"Did you miss me, brat?" The slimy voice brings me back to the worst day of my life.

I can't move.

I can't breathe.

My eyes flash to my brother when the realization hits me. "You raided the warehouse."

Mason shrugs. "No one wants Moreno dead more than Mr.

Singleton. You can't buy that kind of loyalty."

"Do you have any idea what he did to me?"

"From the looks of it, nothing compared to what Moreno did to him."

Tripp's breath tickles my ear as he chuckles, and I writhe in his arms. My head whips back, catching Tripp in the chin, but before I can get anywhere, Mason grabs me in an unrelenting grip. He secures my wrists behind my back before I can stop him.

When Tripp moves into my line of sight, I'm not prepared to see the damage Mason referred to.

This close to him, I can read the words that Ryder carved into his skin. *Coward, useless, nothing, worthless,* and other dehumanizing words line his arms, leading over his chest and up his neck. One hand has no appendages beyond his palm, and his face, which used to only have one single scar across it, is now a mess of light pink markings. Patches of skin are scabbed over in various shades of red and purple that make my stomach turn.

The videos and pictures I saw in Joshua's office couldn't capture the horror before me.

He truly looks like a monster.

"Don't like what you see?"

I don't answer. I can't.

Tripp's lip turns up in a sneer, and he grips my chin with his uninjured hand. "You're really going to ignore me after all we've been through?"

I jerk against my brother, who still holds my wrists, but it backfires when he lets go, and I fall into Tripp's arms. With our noses only inches apart, I breathe in the same pungent scent that takes me back to that horrible day.

"Go to hell."

He pulls my body against his. "Is that any way to talk to an old friend?"

"How's your hand?" As expected, his hold on me tightens.

"You little—"

"Now, now, children," Mason says as he leans against the desk. "Take them downstairs, but in a separate room from the girls."

He ignores my glare and grins as Tripp and Nate lead us out of the office.

The door slams shut, and the sound echoes through the empty concrete room. A metal bar that runs along the bottom of each wall is the only décor in sight. Both Ryder and I are chained to separate walls by handcuffs attached to only one wrist. Even with one hand free, we're too far from one another to attempt an escape.

Ryder slouches against the wall, looking nothing like the larger-than-life man I've come to know. How could I have thought, even for a second, that Ryder was a traitor?

"Ryder, I'm so sorry."

"You have nothing to apologize for," he says in an emotionless, empty tone, not raising his dejected eyes to mine.

"The things I said in the car, the way I attacked you, I never would've done any of it if I'd known about Lyla."

When he finally looks up, he gives me a sad smile. "Under different circumstances, I'd be proud of what you pulled in the car."

"I had a good teacher."

"There was one mistake though."

"Oh?"

His smile falls away. "You should've shot me."

"What?"

"Elli, when your life is on the line, you pull the trigger. It's what you should've done."

"How can you say that?"

Ryder lays his head against the wall. "It's the truth."

I think back to that moment and what had been going through my head. I was so mad at Ryder for his betrayal that I hadn't thought twice about holding him at gunpoint. I even fired a warning shot to scare him.

But could I have made the shot?

"I wouldn't have done it," I tell him.

"I know." Ryder sighs. "Still, I was wrong about you."

"What about me?"

"When Moreno told me he wanted to consider you for the capo position, I thought he was crazy." Ryder looks ashamed to say the words.

"Joshua wants *me* to be a capo?"

My father employs women for two reasons—cooking and cleaning. Joshua's L.A. base doesn't even do that. Even associates, the lowest on the mafia family food chain, are exclusively male.

If Joshua were to name me a capo, it wouldn't just unsettle his family but every crime family in the country once word got out.

Ryder nods. "He settled for having you run the kitchen to start, just to see how you'd do in a position of authority. It wasn't until I watched you snap at Elijah that I got a glimpse of what Moreno was talking about."

My cheeks heat as I try to wrap my head around the idea.

"But after everything that's happened today, I can't believe I didn't see it before. It takes a lot to rattle me, but upstairs, I could barely think straight, and you handled everything. Thank you."

"You don't need to thank me. I would never let anything happen to Lyla."

He only nods, and I know it's time to address the elephant in the room. "Ryder, what happened?"

He shakes his head with a heavy sigh. "During our session, I got a call from Rachel, but when I answered, it was Mason." Ryder spits my brother's name.

"He told me that if I ever wanted to see my daughter again, I needed to go to the garage and wait for instructions, so I did. When I got there, Nate was waiting for me. I was given an earpiece and told not to take it out."

"Rachel's here, too?" I hadn't even thought about Lyla's mother.

Ryder gives me a tight nod. "Mason knows Moreno will call her the moment he sees the footage of me. He'll assume Lyla's in trouble, so Mason will have Rachel tell him everything is fine. I just hope he does a more thorough check than that."

I hope so, too.

"I had to wait until you and Moreno fought, then download the files onto the flash drive and get you to leave the base with me willingly."

"But Nate told me to meet him in the garden at eight. He said he'd get me away from Joshua. How would the plan have worked if I'd actually gone?"

"I was the one waiting for you in the garden. Had you come, I would've told you I work for your father. But when you didn't meet the deadline, I went to find you."

I spend a long moment under Ryder's analytic gaze before asking, "What?"

"Why didn't you come to the garden? You know he lied about Tripp, so why didn't you leave?"

The mention of Tripp's name makes me feel sick all over again, but the ache in my chest is far more painful.

I don't even notice the unshed tears pooling in my eyes until I look up to see a blurry Ryder.

"I love him," I whisper. "I love him so much that it hurts, and I was furious with him for lying about Tripp that I—I just lost it... I said terrible things."

"Like what?"

"That he's a cruel man who ruins everything he touches. That his parents didn't love him, and neither do I."

Ryder shrugs. "That's noth—"

"That he could keep me at the base, but I would never love a monster like him."

"Still, that's—"

"That his sister is better off dead than seeing the man he is today."

Ryder's eyes widen more than I've ever seen before.

"Dammit, Elli."

"I felt horrible about it. That's why I didn't go to the garden. I was on my way to apologize to him when I ran into you."

Ryder mutters a string of profanities.

"He's going to believe the video, isn't he? He's already mad at me, and he's been jealous of you before."

"I don't know, Elli. A few weeks ago, I'd have been sure that Moreno would analyze every second of that video and see through it, but his judgment is clouded with you. Your performance was a little *too* good, and I'm worried he'll stop watching after the kiss at the beginning."

I squeeze my eyes shut, forcing my tears to stop. Now isn't the time to dwell on things I can't change.

"What's our play?"

"There is no play," he says with an undeniable finality.

"What do you mean?"

"I mean, my daughter's life is on the line. Mason already let Tripp mark her up with cuts," he says with a ticking jaw. "She's *three years old*. I won't risk it."

My jaw goes slack. My brother's actions go beyond unforgivable.

"We can't just sit back and let Joshua and my dad have a shootout. Do you have any idea how many lives will be on the line then? We're dealing with the two most stubborn men on the planet. If we don't do something—"

"Elise!" His use of my full name silences me. "I won't risk her life."

"And how do you know she won't get caught in the crossfire? Do you think she's safe down here? You think Mason is above using her

330

as some sort of shield?"

He flinches at my words, but I don't let up. "Her best shot at surviving is if *we* do something to save her and Rachel."

The muscles of his arms tense when he balls his fists.

He knows I'm right.

Ryder gives a deep sigh. "What do you have in mind?"

"I'm not sure yet, but I know that we can figure something out if we just—"

My words are interrupted by the sound of the door opening. Both Ryder and I tense when we see the visitor.

Tripp strides in with a cruel smile and a water bottle in his good hand. "Thirsty?"

As much as I want to spit curse after curse at him, I stay silent.

He waves the bottle like a hundred-dollar bill, and I hate that my parched mouth is begging me to ask for a sip. Tripp chuckles when he reads the thirst in my poorly camouflaged expression.

He takes slow, taunting steps toward me, and I'm ready to tell him to screw off when he sets the bottle of water on the ground and pulls a knife from his pocket. My spine straightens when the blade snaps free, and I can't stop my mind from flooding with the ways Tripp could use it to harm me.

"Why don't you ask nicely, brat?" he says, stopping to stand at my feet so he's towering over me.

I stay silent knowing how badly he wants a reaction out of me.

"Maybe I'll make you beg for it."

I *actually* bite my tongue.

"Back off, Tripp." Ryder seethes, and I notice that he subtly pulls on his cuffs.

Tripp flashes a wide smile at his former underboss. "You're not exactly in a position to tell me what to do anymore. Unless you'd like me to go visit the kid again?"

Ryder freezes at that, his stony features cracking at the mention of harm coming to Lyla.

Tripp turns back to me, crouching until we're at eye level, and I can't help but stare at the knife still poised in his hand.

"I bet you like to beg," he whispers.

I don't have the self-control to stay silent.

"Go to hell, you bastard," I bite out.

He laughs, genuinely amused by my reaction. "And here I thought I broke that spirit in the basement."

I refuse to let him see how much his words bother me, so I make a show of eyeing his fingerless hand and the words etched on his body.

"I'm pretty sure I'm not the one who's broken here." I breathe a laugh, relishing in the fury that dances behind his cold, hard eyes.

In one fast move, Tripp is pressing the blade of the knife into my throat.

"You're a real piece of work, you know that?"

The vengeful gleam in his eyes grows with every second that he pushes the blade deeper, and I can't hold back my wince. The metal slowly pierces my skin, warm blood sliding down my neck and soaking my shirt.

Ryder is shouting at him to stop, but Tripp ignores him so thoroughly that I wonder if he even remembers we aren't alone. I put every ounce of my focus into staying as still and quiet as possible.

He looks down at me with such pure hatred that I realize I'll be bleeding out on this floor in a few moments.

Just before he digs the blade into my carotid artery, he stops, though his rage-filled glare screams that he wants to keep going.

So, why doesn't he?

That's when the plan comes to me.

I force my voice to sound authoritative. "You need to let Lyla and Rachel go."

His billowing laugh makes my skin crawl. "And why the hell would I do that?"

"Because you don't want this."

His raised brow matches his amused sneer. "You chained up and Moreno walking to his grave? I think I've got everything I want."

"You don't want Joshua to have a quick death. You want him to suffer the same way you did. This isn't the revenge you want."

I feel a sense of victory when his eyes spark with interest. "And what exactly is it that you're proposing, brat?"

"Let Lyla and Rachel go, then I'll give you what you really want."

"And that is?"

"Me. I'll let you finish what you started in the basement."

CHAPTER FORTY-SIX

Elise

"What the hell, Elli?" Ryder has abandoned his attempts at subtlety and is now tugging wildly on his chained wrist.

As much as I'd love to send him a reassuring glance, I can't risk giving anything away, so I ignore him.

Tripp analyzes my expression, testing the authenticity of my offer. I repress the urge to cringe when his tongue darts hungrily across his bottom lip.

"And how do I know that you'd cooperate once the kid is gone?"

If I could, I'd stand and match his aggressive stance. Since my restraints make that impossible, I'm left with Tripp towering over me as I focus on maintaining my composure.

"You let Lyla and her mother go, then come back here and beat the hell out of Ryder." My eyes flicker to my friend, who is looking at me like I've lost my mind.

Maybe I have.

"You can tell Mason that Ryder freed them, but you were able to get him back. Once the girls are safe, I won't tell my brother or resist you."

"No way in hell! I won't let—"

"Ryder!" I shoot him a pleading look, which he answers with a scowl.

"You really want this, don't you brat?" I will myself to remain still as Tripp saunters toward me. "I bet you were so disappointed when our time was cut short before."

"What I want is for Lyla and Rachel to be safe."

"Ever the hero," he leers. "If only you were as strong as you are selfless, then maybe you wouldn't find yourself at my feet again."

"Are you going to do it or not?" My tone is measured, not giving away the jumble of emotions threatening to tear me apart.

"You're right." Tripp straightens, taking leisurely steps toward Ryder and gesturing around the room. "This isn't the revenge that I had in mind. I was put through hell by Moreno and this asshole." Tripp lands a hard kick into Ryder's stomach.

By some miracle, Ryder looks at me as he winces, and I silently plead with him to stay down.

He does.

Tripp makes his way toward me, a deadly glint in his eyes.

Lowering once again, he lifts his mutilated arm and gently brushes the rough skin across my cheek.

"I'd love to force Moreno to watch as I defile his favorite toy, but you're wrong about one very important fact."

I play his game. "And what is that?"

Tripp places the flat end of the knife under my chin, forcing my head upward so I'm staring into his manic eyes.

"Your brother doesn't care what I do with you."

After everything Mason's done, hearing those words shouldn't have an effect on me, but they feel like a punch to the stomach.

Tripp drops the blade from my face, letting it roam down my neck and over my shoulder. "Mason only needed you to get Moreno and your father here."

As the knife comes to my breast, I think I'm about to throw up. "But now that they're on their way..."

My heart drops at the implication.

"Why keep us alive at all, then?"

"We won't for long. You're here because you're important to both Moreno and Consoli, which will come in handy if things go south."

He turns to Ryder. "And we've got you by the balls with your kid here. Once this is all over, you'll be killed"—his chilling eyes find me— "and you'll be all mine."

I finally give in to the tiny voice in my head.

Wary of the knife now held at his side, I let my fist connect with Tripp's face, reveling in the satisfying crunch. Before he has a chance to recover, I hold onto the bar behind me with both hands and send my foot into his stomach as hard as I can.

He slides back, wheezing and reaching for the afflicted areas, but I know better than to feel triumphant.

Tripp's chuckle echoes in the room as he stands, drops the knife to the floor, and takes his gun from the holster. The barrel points directly at my head.

"Do it," I dare him.

His smile grows as blood drips down his face, like something out of a horror film.

"I'm not going to shoot *you*." He points the gun at Ryder. "I'm going to shoot his daughter."

"You stay the hell away from her!" Ryder roars.

Tripp weighs his head from side to side. "Of course, I could be persuaded against visiting Little Lyla."

"I won't fight you," I croak. "Just don't hurt her!"

"I think you've proven that you will fight me." Tripp uses the gun to gesture between Ryder and me. "But you won't fight *him*."

Ryder and I share a look.

Tripp tucks the gun under his arm and digs into his pocket, dropping a key onto the ground beside the knife before snatching the gun back up.

"Here's how this is going to work," he says and kicks the key toward Ryder. "You're going to free yourself. Then, you'll take the knife and inflict the damage *for* me."

I can use this.

Ryder shakes his head. "I won't hurt her."

"Either you hurt her, or I hurt Lyla. The choice is yours."

"Do it, Ryder," I tell him.

I've never seen Ryder look more vulnerable than he does as he gives me a desperate look. "I can't."

"You need to," I order.

Ryder studies my eyes, and I hope he can see that I am begging him to trust me.

After a deep breath, he takes the key and unlocks his wrist.

"Watch it," Tripp warns as Ryder stands. "Any sudden movements, and I'll blow your head off before doing the same to the kid."

Every muscle in Ryder's body tenses at the threat.

"Hey," I coax. "It's okay."

When Ryder turns toward me, I'm struck by the pain that I see there as he takes the knife from the ground and lowers himself in front of me.

"Now, since we have the expert himself here, why don't we start with some tattoos?" Tripp holds out his arm to show off the marks. "Let's start with 'brat,' shall we?"

Before Ryder can open his mouth to protest, I reach my free hand out and hold it over his.

"It's okay," I repeat and lower one of my shoulders. I simultaneously turn my head toward the wall so only Ryder can see as I point with my eyes to the cut on my arm that he inflicted earlier tonight.

If Ryder caught my message, his expression gives nothing away. I suppose it's good to remain inconspicuous, but I'm worried he's too worried about Lyla to notice my signals.

I wait for Ryder to make his move against Tripp, but he only looks down at me with grave eyes.

It's like he's moving in slow motion as he takes hold of my right arm and brings the knife to my skin.

I'm not prepared for the pain.

I squeeze my eyes closed so tight that I think they'll never open again. The first slice of the knife is nearly three inches long and placed directly next to the cut Ryder gave me earlier tonight. I can hardly catch my breath as he lifts the knife from my skin, only to bring it down again.

Somewhere in the background, I can hear Tripp laughing, but the sound of my pounding heart is too deafening to be sure. I don't let myself scream since that's exactly what Tripp wants to hear, but I have no control over the whimpers and whines that are brutally pulled from my clenched teeth.

All I want is to beg Ryder to stop.

But I can't.

He needs to do this.

Instead, I picture Joshua holding my head in his lap as we look over hundreds of trees during my birthday picnic. I picture him playfully tossing me over his shoulder to carry me to our room. I picture him holding me in our bed like we're the only two people in the world.

I want to melt into my happy place, but as the blood covers my clothes and the floor, I can't bring myself to escape this horrific reality.

It takes all my willpower to turn my head and see that Ryder has only just finished the R.

I want to sag helplessly to the floor, but that's when I notice

Ryder's eyes.

In all of the pain, I hadn't noticed that his eyes are only half-focused on me. He keeps sending subtle glances to Tripp.

The motion is lightning-fast.

Tripp roars a curse as Ryder's knife sinks into his leg.

In a flash, Ryder darts forward to get to the gun that clatters to the ground.

The relief is so overwhelming that my body begs to curl up for a nap, but the shiny silver key a few feet away catches my attention. Ryder must have kicked it to me before charging Tripp.

I move on autopilot, taking the key and unlocking my wrist in purely mechanical movements.

When it comes time to climb to my feet, I lose vision when I try to use my injured arm. My second attempt is legs only, and I stand just in time to watch Ryder bash the gun into Tripp's head, his limp body crumbling to the ground.

"What the hell?" I say, barely able to get the words out.

Ryder tucks the gun in his belt and removes his button-up, leaving him in a white tee. He tightly wraps my arm with the discarded fabric.

"I'm so sorry, Elli. I needed to wait until his aim drifted. If I'd done it before then, he would've killed one of us."

I pull the wrapped arm protectively to my chest. "Still, that hurt like hell."

"I tried not to cut deep, so hopefully, it won't scar."

A rustle from behind me steals my attention. Tripp's head lulls to one side, then slowly falls to the other. Ryder points the gun at him, but I throw my hands up before he pulls the trigger.

"No! We have no idea how many people are here. We can't draw attention to ourselves." I grab the key from the floor and hand it to Ryder. "Get Lyla and Rachel out of here. I'll finish off Tripp."

He shakes his head. "I'm not leaving you here."

"We don't have time for this. Get your family to safety, then warn Joshua."

I push him to the door, and when we reach the threshold, he turns to me with a gaze that shines with brotherly affection. "Be careful, Elli."

I place a kiss on his cheek. "You, too."

The slam of the door shutting makes me cringe, but not as much as the faint groan from behind me.

Tripp rolls onto his back, eyes fluttering and hands reaching for the knife still embedded in his leg. The floor is covered in a combination of Tripp's and my blood, and I work to ignore the nausea climbing up my throat.

I see the handcuffs against the wall and form a plan in my head. Grabbing them off the floor, I turn just in time to see Tripp's eyes starting to focus.

I'm running out of time.

My heart is a jackhammer in my chest, but I force myself to walk forward. I sink to my knees, reaching out to grab his hand when he suddenly coughs.

When my eyes flash to him, the calculation there is my first indication that something is off.

He moves quickly.

The knife swings upward, missing my throat by a mere inch as I fall back. It takes me a moment to realize that his cough was a diversion to rip the knife from his leg, but I also realize this means he'll weaken from blood loss if I can stall him long enough.

Dodging the knife has left me laid back on my elbows, and Tripp takes advantage of the opening. He darts forward much faster than someone with his injuries should, and the weight of his body pins me down.

His voice is a malicious sneer. "You're going to pay for this."

The forearm of his mutilated hand pushes forcefully on my throat. I try to pry him off of me, but my efforts are futile against his adrenaline-enhanced strength.

He lifts the knife to my arm. "Let's finish this, shall we?"

"Screw you," I rasp.

"Later. I want to leave my mark first."

The blade slips under the makeshift wrap from Ryder's shirt, and I close my eyes.

I'm not sure I can handle much more of this.

I look for anything that could help me, and my eyes fall on the blood stain growing through Tripp's pants. If I can wiggle just one of my legs out from under him, I'll be able to hit that exact spot.

Every fiber of my being aches, but I grit my teeth just in time for Tripp to cut off the last piece of the wrap.

The blade makes contact with my arm, and I writhe in agony.

Through the pain-fueled haze, I work to free my leg, but my struggle only serves to please Tripp. A deep, overwhelming sense of hopelessness threatens me, and I begin to doubt my ability to walk away from this alive.

His smile is vicious, and there's nothing that I can do to stop him from leaning down and licking the tears from my cheek.

The vile action makes me feel as worthless as I did that day in the basement.

My skin burns like it's being held over a flame, and my resolve fades along with my vision.

It would be so much easier to slip into the oblivion that's calling my name. To stop struggling and let Tripp have his way.

Then I see him.

I see him so clearly that my free arm twitches to touch him, but I don't have the strength to reach out.

Joshua doesn't say anything or move to save me. His expression isn't scared or horrified like I would expect right now, and somehow, this look is worse.

He wears the same carefully masked sadness that I left behind in his office.

That can't be our last memory together. Joshua has no idea how sorry I am. He has no idea that I was coming to apologize before everything went to hell. I need the chance to make it up to him.

The vision of the man I love is all I need to remind me what I have to fight for.

Using all the strength in my body, I jerk my leg to the side as Tripp continues his excruciating art, and it comes free.

Raising my knee as high as I can, I bring my heel down on the knife wound.

Tripp wails in anguish, and I buck my hips to roll him off of me. The knife that was in his hand crashes to the ground when his forearm releases my raw throat.

I gasp for air and lunge for the knife, barely grabbing it before Tripp does.

I have the knife. I have the power. Now what?

When your life is on the line, you pull the trigger.

There is no second thought as I spring forward and swing the knife savagely across Tripp's throat.

Eyes wide as saucers stare into mine as blood gushes from my tormentor's neck. His hands shake as he reaches to stop the bleeding, but we both know it won't help.

Nothing will.

I kneel beside Tripp, blood soaking my jeans as I watch the life drain out of him. Perhaps I should feel disgust or guilt.

I don't.

Instead, I see him towering above my helpless, strung-up body in the basement. I see him bringing the whip down against my back. I see him shoving his fingers down my throat. I see him pulling my clothes off of me with a sadistic smile.

"I get it now—why Joshua did all those horrible things to you." I lower myself so that when I speak, it's directly into his ear. "I only wish he were here to enjoy your death as much as I am."

His eyes squint, and I think he means to glare at me, but it's a pitiful attempt.

As the last bit of life leaves him, I *actually* smile.

CHAPTER FORTY-SEVEN

Elise

When I'm sure Tripp is dead, I search him for more weapons, but there's nothing aside from a small radio attached to his hip.

The knife will have to be enough.

Standing takes more effort than I expect, especially when my body would rather curl up and sleep, but there's no time for that—not with so much on the line.

I'm two feet from the door before realizing I have no clue what to do next.

If all goes well, Ryder will get Rachel and Lyla out of here safely, and he'll be able to stop Joshua from coming.

That leaves my father.

I need to tell him to stay away. If both my father and Joshua come here, Mason will make sure they don't leave alive. That means I need a phone, but the only one I've seen is in Mason's office.

Even *I* know it sounds like a suicide mission, but I have to try. Besides, this is what Ryder has been training me for.

Hell, I just killed a man. I can manage to get to an office.

Throwing one last triumphant look at Tripp's lifeless body, I slowly peel the door open and tiptoe into the hall.

I didn't see much of the layout when Ryder and I were brought down here, but I can recall enough to give me a general direction.

The halls are eerily quiet, and I wonder just how many people are here. From the outside, the factory looked huge, so it shouldn't surprise me that the soldiers here are so spread out.

As if my thoughts have jinxed my good luck, faint voices sound from around the corner.

I scan my immediate surroundings and run to a door that looks similar to the cell Ryder and I were kept in. It's locked, and so is the one next to it.

I'm about to resort to running when I see a smaller door to my left. It's the same color as the wall, like no one noticed it was there when they were painting. Even the door handle blends in.

I sprint to it, and by some miracle, it's unlocked. I hadn't considered what I might find in the room, but I'm grateful when it's only a janitor's closet.

I shut the door as quietly as I can and press my back against the shelves.

The voices grow louder, and I can make out the faint conversation.

"I didn't believe it either. I would've put money on hell freezing over before betting on Moreno keeping the girl," one jokes.

"Have you seen her? I'd keep her, too. Tripp had the right idea."

My stomach rolls at that.

"Speaking of, where is that bastard?"

My heart drops. They can't go looking for him yet. I need more time.

"Probably terrorizing the prisoners."

The voices fade as they make their way down the hall.

Even from this distance, I hear their laughter, halted by the sound of radio static. I press my ear to the door, trying to hear the message, but it's too muffled for me to understand.

My eyes go wide when I realize they're coming back the way they came, grumbling as they go.

"I didn't realize they were that close."

"Guess it's go-time," the other soldier huffs.

I hope they aren't talking about Joshua or my father—but since when has anything ever gone my way? For all I know, it's too late to stop what Mason put in motion.

Their footsteps pass the door, and I let my head fall back against the shelf in relief, knocking over whatever cleaning solution was placed there.

"Did you hear something?"

I desperately wish a black hole would replace the floor and swallow me up. It's the only chance I have now. There's no way I can take on two soldiers.

"I don't know. This place is old as hell, Will. It's probably rats."

"No, I don't think so."

Dread settles in my stomach, and I ready my knife at my side. It won't be much help if these men have guns, but it's better than nothing.

"We don't have time for this. We can call animal control when all of this is over. I'm going to the workroom."

"I'll catch up to you."

"Your funeral," the other man mutters.

This I can work with. It'll be difficult to keep Will from alerting the second man when I attack, but it's a risk I need to take.

The handle jiggles only seconds later, and I crouch behind the door.

The door opens slowly, and Will peers inside. Thanks to the darkness, he doesn't notice my small frame hidden in the corner.

When he steps inside the room to get a better look, the light from the hall gives me a clear view of my target, and I strike.

My fist collides with Will's throat, and his eyes bulge as he reaches for his damaged windpipe. His wheeze is louder than I hoped it would be, and I prepare myself in case his friend hears us and returns.

Before he has the chance to process what's happening, I swing the knife, making contact with his chest.

Pride courses through me—until he stumbles into the shelves, knocking over a row of cleaning supplies and filling the hall with the echoes from the crash.

"Will?" His friend's voice is distant, and I don't have long until he's here.

I grit my teeth and give Will the same fatal injury that Tripp received. Blood pools on the ground, and Will's eyes sag lifelessly.

My heart twists at my own actions. It was easy to take Tripp's life because I knew he deserved it. Do these men deserve it, too?

But I can't afford to wonder.

The man's footsteps are getting close, and I scan the room for anything I could use to help me.

A gun rests at Will's side, and I quickly tuck it into my waistband. As good as it feels to have a weapon, I can't use it and risk attracting attention unless I have no other choice.

Just as the man is about to turn the corner, a crazy, dangerous-as-hell plan comes to mind, and I swing the door to hide Will's body.

"Please, help me!" I cry, falling to my knees.

The man comes into view then, gun pointed at my head.

"What the hell?" he mutters, brow furrowing.

I look up at him with pleading eyes. "Please, don't hurt me! They dragged me from my cell!"

He's so puzzled that he doesn't even seem to remember that his friend is missing.

The gun drifts from my body, but I don't trust that my knife-throwing abilities are as precise as Ryder's, so I'll have to draw him closer before I make my move.

I pitifully shuffle forward on my knees. "Just take me back to my cell. Please, don't hurt me."

He nods in a daze. "Hands behind your back."

Sagging my shoulders in relief, I reach behind my back and let my hands rest on the gun hiding there.

The man tucks his gun into a holster and moves toward me.

Exactly two seconds after he lowers in front of me, his eyes widen, finding something over my shoulder.

And that would be Will.

I grab the gun and swing my arm until the weapon connects with the side of his head. The blow stuns him, and he loses balance.

I move to stand, but his leg swings beneath me, and I'm knocked on my ass. When I hit the ground, my gun slides out of my hand and into the hallway, hopelessly out of reach. Before I can orient myself, he's on top of me.

My only sliver of hope is that his gun is a few feet away—he's unarmed, and I still have my knife.

This would be immensely helpful if not for the fact that his knee is pinning down the hand that holds said knife. I try to wriggle out of his grasp, but he pushes into the cuts on my arm with a force that makes my vision blurry.

The pain, mixed with the metallic smell of blood, sends my stomach lurching—a reflex the man must notice because he leans back, nose crinkling in disgust.

I take advantage of the reaction and jerk my arm free, slicing his thigh as I swing the knife upward.

There's a hiss before I feel pain burst across my cheek. My head snaps to the side with the force of the slap, and the man sneers. "No wonder Tripp had it out for you."

If it didn't take all my strength to keep my eyes open, I'd roll them.

He moves to get on top of me again, but I roll out of his reach. My hand makes contact with a rag that must've fallen when Will crashed into the cabinet, and I get an idea.

Rag clutched in one hand, knife in the other, I lunge forward and press my forearm to his throat, using the knife to press into the side of his face.

"Well then, it's a good thing he's dead now, isn't it?"

He opens his mouth, and I shove the rag in before he gets the chance to say anything. I swing the knife downward, leaving a gash from his sternum to his stomach, but not nearly as deep as I needed it to be.

Despite my makeshift gag, the yell is ear-piercing. There's no way it went unheard.

I'm out of options, and I'm out of time.

The next cry that fills the air is mine when the man takes a fistful of my hair and violently drags me to the floor.

I expect him to snatch my knife, but he doesn't. He only turns his head to scan the floor. When he reaches out, I know what he's found.

The next few seconds happen in slow motion.

Only a few feet away, the man reaches for the gun, and the pounding of running footsteps echoes in the hall.

My life is about to end.

With a strength that I didn't know I possessed, I lift myself from the ground despite the death grip the man still has on my head. I feel hair being ripped from my skull as I make one last-ditch effort to save my life.

I lurch forward, dragging the knife across his throat. I'm unable to make a deep incision from my angle, but it's enough to loosen his grip on me.

The second I have enough freedom, I slash again and again until the man goes limp.

The footsteps in the hall grow louder, and I'm out of time. The gun is too far out of reach. Not that it would matter anyway.

I don't have any fight left.

My body sags as the footsteps stop beside me. I don't even look up to see my murderer's face.

"Damn," he mutters, and a wave of relief crashes into me so hard that tears prick my eyes.

Ryder.

He crouches beside me to check for wounds, which must be difficult considering my clothes are blood-soaked, and I take in his appearance, too. Ryder looks infinitely better than me, even with the giant gash on his forehead that's painting the side of his face bright red.

I don't notice my shaking until Ryder takes my jittery hands in his strong ones. The gesture is simple, but it's exactly the comfort I need to take in a full breath of air and get myself together.

After giving me the moment that I desperately needed, Ryder takes rags off of the shelves and helps clean me up.

"You did this?" he asks softly.

I nod. "Did you—"

"Lyla and Rachel are safe, but Moreno isn't. He's here, but I don't know where. We need to find him."

"Why didn't you go with the girls?"

He pulls away like he's searching me for a head injury. "Did you think I'd leave you?"

I did.

I expected him to go with the girls, and I'd accepted that. Seeing him now—when I thought I was on my own—brings on emotions that we don't have time to address.

So, I don't answer the question.

"The packing warehouse," I tell him. "Mason said that's where they'd be."

His eyes narrow in thought. "I might've passed it earlier, but I'm not sure."

"Only one way to find out."

We throw the rags to the side, deeming me clean enough as we step into the hall and close the closet door behind us.

"Lead the way."

Now that there are two of us and we're both armed, we don't move with nearly as much stealth as I had before. Like me, Ryder must have realized that all of the halls are mysteriously empty.

Despite the blood loss and exhaustion, I drink in every detail of the halls we run down, committing them to memory. My senses, which should be shutting down, are sharper than ever, thanks to the adrenaline rush and fear for Joshua and my family.

The words *Packing Warehouse* are written on a door at the end of the hall, and we race toward it. Ryder beats me there, swinging the door open with ease.

The clicking of guns echoes through the massive garage-like room, and my eyes go wide when I realize that every one of them is aimed at us.

CHAPTER FORTY-EIGHT

Elise

If I weren't so consumed by pain and exhaustion, I might have the energy to feel hurt by how little I'm trusted—enough to warrant having two dozen guns aimed at me.

Ryder's body moves protectively in front of mine. Although he blocks most of my vision, it still only takes a fraction of a second for me to find who I'm looking for.

Those dark eyes I've fallen for bore into mine, utterly expressionless.

Did Joshua catch our signals, or does he think Ryder and I are traitors? Is he going to give the command to shoot?

After everything we've been through, I wish I was better at reading him.

Joshua's shoulders tense as he takes in Ryder's defensive position in front of me, but he doesn't give the order to fire.

His gun lowers ever so slightly. "Where's Mason?"

I sag with relief.

He knows.

Joshua knows he can trust Ryder and me. He knows Mason is behind all of this.

I shift to step around Ryder—to run into Joshua's arms like every cell in my body pleads for me to do—but he shifts as I do, blocking my path. I want to tell Ryder off and push him aside, but his smooth voice interrupts my plans.

"He's unconscious in an office on the second floor."

I blanch at that and wonder what exactly happened to Ryder while we were apart.

Joshua looks over his shoulder at a group of soldiers. "Go."

"Wait," I call, shoving Ryder's arm aside and stepping around him. The second I move, I realize why he tried to hold me back.

My sudden movement prompts every soldier to lift his gun in my direction.

Ryder realized what I hadn't—that even though Joshua knows Mason is behind this, we're still not to be trusted.

My heart clenches when I see that even Don and Kade—who stand at Joshua's side—have rearmed themselves.

The only one who doesn't aim his gun at me is Joshua, which would be reassuring if not for the fact that he still doesn't call his soldiers off.

I know that he watched some damning footage tonight, but that doesn't ease my growing frustration. I've had a night from hell, and this is the last thing I need.

I lift my chin and meet their aggression head-on. "Well? If you're going to shoot me, then do it already. Otherwise, back the hell off."

Several men glance at Joshua, waiting to see what he'll do, but I don't wait to find out. I continue walking, Ryder on my heels.

I want to throw myself into Joshua's arms, but his posture is rigid, and his eyes are sharp. Now isn't the time to push my luck, so I stop a few feet away.

When I do, I see the first flicker of emotion in his eyes as he assesses my bloody, bruise-covered body with concern.

"What the hell happened?"

"Not important," I say, then turn my gaze to the group of men Joshua ordered to go upstairs. "You don't have time to get Mason. We need to get out of here right now."

"What do you mean?" Joshua asks.

"My dad is on his way. Mason set this up so neither of you walks out of here alive. We need to leave *now*."

Joshua studies my face, and I, once again, curse my inability to read him.

Never taking his eyes off mine, he tilts his head to the side. "Kade."

"She's right," he says, messing with a tablet that must've been in the backpack slung over his shoulders. "Five vans are heading down the road now."

"How long?"

Kade frowns at the screen. "Maybe three minutes. We won't be able to get away without a confrontation."

Joshua clenches his jaw and closes his eyes. I start to step forward, but Ryder's gentle tug on my shoulder holds me back.

I throw an annoyed look at him but reluctantly obey.

When Joshua's eyes finally open, there's a steely resolve there. He faces the group of twenty or so men around him. "Take cover. This will get messy."

"No!" Ignoring Ryder's advice, I reach out and grab Joshua's arm, forcing him to face me. "You can't fight! That's exactly what Mason wants!"

"Doesn't matter anymore. We don't have another option."

"Let me talk to him!"

"No way. You're taking cover. With me."

Joshua takes hold of my shoulders and pulls me toward a barricade of crates. Every soldier in the room scopes out the best places for defense, and even Ryder is given a gun to replace the one he stole from Tripp.

I struggle against the arms that pull me. "Please, Joshua! I can talk to him! He'll listen to me!"

"No."

Stomping on his foot, I rip myself from his grasp and glare at him. "You're going to die if you do this!"

He stops to look down at me, features softening as he does. "Elise —"

"Please, Joshua. Let me try."

I hold my breath as I wait for his answer, and after a long moment, he finally huffs. "Fine. But I'm going with you."

"He'll hurt you. I can go—"

"Either I go with you, or you don't go at all."

If Joshua goes with me, there's a chance my father will kill him, but if he doesn't let me go, then I'll lose them both.

"Okay," I relent.

"Kade, where are they coming in?"

I don't see Kade when I glance around, but his voice calls out from somewhere behind us. "North. Same way we came in. Thirty seconds."

Joshua leads me across the room to a panel on the wall. He takes one look at it before pressing a blue button that triggers the large double doors of the garage to open.

The grinding of the metal rising is deafening, but it means Dad won't be spooked by our presence when he pulls up.

Joshua doesn't release my hand as we make our way to the center of the room.

This isn't the time to talk, but I can't risk either of us dying when there's still so much left to say.

"Joshua," I whisper, taking hold of his arm.

I open my mouth, needing to tell him how sorry I am and how much I love him, but the crunch of gravel under tires is my ticking clock. With only seconds left, I decide to tell Joshua everything in the way we communicate best.

My lips meet his with all of the desperation and passion that I feel, and he reciprocates in full.

This is far more honest than any words we could've said.

I don't need to tell him that I'm sorry. He doesn't need to tell me he's afraid of losing me.

We feel it as our lips move in perfect synchronization.

It's physically painful to pull away, but I force myself to do it, stepping protectively in front of him.

When the first car comes into view, I lift my chin. I have one chance to save all of the people I love.

I can't mess this up.

When Joshua steps closer, pressing his body against mine, my shoulders relax. Whatever problems we have to solve, my body still knows who it belongs to.

The cars pull into view, but the windows are tinted too much for me to see which one my father is in. One by one, each car pulls up, but no one climbs out until the fifth car pulls in and comes to a stop.

Doors open, and I scan the familiar-looking men until I see him.

Over the last few weeks, I've been so furious with my father for abandoning me that I told myself I would be perfectly fine if I never saw him again. I told myself that he wasn't worthy of being in my life —of being my father.

So then, why am I so damn happy to see him?

Striking green eyes take in the sight before him—his daughter, soaked in blood, standing defensively in front of her alleged captor.

I suppose that would explain the scowl on his face.

A worn, black suit makes him look more fitting to attend a dinner party than a potential shoot-out. His frame, though not as broad as it used to be, is rigid. Like Joshua, everything about my father screams *power*.

I ignore the other soldiers exiting the vehicles, only watching my father as he makes his way toward Joshua and me. When he stands at the edge of the garage door, he stops, and I risk glancing away just long enough to notice that, for the second time tonight, dozens of guns are aimed in my direction.

Also, for the second time tonight, I'm fairly certain no one will pull the trigger.

Damon, James, and Logan come to stand by our father's side, and they all do a poor job concealing their confusion and anger.

"Elise," my father's gravelly voice snaps, "step away from Mr. Moreno."

Here goes nothing.

"Dad, I need you to listen to me—"

"Baby girl, we can talk later. Step. Away. Now."

My hands shake at the order. I've never stood up to my father before, but I don't have a choice now.

I instinctively reach behind me, and Joshua takes my hand without a second thought, squeezing it comfortingly. The action—which felt as natural as breathing—has my family's expressions twisting with disgust.

"I'm not going anywhere," I declare with an authority that catches everyone, myself included, off guard.

My father raises an eyebrow and then directs a fiery glare at Joshua. "What the hell do you think you're doing? You abuse, beat, and brainwash my daughter into being your human shield? What kind of man are you?"

Joshua's body tenses against mine, but I squeeze his hand and press my body into his, urging him to stay in place.

"That's not what happened," Joshua growls, but he doesn't attempt to move around me.

"How else do you explain these injuries?"

This is such a waste of time.

"I killed the man who did this to me, but that's not the point."

Joshua's hand goes rigid in mine. "You did what?"

I ignore the question.

"Mason has been lying to you for years, both of you." I chance a quick glance over my shoulder to Joshua.

"Elise, I don't know what Moreno has told you, but—"

"Just shut the hell up and listen!" I shout, and everyone freezes. I've never spoken to anyone in my family this way, but apparently, it's the only way to get anyone to listen.

"He plans to take over both families, starting by killing everyone here. He has men in both families working for him that will ensure none of us walk away from here alive. We need to leave *now*."

The slight raise in my father's chin is his tell that he's seriously considering my words.

"Moreno has been lying to you, Elise. Mason would never do any of this." Damon says, and when I look closer, I notice the glossed-over look in his eyes.

Mason was right about the alcohol.

"I didn't want to believe it either, but he's behind all of this. You have to believe me." I don't hide my desperation.

They need to see my sincerity.

Logan takes a step forward, cocking his head toward our father but never looking away from Joshua and me. "It's possible that he could be the mole."

"Damn it," Dad says on a sigh.

Tears of joy fill my eyes.

They believe me.

"We need to get out of here," I warn. "There are others here. I don't know how many, but they could come any minute. We're not safe here."

"And him?" my father asks, locking his jaw and nodding to Joshua.

I straighten my back and steel my words. "Joshua stays with me. No one touches him."

He looks like he has a lot more to say about that but he refrains. "Where are his?"

It takes me a moment to realize that he's asking about Joshua's soldiers, but Joshua answers for me.

"In here. Prepared, in case this conversation veers from civil."

I shake my head. "We don't have time for this. We need to hurry."

When my father's eyes fall on mine again, I can see that it's difficult for him to trust me. I want to be mad about that, but how can I be? I'm defending his enemy and accusing his son of betrayal.

I'd be skeptical, too.

That's why it's a damn miracle when my father nods, raising his hand with a slight wave that tells his men to lower their weapons.

The soldiers make their way to the cars, but my brothers don't move an inch.

My father steps forward, closing the distance between us. "You have a lot of explaining to do."

I couldn't agree more.

I step forward to meet him, reveling in the realization that I did it. I convinced them all we need to leave. No one had to get hurt.

That is, until a gun fires—and my father falls lifelessly to the ground just a few feet in front of me.

CHAPTER FORTY-NINE

Joshua

The second the gun fires, I wrap Elise in my arms. I catch sight of Ryder coming from my right, and beyond him, I see the culprit.

Mason.

I spare him only a fraction of my attention, but it's enough to catch the crazed look in his eyes.

I'm pulling Elise with me behind the metal crates when three figures surround me. My hand reaches for my gun before I process who's formed a protective ring around us—Elise's brothers.

The only Consoli brother I've met is Logan. He and his father met me to discuss the negotiation terms, and it's no secret that he isn't my biggest fan. Despite that fact, I know I'm not their target. We may not be allies, but right now, we have a common enemy—and that's enough to know they won't shoot me in the back.

The fact that their sister is in my arms helps, too.

Just seconds after Gabriel Consoli's death, I'm crouched behind the crates, setting Elise down, and allowing her brothers to defend our position.

I get my first good look at her, and my heart drops at the sight of complete horror and disbelief.

"Elise," I call, but she doesn't so much as meet my eye. "Please, baby. I need you to look at me right now."

No response.

The shouts and bullets that fill the room seem to get louder with every passing second, and I don't have time to be sensitive.

With my hands on her shoulders, I shake her hard. "Elise! Listen to me!"

She blinks, and her terror-filled gaze locks with mine.

"Are you okay?" It's a dumb question, considering the situation and the fact that she is most definitely *not* okay, but it's all I can manage right now.

For all my training, being gentle in a hostile environment was never a skill I picked up.

She nods, and I don't push for anything more.

"She okay?" one of Elise's brothers, James, I think, calls.

"In shock, but alright for now."

Ryder slides behind the crates, joining our small group. Elise shrieks in surprise before I clamp my hand over her mouth.

When she sees it's him, she relaxes, but not much.

"Who was it?" she croaks. "Who killed Dad?"

James moves to sit beside her, cutting his eyes at me as he passes, but I don't intervene.

He wraps an arm around Elise. "You were right. It was Mason. He came through a side door, shot Dad, and then soldiers from either side started shooting, but no one knows who's on what side since Mason seems to have compromised a handful of them. It's just open fire right now."

Logan mutters a curse from beside me.

The oldest brother, Damon, who is already coated in a sheen of sweat, sags against the crates. "What now?"

I don't miss the glare Logan throws him before answering. "The traitors are starting to congregate around Mason. We're outnumbered, especially with soldiers from our sides joining him. We need to go before they make their way over here."

With a nod, I push past James and pull Elise into my arms. None of them object, not that it would matter. I don't care if we're facing ten or ten thousand men—I'm not going anywhere unless she's by my side.

I look to Ryder, who's diligently protecting our right side. "Think you can get us out of here once we're inside?"

"The only exit I know is too close to be safe."

"I can get us out," Elise's small but firm voice says from beside me.

A barrage of bullets hits the metal crates, and we all flinch away. The sound brings our grim reality to the forefront of my mind. I've found myself in countless situations like this, but I've never had to worry about the woman I love being here, too. I want her to be as far from this place as possible, but that's not an option.

I pull my radio from my pocket. "Don, you in?"

The response comes only a moment later. "In, but Kade took a bullet to the shoulder."

Damn it.

"Making a move to get out. West side, heading toward the southwest door. Cover and follow."

"Yes, sir."

The Consoli brothers, Ryder, and I shift into formation as though we've worked together for years and not minutes. It goes without saying that Elise needs to be in the middle, and by the time we're ready to go, we protectively surround her.

Elise and Ryder look to me for the order to go, but I nod to Logan. Letting him take the lead is a small price to pay to ensure my focus stays on Elise and her safety.

Logan nods, wordlessly accepting the responsibility.

"Don't break rank, and don't stop, no matter what," he commands.

He flicks his wrist, and we're on the move.

There's no way for our group to move inconspicuously, and Mason knows it. As we run, another wave of bullets flies in our direction, but I take the lack of gasps and groans to mean we're in the clear so far.

Once Logan reaches the door, he throws it open, and one by one, we sprint inside.

As Elise and I enter the hallway, I reach for her hand, and we take the lead. Her brothers throw disgruntled looks our way, but we ignore them.

We follow as she weaves through the hallways with ease, listening for anything that may indicate we're not alone.

We round a corner, and Elise smiles as an intersection comes into view. She slows and turns to face the group just as footsteps echo in the halls behind us.

"Do exactly what I say. Boys"—she looks to Ryder and her brothers—"go left here. The staircase will lead to the exit. Joshua and I will go right and get them off your trail."

Every one of us, myself included, opens our mouths to argue, but Elise lifts a hand with more authority than most of my soldiers possess. "Only I know where to hide to get them off your trail. If we don't do this to split them up and buy time, they'll pick us off once we're outside. Go. Now."

I can't think of anything I want more than for Elise to be safely out of this building, but I bite back my protest. At least she didn't try to get me to leave with the others.

She must know I wouldn't have gone.

Logan snaps to attention first, grabbing his brothers' arms in either hand and pulling them backward.

Ryder begrudgingly follows, but I reach into my pocket before he gets far.

"You'll need this," I say, tossing his phone to him.

He catches it as he turns to follow the others, and they all seem to send the same silent message: *be careful.*

With that, Elise pulls me down a hallway, and I follow as she presses us against the wall. Though we say nothing, both of us seem to understand the need to wait until Mason's soldiers are closer to make our move so we can lead them away from the others.

The thudding of feet gets closer, but I let my eyes fall on the girl beside me. Her clothes, arms, and face are streaked with blood, and I hope it's not hers. I haven't had the chance to assess her injuries, but I take it as a good sign that she's still standing.

The shouts of Mason's soldiers are muffled, but it's enough for me to know they'll be able to hear us, too. In perfect synchronization, we push off the wall and speed down the hallway.

The plan is working.

We're running at full speed when Elise suddenly jerks my arm toward a small, hardly noticeable door on the left wall.

Before opening it, she raises a finger to her lip, uncertainty swimming in her eyes.

Does she think I plan on talking?

The scent hits me first. The absolutely putrid smell fills the small janitor's closet, and it's one I recognize all too well. Before Elise shuts the door, light from the hallway illuminates the space just enough for me to see the horrific scene.

Two bodies lay lifelessly on the floor, cleaning supplies spilled around them and blood covering the floor.

The most alarming part is that Elise isn't shocked.

Damn it.

The footsteps are too close for me to say anything, but I nod toward the corpses in silent question.

She only nods.

Damn it.

I can't ask the extensive list of questions bouncing around my head, so I settle for pulling her into my arms.

"They went down this hallway. Check every cell! They couldn't have gone far." Mason's voice booms from directly outside the door, and I'm certain that if I hadn't been holding Elise, she would've jumped a foot in the air.

Neither of us breathes as we listen to the faint noises from the other side of the door. They don't seem concerned with the janitor's closet, but they're still too close for Elise and me to sneak out.

With nothing else to do, I close my eyes and focus on pinpointing the exact number of soldiers on the other side of the door. If it comes to a fight, Elise and I should know what we're up against.

By the time I open my eyes, Elise's head is cocked to the side.

"How many?" she mouths. "Five?"

Was she counting, too? Pride swells in my chest, and I can't believe I ever made the mistake of underestimating her.

"Seven," I mouth in return.

Her brow furrows, and I lean forward to kiss her forehead, but the voice outside our door halts my movement.

"Sir, we have eyes on the group exiting the perimeter. Your sister isn't with them. Should we follow?"

"Yes! I'll find her myself."

Elise is as tense as a live wire, and I want nothing more than to burst through this door and inflict the most excruciating pain on Mason.

The last set of footsteps fades out of range as Elise whispers, "I think it's safe—"

"How did you do that?" I hiss, nodding toward the corpses.

"A knife and desperation. Now, can we—"

"Did they do this to you?" I ask, making a show of looking over her blood-stained clothes.

She groans in exasperation. "Mason's the one who raided the warehouse and took Tripp. I killed him and these guys on my way to find you while Ryder got Lyla and Rachel out of here. Anything else you'd like to ask, or can we get back to saving our asses?"

Mason raided the warehouse? He would've had access to my house's location and security measures, and I cut off all communication. I wasn't keeping tabs on him to know what he was doing.

I gave him the perfect opportunity.

I take a second to process the information, but I can't help the swarm of images that flood my mind at the sound of Ryder's name on her lips.

Obviously, the video was fake, but that doesn't ease the anger boiling violently in my blood.

I reach for the doorknob when the next part of the video comes to mind.

"What's wrong?"

"The flash drive," I murmur.

"I almost forgot about that," she says. "That was his backup plan."

I nod. "He must've known there was a chance this ambush wouldn't work. The drive ensures he still has power when all this is over."

"We need to find it," she says, and the conviction in her voice is nothing short of inspiring.

"It's not that simple."

"I know where his office is," she tells me. "We can start there."

Maybe it's her confidence or the simple fact that I went hours tonight thinking I'd lost her, but I rest my forehead against hers and let myself hold her. Though we both know time is not something we have an abundance of, Elise doesn't protest. She melts in my arms, and it's the best feeling in the world.

"Joshua, I'm so s—"

"I know, Princess."

And I do. We both said a lot of things we didn't mean in my office today, but that doesn't change how I want her.

How I need her.

"I'm sorry, too. We'll figure it all out when we get home, okay?"

Instead of answering me with words, her lips find mine.

I can feel every bit of the pain her eyes reflected, and she can feel every ounce of my frustration. It's a furious kiss—one that carries the weight of a thousand words unsaid.

Despite the unresolved problems between us, when we pull apart, I know we'll be okay. We've come too far for her brother—or anyone for that matter—to come between us.

"You ready?" I whisper.

She nods, and we're off.

Elise silently peels the door back, and I check that we're clear before moving out of the closet.

The halls are eerily quiet, a fact that keeps both Elise and me on edge as we make our way upstairs. When we reach an intersection, I peer around to confirm we're alone. When I'm sure we are, I reluctantly nod for her to take the lead.

Before she can step past me, I hold my spare gun out to her, and she takes it without hesitation.

"Do you know how many men we're facing?" I ask. It's not comforting that we haven't run into anyone yet.

"No idea. All I know is that before you got here, they were all called to the 'workroom,' whatever that is."

I tuck that piece of information in the back of my mind.

Somehow, our luck holds, and we make it all the way to an office on the upper floor without an encounter. I only hope this doesn't mean everyone is after the rest of our group.

I stand at Elise's back as she opens the door, and we slip inside undetected. The same scent as before reaches my nose, and once the door is locked, I turn to find Nate's body lying only a few feet away. Blood covers the floor around him, and I can see the headshot wound from here.

"We have one fight, and you go on a damn killing spree," I mutter.

She narrows her eyes at me. "That wasn't me. It must've been Ryder."

I shake my head in answer, and we get to work rummaging through the office. We turn over every file and sift through every drawer until there's not an inch we haven't searched.

"Damn it," I grumble.

"What?"

"Mason has the flash drive on him."

CHAPTER FIFTY

Elise

Well, this makes things significantly more difficult.

Joshua looks on the verge of going on a murder spree of his own, so I decide it's best to wait for him to cool down before speaking. However, the longer I stay still, the more my body realizes just how exhausted it is. I've spent the whole night fighting, and it's finally catching up to me.

I let my eyes close, just for a moment...

"Elise!" Joshua's hiss pulls me back to reality, and I blink rapidly as I process that he's holding me up by my shoulders. I hadn't realized that I'd fallen over.

Once I've regained my balance, I look up at Joshua through thick lashes. "I'm okay."

"No, you're not." He pulls me to the couch, and I sit. When he lowers himself in front of me, I repress the urge to fall into his strong arms.

He begins scanning my body, his eyes growing wide as he inspects the torn fabric that only halfway covers the cuts on my arm. I let Joshua lift my arm to get a better look, though the motion elicits a whimper.

Swallowing back the nausea that creeps up my throat, I glance down at the wound. Blood and bruising cover the entirety of my upper arm, but the letters spelling *BRAT* can still be clearly made out. I'd been so focused on escaping that I hadn't realized Tripp actually finished the word. Aside from the top line of the "T" being shortened, the full word is visible.

"Who did this to you?" Joshua's deadly calm tone sends a shiver down my spine.

"Tripp. But I already told you, he's dead now."

He sucks in a sharp breath but doesn't press for more answers.

When I push myself to stand, I'm thankful that Joshua can balance me before I fall on my ass.

He curses under his breath. "You've lost too much blood. I need to get you out of here."

I'm shaking my head before he even finishes the sentence. "We can't leave without that flash drive. As it is, we have no idea how many soldiers Mason has working for him or what kind of resources they have. If he has that information too, we're going to have a huge problem."

"Then it's a problem we'll fix another day," he says, and his resolute tone almost convinces me to back off.

Almost.

"I won't be the reason you lose everything."

Joshua takes my face in his hands. "Elise, I lost everything when you walked out of my office today, and I won't make that mistake again."

I have no idea if the tear falling down my cheek is a product of my pain, exhaustion, or utter relief that Joshua still wants me the way I need him.

I'm about to tell him how much I love him when I'm interrupted by the static of a radio. My body jolts in surprise when the sound comes from inside the office, but it only takes a moment for me to realize it's coming from the radio attached to Nate's hip.

The voice that comes through is unmistakably Mason's. "I want eyes on every exit of this building. They're not leaving this place alive. Do you copy?"

Joshua and I share an apprehensive look. Getting out of here is going to be easier said than done.

An unfamiliar voice answers. "We lost track of the group. Should we keep searching or come back?"

Our apprehension turns to relief. The others are safe. Splitting up bought them the time they needed to make a safe escape.

"I want one unit searching. Everyone else come back now," Mason barks.

"Yes, sir."

With my good arm, I reach for Joshua's hand, taking it in mine.

"There's a good chance we don't walk out of here tonight, and if that's the case, I want to die knowing we did everything we could to stop him."

"Don't say that." Joshua squeezes his eyes shut. "We aren't dying tonight."

His shoulders relax when I rub small circles against his hand.

"Then we might as well take Mason down on our way out."

Joshua's eyes open, and I hate the pain that I see there. His sigh is one of defeat.

He presses a gentle kiss to my forehead, and I stand frozen in place as he approaches Nate's body.

I don't ask what his plan is, and I don't need to.

I'd follow Joshua anywhere.

He stands, bringing the radio to his mouth. "Mason, ready to talk?"

"Moreno. What a pleasant surprise," Mason deadpans only seconds later.

"Likewise."

"Save us both some time and tell me where you and my sister are."

Joshua's fist tightens, but his voice remains perfectly calm. "I want my flash drive, then my fiancée and I are walking out of here." He speaks with such authority and confidence that I half expect Mason to simply agree.

Of course, he doesn't.

Instead, humorless laughter comes through the line. "Over my dead body."

"I assure you, it will be."

Even *I* get goosebumps at the ice in his tone.

"We'll see about that."

A buzzing catches Joshua's attention, and he wordlessly hands me his phone. I take it, checking the notification.

Ryder: We're in the clear. Status?

I turn the screen so Joshua can read it, and I can practically see the wheels turning in his head.

He has a plan.

"Give an update, and tell him to initiate Goliath," Joshua whispers.

I raise an eyebrow, but Joshua doesn't elaborate.

I type out the text saying we're alive but not leaving without the flash drive. I end the message by telling him to initiate Goliath.

"What is it that you want here, Mason?"

Mason's grating voice answers. "You and my traitorous siblings out of the way. With my dad dead, I'm one step closer to taking you all down."

The phone buzzes, and I scan the text.

Ryder: You're sure? Countdown?

I have no idea what to make of the message, but Joshua seems to understand when I show it to him.

"Yes, I'm sure. Fifteen minutes," he quietly confirms before speaking into the radio again. "Oh, please. You're an ignorant, narcissistic child trying to play with the big boys. It's all the same to me, though. You served your purpose."

I type as Joshua talks, and Ryder responds immediately.

Ryder: Done. I hope you know what you're doing.

"And you served yours by giving me unrestricted access to disappointed soldiers looking for a strong leader. Don't worry, I'll take good care of your empire."

"You won't get the chance, kiddo." Joshua's laugh almost sounds genuine. "There's a janitor's closet in the same hallway as the cells. Go there."

I raise an eyebrow, but Joshua only winks.

"This isn't a game, Moreno." Mason seethes.

"But it *is* a game. A game that you were stupid enough to start even though you never stood a chance of winning."

"Are you sure about that? Because the way I see it, it's the two of you against my army."

Joshua nods toward the door. "Get ready. We're about to get out of here." His next words go to my brother. "I would hardly call what you have an '*army*.'"

I wordlessly obey.

"What about the flash drive?" I ask, but my voice is drowned out by Mason's reply.

"You have no idea what you're talking about," my brother spits.

"No need to bluff, kiddo. I saw your *army* in the workroom. I know what I'm up against."

Joshua joins me by the door, tensed for a fight.

"We still outnumber and outgun you," Mason grates out.

I can't believe it worked. Joshua got him to admit to exaggerating his manpower.

He lifts the radio to his mouth. "Are you at the janitor's closet yet?"

A long moment passes with no answer.

"Why do you want him to go there?" I ask in a whisper.

"Now that we're sure his resources are spread thin, knowing he's on the lower floor will mean he's not blocking our exit," he explains.

"But what about the flash drive?"

Joshua's hand squeezes mine, but he avoids my gaze. "Goliath will take care of that for us."

"And what exactly is—"

Mason cuts me off again. "What the hell is this?"

He must've reached the closet.

At Joshua's nod, I slowly turn the handle and open the door.

"A little taste of what you can expect very soon," Joshua warns. He doesn't give my brother a chance to respond because he drops the radio to the ground and stomps his boot over it until plastic and metal shards are all that remain.

Joshua and I exit the office holding hands with our guns ready in the other, and I almost laugh. I always pictured my love story would look a little more like Cinderella and Prince Charming and a little less like Bonnie and Clyde, but here we are.

I'm grateful that Joshua is here because even just by holding my hand, he's supporting my weight more than I care to admit.

I brace myself as we turn the corner and are faced with three armed soldiers. Our not-so-subtle approach gave them plenty of time to point their weapons in our direction.

I suck a deep breath in and let Joshua pull me back behind the wall before a barrage of bullets fly exactly where we'd been standing. Our current position doesn't offer us any real protection, and my mind races to find a way to get past them.

When no ideas surface, I'm about to panic, but Joshua's expression is utterly unbothered. I have no time to react as he releases my hand and launches himself into the line of fire, gun aimed toward our attackers.

My horrified scream bounces off the walls when another round of bullets flies toward the man I love. Seconds later, the gunfire ceases.

Joshua pushes himself to his feet, and I take in the miracle before me.

He's unharmed.

"H-how did you do that?"

Joshua pulls me along. "This isn't my first time, Princess."

I've never truly seen Joshua in action until today. Sure, I've seen him command his soldiers, torture Tripp, and yell at me, but this is different. Watching Joshua antagonize Mason over the radio and single-handedly take out three shooters in under a minute reminds me just how powerful he really is.

And he's mine.

I recognize the end of the last hallway and know that as soon as we turn that corner, we're free. However, the chances of the door being unguarded are slim, so I prepare for another fight. Though—after watching Joshua take out the others—I'm feeling better about our odds.

We share a quick nod and round the last corner, prepared to face the two soldiers who greet us there. I vaguely recognize one of them as someone I've seen around the L.A. base, and I assume from Joshua's muttered curse that he recognizes the man, too.

It's like we're on autopilot as we raise our guns and fire. I barely even process that they fired back until I hear Joshua's hiss beside me.

The blood drains from my face at the sound. When I turn to look at him, he holds one hand against his leg and gives me a pained grimace. "It's okay, it only grazed me."

"Don't scare me like that!"

"You think I *meant* for that bullet to hit me?" He limps toward me, and I watch blood steadily pour from his thigh.

"Can you walk?" I ask, and he nods, letting me wrap my arm around his waist as we make our way to the door that's only a few yards away now.

"Elise!" a voice I haven't heard in weeks calls from behind us. I turn and take in the sight of a panicked Kaitlyn running down the hall.

"Kaitlyn? What are you doing here?"

Her dirty blonde hair is pulled back in a tight ponytail, and her gun is at her side. I can't believe I didn't notice her when she got out of the cars with the rest of my dad's men, but my focus had been solely on my family.

"I've been looking for you! I didn't see where you went when the shooting started, and I needed to make sure you were okay."

Joshua turns with me, watching my friend come toward us with a calculating glint in his eye.

He glances down at his watch and whispers, "Elise, we need to get out of here right now. We only have five minutes."

"Five minutes until what?"

His eyes never leave Kaitlyn's approaching form when he hisses.

"Until this whole building explodes."

Did I hit my head at some point? Because I know there's no way that I just heard Joshua correctly.

"Excuse me?"

"Goliath," he says in explanation.

"Then Kaitlyn needs to come with us!"

Before he can oppose my request, I close the distance and meet Kaitlyn in a hug, and *damn*, it feels good to have an old friend around. If it weren't for the fact that we're minutes from being blown to bits, I'd let myself enjoy this moment.

"Come on, we need to get out of here before my brother finds us."

I step back into Joshua's body, and his arm wraps around my waist.

It's too late when I realize that his arm isn't holding me for comfort but restraining me from interfering as he lifts his gun to my friend's head and shoots.

My scream fills the entryway, and Joshua's hand clamps over my mouth to muffle the sound. Tears are running down my cheek as he limps toward the exit, pulling me with him.

"She was with your brother, Elise," he murmurs.

I shake my head until his hand falls away. "She was my friend!"

"No, she wasn't."

Joshua and I whip around to face the exit, guns at the ready, and come face to face with my brother and three of his soldiers. Four guns face our two, and I'm not feeling nearly as confident about our odds as I had been only minutes ago.

Mason looks horrific. Blood is splattered across his face, his clothes are torn, his hair is disheveled, and there's a manic gleam in his eyes that makes my skin crawl.

"Dad only hired Kaitlyn because I recommended her after a *special screening*. I mean, really, Elise, your ability to still be surprised is admirable."

"Go to hell, bastard," I snap, and Joshua's arm gently tugs me back so I'm tucked into his side.

Mason laughs. "You two really are quite the pair, but personally, I think there's more chemistry between you and Ryder."

I feel Joshua's chest rumble, and Mason's eyes light up at the reaction.

"Three minutes," Joshua practically breathes the words, too quiet for the others to hear.

If we don't get out of here right now, we're all dead.

"Now," Mason purrs, "put the guns down."

Neither of us moves.

"What are you waiting for, Mason? You have us, now what?" Joshua sneers, and I'm forever grateful that I'm not on the receiving end of his wrath.

Mason takes a leisurely step forward, ignoring Joshua and fixing his cool stare on me. "You ruined everything. Years of work and planning—all wasted because of *you*. Well, now you'll know what it's like to lose everything."

Only a few feet away from us, Mason lifts his gun to Joshua.

Most people with a gun in their hand would think to shoot it when they're in danger.

Not me.

I chuck the gun at Mason's wrist before it's fully positioned. My brother grunts as the force knocks his gun to the ground.

That's when the shooting starts.

Joshua is quick to pull me to the floor and cover my body with his own. I don't see how that could help us very much when Mason's men still have a clear shot, but when I look up, their guns aren't aimed at Joshua and me.

Their focus is over our heads, and I watch in disbelief as each soldier falls limply to the floor.

"What the hell were you doing?" a deep voice asks from behind us.

Donovan and Kade jog over to where Joshua and I lay on the floor, their guns poised in case of another attack.

I nearly cry with relief. "You're okay!"

Joshua pulls the two of us to our feet. "None of us will be okay if we don't get out of here *now*. Sixty seconds until Goliath," he explains, and judging by their wide eyes, I gather they know what that means.

We jog to the door as fast as we can with our various injuries, and I think I hear the hum of an airplane growing louder and louder.

I can't help but throw a last look over my shoulder—and wish I hadn't.

Mason lies on the floor, clutching helplessly at his side, which, I can see from here, is gushing blood. What's worse is that his eyes plead with me not to leave him. It's a glimpse of the brother I grew up with. The brother I so desperately love.

The brother that I need to leave behind.

It takes the last bit of strength that I have left to look away and let Joshua lead me through the door.

We run into the pitch-black night, and the whirring of the aircraft is almost deafening. When I glance upward, I see the outline of a helicopter hovering over the building.

Joshua picks up the speed toward the woods, and I barely manage to keep up with him.

Suddenly, he yanks me behind a large tree, and I'm shocked that his voice still carries over the noise when he calls to the others, "Take cover!"

There's a flash so bright that I can almost imagine it's daytime. When the earsplitting blast follows, my body finally decides it's reached its limit, and I fall into the darkness.

CHAPTER FIFTY-ONE

Elise

When I was five years old, my parents took my brothers and me to a lake house for the Fourth of July. It was rare for us to take family trips like that, so it's easy to recall the weekend.

It's among the few memories I have of my mother.

My brothers were having a contest to see who could hold their breath underwater the longest, but they wouldn't let me join because it was a game for *big kids*. In my childish pride, I decided to practice holding my breath so I could impress them.

I swam to the opposite side of the deck so they couldn't see me and submerged myself, glad Mom and Dad weren't outside to catch me swimming without my floaties.

After several tries, my small lungs still couldn't last more than a few seconds, but I was determined.

Maybe, I had thought, *if I swim deep enough, I'll have no choice but to hold my breath, and then I'll get better!*

With my eyes open in the murky lake water, I could barely make out the light from the surface from how deep I was, and for a moment, I was so proud of myself.

Just then, a fish brushed against my foot, and I couldn't help but scream, losing all the oxygen in my lungs. In my panic, I tried to breathe, but the water stung my throat, and the fear that seized me was unlike anything I'd felt in my short lifetime.

As my body screamed for air, I could hear a voice. It was faint and muddled through the water, but I knew, without a doubt, that it was my mother. The relief I felt at the sound of her voice was instantaneous.

"Elise!" she had called. "Elise, can you hear me?"

Darkness threatened to take over my vision, but I could make out the shape of her jumping into the water to save me.

"Can you hear me, Elise? Please, wake up," the voice begs, but it's different now. Still distant and murky from under the water, but less feminine.

I flail my arms, desperate to break through the waterline and find the source of the voice.

"Please, Elise. We can't lose you, too," the voice whispers.

Two things become clear then.

First, that voice isn't my mother.

Second, I'm no longer a child underwater.

Then, why can't I find my breath? Why can't I open my eyes? Why is the faint whisper the only sound breaking through the fog?

With everything I have, I fight through the darkness.

"I think she's starting to wake up," a voice exclaims.

"Elise, can you hear me?"

I want to nod, but I'm not sure how to. I keep forcing my way through the thick haze that holds me captive.

I make a sound resembling a whimper, and a surge of determination shoots through my veins. With all the strength I can muster, I finally feel my eyelids flutter open.

The bright light is harsh against my sensitive eyes, and I cringe away from it.

"Turn off the light. I think it's hurting her eyes."

I want to thank whoever said it, but I'm too busy making my eyes work to find my words.

When I hear the tap of a switch being flipped, I give it another try. This time, it's much easier to peel my eyes open, though it takes a moment to process my surroundings.

I lie in a hospital bed with a white sheet draped over my body. I expect the rest of the room to match the bed, but aside from a few machines around me, it just resembles a bedroom. Plain walls, wooden flooring, a bathroom to the right, and a dresser with a tray of food placed on it.

The two forms looming over me steal my focus, and tears prick my eyes at the sight of them.

"Elise," Logan breathes a relieved sigh. "You're awake."

He sits on my left, hand covering mine, and I'm so glad to see that a bandage wrapped around his wrist and a nasty bruise on his cheek are the extent of his injuries.

James holds my right hand, and he looks more roughed up than Logan—various bandages cover his arms, and a thick wrap peeks out from beneath his shirt, seeming to cover his shoulder.

I want to respond, but my dry throat won't allow it. With a great deal of effort, I nod in the direction of the water, and James rushes to bring it to me, spilling some on the floor in the process.

"How are you feeling?" Logan asks as I take a sip.

Once the water eases my dry throat, I'm able to find my voice.

"I don't really feel anything," I admit in a croak.

They nod in sync, looking every bit like the twins they are. "That would be the morphine."

I glance down at my body, but a sheet prevents me from seeing the extent of the damage. "What's the diagnosis?"

"The most concerning injury is your head," Logan tells me. "You hit it in the explosion. When you weren't waking up, the doctor ran a few tests, but everything looked normal. He said you worked yourself into exhaustion, and your body wasn't ready to wake up yet."

James nods. "There's a lot of bruising around your throat, but no significant damage. Other than that, there's just your arm…"

My eyes fall to the bandage that conceals the vulgar word. "Is it going to scar?"

"It shouldn't," Logan says. "But only time will tell."

I suppose I should be devastated by the fact that I could have the word BRAT etched into my arm for the rest of my life, but I'm not. Maybe it's because I've already been scarred or because I killed the man who inflicted the pain, but I can accept this.

"It's fine," I say, and they turn raised brows my way. "I'm not happy about it, but I'll be fine."

The two share a look, and I'm about to assure them again when I realize that I don't recognize the room we're in. I search for a clock or any way to tell how long it's been, but there's nothing.

"Where are we? And how long have I been asleep?"

"It's been two days since the night at the factory," Logan says, his shoulders tense though his face remains composed. "And we're at Moreno's base."

I shoot to a sitting position, momentarily losing my vision as I do and wincing when I notice the IV attached to my arm. "Where's Joshua?"

"Woah—" James holds his hands out but quickly drops them when he doesn't know how to help. "Calm down, Elise. You need to rest."

"Where is he?"

My brothers share a look, neither of them answering my question, and I imagine the worst.

"What happened to him? Is he okay?" A nearby machine beeps wildly as my heart races.

James sighs, conflict waging behind his eyes. "He's fine."

The knot in my chest loosens, and I lean back in the bed, catching my breath.

"Unfortunately," Logan mutters under his breath.

James shoots him a warning glare before looking back at me. "He left half an hour ago to do rounds."

"He was here?"

"He doesn't leave this room," James complains. "But neither do we, so you haven't been alone with him."

I can only imagine the kind of tension that must have created.

"Will you tell him I'm awake? I really need to talk to him."

They exchange another look, seeming to communicate telepathically.

"What's going on?"

Logan speaks first. "Elise, you're safe now."

He says the statement like I should understand what that has to do with anything.

I don't.

When it's clear I'm not following, James takes over. "Whatever things Moreno told you or did to you, it's over now. You don't need to worry about him anymore."

My first instinct is to jump to Joshua's defense, but I can hardly blame them for their worry. I went missing for two months and was presumed dead. Of course, they want me as far away from Joshua as possible, but they don't get it.

"I promise you, it's not like that. He hasn't brainwashed or forced me into anything."

They don't say anything, and their troubled expressions remain fixed.

I drop my voice to a whisper. "I love him."

That gets their attention.

James pinches the bridge of his nose, muttering to himself while

Logan glowers at me. "You don't love him, Elise. He *kidnapped* you."

"Yes, and that proved to be quite an obstacle, but there's so much that you guys don't know."

"Like what?" James demands. "What could possibly justify what he did?"

"It's a long story that I'd love to tell you, but I really need to talk to Joshua right now."

James shakes his head. "Elise, look at yourself! He's done nothing but hurt you."

This is going to be more difficult than I thought.

"Joshua's done nothing but *protect* me. If you want to blame someone for all of this, then blame Mason. He's the real bad guy here."

"Maybe this wasn't him, but those scars on your back are older. You can't honestly tell me that's from him *protecting* you."

I unconsciously drop my gaze when a wave of shame that I thought I had moved past washes over me.

They've seen my scars.

I wasn't going to keep it a secret forever, but I wanted the chance to tell them when I was ready.

And I'm not ready yet.

"That's a long story, too," I whisper, still avoiding their contemptuous eyes.

Logan puffs his chest out, and for a moment, he looks just like our father. "Elise, we're your family, not him. You don't even know him."

When I laugh, the sound is sour. "I know Joshua better than I know any of you!"

"What's that supposed to mean?"

"It means that Mason was living a double life. Damon's an alcoholic—" their eyes widen at that. They hadn't known Mason filled me in. "You're the family heir, and Dad cared more about his empire than me. I don't know *any* of you! James is the only one that doesn't seem to have a secret." I turn to him. "Do you have anything you want to tell me?"

He lifts his hands in surrender. "Nothing happening here."

"Well then, I guess James is the only member of our family I know."

Logan opens his mouth to speak, but I cut him off. "Just because I didn't want to be a part of the business doesn't mean I didn't want to be a part of our family. Yes, Joshua kidnaped me, and it was certainly a less-than-ideal situation, but being here was the first time in *years* that I haven't been completely alone."

As if they planned it, my brothers shift forward, each taking one of my hands.

"We never meant to cut you out," James says. "We all just assumed you were happy being on your own, and we didn't want to freak you out with all the business stuff."

"I'm tougher than you think."

Logan breathes a laugh. "I think you've proven that. Why didn't you say something sooner?"

"Honestly, I think it took meeting Joshua to really understand it myself."

"You mean being kidnapped," Logan corrects.

It's a miracle I don't roll my eyes.

"I know this is difficult to understand, but you need to trust me. I promise that I'll explain everything to you later, but right now, I need to talk to him."

After a second of deliberation, Logan nods and James leaves the room without another word.

"I don't like him, Elise."

"I'm not asking you to like him. I'm asking you to trust me."

Logan looks like he wants to ram his head through a wall when he tells me, "He does seem to care about you. Actually, everyone here does."

"I care about them, too."

"I was worried that was the case," he grumbles. "Still, I had to be sure you weren't being manipulated."

"And?"

He shrugs. "Jury's still out. I'll keep you posted."

I laugh, and it feels damn good, despite my sore muscles. "If you don't trust Joshua, why did you let him protect me at the factory? You didn't seem to have a problem with him then."

He studies me for a long moment and finally leans back in his chair.

"About a week after you were taken, Moreno set up a meeting to discuss terms. Our siblings didn't know because Dad doesn't normally entertain negotiations. Since Dad is—*was*—grooming me to take over, I went with him, and that was the first time I ever saw Moreno. He was everything the rumors claimed—an insufferable asshole."

I can't help but laugh at the assessment since there are times I'm inclined to agree.

"I couldn't stand the idea of leaving you with him, so I tried to convince Dad to take the deal, but it backfired. Instead of taking my advice, Dad cut me out of his plans completely. When he told us that you were dead, I believed him because I had no doubt that Moreno was capable of doing it."

My brother pauses, brow furrowed, and I give him time to collect his thoughts before he continues.

"When I saw him at the factory," he finally says, "he wasn't the same. Just as intense, but instead of looking ready to kill you, he looked ready to kill anyone who came near you. It was a bit unnerving." He laughs, but it's dry.

"Then all hell broke loose, and he let me take the lead so that he could stay with you. Maybe it was my intuition or just the fact that we had no other options, but somehow, I knew he wouldn't let anything happen to you. Still, one high-risk situation doesn't make up for the hell he put you through."

I can understand where he's coming from, so I don't push him. If my brothers ever do come around to liking Joshua, it'll have to be on their terms.

"Where's Damon?" I ask, only now noticing his absence.

Logan's jaw ticks, but that's the only sign that he's not happy with our oldest brother. "Detoxing. Matteo is here keeping an eye on him until we get things sorted out."

I smile at the mention of our cousin being here. I haven't seen Matteo in years, and I'm looking forward to a reunion. He hadn't been at the factory, so my brothers must have called him here after everything happened.

"Get what sorted out?"

"I'm sending Damon to rehab. Dad was too worried about other families finding out and using it against us, so he always refused."

"You don't agree?"

Logan shrugs. "Doesn't really matter. He needs to get better. He's a good capo when he's sober but a danger to the entire family when he isn't. I need my brother back."

I don't realize tears are running down my cheeks until Logan frowns, gently wiping them away.

"What's wrong?"

"Dad cared so much about the empire he built that he sacrificed the family he built." I give my brother a small smile. "I already know you won't make the same mistakes."

He doesn't return my smile. "I'm so sorry, Elise. I had no idea Dad would abandon you like that. I swear I never would've let him if I'd known."

My heart hurts so badly that it's difficult to draw in air. I didn't forgive my father for giving me up, but in the factory, when he said he believed me, I saw a future where I could.

Now, we'll never have the chance to reconcile.

"I know, and I don't blame you for any of it."

Despite what I'd hoped would be reassuring words, Logan leans back in the chair with a frown. His shoulders sag like he's carrying the weight of the world, and I suppose that, in a way, he is.

With Dad gone, it's time for him to take leadership of the family, not to mention the task of finding the traitors, dealing with our drunk of a brother, and his sister who's fallen in love with a man who was his enemy only three days ago.

It's a lot to manage.

I reach for his hand and take it in mine. "You're going to do great."

A smile breaks his pained expression. "We'll see about that. It doesn't seem like I have much under control right now."

"Well then, it's a good thing you're not doing this alone."

CHAPTER FIFTY-TWO

Joshua

"All I'm saying is that I could've been more useful inside," Alec says for the hundredth time.

Donovan rolls his eyes. "Oh, please. Then I would've had to carry both your injured asses out of that factory."

"I wouldn't be dumb enough to get shot like some people."

"Shut the hell up, Tonis. You literally got shot two weeks ago," Kade points out.

"Well, I wouldn't be dumb enough to get shot *again*," Alec defends.

The rest of their conversation blurs into the background, and I find myself doing the same thing I've done nonstop for the last forty-eight hours—thinking about Elise.

I don't like leaving her side, but I can only sit in stifling silence with her brothers for so long before the urge to kill them takes over. So, I let myself relax on the sofa in Kade's room with the guys—who are trying to keep the conversation light for my sake.

Not that it makes much of a difference.

Kade lies in his bed, still too injured to return to work. Alec, whose leg is freshly uncasted, leans against the far wall beside Donovan.

No one mentions the missing piece of the group, but that doesn't make the emptiness any less noticeable.

I haven't talked to Ryder since we got back from the factory.

The first day here was pure chaos, and I didn't have time to deal with it, but now that things are starting to settle down, I can't push it off much longer. What he did was unforgivable, though I know Elise would say otherwise.

The only thing stopping me from putting a bullet in his head is that she'd never forgive me for it. That only makes it more difficult to decide how to handle it, especially considering that there are hours from that night that are unaccounted for. I have no idea what Elise and Ryder endured in the time before we arrived and I'm not going to be able to make a decision until I know all the facts.

But Elise is still unconscious, so if I want information, I need to talk to Ryder.

I push out of my chair without warning, ending the conversation around me.

"I'll see you guys later," I say without looking back as I leave the room.

I head toward my office and send a quick message telling Ryder to meet me there. His confirmation is instant.

He's already at the door when I arrive, and I'm hit with a sickening sense of irritation as soon as I see him. Maybe I should take time to calm down before doing this, but I'm too eager to get it over with.

I push past him and round the desk as he closes the door behind us.

We stand in thick silence for several seconds before I even know where to start, but I finally take a seat and face the inevitable head-on.

"What happened that night? Tell me everything from the moment you heard from Mason to the moment I got to the factory."

And he does.

He tells me how he received a call that Rachel and Lyla had been taken. About how he got Elise to come with him by telling her that I left the base. About how she attacked him on the side of the road after realizing she'd been tricked. About how Mason forced them to make that video by threatening Lyla.

"We were taken to a cell, then Tripp came in."

It's then that Ryder stops to take a seat across from my desk. His breath hitches, and there's a tremor in his hand.

Ryder rarely shows emotion, so I know the grief must be overwhelming if I can see it.

"I didn't want to do it, but there was no other way."

"Do what?"

"Her arm."

My stomach twists, and it's through gritted teeth that I ask, "What about her arm?"

He searches my face. "You didn't see the cuts?"

I squeeze my eyes closed and force myself to take a deep breath to stop from reaching for my gun.

I shouldn't be surprised that Elise lied to me. She knew how I'd react; she knew I'd want to kill Ryder for this.

And she was right.

"She told me it was Tripp," I bite out, squeezing my fists so tightly that my fingernails draw blood.

Ryder seems just as surprised by the news as I am.

"He knew she wouldn't fight me, so he held us at gunpoint and told me that if I didn't do it to Elise, he'd do it to Lyla. As soon as his aim drifted, I threw the knife, and that's it. I didn't even write the whole word—"

"Don't you dare lie to me, Ryder. I *saw* the whole word."

He freezes, and the blood drains from his face. "No."

My chest constricts, and I slowly push to my feet so I can look down at him. "What?"

"I swear he was unconscious when I left." His voice breaks on the last word, but his pain does nothing to ease my fury.

I slam my fist onto the desk, and everything on it shakes. "You left her alone with him while he was still alive?"

He shoots to his feet, but there's nothing defensive about his countenance. "When I heard she'd killed him, I assumed she'd just finished the job. I never thought there would be another fight."

It takes a conscious effort to stop myself from lunging over my desk to strangle him. How could he leave her there with the man who tortured and almost raped her only weeks ago?

"I had to go to Mason's office to find a key to Rachel and Lyla's cell, but he and Nate were in there. I took Nate out, but that was my last bullet, so I fought with Mason. He fell back and hit his head on the desk. It knocked him out, and I left him there. I found Lyla and Rachel, got them out of the building, then went back inside to find Elli. She was in this janitor's closet. Damn it, Joshua, she killed two of Mason's soldiers with only a knife."

I recall how surprised I'd been when I saw the corpses myself.

"After that, we went to find you. You know the rest from there."

Neither of us says a word.

We catch our ragged breaths. After a few minutes, I let myself sit back down, and Ryder does the same.

"He had your daughter, I get that, but that doesn't justify what you did."

"I know."

And my decision is made.

"I'm transferring you," I tell him. "You'll accept a capo position at the base in Sacramento. It's the closest one to Rachel and Lyla."

Ryder looks at me with warranted disbelief. "A transfer? That's it?"

I'd laugh if it weren't for the venomous bile crawling up my throat.

"Would you like me to do worse?"

"I deserve worse."

"Yes, you do," I agree.

"So, why don't you?"

No one has ever used the word merciful to describe me, and rightfully so. Ryder deserves a bullet to the head, and we both know it, but there's one very important reason I can't bring myself to hurt him.

"Elise," I answer. "She cares about you too much, and I'm not willing to hurt her. She's been through enough."

A million words pass between us in this silent moment.

My best friend and I stand across from one another, separated by far more than a desk. This man stood by my side through the best and worst days of my life. He's seen me at my lowest, celebrated with me at my highest, and watched my entire world shift on its axis when Elise came into my life.

I trusted him with everything I had, and he stabbed me in the back.

"I suppose I owe her my life then."

"Don't make me regret this, Ryder."

"Yes, sir."

He stands, nodding respectfully, before leaving the room.

Before the door shuts behind him, a hand shoots out to stop it. No one comes into my office uninvited, especially without knocking, so I'm about to lay into the intruder until I see who it is.

I'm on my feet when James Consoli steps cautiously into the room, and he says the words I've been waiting to hear for the last forty-eight hours.

"She's awake."

The second my eyes meet hers, it's like breathing fresh air for the first time in days. My chest loosens, my shoulders sag, and my heart pounds expectantly.

Her skin is pale, highlighting the bruising around her throat. Her lips are cracked and chapped but still pull into a small smile at my entrance.

"Joshua," she breathes, and it feels like years, not days, since I've heard that melodic voice say my name.

I rush to her side, ignoring how Logan glowers at me the whole way.

"Damn it, Elise. I'm so sorry I wasn't here when you woke up."

With so many parts of her injured, I can't exactly pull her into my arms, so I settle for taking her hand.

She holds mine like it's her lifeline, and her eyes pool with tears. "I'm so sorry. Those things I said in your office. I didn't mean any of it. I was on my way to apologize when—"

I silence her with a gentle hush. "You have nothing to apologize for, Princess."

A gagging sound interrupts our reunion, and Elise glares at Logan. "Could you give us a moment?"

James, who still stands at the door, nods, stepping out of the room without another word. Logan, however, doesn't move an inch.

"Logan, please?"

When he looks at her, his stony glare falls away, and I wonder if there's anyone who could withstand the power of her big, brown eyes.

I doubt it.

He huffs a sigh. "Fine, I'm going to check on Damon. If you need anything, call, and I'll come right away."

Does this asshole think I'd hurt her? Just the thought pisses me off.

I take both her hands in mine once the door closes behind him. "I don't think your brothers like me very much."

Her breathless laugh is the sweetest sound I've ever heard. "Doesn't seem like you care for them, either."

I shrug off the observation. "How are you feeling?"

"I'm on some pretty strong pain meds, so I don't feel much of anything. What about you? How's your leg?"

I'd almost forgotten about my graze wound.

"I'm fine, Princess. It'll take a lot more than a shootout and an explosion to take me down." I wink to emphasize my point.

Her no-nonsense glare doesn't falter, and I give in. "My leg really is fine, but I have a few broken ribs from how I landed in the explosion and a ruptured eardrum."

"I guess we got lucky then."

My eyes fall to the wrap covering her arm. "I wouldn't go that far."

"Don't worry," she says as she holds up her arm, turning it to either side for closer inspection. "I'm sure it won't scar."

"You lied to me."

She doesn't need me to elaborate, and she doesn't deny it. "It wasn't a complete lie. Tripp *made* him do it."

"That doesn't change the fact that he did it to you. I should've killed him for this." I reach out, gently grazing the bandage with my fingertips.

"Hence, why I didn't tell you."

"Elise—"

"No, Joshua. Everything he did, he did for his daughter. I don't blame him, and neither should you. Did he tell you that I begged him to do it to protect Lyla?"

No, he didn't. Probably because he knows I wouldn't have believed it.

"You might not be mad at him, but that doesn't change the fact that he betrayed me. I can't ignore that sort of thing—not even for him."

Her already pale face loses the tinge of pink, and her eyes widen. "What do you mean? What's happening to him?"

I rest my palm against her cheek, and she leans into it, relaxing as she does. I'd been right to handle the situation with Ryder like I did. There's no way Elise would've forgiven me if I'd punished him the way I'd wanted to.

The way I still want to.

"I'm transferring him to a base close to Rachel and Lyla, which was generous after everything he did."

Though her tensed muscles relax with the news that I don't plan to kill him, she doesn't look any happier.

"He's leaving?"

"I can't work with a man I don't trust—and I don't trust him after this, Elise."

"But that doesn't mean he has to leave."

It takes me a moment to repress the frustration threatening to break through my composure. The only way to handle this is to tell her the truth.

"I want to kill him," I admit. "Every time I see his face, all I can see is the fact that he betrayed me and hurt you. He needs to leave the base, so I have time to convince myself he doesn't deserve to die for what he did."

Elise goes so still I'd believe she wasn't breathing if it wasn't for the fact that the monitor beside her says otherwise.

"I know what he did wasn't okay, but I wouldn't have survived in there if it weren't for him."

"You also wouldn't have been there in the first place if it weren't for him."

She softens her voice to a whisper. "He did exactly what my dad should've done for me. He fought for his daughter."

Of course she'd feel this way.

Elise knows betrayal better than most. Her brother handed her over to her enemy, and her father left her there. It doesn't surprise me that she can so easily forgive Ryder. I just can't do the same.

She lays her hand over mine. "You know the video was fake, right? Nothing in that was real."

As if I needed another reason to kill Ryder.

"Obviously, the video was fake," I mutter, running my thumb over her bottom lip. "But if I ever see your lips on another man again, I *will* kill him. These lips are mine, understood?"

Despite the dark threat, she smiles.

"All yours," she assures me.

The urge to take those lips now is nearly irresistible, which she must see because she blushes furiously and asks, "What about Rachel and Lyla? Are they okay?"

"Lyla has a few cuts on her arm, nothing vulgar like yours, but it'll probably scar. She doesn't understand much of what happened aside from the fact that some bad people had them, and her dad saved her. Kids are resilient. She'll be fine."

"And Rachel?"

"She'll be okay too, but she's pretty roughed up. She wasn't exactly the most cooperative captive. She has severely bruised wrists from struggling against the cuffs, a cracked rib, and bruising along her cheeks and throat."

Just as I suspected, Elise's eyes go wide with concern.

"Where is she now?"

"She and Lyla are staying in Ryder's room. I'm sure you'll get to meet them soon," I tell her, and she seems to cheer up at the idea.

"What about everyone else? Wasn't Kade shot? Is he okay?"

Now that the conversation has veered from anger-provoking topics, I reclaim my place at her side.

"Kade is better now. The bullet went in and out of his shoulder, so the real problem was blood loss, but Donovan did a good job patching him up in the field to minimize the damage. It's a miracle that he didn't get more injured in the explosion. Donovan managed to walk away from the experience without a scratch."

"For some reason, that doesn't surprise me," she says with a shake of her head. "So, *Goliath* is just blowing up the entire place?"

I shrug. "The Sacramento base used to be a military base. I pulled some strings to get my hands on some of their explosives. It's a last resort."

Elise's eyebrows knit together. "What about Donovan and Kade?"

"What about them?"

"If they hadn't found us in time, they would have died too."

"Calculated risk."

She pulls her hand from mine. "*Calculated risk?* You almost killed them!"

Every muscle in my body twitches to take her hand back, but I answer in the most controlled tone I can muster.

"Sometimes I need to make choices like that, Elise. It comes with the job. Don and Kade know that."

She opens her mouth to respond, but nothing comes out. She closes it with a sigh and returns her hand to mine, her way of showing me she understands even if she doesn't like it.

"We got lucky that they found us when they did," I note. "Mason almost had us, which wouldn't have been the case if it wasn't for your *friend*."

Elise stiffens, and I figure she hadn't remembered that part.

"How did you know Kaitlyn was working for Mason?"

"She didn't get out of the vans when your dad showed up. I figured the chances of her being a traitor were higher than the chances of her coming in as backup."

Elise's hand tenses in mine, and I rub soothing circles there. "I'm sorry, Princess. I know she was your friend."

"Clearly not."

I lean my forehead to hers. "You have friends here. Real friends."

Those beautiful brown eyes finally open, and I swear I could stare at them all day long if she'd let me.

"I have more than just friends here," she mutters, bringing her lips to mine.

CHAPTER FIFTY-THREE

Elise

After getting the all-clear from Dr. Hanes, Joshua insists on carrying me to our bedroom—not that I put up much of a fight.

The second we step into our room, he's kissing me.

His lips move slowly against mine like he's committing this moment to memory. The tender kiss is in striking contrast to the firm grip he has on my waist.

Patient, yet demanding.

After a speedy shower, I feel brand new, albeit completely and utterly exhausted. Somehow, sleeping through two entire days was not enough.

Joshua and I climb into bed, letting our limbs tangle until we're wrapped up in one another.

I haven't felt so peaceful in days.

Of course, that's when we hear a violent pounding at the door.

"Open the hell up, Moreno! I know you have my sister with you!" Logan's voice booms from the other side of the wooden door.

I relax when I realize it's only my brother, but my relief is short-lived when I glance at Joshua's locked jaw and narrowed eyes.

Men and their egos.

Joshua climbs out of bed and stalks toward the door as I sit up.

I won't get any rest until this is dealt with.

When it opens, an irate Logan stands red-faced in the doorway, with James standing expressionless at his side.

"Did you seriously think you could just steal her away to your bed?" Logan seethes.

"I can, and I did." Joshua's voice is abnormally calm—a front meant to irk my brothers.

It works.

Without warning, Logan's fist connects with Joshua's jaw.

"Joshua! What the hell, Logan?" I shout, eliciting a throbbing in my head as I work to pull myself from the tangle of blankets on the bed.

Joshua doesn't so much as stagger and neither of them acknowledges me.

"I'll remind you that you and your men are here as guests, but I can change that very quickly," Joshua says, and his voice carries a deadly promise.

"Stop it!" I throw the covers off and stand faster than my concussed head can handle, causing me to fall to the wooden floor with a loud *thud*.

I cry out, tears filling my eyes when my injured arm collides with the floor.

"Elise!" James gets to me first. "Are you okay?"

"No, I'm not okay!" I grate as James helps me to my feet and wraps a supportive arm around my waist as I glare at Joshua and Logan. "You two are acting completely ridiculous!"

"Elise, get back in bed," Joshua says.

"Don't tell her what to do," Logan snaps.

"Stop it!" I snap. "Joshua, these are my brothers, and they're only looking out for me. There will be no threatening them or any of their men during their stay here."

Joshua's eyes darken with the promise that we'll be discussing this later, but I ignore him and face Logan, who wears a smug grin. "And Logan, you might not like Joshua, but while you're under his roof, you'll show him respect. You will *not* lay a hand on him again, or I'll kick you out myself."

Both men open their mouths to speak, but I silence them with the wave of my hand.

"I get it—you have reputations to uphold, and you don't like each other, whatever. But if either of you cares about *me*, you'll figure out a way to get along." I drop my scowl. "Please, don't make me pick between my family and the man I love."

"Elise, you're not going to stay in his room," Logan says.

"You're right." I step out of James's hold, and Joshua's arms take me in as soon as I'm within reach. "I'm going to stay in *our* room, just like I have been for weeks."

Logan's expression only hardens.

"It was her choice," Joshua tells him. "I never forced her into anything."

"You quite *literally* kidnapped her," Logan bites.

Joshua stiffens, and I place my flat palm against his chest.

Thankfully, James decides to cut in. "Logan," is all he needs to say.

The two look at each other for a moment before Logan sighs. I expect him to agree and go, but he doesn't.

"I need to hear the story," he says. "You said that what happened between you two is a long story. I need to hear it."

I sigh in relief, and the invisible weight that's been on my chest since I woke up finally eases. He's *actually* willing to listen.

"I think that's a great idea." I gesture to the table across the room, and Logan and James go to it.

Joshua remains in place.

"You need to be resting, not storytelling."

"Everyone will rest better when this is handled."

Joshua's phone buzzes, and he pulls it out with a grimace.

"Take it," I tell him. "I'm good here."

Joshua's conflicted gaze flicks to my brothers, who are caught up in their own heated conversation.

"I don't like leaving you," he says, omitting the implied, *with them.*

"They're not going to hurt me, Joshua."

"I'm not worried about them hurting you."

Though he doesn't say the words, I can see his real concern hiding behind his signature stony expression.

I wrap my arms around him, laying my head on his chest, and breathing in the perfect scent of him. "No one is going to take me from you, okay? I'm yours."

His arms hold me, and his lips press gently to my forehead. "All mine."

I spend the next hour reliving every moment of the past two months, good and bad.

Though I desperately want my brothers to make peace with Joshua, I don't edit the story. They deserve to hear the truth, even if it's messy and difficult to come to terms with.

The only parts I tweak are the less-than-appropriate ones. I want them to understand that I love Joshua, but they don't need to know *how* I love him.

I expect Logan and James to interrupt as I go on, but neither says a word. Their expressions remain controlled and calm throughout the entire story.

Well, almost the entire story.

Telling my brothers about Tripp assaulting me in the basement is a difficult experience for all of us. Talking about that day is still a physically difficult task, and my brothers aren't handling it any better. Balled fists, red faces, and clenched teeth stop them from bursting as I explain.

Though Tripp is the culprit of that particular part, I know their anger is directed at Joshua for his lack of protection, and I can't blame them. It's the same reason I couldn't even look at him for days afterward.

The rest of the explanation is much easier to get through, and I find myself smiling at the memories as I tell them.

Life with Joshua is so much more than I ever imagined it could be. I'm not just at peace with it—I'm *happy* here.

Logan and James are surprised when I tell them about my training with Ryder, but that's nothing compared to their reaction to what happened before they got to the factory.

The entire Consoli family saw my blood-covered clothes when I pleaded with everyone to leave the factory, but none of them knew what led to that point.

Suffocating silence follows the end of my story, and I wait on bated breath for their response to everything I've told them.

James goes first. "Dad messed up by sending you away. He should've been training you all these years with the rest of us."

Logan nods but says nothing.

"Well, it's not like I was ever interested anyway."

James shakes his head. "I don't understand how he never saw your potential—how none of us did."

My cheeks heat at his words, and I look to Logan, who avoids meeting my eye.

"Logan, I—"

"You love him," he says.

I slowly nod. "I do."

When his green eyes look up, I'm struck by just how much he looks like our father. Though the boys are identical twins, Logan's resemblance to our father is far more prominent.

"Well, I love you," he tells me. "So, if Moreno is what you want, I won't stop it."

I smile despite the tears welling in my eyes. This understanding is all I hoped for from my brothers, and it means the world that they're giving it to me.

"But if you ever change your mind, we'll drop everything to come and get you," he promises.

As if the timing had been planned, Joshua opens the door, taking in the scene before deeming it safe to come in.

"You told them everything?" he asks, coming to stand at my side.

"Everything."

The attention falls on Logan.

My brothers stand, and Logan squares his shoulders as he levels Joshua with a grave look.

"If you ever hurt her, I'll make it my life's mission to inflict the most excruciating pain imaginable on you."

"Logan!" I exclaim, but Joshua only chuckles.

"Good luck beating her to it," he says, bringing me closer by wrapping one arm over my shoulder.

I expect Logan to snap at Joshua's sarcasm, but he nods, and I wonder if they actually agree on that fact.

Joshua and I walk my brothers to the door, but Logan pauses before leaving.

"You're not good enough for her."

I want to object again, but Joshua answers without hesitation.

"I know."

Joshua and Logan share a tight nod before the door closes, and we're finally alone.

"Are you sure you're up for this? No one would blame you if you decided you'd rather rest."

"I'm sure," I tell him for the third time. "I can't think of anything I'd rather do."

"I can think of a few things," he mutters, but there's a knock on the door before he can make any suggestions.

Joshua opens the door, and Donovan leads the group—likely due to the fact that he's the only one of us not sporting a major injury. It's one of the rare days his long hair falls around his face, and he's dressed in black sweats and a tee.

Alec follows, and the first thing I notice is that his leg is cast-free. He carries a tray, which I can see from here is full of various desserts.

Kade brings up the rear of the group, and he's traded his typical slacks and button-up for jeans and a tee, thanks to the obnoxious sling securing his left arm. Without the full use of both arms, he must've given up on shaving because his stubble is longer than I've ever seen it.

As soon as he reaches the bed, Donovan wraps me up in a bear hug that provokes a scowl from Joshua that we both ignore. "How do you feel?"

"Better now that you guys are here."

Donovan smirks. "I tend to have that effect on people."

"She meant me, dumbass." Alec unceremoniously pushes Don out of the way and sits on the bed beside me. "I come bearing gifts," he announces, holding the tray out as an offering.

"Don't be a prick, Tonis," Kade says. "It's from Jay."

I eye the selection of cupcakes, pie slices, cookies, and brownies. It's an overwhelming gesture.

"If you think I can eat all of this, you're insane. Please, take some."

"Thought you'd never ask." Alec leans in to grab a cookie, but his hand is smacked away by Kade.

"No way. These are yours, Elli."

"I don't need all of these," I assure them. "I didn't do anything more than anyone else here."

The three share a look.

"I didn't fake an affair on the spot to save a child's life," Don says.

"I didn't kill three trained fighters with nothing but a knife," Kade adds.

"I didn't convince two enemy families not to kill each other in less than five minutes," Alec finishes.

"Don't forget how she assaulted me on the side of the highway after pretending to be carsick."

My eyes flit to the owner of the honey-smooth voice at the door. "Ryder!"

He stands in the doorway, and though my view is partially blocked by Kade, I assess his injuries. Other than a bandage covering a large part of his forehead and a few stitches on his lip, he looks perfectly healthy, but he doesn't make a move to come inside.

"What wouldn't I give to have watched Elli kick your ass?" Alec clutches his chest dramatically.

"If you don't come hug me, I'll have to do it again," I threaten.

I don't miss Ryder's eyes flitting to Joshua or Joshua's subtle nod of allowance, but the others don't seem to notice.

Kade steps aside for Ryder to come through, giving me a full view of the stunning woman with a small child in her arms. She must've been hiding in the hall because the others don't seem to notice her until now, too. She captures the attention of the whole room as soon as she steps inside.

Her silky black hair is pulled into a slick ponytail, and even though she wears leggings and a sweatshirt, she looks runway-ready. Flawless, dark skin and softened features give her no need to wear makeup since everything about her is already naturally beautiful. Even the bruising along her cheeks and throat has lightened to a barely noticeable degree.

This must be Rachel.

The little girl she holds has tiny arms wrapped so tightly around her neck that it's a miracle Rachel can breathe. Her tightly coiled hair is pulled into two buns on the top of her head, and a pink, Barbie-themed bandage peeks out from the sleeve of her T-shirt.

"Elli, this is Rachel and Lyla," Ryder says, gesturing between us before coming to give me the hug I demanded.

Alec moves off the bed as soon as Rachel enters the room, and I think he's going to hug her, but he holds out his arms to the little girl.

"Uncle Alec!" The shy look melts away as Lyla's features soften with a smile.

Rachel releases her into Alec's arms, accepting a chaste kiss on the cheek from him as she does.

"I thought you and Lyla were going back home today," Donovan says, standing to mimic Alec's greeting, then moving aside for Kade to do the same.

Her kind eyes look to Joshua, then back to Don. "We were, but I decided to push it back when I heard Elli had woken up."

He nods, but then all three capos focus their attention on Lyla. They fawn over the girl, asking her about school and her best friend, Dominic. Her laughter breaks any remaining tension in the room.

Ryder stays at Alec's back, as close as he can be to Lyla without taking her out of his arms. I don't miss how her eyes flit to her father's every few seconds, making sure he doesn't go anywhere.

Joshua watches the group but makes no move to participate—and he doesn't acknowledge Ryder.

I don't have the chance to attempt easing them into interacting because Rachel sits on the bed beside me, taking both my hands in her own.

"It is so nice to finally meet you," she says in a low, smoky voice.

"You too. Ryder speaks so highly of you."

Her eyes drift to where Lyla is trying to grab a brownie from Donovan's hand, but he keeps pulling it out of her reach at the last minute. Kade suddenly snatches it from him and gives it to the girl, who smiles at him like he's lassoed the moon for her.

"I can't thank you enough for what you did for my daughter and me. It couldn't have been easy, but I'm so grateful."

I shake my head, ignoring the pain it inspires. "There's no need to thank me. I'm so sorry for what my brother put you both through."

"That's not your fault," she assures me, but the guilt in the pit of my stomach is unmoving.

She looks to where Joshua leans against the wall across the room. He's too far away to hear us, but his eyes watch me warmly. "I've known Mr. Moreno for years, and I have never seen him like this. I've only been at the base for two days, but it's impossible to miss. He's crazy about you."

If I blush anymore, I'll permanently turn red.

"The feeling is mutual," I admit. "It's so good to talk to another girl. I've been surrounded by guys for way too long."

"Try doing it for nine months when your hormones are already out of control," she mutters.

My eyes nearly pop out of my head. "What?"

"Ryder never told you? I stayed here during my whole pregnancy. Mr. Moreno was traveling back here for the year and needed Ryder to come, but he refused to let me out of his sight, so I was brought along."

I try to imagine it—nine months surrounded by nonstop testosterone while pregnant.

"You're kidding, right?"

She shakes her head. "Once Lyla was born, I put my foot down and moved back home. So, I know a little bit of what you've been through. Of course, I wasn't kidnapped, but I do get what it's like to crave girl time."

"Rachel," Joshua calls from across the room. When we look up, he's inspecting his phone with a furrowed brow.

She stands but doesn't go to him right away. "I had Moreno put my number in your phone. If you ever need anything or just want to talk, don't hesitate to call, okay?"

I nod, and she squeezes my hands gently before going to Joshua, stopping to pick up a brownie-covered Lyla on her way.

I expect Lyla to resist being taken from Alec's arms, but she eagerly accepts her mother's embrace. In fact, it's the boys who look disappointed. Each of their faces falls as they wave to the girl being carried away.

"Have you looked at it yet?" I'd been so focused on the capos that I didn't see Ryder's approach. His eyes are fixated on my bandaged arm.

"Not yet."

Ryder is excellent at hiding his emotions, so I'm shocked to see pain openly creasing his face.

"I don't blame you for anything," I tell him.

"You should. If I hadn't been so rattled, I could've come up with a better plan. I could've—"

I pull on his hand until he sits on the bed beside me, and he finally meets my gaze. "Ryder, I'm *fine*. I'm safe, and so is your family, which means you did everything right."

His lip twitches up, and it's such a relief to see his smile again, even if it is a small one.

Ryder glances over his shoulder, and I follow his gaze to where Joshua and Rachel are huddled, deep in conversation. "It'll take a long time to get back to normal."

"A price worth paying for your family," I remind him, and he nods. "I'm glad you're okay."

His smile is natural now. "You too, Elli."

CHAPTER FIFTY-FOUR

Elise

"Ready?"

I look up at Joshua through thick lashes. "No."

His low chuckle eases only a fraction of my nervousness. "Come on, Princess."

I was surprised this morning when Joshua told me that I was going to join him today, especially considering it's only been two days since I woke up, and I'm nowhere near healed from my concussion. Still, he insisted on my attendance, promising to take me back to the room if I was in too much pain.

Pain is the least of my worries.

Today, Joshua's capos are meeting with my brothers and their capos to establish the terms of their alliance. I should be thrilled that both parties are willing to compromise for peace, but I know better than to expect this to go smoothly. Logan and Joshua are bound to butt heads.

We walk into the conference room and find everyone is already seated and waiting for us.

It's a long rectangular table, with Logan sitting at the head of the farthest end. Beside him sits James, Damon, our cousin Matteo, and Jace—the capo charged with cybersecurity for the Consoli family. The end chair closest to us is empty, clearly meant for Joshua, and to the right sits Ryder, Donovan, Alec, and Kade.

All eyes are on us.

"Elise? Is everything okay?" Logan stands at our entrance, concern etching his face.

"Uh, yeah, everything is fine."

"Then what are you doing here?"

My eyes snap to Joshua's, and I realize that none of them were expecting me. He made it seem like my attendance was a unanimous decision, but the only person who doesn't look surprised is Ryder.

I'm glad Ryder was still invited to this meeting despite his transfer. He doesn't leave for Sacramento for two weeks, so he has plenty of time to train Donovan, who will be named underboss in his absence.

Joshua doesn't seem at all bothered by the bewildered gazes. "Elise is here for the meeting."

"Mr. Moreno, this isn't how we do things." James looks ashamed to say the words, and he doesn't meet my eye.

"She doesn't need to be involved in this," Logan agrees.

"I—well—" I unconsciously step back, but Joshua wraps an arm around my waist to hold me in place.

"Elise has more than proven herself, and every man here has seen it firsthand. If you have a legitimate reason to believe she can't handle this meeting, go ahead. I'm all ears."

No one says a word.

Though most of the men keep their composure, Damon, Ryder, and Donovan are all suppressing smiles.

Logan falls back into his chair.

"It's settled then," Joshua says. "She stays."

Joshua leads me to the table, but there's only one chair available. I'm about to ask if I should go get another when Joshua sits and pulls me onto his lap.

"This is hardly appropriate," Logan grates out.

Despite my brother's mood, I can't help but tease him.

I point to where I sit on Joshua's lap. "I'm sorry, did you have dibs?"

Logan's face turns bright red, and I can almost see the steam coming out of his ears. There are snickers to my right, and Damon doesn't even try to hold back his laughter.

James places a calming hand on Logan's shoulder, glaring at me for the unnecessary riling. "Mr. Moreno, please get us started."

"We have two main issues to address today. First, the terms of the alliance."

Logan, having composed himself, straightens his back. "The Moreno family will be granted access to the territories you originally wanted, provided the Consoli family is entitled to fifty percent of the profits."

Jace begins to write as Logan talks.

Joshua scoffs. "That's completely unreasonable, and you know it. Fifteen percent."

"Seeing as you have no bases close to those territories, we'd also grant hospitality. Fifty percent."

"And I'm fully capable of establishing a base in the area. Fifteen percent."

As their voices harden, I want to cut in and help reach a compromise, but the subtle shake of Ryder's head halts me. He's probably right. This is how negotiations work, especially between two men as stubborn as Joshua and Logan.

"Mr. Moreno, I'm sure you're aware that the Diaz family has launched several attacks on the minor bases in our territories."

"I am."

"Then you know it's only a matter of time before they make a move against us. If you establish a base in a high-risk area to intimidate the Diazes, then I'll agree to thirty percent."

I keep my face composed like the other men at the table, but I can't help but wonder why Logan didn't open with that.

"This puts my soldiers on the front lines of a potentially messy fight. The base will need heavy artillery." Joshua looks at Donovan. "Get me a full report of what we'd need for security in such a high-risk area."

"Yes, sir." Donovan starts taking notes.

Joshua's attention is back to Logan. "If you agree to provide the necessary weaponry for the base, I'll agree to thirty."

The smug looks on both their faces answer my question.

Neither of them will risk looking weak by agreeing too quickly. This means that instead of outright saying what they want, they'll dance around the real objective until they're able to state it without hurting their egos.

"Deal."

The next thirty minutes drag, and I'd be lying if I said I didn't zone out. I could blame my short attention span on my concussion, but in reality, it was just boring. It makes me feel better that I caught capos from either side of the table staring off into space, too. I'm not the only one having a hard time staying interested.

Of course, it doesn't help that Joshua rubs my back in slow, soothing circles.

"Well," James says, and the liveliness in his voice brings me back to the conversation. "Now that we have the terms figured out, we'll have Jace print the official documentation."

Joshua nods. "The second order of business—establishing a procedure for weeding out the traitors who aligned themselves with Mason Consoli. There's currently no way of telling how many people he had working for him on either side, so this needs to be a top priority. For this to be successful, we will need the full cooperation of both families."

Logan nods. "I'll be pulling some of my best soldiers together for a task force that will be dedicated solely to finding these individuals."

"And what kind of assurance do we have that your task force is clean?" It's the first time Ryder's spoken the whole meeting.

Logan's jaw ticks. "I'll interview them myself."

"These guys aren't stupid," Ryder says as he leans back in his chair. "They know what will happen to them if they're found, and with Mason gone, there's no one to incriminate them. I don't think a good old-fashioned interrogation will be enough to crack them."

"Well, we can't torture everyone and hope the right guys break," James notes.

"All I'm saying is that we may need a more aggressive approach."

Donovan looks between both parties. "If we aren't careful, this will turn into a witch hunt that will tear both families apart from the inside out."

"We need to find how Mason communicated with them," I say, hating how shaky my voice sounds.

Questioning eyes turn my way, and I look to Joshua, who nods for me to go on.

"Mason had to communicate with his soldiers somehow, and if we find that source, it'll lead us right to the traitors."

Logan arches a brow. "And how do you suggest we do that?"

I carefully consider his question before responding. "Kade, didn't you backtrack the activity on the server after Ryder copied files?"

He nods.

"Mason was able to make a lot of the security footage go missing, which means one of two things. Either he hacked into the system, or he had an inside man do it for him. Either way, there's a digital footprint somewhere. We just need to find it. I say we start there."

I wait for the critiques and flaws of my plan to be spoken, but when I look around the table, there are only nods of agreement.

James folds his hands on the table. "Once we can identify all the traitors, word will travel fast when we start to round them up. It could turn ugly fast, especially if they work together."

He has a good point.

Both Joshua and my brothers have multiple bases, meaning Mason's followers are likely spread across the country. Without being properly prepared, the whole operation will fall apart.

"What if we pick up where Mason left off?" I ask.

Logan tilts his head from one side to the other. "That could work. Using the communication system to rally the traitors under the impression that it's someone finishing what Mason started."

I nod. "We could give directions to have them all meet at a certain base, so we can isolate them."

"We can send out several units of soldiers around the same time to allow the traitors to get to the designated location," Joshua adds.

"It's settled then," James says. "We find the source of communication, draw out the traitors, and take them out all at once."

"What about their resources?" Ryder asks.

Joshua turns to him. "What do you mean?"

"You all saw the factory. He had weaponry, ammunition, vehicles, and who knows what else. With all the connections he had through both families, it's unlikely that he found an independent supplier. Somewhere, there's a leak that he was exploiting. If we don't find it and fix it, we might be in danger of the traitors getting to it first."

"It has to be one of ours," Joshua sighs. "It's not a coincidence that the factory was only a few miles from here. He couldn't have been using the main base since we would've noticed things going missing, but it's likely one of the others."

James taps two fingers on the table. "Okay then, the Consoli family will work to uncover the communication program, and the Moreno family will track down and cut off the resource leak."

I wait for the arguing between Joshua and Logan, but they share a single nod of understanding while all the capos murmur their agreements.

"There's one more matter I'd like to address before we disperse for the day," Joshua announces. "At the end of this week, I'll be making an announcement to officially appoint my newest capo. After recent events, it's abundantly clear that Elise is the best person for the job."

I whirl around on his lap to face him. "Excuse me?"

"What?" my brothers exclaim in unison.

His lip turns up, and he presses a kiss to my temple. "I've been planning to bring her into the family business for a while now, but after everything that happened at the factory, I have no doubts. She's the perfect candidate."

I study Joshua's expression with all the brain power my concussion will allow, looking for any sign that he's joking—but there's none. His gaze is earnest, shining with certainty.

I look to my brothers next.

Damon leans back in his chair, a slight smile on his lips like he's watching me win an award. James's stare is trained on me, and I can practically feel the waves of wariness rolling off of him. Logan doesn't shift his gaze from Joshua's, testing the sincerity like I had.

"You should do it," Damon states, and it's the first time he's spoken to me since I woke up.

I smile my gratitude to my oldest brother and look to Logan, waiting for his objection.

Instead, he sighs. "Elise, what do you want to do?"

Everyone looks at me expectantly, and I realize that I don't have an answer to that. I'd been so focused on their reactions that I hadn't considered the actual proposition.

My whole life, I've been running from this very fate. I spent years searching for something better—something *normal*—but I never found what I was looking for. Sure, I could fill my time and tell myself I was happy, but there was always something missing.

Now I know that it was *me*.

I suppressed so much of who I am in the name of freedom, and in the end, I was only holding myself hostage.

In some strange twist of fate, when Joshua kidnapped me, he also set me free.

I look to Joshua, who is practically beaming at me with love and pride.

My smile is wide. "I accept."

It's been hours since the meeting, but I'm still riding the high of accepting my new position. Joshua tried to convince me to go back to our room and rest, but sharing a celebratory drink with the other capos was too enticing to pass up, even if I had to drink water and take a three-hour long nap afterward because of how exhausted I was.

I've only been awake for an hour, despite the fact that it's now early evening.

"Why don't we go on a walk?" Joshua asks, placing a sweet kiss on my forehead.

"You're the one badgering me to stay in bed," I remind him.

"Who said you'd be doing the walking?"

Careful not to jostle me too much, Joshua scoops me in his arms so I'm cradled against his chest.

"Ready?"

"Lead the way," I say with a laugh.

The gentle rocking is so calming that it almost lulls me to sleep.

When we step into the garden, the first thing I notice is the sky. Dark purple, orange, and blue color the vast space, and the sight is absolutely gorgeous.

I'm captivated by the view, which is probably why I don't notice my surroundings until Joshua stops walking and gently places me on my feet.

If I thought the sky was beautiful, then what I'm looking at now is breathtaking.

We're at the base of the gazebo, but the smooth stone is no longer bare. Candles line either side of the staircase with string lights wrapped around the handrails and Roman-style pillars. Their illumination blends seamlessly with the dusk lighting. Hundreds of flowers that I can't even name line the inside of the structure, and rose petals have been sprinkled over the ground and stairs.

I'm speechless.

Joshua takes my hand, and we ascend the stairs until we're standing in the center of the lights and flowers.

As he faces me, taking my hands in both of his, I find my voice. "Joshua, what—what is all of this?"

He smiles, and it's a sight that rivals the beauty around us.

"When I walked into that bakery, I knew that I was about to change your life, but I had no idea that you'd flip mine upside down. I spent months creating the perfect plan, and within twenty-four hours of meeting you, it was already going off the rails."

He shakes his head. "Every time I saw you, it was like I was losing control of the situation—like you were breaking my walls and stealing every last bit of my sanity. It pissed me off that anyone—let alone some girl—could have that kind of effect on me. It wasn't until that night in the garden that I realized I had it all wrong. You weren't breaking or stealing anything. You were giving pieces of yourself to me. I had no idea what to do with the hope and trust you were putting in me despite everything I'd done to you. All I knew was that I needed to protect it. Then Tripp attacked you…"

Joshua's gaze, overflowing with sincerity and love, locks on mine. "I let you down, and I'm not sure I'll ever fully forgive myself for that."

I open my mouth to tell him that I've already forgiven him, but he silences me with a peck on the lips before going on.

"When you agreed to stay with me for the month, I promised myself that I'd be worthy of the chance you were giving me. I never wanted you to look at me the way you did in that basement ever again… But you did after you saw what I did to Tripp."

He goes on. "I lashed out because I was pissed at myself for breaking that promise *again*. It felt so hopeless to keep trying to make this work when I clearly couldn't get it right."

He drops my hands, only to wrap his arms around my waist and pull me to him. I instinctively wrap mine around his neck so our foreheads rest on one another.

"But the idea of losing you…" He shakes his head. "The idea of you being out in the world and not being mine? That's worse than anything I could imagine."

He places a long kiss on my forehead.

"I've screwed up more times than I can count, and I can't promise that it won't happen again. What I can promise is that I will never stop trying to be the man you deserve. Being without you isn't an option anymore, so I'll do whatever it takes to have you. You are my light, my life, and my heart."

He releases my waist, slowly lowering himself to one knee. I feel a single tear sliding down my cheek as Joshua reaches into his jacket pocket and pulls out the familiar box.

"Exactly one month ago, I asked you to stay with me, and I told you that at the end of that time, I'd be making you my wife."

When he opens the box, revealing the stunning ring, I realize I haven't felt complete since taking it off.

"Elise Maya Consoli, will you do me the honor of being my wife?"

I fall to my knees, wrapping my arms around him and bringing my lips to his.

"Is that a yes?" Joshua asks through kisses.

"That's a yes," I confirm, smiling against his lips.

He's kissing me again before the word is even out.

As the sun sets over the flower-filled, dreamily-lit garden, I lose myself in the complete and utter perfection of this moment.

Joshua Moreno is the love I never saw coming. He came crashing into my life like a hurricane—brutal and destructive. I thought he was stealing my life away from me, but he's given me more than I ever imagined I could have.

He says that I'm his light, his life, and his heart, but Joshua Moreno is my *everything*.

Epilogue One

Elise
Four Months Later

"For the first time ever, I present to you, Mr. and Mrs. Joshua Moreno!" The DJ's voice booms through the speakers of the botanical gardens as my husband leads me through the grand doors.

Cheers erupt from all around, but I barely notice the chaos as Joshua pulls me to a stop, dipping me for yet another breathtaking kiss. I feel, rather than see, the flashes of the camera capturing the precious moment in all its candid glory.

Thoughts of ditching this party to find some privacy are almost overwhelming by the time Joshua pulls away with a wicked smile that says his thoughts mirror mine.

The cheers finally subside as we take our place on the dance floor. Guests whisper amongst themselves, no doubt questioning the song choice, but it had been a no-brainer for me.

An orchestral rendition of Hostage, by Billie Eilish, plays through the speakers, and its violin intro romanticizes the originally gloomy song.

However, it's difficult to focus on the music when my husband's hand holds my lower back and his lips brush the shell of my ear.

"Have I told you how stunning you look?" he murmurs, eyes devouring me in a way that heats my cheeks.

I follow his gaze to the white dress that clings to my body like a second skin. I hadn't thought the mermaid style would be for me, but something about the intricate lace and pearl beading had called to me the moment Rachel and I stepped into the bridal boutique.

"Only a million times," I answer, biting back my wide smile while trying not to mess up my meticulously applied makeup.

"Never enough, Mrs. Moreno."

Mrs. Moreno. Though it's only been accurate for an hour, it feels more right than my birth name ever did.

As Joshua turns us on the dance floor, I take in the smiling faces of our friends and family.

Rachel and Ryder sit at a table with the other L.A. capos, and they send warm smiles our way. He and Joshua aren't back to normal yet, but they've been closer since the incident two months ago, and it gives me hope that a full recovery is possible.

Damon is sitting with them too, a bottle of water in his hands as he tells an animated story to the other capos, who are laughing heartily with him. He hasn't touched alcohol since our father's funeral four months ago when Logan, James, and I told him we'd be sending him to rehab.

James sits at a table with the Consoli capos, who seem content to talk amongst themselves. The only person who isn't smiling sits to James's left.

Logan.

He's leaning back in his chair, gaze focused on the amber liquid that fills his glass. The past few weeks haven't been easy on him for more reasons than I can count, but it means the world to me that he not only came today but gave me away at the altar. He and Joshua are on barely civil terms, but they've managed to make it this far without maiming each other, so I'll take what I can get.

The music fades, and Joshua leads me by the waist to our table. He pulls out my chair, and I wonder if I'll ever get used to how effortlessly chivalrous he can be. I hope I don't. I hope these moments still feel like walking on water, even when we're old and gray.

"And now, the maid of honor and best man have a few words they'd like to say," the DJ announces, and Rachel takes the microphone from him.

She looks beyond stunning in her pale-pink silk gown, her hair falling in straight sheets halfway down her back. I glance at Ryder, who's watching her with awe and admiration.

She takes a deep breath, giving me a *you're lucky I love you because you know I hate public speaking* look that makes me smile.

"I want to welcome you all here tonight and thank you so much for taking part in this special celebration. I'm Rachel, the maid of honor," she begins, taking a long look at her note card before letting it fall to her side. "Elise and I met four months ago, and though that might not seem like a long time, it feels like I've known her my whole life. Elli is just one of those people that skips over the superficial and the small talk. She gets right to who you are and accepts you no matter what—which came in handy for Moreno."

That prompts a round of laughter that even Joshua joins in on.

"I've known Mr. Moreno for four years, and I can honestly say I never pictured him settling down, especially with someone as strong-willed as Elise. But, as I'm sure you can all agree, I've never seen two people more perfectly matched for each other."

Joshua squeezes my hand in agreement, and I return the gesture.

"It's not that you always agree or get along—we all know you do *not*." She pauses for the chuckles before fixing us with a smile. "It's that, even in the worst arguments, you're fighting *for* each other, not against each other. A love like yours is rare—the kind of thing people spend their whole lives searching for—and I hope you never take it for granted."

Rachel sets the note cards down and raises a glass. "To the bride and groom—I can't think of anyone who deserves a happily ever after more than you two."

We all raise our glasses and I mouth my thanks to my best friend.

Rachel returns my gesture with a small nod and hands the microphone to the best man.

"Well, this should be good," Joshua mutters, and I can't help but agree as my shoulders tense.

"Did anyone approve his speech?" I whisper, though I'm fairly sure I know the answer.

Joshua shakes his head. "Like I said, this should be good."

Damon clears his throat, his smile widening as he takes in the guests who are waiting on bated breath to hear what he has to say.

When the time came to name our wedding party, I hadn't been surprised when Joshua picked Damon. Though a part of me was sad that Ryder wasn't his first choice, I can't say I'm upset that Joshua and my oldest brother have formed such a close friendship.

A week after our father's funeral, Damon attended a rehab center in California. Once his two-week program was over, he wasn't ready to go home, so Joshua and I happily agreed to let him stay with us for a while—well, I happily agreed, Joshua was more or less forced into it. Based on that reluctance—and the fact that he and the twins don't get along—I was fairly certain Joshua and Damon would share the hostility.

I've never been happier to be wrong.

Since his first day with us, Damon and Joshua have clicked unlike anything I've ever seen. It's different than his friendship with Ryder since there's no business talk allowed—per Logan's rule for allowing him to stay with us—but I think Joshua prefers it that way. Having that boundary stops him from feeling like he's replacing his former best friend.

My brother gives me a look similar to Rachel's, only his says *you're going to regret giving me a microphone*, and I have a feeling he's right.

"For those who don't know who I am, my name is Damon Consoli. I am the bride's oldest brother and the groom's biggest pain in the ass," he says with a wide grin.

"Most big brothers would take it upon themselves to threaten their little sister's boyfriends, but since Moreno skipped the pick-up lines and went straight to kidnapping, I didn't exactly get the chance."

My cheeks flame red, and Joshua chuckles.

"By the time I finally had the opportunity to threaten him, she was wearing a ring, and he was wearing a leash, so it seemed like a moot point." The guests erupt with laughter, but Joshua's laugh lines are replaced with a daring glare that Damon waves off.

"All jokes aside," Damon says, face taking on a rare seriousness. "I couldn't have asked for anyone better to marry my sister. Sure, at first, I would've rather cut my own hands off with a dull knife than watch her tie her life to yours, but the weeks I've spent with you have proven three things to me. First, love isn't found, it's built. Two people have to mutually agree to put in the work every day. Second, last names can't dictate matters of the heart. When love and blood clash, love will always win. And third, never walk into a room without making a lot of noise first. These kids are still learning how locks work."

I'm certain my face couldn't possibly turn any redder, and I use both hands to cover my mortification, though Joshua seems to be muffling his amusement.

"To the bride and groom!" Damon announces, and the crowd cheers.

Joshua's hands peel mine away from my face, and his lips hover just close enough that we share a breath. With each inhale I take in that scent that's all him, and it eases the embarrassment.

"It honestly wasn't as bad as I thought it'd be."

I laugh. "I'm glad someone enjoyed it."

His lips brush against mine. "Just think about it this way— speeches being over just got me one step closer to getting my wife home and all to myself."

I hum my approval and steal a kiss, basking in the electricity that hasn't faded since our first touch.

And somehow, I know that it never will.

Epilogue Two

Joshua
Four Years Later

She looks up at me with those big brown eyes that always seem to render me helpless. It doesn't matter how much time passes—I'll never grow immune to her pleading gaze.

She has her mother's eyes.

I stare down at my two-year-old daughter, holding her arms out for me to lift her up, and, naturally, I do.

"Help?" she asks, lifting the star in her tiny hands.

"Of course, Princess." I kiss her rosy cheek before lifting her over our almost fully decorated Christmas tree. She wiggles in my arms as she spends several moments trying to place the star in just the right place.

"There!" she announces, and when I pull her back to my chest, the golden star is so crooked it's a miracle it's not falling over.

Her beaming smile is the most beautiful thing I've ever seen.

"Want to show Mom?" I ask.

"Yes!" she exclaims, squirming out of my arms. The second her feet touch the tile, she's racing into the kitchen.

"Mama! Come look what I did! I finished the tree!"

"Without me?" The melodic sound of my wife's voice drifts to my ears, and with it, a sense of bliss hits me. The feeling intensifies when the two girls I love most in the world walk into the living room, hand in hand.

My wife is as beautiful as ever. She wears a red shirt with a gray cardigan falling to her knees and a Santa hat that matches my own, courtesy of our daughter. Her skin is still tan from our trip to Greece last week—practically glowing in the firelight. We'd taken the trip with the knowledge that it'll be a while before we're able to travel again.

My girls stand beside me in front of the tree, and Elise smiles down at our little girl.

"Vanessa, you did a great job putting the star up," she coos. "It's perfect."

Ness smiles her toothy grin before leaning into her mother's stomach. "I'll teach you to do the star, too!" she promises her unborn siblings.

I wrap an arm around Elise's waist, pulling her into me and placing my palm over her 20-week pregnant belly.

We announced the pregnancy to our family a few weeks ago at Thanksgiving, though many of them had suspected it since it was no secret we'd been trying. What was surprising, however, was the news that we're having twins.

I lead my wife to the couch, ensuring she's comfortable before finishing the mugs of hot chocolate she'd started before Ness went to get her. Before I go back to the living room, I take a detour to my office, grabbing the wrapped box that's been sitting there for a week now.

I finally get to give it to her.

When I come back to the living room, I stop in the doorway, just watching Elise with Ness.

She's the perfect mother. I'd always known she would be. Even when I wasn't sure I'd ever want kids, I never doubted that she was exactly the kind of woman I'd want as the mother of my children.

I hadn't thought there was much hope for me as a father—despite Elise's assurances—but once our girl was born, I knew she'd have a better father than either of us did.

When my eyes first fell on Vanessa Maya Moreno, I realized that my heart is a lot bigger than I thought.

I take a seat on the floor beneath Elise and pull Ness onto my lap as I hold out the box.

"What's this?"

"Open it," I tell her.

She takes it, giving me a side glance as she pulls the top off. After lifting the first layer of tissue paper, her mouth falls open, and her eyes widen. It's exactly the reaction I'd been hoping for.

She pulls out the first piece, a flat, circular ornament, pearl white with fine script writing.

R. R. Bates, with the wedding date of our best friends beneath it.

Elise looks at me with awe-filled eyes. "Is this—"

I nod. "Keep going."

She presses her lips together, trying to control her smile as she moves another piece of tissue paper and pulls out the next ornament.

L. K. Consoli. And the next.

J. I. Consoli. And the last.

D. S. Consoli.

All with their designated wedding dates beneath them.

Elise used to tell me about her dreams of big family gatherings. She hoped her brothers would one day find the same love we have—and eventually, they did.

Our family has grown a lot over the last four years—more than I ever thought possible—and I know the journey has meant the world to Elise.

When my wife's eyes meet mine, tears stream down her face, and though she'll blame them on the hormones, we both know she would've reacted this way regardless.

Elise slides onto the floor, where I sit with a sleepy Ness lying on my chest.

"Joshua, I love them," she whispers.

Careful not to disrupt Ness, I reach up and stroke her face. "It's our first Christmas without the rest of our family. I know you're missing your brothers and won't be able to see them until after the twins are born, so I thought these might help."

"They're absolutely perfect."

Elise's smile still takes my breath away despite the fact that I have the honor of seeing it every day. My wife is the most beautiful woman in this world—her only rival being our own daughter.

This life that we've built isn't what I imagined for myself. It's not what I pictured when I made plans to expand my empire and influence. It's not what I deserve.

But it's a damn good life.

THE END

Bonus Chapter

Ryder

"Be careful, Elli," I tell her, every bone in my body hating the idea of leaving her behind.

She rises onto her tiptoes and presses a kiss to my cheek. "You, too."

Her reassuring smile hits me like a bat to the head. Her eyes shine with relief and hope—neither of which I deserve.

Elise may be able to see my motives for hurting her as noble—justified even—but they aren't. I didn't just choose to save Rachel and Lyla.

I chose to betray Joshua.

Moreno isn't just my boss—a man I respect and would follow into fire—he's also my best friend.

But not after this.

The penalty for betrayal is death—I know that. I accepted that the second Mason called me.

What I cannot accept is Rachel and our daughter facing the same fate.

I race down the hall to the cell Nate took me to earlier. There are no guards at the door, and I'm tugging at the knob the second it's within reach.

It doesn't budge.

It does—however—inspire a shriek from inside the cell.

"It's me," I call as softly as I can. "It's okay. I'm going to get you out of here."

"Ryder?" Rachel calls, her voice low and strained, and the sound of it eases a fraction of my panic.

It's been years, and her voice still has the same effect on me.

"I need to find the key to get you guys out," I tell her, stepping back to assess the door. There's a sliver of space beneath it—just enough room for the cuff keys. "How far are you from the door?"

A brief pause. "Maybe ten feet," she says with an edge of uncertainty. "Why?"

"Left, right, or straight ahead?"

"Your left," she answers. "What's going on?"

"I have the key for your handcuffs. I'm going to slide it under the door, and then I'm going to find a key for the cell. I'll be back as fast as I can. Be ready to run when I'm back, okay?"

I can just barely make out her shaking voice as she answers, "Okay."

I slide the key under the door to my left as hard as I can.

"I got it!" Rachel calls, and for the first time tonight, I feel like everything might just turn out okay.

"I'll be right back," I promise, then turn to go.

I need to find Nate. He had the key to their cell, and I'm willing to bet he still does. Still, I have no idea where the hell he could be.

This factory is big—but I have no idea how big. He could be anywhere, and he's probably not alone.

Still, I need to find him.

I move through the maze of hallways as quickly as I can without making too much noise. I'm itching to fly down the halls and shoot every bastard in my way, but without any backup, I can't risk it.

Muffled voices stop me in my pursuit, and I pause outside an unmarked door to listen. I can't make out the words being spoken, but there are three distinct voices—all expressive and buzzing with excitement.

Moving slowly, I peer through a small window in the door. It doesn't give me a full view of the room, but as far as I can tell, only three of them are inside.

With one last glance ensuring the halls are clear, I flatten my back against the wall beside the door and flick my hand over the knob, tugging the door open.

"What the hell?" One of them mutters, and anger buzzes through me when I recognize the voice—Guy, a soldier from the San Diego base.

"Must be a busted doorknob," another says.

Slow footsteps creep closer to the door, but I remain perfectly still until the figure reaches it. When he does—I don't give him a single second to process what's happening.

I grab him by the shoulder, shoving him back into the room as my human shield. I raise my gun over his shoulder and fire twice. One of them collapses.

Guy is on his feet in an instant, firing at me—and hitting his own friend. He realizes his mistake too late as I shove the groaning body into him.

Guy stumbles back at the force, and I kick the gun from his hand as he hits the ground. I fire one more bullet in my human shield's head —effectively silencing his shouts.

The entire ordeal takes place in a matter of seconds, but I'm not under any illusions—I've just made a hell of a lot of noise, and backup is probably on the way.

The smirk on Guy's face is all the confirmation I need of that.

No time to waste then.

"You've got thirty seconds before this place is swarming with soldiers," he sputters, shoving his friend off of him.

"I only need ten," I tell him and kick his stomach as hard as I can. Once he's sufficiently out of breath, I stomp on his foot. The snap is music to my ears as his foot bends in a direction it was not made to go.

His wheeze smothers his scream, and I grab him by the throat.

"Where's Nate?" I emphasize the question by kicking his broken foot.

He's sputtering for breath, but the pathetic bastard doesn't even attempt to fight. "Office," he wheezes. "Mason's office."

I slam his head against the wall twice, and I'm running from the room before his lifeless body even hits the ground.

The factory is a maze of hallways, but I've already walked to and from the cells to Mason's office, so I know exactly where I'm going.

I pause at an intersection and glance down the halls to ensure they're clear—they are, but I don't let myself relax. This factory is big— but I have no idea how big. Just because I'm not seeing them doesn't mean there aren't hundreds of soldiers roaming the building. Since I have no idea what I'm up against, I need to be on full alert.

I race down the halls as fast as I can while staying quiet and eventually make it to the staircase that leads to Mason's office.

When I reach the door, I lean in to listen, but I don't hear anything.

I have no idea what I'll do if he's not inside.

I need to get my girls out of here.

Bracing for the worst, I kick the door open and fire at Nate before he can even look up from the tablet he holds. The bullet lodges in his head, and he goes down with a thud that I commit to memory.

It's not the revenge I wanted, but I'll take it.

I've taken a single step toward him to grab the keys when movement from my side registers just as a blinding pain reverberates across my head. I fire another bullet at the shadow, but I know I've missed as soon as it fires. I pull the trigger again, but nothing happens.

Five bullets.

That's all Tripp had in his damn gun.

I should've checked before now, but why the hell wouldn't he have had a fully loaded weapon?

A damn idiot.

Blinking rapidly, I barely duck out of the way of Mason's second punch. Blood pours down my face, making it harder for me to notice that Mason is now moving for his desk—or rather, the gun sitting on it.

I launch myself forward just as he grabs it. Before he can cock the gun, I'm over the desk, slamming into him.

The gun clatters to the ground, sliding under a cabinet and hopelessly out of both of our reach.

Fine by me.

I send my fist across Mason's face—just like I've imagined doing for years now.

His bloody lips pull into a malicious sneer, blood filling the crevices of each tooth, making the bastard look as demented as he is.

"You're too late," he says with a biting laugh. "Moreno's already here, and my dad isn't far. There's no stopping this now. Your kid is as good as dea—"

I send my fist to his face again—and then two more times for good measure.

I'd love nothing more than to sit here and beat this bastard to death, but I don't have the time. I'll have to settle for his being unconscious.

I grab the keys off Nate—who's somehow unarmed—and run from the room again.

By some miracle, I don't encounter a single soldier on my run through the base. Even as I pass the room with Guy and his friends, there's no one there.

No one even came to investigate the gunshots.

That fact brings me no comfort. If the soldiers aren't here, they're with Moreno—or at least preparing to be.

But it just might give me the time I need to get my girls out of here.

I reach their door in record time—taking better care not to scare them this time.

"It's me," I call, tapping the metal door before sliding the key in and opening it.

The sight guts me to my core and fills me with so much hope at the same time.

Rachel stands several paces from the door, holding Lyla, no doubt prepared in case I hadn't been the one at the door. The bruising along her wrists and throat fills me with the most potent rage I have ever known. Maybe it would've been better to take the extra few seconds to end Mason's life.

Just then, voices echo down the hall, and I know we don't have any extra time to waste.

Rachel's eyes go wide at the sound of voices, and I'm pulling her into me in the next second.

I cradle her face in one hand. "We're getting out of here."

She nods in a jerking motion, and I know she's having a hard time getting words out between the fear and the bruising.

I hold my arms out to take Lyla from her, but she doesn't pass her over right away. Studying her gaze, I know there's more to her hesitation than fear.

But we're low on options, so she releases Lyla into my arms, and I cradle her to my chest.

"Hey, Tiger," I whisper with a soft smile.

My daughter's hollow, fear-struck expression sears itself into my memory.

"I need you to do something for me," I say gently. "Close your eyes and don't open them until I tell you to. Can you do that?"

My three-year-old nods in a robotic motion as she squeezes her eyes shut and buries her face in my chest. I take Rachel's hand and press a kiss on her forehead.

"Stay at my side," I whisper against her forehead.

"Ryder," she says in a hoarse whisper, and she's trembling under my touch.

I pull back just enough for her to meet my eyes, overflowing with panic and heart-wrenching fear.

"Hey," I gently coax. "Do you trust me?"

Her pause is brief before she nods. "To get us out of here."

I deserve that—I know I do.

After all, this isn't the first time their lives have been on the line because of me.

I gently squeeze her hand and pull her closer to me.

Whether Rachel forgives me or curses me to hell and back, it doesn't matter.

"I'm getting you both out of here, okay?" I promise her.

She nods again, and with a deep breath, she's as ready as she'll ever be.

With one arm wrapped around Lyla, holding her to me, and Rachel holding my other, I peer into the hall to ensure the coast is clear.

It is, and I don't hear the voices from before anymore, so I pull the girls with me as I race through the halls.

Time is not a luxury we have. With Moreno here and no weapon to protect the girls in the event of an encounter, getting them out as fast as possible is all that matters.

I spot a window down a hallway at an intersection, and I run to it. Three cars are just barely in view, and I can spot an exit from here that would let out near them. I mentally calculate how to get to that side of the factory. I have no way of knowing if any of the doors I'll need to go through are unlocked, but it's the best plan I have to work with.

Voices echo down the hall, and Rachel's hand goes stiff in mine as Lyla tightens her hold on my neck.

"I see an exit that'll get us out," I tell them, giving Rachel a look that I desperately hope comforts her.

The fear in that beautiful gaze is unbearable.

We're moving through hallways as fast as possible. The mental route I calculated was generally accurate—aside from a few times we hit a dead end, and I had to track back and figure out where we went wrong.

Roughly five minutes pass before I spot the neon red EXIT sign.

Relief crashes over me as I usher my girls out the door and into the cool night.

I don't stop until we've reached the car, and I'm met with Alec stepping out from the car with his gun and a glare.

Then he sees the girls.

Whatever Alec thinks of me and my loyalties, he'd never hurt Rachel or Lyla.

He casts me a warning look before tucking his gun away—just in time for Lyla not to see.

"Get them out of here," I bark at him, cringing when Lyla goes rigid in my arms.

I soften my tone. "It's okay, sweetie. You can open your eyes now. You're safe. Uncle Alec is here, and he's going to take you and Mama somewhere safe."

Her eyes open and lock on Alec's softened smile, and I feel my daughter relax in my arms.

"What about you?" Rachel asks as she takes Lyla from my arms and holds her tight.

Alec wraps a secure arm around Rachel—his attempt to comfort her and ease her tremors—even as he levels me with a hard look.

"Ryder," he warns.

He doesn't say anything else, but he doesn't have to.

The message is clear: I'm to be treated as a prisoner until further notice.

I look over Rachel's head, telling both of them, "Elise is in there. I can't leave her. It's because of her that I even had the chance to get you both safely out."

Alec's features soften to reluctance, and I know he won't stop me. My gaze drops to Rachel, and I wish it hadn't.

The look on her face guts me.

It's a look I've seen before—on that day three years ago.

She wants to ask me to stay, but she doesn't.

Not this time.

Leaving her and Lyla is the last thing I want to do, but Elise is still inside, and she's alone. I owe her my life—my family's lives.

I pull Rachel to me, relishing the feel of her as I press a kiss to her forehead.

"I'll meet you at the base," I promise her, then look to Alec. "Take care of them."

He still looks reluctant to let me go, and that's fair enough—I'm a traitor to our family right now. But he sighs, giving me a sharp nod as he ushers the girls into the car.

"Good luck," he says.

I steal one last glance at my daughter and the woman I love—the one I lost once already. Then I run back into the factory, hoping I don't lose them again before I get the chance to make things right.

Acknowledgments

Thank you so much for reading *Loving Elise*!

This book started as a pandemic-driven hobby and quickly became an obsession, and I'll forever be grateful to the many people who supported me on this journey.

First, thank you to my husband, who wholeheartedly supported my decision to pursue publishing this book instead of my degree—and who continues to encourage my dream in every way imaginable. This book simply could not have happened without him.

Next, thank you so much to my mom and sister for being the first people to read this story and for making me realize that I might have a knack for this whole "writing" thing after all.

My incredible book cover was designed by Lena Yang—who brought to life a vision so much more beautiful than anything I could've imagined. Seriously, you're the best.

A huge thank-you to Kelly Graman for helping me edit this book. It would not be readable without you!

Another thank-you to Savannah Gilbo, whose podcast *Fiction Writing Made Easy* inspired me to pursue publishing—and whose course, *Notes to Novel*, gave me the tools to achieve that goal!

And finally, thank you to everyone who has supported me—whether by writing a review, referring a friend, or just by reading. You mean so much more to me than I could ever put into words.

Made in the USA
Monee, IL
10 May 2025

17133623R00246